The Dating Pact

LULU MORRIS

CANELO

First published in the United Kingdom in 2026 by

Canelo, an imprint of
Canelo Digital Publishing Limited,
20 Vauxhall Bridge Road,
London SW1V 2SA
United Kingdom

A Penguin Random House Company
The authorised representative in the EEA is Dorling Kindersley Verlag GmbH.
Arnulfstr. 124, 80636 Munich, Germany

Copyright © Lulu Morris 2026

The moral right of Lulu Morris to be identified as the creator of this work has been asserted in accordance with the Copyright, Designs and Patents Act, 1988.
All rights reserved. No part of this publication may be reproduced or transmitted in any form or by any means, electronic or mechanical, including photocopy, recording, or any information storage and retrieval system, without permission in writing from the publisher.
No part of this book may be used or reproduced in any manner for the purpose of training artificial intelligence technologies or systems. In accordance with Article 4(3) of the DSM Directive 2019/790, Canelo expressly reserves this work from the text and data mining exception.

A CIP catalogue record for this book is available from the British Library.

Print ISBN 978 1 83598 317 1
Ebook ISBN 978 1 83598 318 8

This book is a work of fiction. Names, characters, businesses, organizations, places and events are either the product of the author's imagination or are used fictitiously. Any resemblance to actual persons, living or dead, events or locales is entirely coincidental.

Cover design by Kah NS

Printed and bound in Great Britain by Clays Ltd, Elcograf S.p.A.

Look for more great books at
www.canelo.co | www.dk.com

For my mum, Moira. I wish you could have read this, you'd have loved Ellie!

Chapter One

London

March

The bar was so tightly packed that it seemed to Ellie as if the crowd was giving birth to her friend. First, Hannah squeezed her head between a tiny gap in a sea of shoulders, and then she had to rotate her body and twist her shoulders to break through.

'It's closed!' gasped Hannah, as she managed to grab the bar with one hand and pull herself to Ellie's side with a grunt.

'What?' mumbled Ellie, so distracted by the disturbing image that she had to shake her head to clear it.

'The roof terrace – it's closed. All of it. There's a sign saying it's reserved for a private party; they've got bouncers and everything.'

Ellie's heart sank. The terrace was the only reason for them coming here in the first place. 'That explains why it's so rammed in here.' She glared pointedly at the sharp suit who'd elbowed her twice since he'd shoved his way to the front of the bar five minutes ago. If that hadn't been enough for her to loathe him, he was also waving a twenty-pound note at the staff every time they passed, apparently oblivious to the fact that they were still serving another customer.

The barman looked over at them. 'Who's next?'

Ellie gave him a bright smile, conscious that the staff might appreciate a friendly face after being run ragged. He shifted towards her and she leaned over the bar, so that he could hear her over the thumping house music.

A twenty-pound note flapped in front of her nose before she had time to open her mouth. 'Double Grey Goose, on the rocks, and make *sure* it's Grey Goose. I don't want any of that communist shit,' said the suit, an LA twang to his accent.

'Sorry,' Ellie said. Not sorry at all. 'I was next.'

'I don't think so. I've been here for at least twenty minutes.' He gave her a quick up-and-down appraisal that was so filled with disdain, it made her jaw clench. She was used to sneering looks; it came hand in hand with being plus size.

Returning the favour, she gave him the same scornful appraisal. Middle-aged with greased jet-black hair that had obviously come from a bottle. His expensive suit fitted perfectly on his thin frame. Beneath the spray tan, his complexion was sallow, like she'd seen in her alcoholic patients. He was the type to tell her to consider her health, while he trotted around with cirrhosis of the liver.

Ellie lowered his note with a firm press of her index finger. She usually dealt with rudeness with the forbearance of a saint, but tonight was Hannah's last night in London. Tomorrow her best friend since primary school would leave her to go and live in Australia for a year. This man wasn't going to push in front of her and get away with it.

Not today, Satan!

'I *was* next.' She stared him down with her best *Nurse Ellie takes no prisoners* glare.

He looked away first. Wimp.

Turning back to the confused barman, she flashed her pearly whites. No way was she going to let some fatphobic snake ruin her night. 'Two raspberry gin fizzes, please.'

There was an exasperated huff beside her, but she deliberately ignored the slimy suit.

After their drinks were made and paid for, she handed one of the massive candyfloss goblets to Hannah and sashayed away with a toss of her freshly blow-dried hair. Leaving the bar area was significantly easier than arriving.

However, her victory was short-lived, as there was nowhere to sit and barely anywhere to stand. The growing throng of customers grew more and more intense, packed into the small cocktail bar like sardines. Hannah, who was tiny, kept being knocked by a lady's designer tote that probably cost more than their monthly nursing salaries combined.

'It's not normally this busy, is it?' asked Hannah, dodging another swing of the luxury bag.

'No. But I guess with the terrace closed…' They both looked longingly at the closed doors, which were black-lacquered and inlaid with mother-of-pearl to fit with the Asian fusion theme of the restaurant. Chopsticks was a swanky high-rise restaurant, with a tiny cocktail bar serving overpriced drinks, and terrible music. But the roof terrace by contrast was a lush, calming oasis with comfy seating and stunning views of the city.

Ellie twizzled her cocktail stirrer, her heart and hopes for the evening plummeting with each beat of the woman's tote against Hannah's head. 'I'm sorry.'

Hannah gave her arm a light squeeze. 'Don't be. It's still lovely to have one last cocktail with you before I go.'

'When's your dad picking us up? We could try somewhere else, the Gun maybe?' she asked, knowing she was clutching at straws and trying to halt the inevitable.

Soon, Hannah would be gone, and Ellie would be left behind. Nothing but the hospital and helping her family with their flower shop to fill her days. She really needed to get a life – except, she couldn't afford one.

Hannah checked her watch. 'Thirty-five minutes?' Her dad had been a black cab driver for over thirty years, and he was never late.

Ellie did a quick calculation in her head. By the time they'd queued up for the super-fast lift to the ground level, walked to the nearest bar and ordered drinks… Well, they'd only have five minutes left together at best. 'I can't persuade you to stay out a bit longer?'

Hannah shook her head sadly. 'Six a.m. flight. Pretty much have to leave as soon as I get in.'

Ellie sighed. 'We shouldn't have stopped for dessert.'

'And miss the best ice cream sundae in London? No way.'

'But this place is rubbish without the terrace.' Ellie shuffled out of the way of a waitress who was carrying a platter of steaming noodles through the crowd. This really was the worst end to an otherwise perfect farewell.

'Stupid private party,' she grumbled, as she mentally tortured herself by remembering the terrace only a few steps away. With acres of squishy seats and low tables, the terrace's roof garden was not only beautifully landscaped with magnificent views, but it also had a huge cherry blossom tree planted in its centre. How the hell they'd hauled a massive tree up here in the first place was beyond her, but they'd somehow managed it. At night the tree was lit up with hundreds of fairy lights, and she could just make out the twinkling glow of it beyond the steamy windows.

Hannah's voice interrupted her thoughts. 'Don't be disappointed, you've given me the best send-off imaginable. We've done the best tea room, the best dim sum, the best ice cream. It's been the *perfect* day. After all that food and walking, I'm going to sleep like a baby through the whole flight.'

She was still leaving. Ellie had planned this day half hoping that showing off everything that London had to offer might make Hannah change her mind at the last minute. A futile hope.

'You're going to sleep the whole twenty-five-hour flight?'

'With two stops,' Hannah reminded her with a twinkle in her eyes.

'With two stops…' Ellie chuckled. Resigned to her fate, she stomped down her disappointment and forced herself to be enthusiastic for her friend. 'You're going to have the most amazing time, babe.'

Hannah's own smile faltered for a moment as tears gathered in her eyes. 'I wish you were coming with me.'

Ellie longed to shout, *Please, don't go!* But she knew that confessing her misery would only make Hannah feel worse, and she knew that her friend already felt terrible. Hannah's decision to go travelling had meant Ellie had had to move back in with her family temporarily. And it *would* be temporary, she reminded herself.

Instead, she gave a dramatic gasp, and pretended to clutch her pearls. 'Australia! With all those spiders and creepy-crawlies? No thanks.'

'Well... maybe you could come and visit me. Have a little holiday?' Hannah asked hopefully, tucking a long strand of mousy-blonde hair behind her ear.

Always so unsure of herself, Hannah's travelling plans were a strange role reversal between them. They had been best friends since Ellie had grabbed shy little Hannah's frightened hand on the first day of school. Now, she who always followed loud, bolshie, risk-taking Ellie with good grace, was taking the bravest step she'd ever made – alone.

'If I don't do it now, I'm afraid I'll never do it.'

How could Ellie argue with that?

She would have been proud of her, if Hannah wasn't leaving her behind and taking half of their flat deposit with her. There was no way Ellie could afford a 'little' holiday to the other side of the world, but she wouldn't tell Hannah that. 'Maybe... It might be easier to save at my mum's.'

Hannah's eyes lit up. 'Please, I'd love to see you, and I'm so sorry I ruined everything for you. You had your heart set on that flat—'

'It's not your fault,' Ellie said. Although it kind of was. Now wasn't the time to dwell on it. Hannah would be leaving tomorrow, and twenty-five years of friendship was worth more than her personal disappointment.

Hannah beamed at her. 'You can stay with me and get a cheap flight. It won't cost much.'

Ellie nodded, almost believing it might be possible, until she remembered she'd already had to pay her mum's phone bill this month.

God, it was all so depressing! She was sick of being skint, of doors being constantly closed in her face, of people – like that suit – looking down on her, just because she dared to stand up for herself and exist in a bigger body.

Another waitress with a black jacket and chopsticks in her hair struggled through the crowd with a full platter. Ellie and Hannah leapt into each other's arms to avoid being smacked in the head.

'Right, I've had enough of this. Knock back your drink.' Ellie downed the last of her pink fizz and placed it on a nearby table. Then she tied up her hair in a makeshift bun, mimicking the waitress's hairstyle. *Needs must.* She grabbed the stirrer from her cocktail and then Hannah's and grinned at her friend's confused face as she stuck both stirrers in her hair. 'Can I borrow your jacket?'

'Sure…'

Hannah was at least five sizes smaller, but after some wiggling she managed to squeeze into it. It didn't matter that it wouldn't do up, or cover her breasts, she just needed to look the part. She dug in her handbag for her work name tag and stuck it on the lapel, then handed her bag to her friend. 'Hold these and follow me. Act like you know what I'm doing.'

'What *are* you doing?'

'Getting us onto that bloody roof terrace.' Ellie strode forward, grabbing discarded menus from a nearby table as she passed.

If her best friend was going to leave her, she'd at least give her the perfect memory of her last night here – perhaps it would bring her back sooner?

Fuelled by pink fizz confidence, they wound through the crowd with surprising efficiency, Ellie holding up the menus and barking, 'Excuse me,' until they were in front of the pearly gates, guarded not by angels but two stocky guys with designer stubble.

'I've got a late arrival,' she said with an air of authority she didn't feel, and was secretly pleased when he didn't look too closely at her NHS name badge, and instead was distracted by her cleavage.

Thank you, favourite corset dress!

He opened the door for them and they walked straight into heaven.

Chapter Two

A pair of shapely legs sauntered past Alex, attached to hips with enough sway to make him sit up and take notice. She was one of the waitresses, a stack of messy menus in her arms, and he wondered how he hadn't spotted her until now.

The woman was tall with a well-rounded hourglass figure, a sexy Marilyn Monroe wiggle to her walk. A long strand of her chestnut hair swung down from her messy bun pierced with two flimsy chopsticks. It swung from side to side as she walked, begging for someone to give it a playful tug. He shook his head, amused by his runaway thoughts.

She was leading another woman he didn't recognise, a tiny sparrow in comparison, with mousy-blonde hair and nervous blue eyes. Maybe she was one of the backstage crew? A pang of guilt twisted in his gut. He'd sworn to himself that he would be the kind of director that knew everyone by name, and yet it was opening night and he had no idea who this person was.

On the other end of his mobile, his mum was still speaking, reminding him of his greatest and most humiliating failure.

'...Savannah and Liam are arriving on the Thursday before, with the rest of the wedding party coming on the

Friday. But you still haven't said when you're coming. You will let me know, won't you?'

Distracted, he answered without thinking, 'Do I have to go?'

'Oh, sweetheart. You can't let all of this affect you – it will only add more fuel to the fire.'

He rolled his eyes at his mother's tone. How did she manage to make him sound both pitiful and a pain in her ass?

I guess it was that acting range that won her two Oscars.

She battled on, ignoring his silence. 'I know it's difficult. But at the end of the day, it's your brother's wedding. You *have* to be there, despite how things began.'

What a fucking joke. 'Things' began with the biggest Hollywood scandal of a decade, and, like an uncontrollable wildfire, he'd been unable to escape its flames even after moving to London. His mother was crazy if she thought a quick wedding would erase the past.

He took a deep breath to compose himself. 'It might be easier, for everyone, if I didn't come.'

'Nonsense. The more you avoid them, the more awkward it becomes – and then people make up stories…'

His mother went into her usual speech about the importance of King family solidarity, and Alex switched off, staring blindly ahead, allowing her words to wash over and through him. There had been a time when he'd believed firmly in family loyalty, that, no matter what lies the press printed, his parents and brother would always have his back. But even that had been a lie; he couldn't rely on any of them. They had chosen Liam – the golden child – over him, and it burned Alex to the core that he wasn't even allowed to be upset about it.

Movement to the side of him caught his eye. The waitress looked over her shoulder and grinned. Not a polite and professional gesture, but a genuine smile of pure delight and joy, as if she'd just won the lottery.

Damn, she was cute. Full red lips, high cheekbones and smoky brown eyes that lit up her face like fireworks. His body jolted with a sudden arousal he'd not felt in years.

It was a welcome distraction. Even though the party had been his idea, the constant charm he'd had to force was exhausting. So much so that he'd even welcomed a call from his mother as an excuse to escape it... which he now regretted.

The waitress tossed the menus onto the table in front of him without looking at where they fell. She grabbed the little sparrow in a bouncing hug. 'Oh my God, we did it! I can't believe we got away with it.' She laughed, and the corners of his mouth twitched as he realised they were gate-crashers. Usually, fans were quick to seek him out and he was just as quick to call security. But if the women had been after him they wouldn't have passed him without a second glance.

'Ellie, shh,' said her friend, darting a concerned look in his direction for the first time. He ducked his head, pretending to be engrossed in his call.

Ellie. He wondered what it was short for. Elizabeth? Eleanor? Eliza? From the twang of her cockney accent, Eliza suited her.

'Are you listening, Alex?' asked his mother curtly.

Oh. 'Yes?'

'Good, so you'll come on the Sunday, in plenty of time for the rehearsal dinner.'

Wait... How had he agreed to that? The rehearsal dinner was five days before the wedding; he could end up spending nearly an entire week with his family and the hideously happy couple in one of the most romantic locations on the planet. He didn't think he could survive it.

'I might need to stay in London.'

'Nonsense, you're the director. Richie says once the show's up and running you don't need to stay, and you're not acting in it either. So, you'll hardly be exhausted.'

Typical – his mother only ever saw the strain of a project on actors like herself. Never thought of how it might affect any of the other hardworking people behind the scenes.

'Well, I'm not making any promises, not until the reviews for tonight's performance come in.' Reminding himself of the reviews made him bad-tempered, because everything he touched lately seemed to turn to shit. The press were determined to paint him as the villain in his own miserable story.

'Very well. Just let me know so I can arrange the jet—'

'I've got to go.'

'Okay, we'll speak again soon?' She paused. Her next statement was gently coaxing. 'Love you…'

'Love you too, Mom,' Alex sighed, then quickly hit the red button and put away his phone.

The curvy brunette was instructing her friend on how best to pose in front of the iconic blossom tree. It was the main reason why he'd picked this venue, listed as the best rooftop bar in London, for the opening night party. When he was feeling ridiculously romantic, he liked to think of himself as an old tree finding roots in a new setting. Not that he was old, he was only thirty, but these days he felt ancient. The pressure of the last few months with his family and the play had been suffocating and lonely. But these two women giggling over something as silly as gate-crashing a party for a photo in front of a tree significantly cheered him up.

'Not like that, Hannah. Put your hand on your hip and stick your bum out. Yeah, just like that. You can use it on your new Aussie dating profile.'

Hannah blushed, but tried her best to hold the pose. 'I thought you said Tinder was a waste of time? That it was all dick pics and time-wasters.'

Ellie bent at the hips slightly, trying to get the best angle while she backed up towards his table. Alex's throat dried as he watched her beautiful ass wiggle towards him.

'Oh, it is. But aren't there more men in Australia than women? It'll be like a party in a sausage factory. I wonder what dating apps are called in Australia. Is there a down-under-the-covers app? Fair-Dinkum.com?'

The blonde sparrow threw back her head with a laugh, her blue eyes sparkling and her face shining with a sudden inner confidence. A startling change from the shy woman she'd been moments earlier. Ellie was quick to take her photo, and then gazed in triumph at the image on her phone. He needed a friend like that, someone who brought out the best in him.

'Would you like me to take a picture of you both?' he asked, trying his best to untangle himself from the low sofa – not his usual suave manner of entering a conversation. A quick glance around reassured him that the rest of the cast and crew were still happily chatting in their little bubbles. No one noticed as he made his way towards the two women.

The way Ellie's scarlet lips spread with delight made him grateful he'd asked. In fact, it made him grateful to be alive.

Huh… that's a nice change.

As he moved to her side, her perfume drifted towards him, rich and musky, dark chocolate spiced with cinnamon. He breathed it in deeply, allowing her scent to wrap around him like silk. He'd not been with anyone since the break-up, and it felt good to admire someone else. Especially someone so very different from his ex.

'Yes please, that's so sweet of you.' She handed him her phone and their fingers fumbled against each other, causing her to giggle. The sound rippled through him on a wave of heat that quickly vanished when she bounced over to her friend.

He took a few photos and then offered the phone back to her. After she'd checked them over, she gifted him with another megawatt smile.

'Thanks so much.' She paused, rolling the phone in her hand thoughtfully. 'Do I know you from somewhere?'

Oh man, she didn't want him to answer that, did she?

'*Oh, I'm pretty famous. You may have seen me in a couple of films and TV shows. Or advertising this play that I just produced and directed and whose party you're currently gate-crashing.*' He'd sound like a complete asshole. And he'd been accused of that enough times to last him a lifetime.

'Err…'

'You been to the Royal Hospital lately? That's where we work. Well, where I work – Hannah's escaped.'

He practically melted with relief. Could he pretend to be someone else for a short while? Imagine what his life could be like, if he wasn't the most pitiful member of a famous acting dynasty.

'Dad's just texted. He's about twenty minutes away,' said Hannah, and Ellie turned away, taking her warmth with her.

'One for the road?' she asked hopefully.

'And queue at that bar again?'

They both grimaced. 'We should probably head down,' said Ellie glumly.

They turned to walk away and Alex's chest tightened. He felt unwilling to let her leave. He stepped forward and indicated the little drinks stand set up a few metres away. 'Why don't you get a drink from the stand?'

They glanced at each other as if uncertain.

'It's only prosecco, some house wine and beer, but it's got to be quicker than waiting at the bar.'

Ellie looked at her friend and then at him before taking a step towards him and lowering her voice to a conspiratorial whisper: 'We're not actually invited to this party... We snuck in.'

'I know. Don't worry about that.'

Ellie winced. 'How did you know? Is it that obvious?'

'I know because I didn't invite you.'

Her mouth gaped with horror, and he wished he could slap his forehead for being such a jerk. He tried to reassure her. 'Like I said, don't worry about it. It's only a work thing. What can I get you?'

'Ermm...'

'Prosecco? I don't think I've met a single Brit who doesn't like prosecco.'

They both nodded dumbly in response, and his need to charm them was almost overwhelming. He walked over to the stand and swiped three glasses of prosecco.

'That's really nice of you,' said Hannah, taking one of the glasses gingerly from his hold.

'I'm Alex,' he said with his best Hollywood smile.

'I'm Hannah, and this is the wonderful Ellie,' said Hannah, and he nodded as though he didn't already know she was wonderful.

Ellie suddenly looked very pale. 'Oh my God, Alex King!' she gasped. 'That's how I know you.'

His heart sank to the pit of his stomach as he waited for the awkwardness to begin. Would she know about Savannah? His earlier confidence shrivelled but he maintained his placid facade, something he had years of experience doing.

To his surprise, she laughed, a joyful and unrepentant sound that gave him hope. 'I am so sorry! I don't watch a lot of films. But I think I saw one where you were an archaeologist solving murders or something? I'm a nurse, I see so many faces. And my hours are a bit weird, so I tend to fall asleep halfway through most films. Hannah's also a nurse.' She leaned closer again, with that conspiratorial hushed voice. He decided he liked being invited into her inner circle. 'Thanks for not kicking us out, especially as it's your party. I feel terrible. It's just… it's Hannah's last night before she goes to live in Australia for a year, and, well, this is such a beautiful place – it's one of our favourite spots.'

He was utterly enthralled by the melody of her accent, the way her words tumbled out of her like pebbles rolling down a hill, hitting some T's sharper than others, while fudging together some of the vowels. She spoke with passion and self-assurance, two things he'd found himself lacking in for a long while.

'Mine too, actually,' he said, dropping his voice to a low and flirtatious rumble. 'And now that I know it's a special occasion, I'm relieved you were able to sneak in. Good acting, by the way. Maybe I should get you to audition for my next play?'

Hannah gave him an enthusiastic nod. 'She'd be great! Ellie could blag her way into anything.'

'You gotta fake it to make it!' Ellie said with a cheerful shimmy of her hips. 'So is that what you're celebrating, your play?'

'It's our opening night. A modern retelling of *The Great Gatsby*, set in Wall Street.'

'Oh, I love that book. But it's so sad.' She sighed dreamily.

'It is. Gatsby's a tragic character.'

'Not *just* Gatsby. All of them. They're all their own worst enemy, don't you think? Gatsby pining for Daisy. Daisy losing the love of her life only to marry a man who sees her as a trophy. Honestly, I think neither Gatsby nor Tom love her, not really. They love the *idea* of her. Not to mention the narrator Nick, he's so lonely, and poor Myrtle. It's all such a tragic waste.'

Alex couldn't help but be impressed by her insight, but something about her words made him internally flinch, although he couldn't think why. 'Most people who say they love the book have never even read it. You clearly have.'

She blushed under his stare and cleared her throat. 'I like to read. You play Gatsby, right?'

'Oh, no. Isaac plays Gatsby. He's talking over there with John, who plays Nick Carraway.'

'Then who do you play?' asked Ellie with a frown.

'No one. I wrote the script and directed it.'

'Impressive! Now I really have to come and see it.'

'I'd love that.' For once, he meant it. He was oddly flattered by her praise and genuine enthusiasm. He'd secretly hoped his family would react the same way as Ellie when he'd first announced he was quitting acting and taking to directing. Instead, they'd exchanged worried glances and mumbled something about being happy for him as long as he was happy. Except, of course, he wasn't.

'My dad's here,' said Hannah quietly, breaking the odd intimacy that had grown between them. Ellie turned to her with a start.

'Already? Why's he always so early?' she cried. With a reluctant expression, she said to Alex, 'We've got to go. It was lovely meeting you—'

'Oh, she's staying,' Hannah said firmly, surprising them both. When Ellie opened her mouth to speak, Hannah quickly silenced her with a raised palm. 'I have an early flight tomorrow, and I'm going straight to bed. I've had the best day, Ellie. So please stay out and have one more drink for me. In fact, I insist you stay out. You bloody deserve it.' She fixed Alex with an unnervingly fierce look that he never would have expected from her. 'I'm trusting you to show this wonderful woman a good time. Understand?'

He was a little afraid to disagree with her, but also more than a little pleased that Ellie wouldn't be leaving after all.

She turned to Ellie and opened her arms. They hugged tightly for a minute, their heads buried in each other's necks. When they pulled apart, he could see tears on both of their cheeks.

'I'm going to miss you so much,' whispered Ellie.

Hannah pressed trembling lips tightly together. 'Thank you. I couldn't have done this without you. If you'd not been so understanding—'

Ellie interrupted her. 'Just promise me one thing.'

'Anything.'

'Have the best time. Go everywhere, drink all the drinks, eat all the food, go on all the trips. Just have the *best* time. Promise?'

'I promise.'

They hugged in a touching display of friendship that he felt privileged to witness. His chest tightened as he thought of Liam – the brother he'd once thought of as a friend, but who had betrayed him in the worst possible way.

The two women separated and Hannah left, leaving him and Ellie alone.

Chapter Three

Ellie gave her unexpected companion a quick and furtive smile before looking around aimlessly in an attempt to not seem awkward. She immediately wished she hadn't. People were beginning to stare at them. No one had looked their way until Alex had stood up, but he was like a magnet drawing them in. Some were just curious, others a little envious, but the worst ones were the sneers. She knew what they were thinking – what's he doing with *her*?

Her stomach clenched at the silent judgement, but she forced herself to turn away from them and gaze out at London's skyline instead. It had taken her years to ignore people like that, and, even though she refused to show it, their judgement still hurt.

She was convinced Alex would make an excuse and leave, so she was surprised when his body shifted closer.

This evening was getting more surreal by the minute. Not only was Alex ridiculously handsome, but he was also a film star, and he seemed more than content to ignore his fabulous friends to hang out with her.

'Sorry, this is so weird. You don't have to stay with me.' She gulped back some more prosecco, aware that the buzz from her previous drink needed topping up, for her sanity more than anything else.

Alex was very tall, at least three or four inches over six foot, and even in her heels she reached just below his broad shoulders. His jet-black hair was cut in a rock and roll style, loose and choppy, curling around his forehead and neck in an effortlessly cool look. Occasionally, he ran his fingers through the silky strands, sweeping them out of his heavenly blue eyes, and her fingers itched to do the same, to stroke through his dark hair and entwine her arms around his neck.

She liked the cute, nerdy glasses he wore. He was every inch the Hollywood star turned theatre director, so much so it was almost like a costume. She was surprised his glasses weren't held together with a piece of tape.

A Hollywood Clark Kent. No wonder it had taken her a while to recognise him. The last film she'd seen him in, his hair had been much shorter, and he'd played a sophisticated jewellery thief. She knew from the film that there was an impressive physique beneath that cotton polo shirt. He had a warm Californian accent that she found really appealing – the type of voice that made her melt like butter on hot toast. But there was also a depth and thoughtfulness to his manner. He seemed the type to read a Penguin Classic in the morning and ride a Harley in the afternoon, or surf some waves – something cool, anyway.

Which raised the question, why the hell was he still talking with her?

'I think I'll have more fun if I stay with you.' At her raised eyebrow, he added, 'I'm not very good at mingling. Honestly, you're doing me a favour.' He gave her a lopsided smile that cut off the oxygen to her brain for a full five seconds. 'Some people find me a little… intense. I'm not exactly the life of the party lately.'

He looked so sad, she almost reached out to squeeze his thick bicep. But she was able to stop herself because that *would* be weird. 'What happened?'

He looked away to the city sky. 'You really don't know? I thought it was on the front page of every gossip rag and website, I think there's even a dance trend in my honour.'

'Ah, I don't really follow social media or gossip mags. They're not good for anyone's mental health. All those red circles of shame, all that rumour and click-bait? I spend most of my working day dealing with the fallout from poor mental health, I don't want to add to it.' She paused and then added gently, 'You don't have to tell me if you don't want to.'

His gaze shifted towards her, and he hesitated, biting his bottom lip for a moment, before speaking. 'You'd probably think me pathetic. So, let's just call it a bad break-up.'

The way he said it made her heart ache. He sounded broken and exhausted, and she wanted to take whoever had ripped up this beautiful man's heart and snap them in two. But she doubted she would ever meet them, so she decided to cheer him up instead.

'Pathetic? Oh, well, if I'd known this was going to be a pity party… The gloves are off, because I can beat your story,' she teased, before taking a deep breath. 'So, my best friend has left me to go live in Australia for a year – who knows, she may never come back…' She tried to ignore the icy shiver that ran down her spine. 'And I'm gutted. Not only because I'm going to miss Hannah like mad, but because it also means I've lost my flatmate, and I can't afford to rent a place on my own. Or buy, as I'd hoped. We'd been saving towards a mortgage deposit for years. We're best friends, single and earn the same crappy salary, so it makes sense to buy a place together. I'd even picked out the best block of flats for us, and we'd just been waiting for something to come up for sale. Except, Hannah suddenly realised she'd much rather spend her money on expanding her horizons – and who can blame her? But now I don't have enough of a deposit to buy on my own. So, while Hannah's going to explore the other side of the world, I'll be back at home with my mum, nanna and brother while I save up the shortfall. It's a huge step backwards that I'd hoped never to make, and it's kind of depressing. But that's nothing compared to my love life, which is the *worst*. The last date I went on, he stood me up halfway through the meal.'

Panic suddenly struck her dumb and her eyes flew wide in horror. Talk about over-sharing – what the hell was wrong with her?

'What?' Alex looked as horrified as she felt.

She should shut up, but her mouth couldn't be stopped, because a moment later she was already jumping back onto the juggernaut of humiliation by declaring, 'No matter how pathetic you think your story is, I can promise you mine is *much* worse.'

'I don't understand. How can you be stood up halfway through a date?' To his credit, he seemed genuinely confused that someone would leave a date early. She doubted he'd ever been on a date with anyone who wasn't a model and/or desperate to marry him.

'He went to the bathroom and never came back. I think it was because I told him I wanted to get married and have kids…' Alex raised a sardonic brow and she threw up her hands. 'I didn't mean immediately! But he did ask. He wanted to know where I saw myself in five years and, well, that's what I'd hoped for. Not necessarily with him, of course, just generally. But it still spooked him.' *Jesus, Ellie, it'd spook any man.* 'I wish he hadn't ordered fillet steak, because I had to pay for it. I'd like to say that's my only pathetic example, but I've been ghosted more times than I'd like to admit, encountered some scary weirdos, been stood up loads and...' She paused, her mind immediately flashing to her most humiliating dating experience. Damn it, she'd managed to not think of David for months. She shook her head vigorously to clear it. 'Anyway, modern dating... it's tough out there.'

'That guy who stood you up was an asshole.'

Ellie blinked, her shoulders immediately relaxing. 'Thank you, that's actually really nice to hear another man say that.' She let out a cleansing breath, feeling surprisingly at ease with this Hollywood star. 'Anyway, I made a resolution this New Year. Absolutely no more dating. I'm going to concentrate on sorting myself out first. Buying my own flat, having a cat, settling down.' She winced at how miserable her goals sounded, especially now that the most important one was a dead end, with Hannah leaving. 'I'm sure your break-up – even if it was posted everywhere – isn't pathetic.'

Alex took a deep breath and stared straight ahead as if he were in the confession box and knew he was going to get a thousand Hail Marys. 'My ex-girlfriend cheated on me with my brother for years and now they're getting married. The gossip columns are saying that I'm toxic and jealous, and keep trying to split them apart. That I am an emotionally abusive bastard who never deserved either of them in the first place.'

Her mouth fell open. 'Oh.'

'Exactly.' Bitterness radiated off him, and she couldn't blame him. Hadn't a hidden part of her begrudged

Hannah for leaving? Sometimes life kicked you down and then stood on your fingers as you tried to get up again.

'Screw 'em,' she declared loudly, with a dismissive flap of her wrist. 'I mean it. I bet you were too good for her anyway.'

'Savannah is a supermodel, film actress and UN ambassador. Liam just won an Oscar and donates most of his earnings to charity.'

'Fuck me.' It came out before she'd had time to stop herself, and even clamping her hand over her mouth didn't stop her in time. Alex's answering chuckle was enough to reassure her that she hadn't mortally offended him.

He clapped his hands together firmly. 'Let's get some more drinks. I think we deserve them.'

They grabbed fresh glasses and walked over to one of the large squishy sofas under the twinkling lights of the tree, the blossom draping down around them in a heavy curtain of foliage. It was almost unbearably romantic and Ellie cast around for something to dispel that thought quick-sharp.

'You've got to love a precocious tree,' she said. 'The weather has only just warmed up and it's already out in full bloom.'

'Precocious?' he asked, his head tilting, allowing his hair to flop forward adorably. 'I've never heard a tree called that before.'

'You pick up a few bits when your family own a flower shop. Cherry blossom flowers early, that's why it's called precocious.' She gave him a teasing look. 'I think that's what I love the most about them. They don't give a f—' She stopped herself from swearing like an old fishwife just in time, squirming in embarrassment at the near-slip, her movements resulting in a gassy wheeze whistling from the cushions. She grabbed his thigh to balance herself and then quickly let go, her face flaming with embarrassment.

'I'm so sorry,' she gasped, absolutely mortified by her thigh-grab. The cushions added further insult to injury by making a plastic squelching sound as she shifted back in her seat.

Bloody low sofas! They were worse than beanbags, which until now she'd always considered her arch-nemesis.

Alex wiggled his bum and the seat made more fart-squeaking sounds that made them both giggle, and Ellie felt distinctly more comfortable about her awkward behaviour.

This would go down as number one on her list of heroic acts performed by ordinary men. Except, of course, he wasn't ordinary. Again, she noticed the peripheral stares, and wondered if their audience were somehow edging closer towards them.

It was strange and yet not. Alex was a global star, but she was so at ease with him that she kept forgetting. Plus, he really didn't look the same as he did on the silver screen. Was that deliberate – was he trying to escape the attention of the media by changing his appearance?

However, she preferred this man to any movie poster version. He was more approachable, more human. She'd never have thought that someone like her would end up feeling sorry for someone like him, but she did, and more than anything she wanted to cheer him up, even if it meant accepting a few spiteful stares.

'How long have you been living in London?' she asked, taking a much smaller sip of her prosecco, as she was beginning to feel a little light-headed. Maybe she should rein herself in a bit. This was the most she'd drunk in months and she didn't want to make a fool of herself, not in front of Alex and his glitzy actor friends.

'Since rehearsals started a month ago. I really should get an apartment, if I'm going to stay long term.' His eyes locked with hers. 'Which I hope to do, now.'

Ellie resisted fanning herself, but she had to clear her suddenly dry throat. *He's not flirting, you fool, he means now that his play has started.* 'Where have you been staying?' she squeaked.

'A hotel. I've been back and forth from LA for a while. But really I should lay down some roots, especially if all goes well with the play. I just don't know where to start with the house-hunting.'

'What area were you thinking of?'

'I've no idea.' He blew out his breath with an overwhelmed pout that drew her eyes to his lips, firm, plump and kissable.

With a quick shake of her head, she tried to focus. 'Well, I've lived in London all my life. I can tell you about all the different areas.'

He grinned at her, turning fully to face her, his knee brushing against hers, sending shivers of excitement up her thighs. *Focus, Ellie!* But she couldn't, not with those ocean eyes staring back at her, drowning her senses with wicked thoughts.

'That'd be great. Thank you, Ellie, I'm so glad I met you tonight.' Her pulse quickened. He was so close she could feel the warmth of his breath against her face, smell the sandalwood and spicy aftershave on his skin – the type hand-crafted by a real perfumier and not bought from duty free.

'I think we're going be really good friends,' he said, taking a large swig of his drink.

Reality crashed over her like a wave of icy water. Of course he thought of her as a friend. What on earth made her think Alex King would see her as anything different? She reminded herself that she couldn't be upset about something that had never existed in the first place.

'I think so too,' she said, knocking back the last of her drink.

'The first review is in,' screeched a pretty blonde, practically sprinting over to them despite her skyscraper stilettos.

Heads all snapped towards them, and the entire party of people hurried over in a rush of anxious excitement.

'I should go,' said Ellie, reaching for her bag.

Alex grabbed her wrist, his face pale. 'Please stay.'

She could never say no to someone who said please. Especially when they were gorgeous and vulnerable. She settled back down beside him and his fingers relaxed, the heat of his body keeping away the chill of the spring night. 'Okay.'

One man barrelled to the front of the ever-increasing crowd and firmly took a seat opposite Alex. Ellie recognised him immediately. It was the rude suit from the bar who'd shoved a twenty-pound note in her face. Her throat tightened under his reptilian gaze.

When he spoke his tone was mild, but his eyes remained deadly sharp. 'Who's your friend, Alex? I don't recognise her from the theatre.'

Alex draped a casual arm around her shoulders and gave her a warm squeeze. 'This is my friend, Ellie. Ellie, this is my agent, Richie. My whole family is on Richie's books – we keep him very busy.' *And very wealthy, too, by the looks of it*, thought Ellie, not able to shake the man's earlier entitlement from her mind.

'Five stars,' screeched the blonde again, drawing everyone's attention back to their phone screens, which were all lit up with the same website.

'Thank fuck for that,' crowed the actor who played Gatsby, and there were hoots of agreement.

Cheers and whoops rang out as everyone shared and quoted from all the online reviews they could find. Alex ordered more bottles – this time magnums of the finest champagne – and the night air was filled with the sound of corks popping and glasses fizzing.

Richie didn't seem quite as delighted by the news as the rest of the cast and crew. He offered a weak, 'Congratulations,' then walked off to make a phone call.

Alex slumped back in his chair and drained his glass. 'Thank God. Hopefully the ticket sales will improve now.'

'It's not been selling well?'

'Tonight is the only night we've sold out. It doesn't bode well for the rest of the run.'

'Well, I'm sure that will change now,' Ellie reassured him, patting his arm.

His answering smile seemed even more devastating because of his earlier uncertainty. She wanted nothing more than to reach out and hug him, was even leaning forward to do so when a flashing light blinded her.

'Alex! Great news on your reviews! How do you feel about Savannah and Liam's engagement?' a male voice shouted over the sounds of celebration, the light continuing to flash and the incessant clicking of a camera shutter punctuating more shouted questions that Ellie could no longer understand as the people around them roared with disapproval.

Ellie flinched from the glare of the flash and looked at Alex, whose face had flushed with anger. He stood up to his full height, fists clenched, and Ellie realised with a gasp how tall and intimidating he could actually be. If he wasn't so upset, she'd have found it indescribably hot.

'Get out!' he roared.

'How do you feel about Savannah wearing your grandmother's ring?' continued the paparazzo, unashamedly taking more photos as he prodded Alex for a reaction.

'Security!' bellowed one of the actors, running towards the bouncers, who'd finally woken up to the chaos unfolding and had stumbled out onto the roof terrace to help.

The bouncers grabbed the paparazzo by his arm and started to drag him out.

Richie rushed over. 'How the hell did he get in here? I told you the theatre would have been a better venue!'

Alex sat back down, sinking into the cushions like a rock.

'Are you okay?' she whispered, and he nodded, though she could see a vein pulsing in his neck.

'I'm going to speak to the manager,' still barking, Richie charged away, 'this is unacceptable!'

'Wow,' said Ellie slowly, looking around the suddenly glum faces of the cast and crew. She had to break the tension. 'Security really is lax here, isn't it? They just let in any old riff-raff!' Alex was still raging by the flex of the muscle in his jaw, so she touched his arm gently until he finally looked at her. 'How about a drinking game? Take a sip every time security lets in a random person? Too soon? How about when someone says five stars, or quotes from a review. And...' She paused to think, glad that the previous tension in Alex seemed to be slowly melting away. 'Down your drink if Richie gives me the stink-eye!'

'What do you mean?' asked Alex, following her pointed gaze to Richie, who even while he was yelling at a frazzled-looking manageress took a moment to cast one last dirty look in Ellie's direction.

'Oh,' Alex said, with an apologetic look, and Ellie clinked her flute with his.

'Bottoms up. Fannie's your aunt!'

Alex appeared confused for a moment, before throwing back his head with a deliciously wicked laugh. 'If you say so!' He downed the flute in one go and reached for the bottle to fill them again.

'Five stars from the *Guardian*!' shouted the blonde.

'Five stars from the *Stage*!' cheered Isaac.

Oh God, what had she done? The hangover tomorrow was going to be brutal.

Chapter Four

'Who's the stray sleeping in the lounge?' Mark walked into the kitchen and sat down at the breakfast table with a thud.

Ellie winced as her mum's head snapped up from her entertainment rag like a bloodhound catching a scent. Her nanna shifted closer to Mark and whispered with barely contained excitement, 'It's not Hannah?'

'She'd have missed her flight if it was,' her brother said.

Her mum and nanna exchanged shocked looks, and then stared at Ellie expectantly.

It was too early for this.

The soft light from the kitchen balcony was far too bright. Her head was pounding and her mouth was as dry as the Sahara. She could hear a siren in the distance. Hackney was already abuzz with activity. Hangovers were definitely worse after you turned thirty.

She'd hoped to get away with Alex staying over – her family never sat in the lounge on a Saturday morning, as it was their busiest day and they were always up and out early, either to open the shop or to run their errands.

'A friend,' she mumbled, not daring to look at them as she prepared tea and toast in her pink dressing gown and fluffy bunny slippers. She'd wanted to grab a tea and slink back to shower and dress before checking on Alex.

'He looks familiar,' said Mark.

'He?' gasped her astonished mum, and Nanna clutched the waxed tablecloth.

Ellie's teeth clenched. 'You won't know him. Is he up?' She'd half expected him to have been gone already.

'Sleeping like a baby. A big one.'

The mugs clattered together in the cupboard as she tried to prise her favourite one from the pile. She winced at the horrible sound they made. Every day was like playing Jenga with the crockery, especially now all her stuff was mixed up with her family's.

'Is he one of Hannah's friends?' asked Mark, still puzzling over the conundrum of his sister managing to bring a man home with her.

'No,' she snapped. *Why the sudden interest?* Mark usually didn't give a toss about her personal life. 'As I said, you won't know him.'

'Then how do you know him?'

'I met him last night.'

Her family stared at her in shock.

'Jesus, Ellie! You can't just bring a random man back to our house. You're not Mum.'

'Excuse me,' growled her mum, and Nanna cackled.

'What if he'd robbed us?' Mark glared at her as he began tearing open the post, only to discard the contents in a scrunched-up pile.

Her mother seemed alarmed by the prospect, while Nanna's lips twitched with amusement as she sipped her tea. 'Good luck finding anything worth pinching.'

'Nanna's right, and believe me he's got no reason to rob us.' Ellie turned away with a roll of her eyes. Unfortunately, the swift movement only made her stomach roll, and she had to take a steadying breath.

'How do you know, you only met him last night.'

Her patience broken, she turned on Mark like a provoked animal. 'Because he's Alex King, for fuck's sake!'

'Language,' Nanna reminded her firmly.

'Sorry,' Ellie mumbled, before scowling at her brother with full force. 'He's Alex King, the movie star. What would he want to steal from us? Flowers? Gift bags? Maybe our excess supply of novelty tea towels?' She pointed at an offensive example by the sink that depicted the royal family as corgis.

For the second time that morning, Ellie enjoyed the stunned faces of her family. Or she would have, if it hadn't led to even more questions.

'Alex who?' asked Nanna, apparently baffled.

'Oh my God!' gasped her mum, quickly making the sign of the cross. She leaned forward, her voice a whisper. 'Really? Alex King?'

'Yes,' Ellie huffed, finally managing to tease out her favourite mug, shaped to be a black cat's head. She held it close to her chest for a moment as if it were a security blanket.

'Really?' cried her mum, making Ellie question the wisdom of her revelation for the hundredth time. But she supposed this was better than Mark calling the police.

'Yes, really. Now, be quiet before he hears you.'

'Morning, everyone,' came a sexy voice from the doorway, and Ellie died a little inside.

She spun to face him, still clutching her favourite mug to her chest.

Alex looked... *glorious.* His hair was mussed, his clothes rumpled, but he still looked as if he'd fallen out of a magazine shoot.

'Hi,' she squeaked. Why the hell was she nervous? *Perhaps, Ellie, because you agreed to go on a date to an awards show with a Hollywood star last night?* She shook her head. He'd probably forgotten all about his drunken invitation, or more likely she'd imagined that part of the night; the drinking game had been a bad choice.

'Hiya, my name's Angela,' her mum said, and Ellie frowned at the breathy softness of her voice.

Oh God, she wasn't going to chat him up, was she?

'Hello.' Nanna grinned and offered a little wave, enjoying this far more than was seemly for a woman in her eighties.

'All right, mate?' said Mark, with a gruff cough.

'I'm good, thanks,' replied Alex, oblivious to the fact it was a greeting and not a question. 'And you?'

'Yeah… erm… All right.' Mark grabbed a slice of toast from Mum's plate and made his way out. 'Best get opening the shop. Nice to meet you, Alex.'

Nanna patted the vacant chair beside her as Mark left. 'Alex, come and sit down, love. After a night out with our Ellie, I'm thinking you could do with some tea and toast.' She appeared so innocent in her rollers and flannel. Ellie was immediately suspicious but, at Nanna's pointed look, she quickly got to work making some breakfast for Alex. Lack of hospitality was a crime against nature in her nanna's book.

'You guys are all up early on a Saturday,' remarked Alex with a faint blush, sweeping back his hair with a brush of his hand that made her stomach flutter.

'Mum, Nanna and Mark run the flower shop together. They're all early risers.'

'Ah yeah, it looks awesome, I caught a peek last night. Ellie tells me it's been in your family for several generations, that's amazing.'

Nanna's face lit up like a winning slot machine. Alex couldn't have said anything better to get her on his side. 'We're very proud of it, thank you. It's been in my family since before the First World War, and before that we had a flower stall…'

Ellie watched Alex over the mug's pointy cat ears while Nanna told him all about the history of their shop. He listened with genuine interest, asking questions and chuckling appropriately at all of Nanna's silly stories.

After their breakfast was finished, Alex turned and gave her a bright smile that almost burned out her retinas. 'Thanks so much for letting me stay, but I need to make a move. I've got another show this afternoon.'

'Of course.' Ellie hustled to a stand, her chair scraping loudly on the tiles. 'I'll show you out. Mark's opening the shop, so we'd better go out the back.'

'It was nice meeting you both,' he said to her mum and nanna, who beamed dumbly back at him as he stood up to leave.

They made their way downstairs, passing the family photos, including the God-awful school portraits of herself and Mark, her weight yo-yoing so much that they must look like a series of before-and-after pics.

'You have a lovely home,' he said.

'Thanks. Some people find it a bit weird what with the layout. Topsy-turvy.'

The shop and storage room took up the entire ground floor, while on the second floor were three bedrooms and a snug-lounge, and their kitchen-diner, bathroom and Ellie's box room sat on the top floor in what used to be the attic.

'It's cool,' said Alex, and she beamed with pride, even as they picked their way through the piles of boxes and clutter to reach the back door.

The yard backed onto an access road followed by more Victorian terraced houses. Their house was in a tiny patch of East London that had been largely unaffected by the Blitz, demolition of the slums, and any other form of modernisation.

Like my family, she mused as they passed the black-and-white photograph of her nanna as a little girl sat on the front step of their shop, the same sparkling eyes and cheeky grin plastered on a much younger face. Their history was stamped in the worn-out cobbles and graffiti sprayed buildings of the East End.

Dirty, beautiful and timeless.

Home.

A way of life preserved through the changing years. They could have sold up and moved out to the suburbs at any time over the years, as many families had, and they would have made a good amount of money doing it too. But they never had. It would have felt wrong, like selling a member of their family. This corner of London was all they had ever known or wanted. Even when Ellie had wanted to buy her own place, she'd not looked further than a short walk away – it was one of the many reasons why she was thirty and still saving to buy her own flat. As much as her family drove her mad, they were hers, and they lived here in the heart of the East End. She couldn't leave, but she couldn't stay either.

She began fumbling with the huge pile of keys they kept in the lockbox.

'You must think me an idiot, forgetting where I'm staying.' Alex's deep voice was so close to her neck that it sent shivers of longing down her spine.

'Did you remember it this morning?' she teased, and laughed at the sheepish cringe he made. He'd not remembered much last night, like the name of his hotel or his driver, and Richie had left early. Probably because, whenever he'd looked their way, they'd downed a glass of fizz.

'No, but I remembered how to check my booking information on my cell.'

Ellie continued to look for the right key, more aware of the tight space and Alex's big body with every passing second. She had no idea what half of them were used for, and suspected most were for locks they no longer had. 'That's good. Although I think Nanna would adopt you given half a chance.'

'Sounds good to me,' he said, a layer of sadness sitting beneath his humour.

She looked up with a twinge of concern. 'It'll be okay, you know.'

'Thanks for saying that.' He swept a hand through his hair, not quite meeting her eyes. 'Can I have your number? You promised to come with me to the Olivier Awards, remember?'

Her stomach dropped to her bunny-eared feet. 'Do you still mean that? I mean… we both had a lot to drink…'

'The offer stands – if you want to, I'd be grateful. I don't have any friends this side of the pond.'

Her heart expanded and contracted painfully with a mixture of excitement and hope that made her uncomfortable. *He wants a friend!* she reminded herself sternly.

Concentrating on finding the key, she shrugged lightly. 'Sure.' But she doubted it would really happen. It was a drunken promise. If he found someone better, she was sure the invitation would be quickly rescinded. She'd been here before, making arrangements for dates that would never happen. She swore men liked to suggest another date just to avoid an awkward goodbye. Frankly, she wished the cowards were just honest from the start. She was sick of false promises – she'd had enough of them with David to last her a lifetime.

All the flowers and gifts, the sweet words and promises – all made in private, of course. Had David meant any of it? Or had he simply been lonely? Desperate for someone to shower with love, and like a fool she'd taken all of the lies he'd fed her, because she was desperate to love and be loved in return?

Never again.

'Ah-hah!' Grateful to have finally found the right key, she unlocked the back door, and then turned to face him. 'I gave my number to you last night, remember? When we were promising to be best friends for ever. I'm under, Ellie BFF.' Good old Ellie, always the reliable friend.

Alex blushed, a sweet rush of pink painting his gloriously high cheekbones. 'Of course. Best friends for ever.'

Why did that make her feel so sad? Maybe because she'd already had a best friend and she was currently flying thousands of miles away from her. Alex would do the same, sooner or later.

'The lock on the gate is a bit dodgy.' She walked out into the yard, her ridiculous slippers slapping against the flagstones as she moved.

As usual, the latch stuck and the rusty bolt refused to budge. She wiggled it from side to side and then pulled at the same time as she threw the bolt. 'There,' she said triumphantly, throwing open the gate.

A flashing light and a shouted, 'Alex!' blinded her as she froze in mortification, like an actual rabbit caught in the headlights. A horde of photographers stood in front of her, and with a leap forward they all shoved their cameras in her face.

Chapter Five

Alex slammed the gate shut with one hand and grabbed Ellie's elbow with the other. 'Back inside! How did they know I was here?'

Did they follow me last night? But there'd been no sign of them when he'd checked the window first thing this morning.

Brown eyes shining with tears and horror stared back at him. 'Honestly, I have no idea!'

He squeezed her arm gently. 'I know.'

'*Alex? Who is she? Are you over Savannah?*' shouted a voice from above. The cockroaches had scaled the wall and were leaning over it precariously, trying to take more photos.

'This is *private* property!' Ellie shouted back, the shock obviously giving way to anger as she began to rattle the gate, causing the paparazzi to wobble. 'I'll call the police! Get off my bloody wall!' Her eyes were spitting deadly fire and he wouldn't have been surprised if she'd thrown her slippers at them.

He tugged her away and she stumbled after him, the soft fluffiness of her dressing gown brushing against his arms and chest. His lips twitched with amusement as he bundled her back inside. Her outrage on his behalf was kind of flattering.

With a bang, he shut the door, relieved that there was only one tiny window in the dim corridor and that the glass was warped to provide privacy. A firm barrier between them and the outside world. The Victorian brick smothered the shouts of the paparazzi, until he could almost believe they were alone.

Their breathing was heavy from the run and the panic. Ellie clutched the collar of her fluffy dressing gown closed, her face flushed and her hair tumbling around her in messy waves, a few pink petals still tangled in her hair from last night. The sweet, heady scent of Ellie and *precocious* blossom clung to her skin. He wanted to wrap his arms around her, reassure her that everything would be all right, but he knew that would be a lie.

Once the media had a story they were like a dog with a bone. He needed to speak with Richie – he'd know how to handle it. 'It's best not to engage, that's what they want,' he said.

Dismay filled her eyes, and she glanced fearfully at the window. 'Is this what it's like? People chasing you, shouting personal questions at you?'

'Sometimes.'

Her expression softened with sympathy. 'It must be horrible. Almost makes me glad I'm a boring old nurse.'

'It's not always like this. Most of the time I'm not even recognised. It's because of Liam and Savannah. They're the big stars, and I'm just the villain. I guess the love triangle makes for a juicy story, and they're trying to get a rise out of me, that's all. They'll get bored eventually.'

'That's awful.'

He sighed, because it was awful – and he'd dragged Ellie into his mess. Being with her had almost made him forget the bitter truth: that he didn't belong anywhere, not even with his own family. For years he'd been playing a part, and now that everything had gone to shit he wasn't sure who he was any more.

'What's going on?' called Ellie's mother as she and her nanna came hurrying down the stairs. Mark opened the door beside them. It looked as if he hadn't opened the shop yet – which was a good thing, as Alex was sure the photographers would try the front next. He couldn't hide inside for ever – they had a business to run.

Guilt gnawed at his insides. None of them deserved any of this. He should have left as soon as he'd woken up, but he'd wanted to see Ellie. Hadn't wanted their time together to come to an end. Now, his selfishness was costing a whole family their privacy.

'There are photographers outside the front too,' said Mark, giving a fearful glance at the half-raised metal shutters and the moving shadows beyond.

Ellie's brow furrowed. 'I don't understand how they knew you were here. Unless they followed us? But there wasn't anyone around when we got home last night… Was there?' He shook his head and her frown deepened in thought. 'Unless someone tipped them off?'

'Don't look at me!' cried Mark.

Everyone looked at him.

Alex took pity on Mark and retrieved his phone from his pocket. 'I'll call my agent. He can get a car out to me in no time. What's your address?'

'Why don't we call Martin instead?' asked Ellie's nanna. 'I'm sure he could help us out. He could even help create a diversion.'

Ellie nodded enthusiastically. 'Yes! He only lives around the corner and he drives a black cab. I'm sure he could get a friend of his to help as well. If we have one cab pull up out the front first, that'll distract them while you get into another out the back. Maybe Mark could go out with a hoodie and sunglasses on – he's almost the same height as you.'

'Yeah, I can do that. Happy to help.' Mark shrugged sheepishly.

Alex looked around at their eager faces and tucked his phone away. They were so desperate to help, he didn't want to disappoint them. 'Sure, let's do this.'

—

It all went according to plan, which was a miracle in itself.

Martin was happy to help. He called a buddy of his, and one black cab rolled up out front, followed by another two minutes later down the back alley. The photographers had all swarmed to the front of the building as planned, not realising there was a second cab arriving. Mark distracted the crowd further by walking out front in a pulled-up hoodie and shades, while Ellie's nanna opened the shop. It all happened so fast that in no time Alex was waving goodbye to Ellie through the back window as his black cab sped off down a side street.

'Thanks for doing this,' he said to the driver, a bald man in his late fifties.

'No worries, mate, anything for Ellie. She's been my girl's best friend since they were kids – been through thick and thin together. She's a good girl.'

'Yeah, she's awesome,' Alex agreed, relaxing into the leather seat.

He only hoped this wouldn't be the last time he saw her. Ellie had agreed the previous night to come to the awards with him, but she'd seemed reluctant when he'd mentioned it this morning. Understandable really, considering she barely knew him, and she'd now experienced the chaos of his life first hand.

Should he leave her be? Forget taking her to the Olivier Awards and let her live her life?

Why had he even asked her in the first place?

He thought of how his blood heated every time he was near her, the tempting curves of her body and the playful gleam in her eye. And then he thought of how Ellie had been the first person to form any sort of connection with him in months, possibly even years, and how the weight of his loneliness lifted in her company. But hadn't he moved around enough as a kid to realise that no relationships were ever permanent? Especially under the glare of public scrutiny. He should focus on finding his feet, rebuilding his life, not dragging someone else into his mess. Besides, he was asking too much of her, and she was vulnerable after losing her friend.

'Is your daughter called Hannah?' Alex asked curiously.

'Yes, that's her. Had to drop her off at Heathrow very early this morning. Not ashamed to say it, we shed a fair few tears saying goodbye to her. Me and the wife are going to miss her like mad. Yer lucky the traffic was good and I was back in time to help ya.'

'I'm sorry, you must be exhausted.'

'Nah, yer all right,' said Martin with a shake of his shiny head. 'Happy to help. Sometimes it's best to keep busy – a welcome distraction, honestly. I'll be worried sick until I know she's landed safe.'

Alex settled down and listened to Martin chat about his family and the unseasonably warm weather they'd been having, while they wound through the grey London streets. But his mind kept returning to Martin's earlier words: *a welcome distraction.*

Had he been wrong to hide away and avoid the press? Wouldn't it be better to give them something – positive – to focus on? A welcome distraction?

But what could possibly distract the paparazzi from Liam and Savannah's wedding and turn the tide of bad feeling towards him? Fame was a double-edged sword. He hated it, but he also knew he would have no work without it. Even this theatre-directing gig would have been impossible without his connections and celebrity status.

Which again raised the question: who would he be if he wasn't part of the King family legacy?

'Here you are,' said Martin, bringing him back down to earth, as they pulled up outside his hotel.

'Ah, thanks man,' Alex said, getting out his wallet.

'No need.'

They had a good-natured battle for payment for a few moments. Eventually Martin accepted the notes Alex thrust at him, and gave him his number in case Alex got stuck without a driver again.

Alex's phone began to ring as he entered his suite. A quick glance at the caller ID showed that it was the theatre's executive director.

'Hi, Russell, what's up?' he said, with a brightness he didn't feel as he lowered himself into a nearby armchair in his lounge. Absently, he took off his glasses and rubbed the bridge of his nose.

'Good morning, Alex, how was the party, I hear it was a late one? Hope you're feeling well enough to attend the matinee.' Russell's voice was crisp and polished, as if he'd had elocution lessons from the King of England.

Shit, had he heard about last night already?

Alex couldn't remember talking to anyone much except for Ellie, but his memory was like Swiss cheese.

'Of course,' he answered, part of him bristling at the implied censure. Who was Russell to question his lifestyle? Except he was, in fact, his boss. He wasn't in LA now, he couldn't just expect people to bow and scrape around him. 'I'll be in by twelve, plenty of time for the matinee,' he said, keeping his voice light and relaxed.

Russell chuckled good-naturedly. Thankfully, he wasn't the type to hold a grudge – just quietly point out his disapproval. 'Good, good. I wasn't sure, you see, when you didn't come in at your usual time. But always nice to celebrate opening night. Let off a little steam and all that. Then straight back to work, hey? Focus on the run and keeping up those five-star reviews. I said as much to the cast and crew this morning.'

Alex's stomach twisted with guilt, but he'd never agreed to come in at the same time during the run as he had during rehearsals. 'Well, best get going, I'll see you soon anyway...' He waited expectantly for Russell to agree and end the call. Unfortunately, he didn't.

Russell cleared his throat dramatically – definitely a Royal Shakespeare Company-approved cough. 'Ah-hum... Just a couple of things while I've got you.'

Alex crossed his fingers and prayed that Russell wasn't going to shorten the play's run any further. 'Yeah?'

'I know you don't want any fuss with marketing and promotion. But... we could really do with some publicity to promote the play.'

Alex gritted his teeth until his jaw ached. But he tried his best to remain in character as Alex the relaxed and always-in-control director. 'I'm sorry, man, but Richie's contract is quite clear. You can use my name, but all interviews must be with the actors only.'

Russell's reply was professional and direct. 'Indeed, and I commend your artistic integrity and strict privacy rules, of course I do.' He took a breath. 'That being said...'

Here we go.

Russell cleared his throat again, and Alex had the uneasy feeling his character had slipped for just a moment, and maybe, just maybe, he'd inadvertently muttered those internal words out loud. He cringed.

'That being *said*,' Russell continued, more sharply this time. 'This is a theatre, and we need to promote our plays to sell tickets. Especially as it's only a short run. Now, it's a great play – wonderful, even – but how will people know that unless they hear about it? And *how* will they hear about it if the biggest name behind it refuses *all* interviews with the press?'

Alex opened his mouth to speak, but couldn't think of an appropriate response. It was true, he'd insisted on cast approval in his contract, and had chosen relatively unknown actors to star in his play. He'd wanted to help launch careers – but had that been a mistake? Theatre audiences loved big names.

'I have a reporter from the *Arts Review* keen to interview within the next day or two,' said Russell firmly. 'They're not tabloid, they're aimed at our core audience. So, their questions will be focused purely on the play. It's up to you – this is a fabulous production, but it needs exposure, and who better to do that than its director, hmmm?'

Russell had a point. Alex took a deep breath and chose his words carefully. 'My contract was clear. But I will think about it, and I'm sure we can work something out.'

'Good, good. Glad to hear you're considering the needs of the production first. The cast is full of bright fresh talent, and their careers could rise or fall because of this.' Russell's tone had hardened by the end of his speech, and he left Alex hanging in the silence.

'I understand.'

The good-natured boss returned with a cheerful, 'Good, good! Glad we understand each other. Cheerio,' before he promptly ended the call with a hard click.

Alex's aching head dropped back against his armchair. He had the uneasy feeling he'd just said yes to the interview without actually saying yes.

Chapter Six

Ellie only had two more days off until she was back at the Royal and working seven nights straight, followed by days, then more nights. It was meant to distract her from Hannah's leaving, but, rather than luxuriating in the last moments of her freedom, Ellie was restless.

She floated around the house doing anything to distract herself from looking at her phone. After putting on a couple of washes, dusting the shop and cleaning the bathrooms, she'd decided to reorder the mugs so they would be less higgledy-piggledy the next time they had guests – for goodness' sake, how many celebrities did she expect to bring back each night?

Halfway through the sorting, she discovered some dusty mugs at the back and decided to wash them first before tidying them away. She glanced at the black mirror of her phone, perched against the wall and counter. As always it remained blank and silent. She checked it anyway. Maybe a text had come in while she hadn't been looking?

Nope. You're officially delusional.

Alex wasn't going to call or text her. He probably never wanted to see her again after the fiasco with the press this morning, let alone take her to the fanciest theatre awards ceremony in London. It really shouldn't be a surprise that Alex had behaved like all the other men she'd met in the past – seeming to lack any sense of object permanence. When a woman was out of sight, she was out of mind, and Ellie was sick of having her hopes raised only to have them stomped on moments later. Hadn't she sworn to herself that she wouldn't prioritise men any more? To focus solely on the areas of her life she could control, like owning her own home?

The last guy she'd messaged on a dating app had seemed really sweet at first, until he'd told her bluntly that *'luckily for her, he was into thicc women. But he was a bit skint at the moment, so did she just want to have phone sex rather than go on a date?'* She'd promptly blocked him and deleted the app.

After David, that creep had been the final straw, and she'd made her New Year's resolution not long after.

Damn David! He had been like the scorched earth of her love life, turning her once hopeful and romantic dreams into an embarrassment. He'd love-bombed her – that was what Hannah had called it – with over-the-top gestures and lightning-speed love declarations; flowers, gifts, intimate weekends away. He'd been gorgeous, and she'd been so blinded by all of his attention that she hadn't noticed all of the red flags – his secretiveness, the fact that he wouldn't allow her to post anything about them on social media, the distant way he treated her in the gym in front of his friends, because he 'liked to concentrate on his workout'.

All lies. The truth was he'd been ashamed of her.

She was spiralling, and she gripped the counter to steady her racing thoughts.

Alex was a friend, and, if nothing else, Ellie was always a good friend. She turned to look at Mark, who'd made a mess of making his lunch. But she couldn't even be mad about that because it had given her something else to clean. Although, there was something else she could be mad about – if her suspicions were correct.

'Stop glaring at me,' said Mark, avoiding her eyes as he ploughed through his lunch, a bacon baguette the length of a baby's arm.

She didn't even blink. Instead, she continued to dry the chopping board with the corgi tea towel. Slow methodical movements just to irritate him. 'You were really shifty earlier,' she said mildly.

He stopped chewing and finally looked up at her. 'What do you mean?' he grunted through a mouthful of food, deception clearly written all over his crumb-covered face.

God, were all brothers this disgusting?

'Don't look at me!' she mocked in a high-pitched voice, waving the tea towel for dramatic effect.

A telltale flush began creeping up his neck – caught red-handed, or red-faced, she supposed.

'I knew it,' she snapped, whipping the tea towel against the kitchen table. Mark jumped, which was satisfying in itself.

'Look, I'm sorry, I didn't think it would blow up as it did. I thought it'd just be one, maybe two.' He put down the baguette with a miserable grimace.

'Why? Why would you do that?' Mark was many things, but deliberately cruel was not one of them.

He crossed his arms and pretended nonchalance. 'Oh, come on. I'm sure he's used to it. What does it matter if a few people got his picture?'

'He was my friend,' she said sharply, refusing to back down.

And there it was, the unspoken rule. You didn't mess with your siblings' friends. You didn't date them, you didn't slag them off, and you *definitely* didn't hurt or embarrass them.

Mark couldn't meet her eyes.

'Why?' she repeated, softer this time, as a horrible feeling began to churn in the pit of her stomach.

He looked pointedly at the closed door and then back at her. Whatever it was, he didn't want Nanna or Mum to know.

This is going to be bad.

'Nanna's out, and I presume Mum's watching the shop while you eat? So, come on, spit it out.' She noticed the worry lines on his forehead. Her 28-year-old brother suddenly seemed a lot older than he actually was.

'I thought I could make some money.' She continued to stare at him, and he twisted under her gaze like a spider under a magnifying glass. 'We had a tough time last year.'

'Understatement.' Mum had told her they hadn't made any profit last year. Small businesses like theirs were struggling. They'd taken a massive hit during the pandemic, then there'd been the credit crunch, the astronomical rise in the cost of living. One disaster after another. Thank God they owned the shop and house outright.

'Well, the rates and insurance have gone up, and the tax bill was double what I expected. Sales are still bad. I thought if I sold them the story of Alex being here, then I could keep us going for a bit longer, but turns out they don't pay much anyway, so it wasn't even worth it. If things don't improve, we might have to close the shop at the end of the month... For good.'

Ellie flinched as if he'd struck her. They couldn't close the shop. It was their family's pride and joy. 'No, absolutely not.' She stepped away from the counter, her fists clenched tight, as if she were about to fight back. But who was she going to fight? Mark? Yes, he was useless at keeping track of the accounts, but the shop was his life's blood. Whatever risks he'd taken, they would always have been for the good of the shop. For all his faults, Mark loved the shop, just as much as – probably more than – she did.

Mark ran his hand through his hair and pushed away his half-eaten baguette. 'Well, we might have to.'

Ellie's heart broke. She couldn't let this happen; this was their home, her family history and future. 'I can give you my flat deposit,' she blurted out.

He blinked. 'I can't ask that of you – that's your savings, your future.'

Her jaw tightened. He was right, but it was still the right thing to do. She *had* to help her family. Yes, it would mean the end of her dreams for her own flat, but if it saved the shop? Their family home? There was no question about it. 'You're not asking. I'm doing it.'

Mark looked miserable, and she suddenly felt very sorry for her idiotic brother. How long had he kept this burden to himself?

'You'd just be throwing good money after bad. It might keep us going for another six months, a year maybe, but the business just isn't profitable any more.'

'Then we should make it profitable. Our family's done it before, we can do it again. Change, diversify. Try something new. We can't give up.'

He blinked up at her as if seeing her for the first time, a glimmer of hope in his eyes. 'Maybe. I mean, I had one idea…'

Ellie sagged with relief. She'd say this for Mark, he always had decent ideas… mostly. The personalised balloons hadn't worked out well. No one needed to see themselves in balloon form – it was the stuff of nightmares. But it boded well that he'd at least considered some changes to save them.

'I wondered about becoming a cafe, or maybe starting a personalised gift delivery service. But don't mention it to Mum, you know how she gets about change and I need to think it over first. Oh, and don't mention it to Nanna either. I don't want them to worry, not yet at least.'

Ellie tried not to roll her eyes. Nanna was tougher than he thought, but he might have a point about Mum – she never took bad news well. 'Will do.'

Mark winced. 'Especially… as it might mean an initial investment.'

Well, she had offered. 'Okay, sounds great. Have a think about it. Do a business plan or whatever. I'm sure we can sort something out, and I'll send you the money.'

The worry lines on Mark's forehead relaxed, and in one quick motion he stood up and wrapped her in a fierce bear hug. 'Thanks, Sis.'

Swatting his arm playfully, she untangled herself from him. 'No problem. Everything is going to be fine. So, don't worry.' She tried not to show how gutted she was. Her own dreams were nothing but ash now. Why couldn't someone take care of her for a change, instead of her having to constantly tear chunks off herself to make other people happy?

'And that thing with Alex? I won't do it again, I swear,' said Mark solemnly, his head low.

She snorted lightly. 'I doubt I'll ever see him again. But it's good to know there'll not be another picture of me out in my slippers and dressing gown.'

He grinned. 'You're safe. Besides, the money was rubbish. Nanna's brought home more from bingo.'

They both laughed because Nanna never won anything at bingo, and had more than once complained about it being '*ruddy fixed by that sodding Kathleen*'.

'Right, best get back to work,' Mark said, and walked out of the door, with more of a spring in his step.

When he was gone, she finally allowed her disappointment to show, slumping down at the kitchen table with a heavy sigh. She was still holding the damp corgi tea towel, and now she dropped it with a soft splat that echoed her mood. She'd never afford a place on her own now. This was like watching paper catch on fire; in a matter of moments, her revised plans had been eaten away and turned into smoke.

So, what now? Renting? She couldn't even afford that on her own; she'd have to find a flatshare. Living with strangers, who would be weird, or too young to understand that she didn't want to party every night.

Nope, her only option was to stay at home with her family and help out with the shop occasionally... for ever.

Unless she was really *lucky* and settled with some boring bloke who liked *thicc women* and was generous enough to buy her a coffee. Her stomach flipped. Hadn't her mum done that with her dad? Settled, only to be divorced with two kids after only a few years? No thanks. Perhaps she could save some money and join Hannah in Australia. But that had been Hannah's dream, not her own.

Damn Mark. Damn Hannah. Damn her poorly paid nursing job!

'Damn!' She picked up the soggy tea towel and whipped it against the table. When that didn't help, she whipped it again and again. Punctuating every crack of her whip with another, 'Damn, Damn, Damn, Damn, DAMN!'

'You all right, love?' Her mum stood in the doorway looking concerned.

She threw aside the tea towel and busied herself tidying up her brother's lunch. 'Yeah, I'm fine.'

'Hmmm, okay. Well, Alex seems nice. Shame he didn't stay...' she said, clicking the kettle on before she began to help Ellie tidy up.

Subtle, Mum, real subtle. 'Yeah, he's lovely.' She refused to rise to the bait.

'Has he got a boyfriend?'

Ellie stopped still. 'What?'

'Well, I just presumed he was gay,' said her mum with a defensive shrug of her shoulders.

'Why? Because he came home with me and that must make him gay?' Ellie asked waspishly, already irritated that she had, as always, risen to the bait.

'Of course not,' snapped her mum. But Ellie knew the truth. Her mum was tormented by her own body issues, and unfortunately that had had a knock-on effect on Ellie. She'd been able to ignore most of it when she'd left home, had even repaired some of the damage caused by her mum's dieting obsession. But now she was home, it felt like death by a thousand cuts.

She grabbed her phone from the side, trying not to feel disheartened at the lack of notifications. Brutal confirmation of her one-way ticket to Delulu-loser-ville.

'He's just very polite and sweet. You were the one that said nothing happened between the two of you. What else was I supposed to think?'

Ellie rolled her eyes – and almost dropped her phone when it started to ring.

Her mum watched her with wide eyes and growing excitement as Ellie listened to the person on the other end of the phone.

'Sure, why not, seven p.m. is fine,' she said, and ended the call.

Her mum clutched the kitchen counter as if to steady herself. 'Was that…?'

Ellie put her out of her misery. 'Work. There's an extra shift going.'

'Oh.' Her mum's shoulders slumped. 'But you're doing nights next week, aren't you? That's not very fair.'

'They need me,' Ellie said with a shrug, and tried to ignore the cat's bum her mum's mouth was making and left the room to put on her uniform.

–

Ellie deeply regretted saying yes to this last-minute shift within an hour of arriving. The night was slow and boring – much like her love life. But they were short-staffed and she needed the money.

As happened quite often in A&E, things changed rapidly. Her quiet shift turned into a shit-storm of epic proportions. She had a series of people from a bar stabbing, followed by a car crash involving a bus. But the hardest moment of all came, as it always did, out of the blue.

An alcoholic and homeless man called Bob came in suffering from bronchitis and chest pains. Nothing new, as he was asthmatic and came in most weeks with breathing difficulties. Usually, he was checked over and sent back out again with nothing more than a prescription. He was polite and sweet, with a dry sense of humour, and all of the nurses liked Bob and didn't mind that he was in and out of their care like a bad penny.

Tonight, he died in triage, before anyone had had time to examine him properly. He died as he lived, quietly and without much fuss. Alone.

Ellie finished her shift with a heavy heart, and, as she stepped out into the brisk early morning air, every ache and pain of the last twelve hours hit her with full force.

She quickly checked the Australian time difference on her phone, then called Hannah while she walked off the stress of her long shift. The morning light was weak and milky against the backdrop of the surrounding red and cream brick buildings.

She passed the rainbow signs asking people to respect NHS staff – because yes, people did apparently need a reminder – and walked past the quiet Victorian warehouses, pubs, graffiti-splattered walls and huddled shops towards home. The skyscrapers of the City sparkled in the distance, a world away from here, and yet always present. The rich and the powerful staring down at her like the little worker-ant she was.

Depressing.

In contrast, Hannah's voice was bright and energised. It reverberated down the line to her, as if she were shouting down one of their old string-cup phones. 'Oh my God, hi! How was your night with *the* Alex King? I swear he fancied you!'

Ellie tried to match her enthusiasm and failed. She didn't want to think about Alex. 'Oh, don't be silly, nothing happened. Besides, I'm strictly off men, remember? Especially the handsome ones way out of my league.'

Hannah made a tutting sound. 'No one is out of your league.'

Ellie was quick to move on. 'Anyway, how's life down under? You arrive okay?'

'Yes, and it's wonderful! My cousins took me to the beach as soon as I arrived. Although my surfing skills need improvement.' Her merry laugh blended with the sound of ocean waves crashing in the background. 'I wiped out more times than I can count.'

'No jet lag then?'

'I'm running on adrenaline.'

This conversation was the opposite of what she needed right now, but she grimly battled on. 'Sounds amazing! Send me plenty of pics, I bet the beaches are stunning. Well, I just wanted to check in and see if you arrived safe. Glad you're having fun.'

There was a crackling pause. 'Are you okay? Has something happened?'

'Nothing major... just, well, No-One Bob died. Cardiac arrest.' Their bad-taste nickname stuck in her throat. They'd called him that after so many times, writing *No one*, on his next-of-kin forms.

'Oh no, poor Bob. Are you okay?' It was all Hannah could or needed to say. Unlike anyone else, she knew how Ellie felt. The quiet grief beneath the professional face was hard, but it was also normal.

She was about to paste on some fake joviality and pretend everything was all okay, but she found she couldn't. With every step the sparkling towers seemed to loom closer, and her ability to hide behind her usual confidence crumbled.

'I don't think I can keep up with this any more...'

There was silence on the other end of the phone, but she could hear Hannah's patient, even breath, giving her the time to talk.

'Working every shift and every bit of overtime that I can get... and what for? A bad back and no one to go home to? I just... I don't think I can take it any more.' She sighed, feeling better now she'd dragged out the truth. To be honest, it surprised even her to say it out loud.

'What else would you do?' Hannah's voice remained calm. She'd already realised this, of course; it was why she'd left. 'Forget about everything else for a minute. What would you want, if you could have anything? How would your life look?'

She nosedived into the endless possibilities, but they only frightened her further. 'I don't know... More free time, a cute cat to snuggle up with at night...' *A family of my own.*

'Would you give up nursing?'

'No.' The answer was quick and certain, a relief. 'But maybe fewer hours, or more reasonable hours.'

'Move departments? Go into teaching or community nursing?'

'Maybe...'

'Well, that's a start. Something for you to think about.'

'If I had the time,' she grumbled.

'Make the time,' snapped Hannah, and Ellie was surprised by the strength in her docile friend's tone. 'I'm serious. If you're about to burn out, you need to take some time out and think about what you really want. And then sort a plan, and *make* it work.' x 'Maybe...' She hated to admit defeat, but Hannah was right. She'd worked so hard for the goal of her own place. But with the fate of the shop at stake, she'd given it all up in a heartbeat. Which left her working her arse off for nothing. She needed to slow down, to rethink.

'You need a holiday, Ellie, and I'm not saying that just because I want you to come out here and visit me. I'm saying it because I was about to burn out myself. Coming out here, that's part of my plan. I think things are going to be better for me over here. I might even try nursing here. The pay is better, the patient ratios… I need to look into getting my registration, but I'm feeling… hopeful.'

Ellie wiped away a tear. She hadn't realised she was crying until she'd felt the wetness on her cheek. Hannah seemed so confident, so certain, and she wished she could feel the same, but she didn't. Despite her bravado, Ellie was lost. Not quite as alone as Bob, but almost. She tried to gather her strength, but the idea of Hannah living in Australia permanently was another bitter blow. She resolutely brightened her voice. 'Now, tell me more about you learning to surf.'

—

When she got home, Ellie couldn't face her family. She decided to go to bed, sleep and then go straight out again.

Not to work though.

She wanted to relive the fantasy of being friends with Alex King. She was like Gatsby, staring out across the void, longing for a life she could never have.

No, she would put on her glad rags and go see his play. Pretend she lived in a nicer world.

How cool would it be to have someone as interesting and gorgeous as Alex as her boyfriend? She could pretend in her mind that she was going to see her boyfriend's play, and imagine a life where she wasn't single, skint, and living at home in her thirties.

She only hoped Alex didn't see her and think she was stalking him.

Chapter Seven

Following the matinee performance, Alex met with the *Arts Review* journalist and photographer for an interview. Russell had pretty much taken their conversation this morning as a green light and had been quick to arrange it before Alex could think of some excuse to wriggle out of the meeting.

The photographer was taking shots of the actors on set, while the interviewer, a cheerful Asian woman in her mid-fifties called Mei, sat with him in the front of the auditorium.

She crossed her legs and turned her platform heel towards him. Her phone rested on the arm of her chair, recording their conversation – she may as well have placed a cobra next to her; he would have been less nervous.

Mei wore a smart and fashionable pink trouser suit that reminded him of some of the play's costumes; bright and stylish, it screamed corporate glamour. 'Thank you so much for agreeing to speak with me, Alex.'

Russell beamed at them from across the auditorium like a proud stage mom. Alex suspected he hadn't run this past Richie, but then again his agent rarely came to the theatre. In fact, he was a little surprised Richie had come to London at all, considering how little he saw of him normally. Still, Richie – despite his faults – had shown far more loyalty than the rest of his family, none of whom had taken a day or two out of their busy schedule to come and see his play.

Alex stepped into the charming persona he always wore during interviews. Friendly, yet professional. 'Did you enjoy the performance, Mei? By the way, love your suit. You look like you could be part of the show.' He was careful to give her a compliment early on. A trick his mother had taught him to help make a connection with journalists, and hopefully keep them on your side.

Mei beamed with enthusiasm. 'I loved the performance, and thank you. You've certainly brought the luxurious glamour of New York to the West End.'

The interview started well, plenty of questions about the actors and his artistic choices, and Alex quickly relaxed.

His first mistake.

'How did your own experience growing up in a famous Hollywood family inspire your interpretation of Gatsby's parties?' Mei blinked wide, innocent eyes at him.

He laughed to hide his building anxiety at the more personal question, and then gave a couple of sweet anecdotes about his mom's star-studded Halloween costume parties, all while being careful to steer it back to the costume and set designers he'd chosen for the production.

However, the next question tested his acting skills and patience to the max.

Mei tilted her head thoughtfully. 'Did your recent break-up influence your direction of this production?'

Alex glanced at the recording phone, an unspoken threat. To buy time and collect his thoughts, he sipped from his water bottle. If he denied any heartache or refused to comment, it might be viewed as confirmation that he was the callous villain after all, but if he told the truth and explained the situation it would paint his family in a poor light – or, worse, be viewed as defensive lies.

'Mei…' He purred her name, in a subtle rebuke, fixing her with a firm look that made her shift in her seat. He waved his hand dismissively. 'I don't really know what you mean. I'm at an exciting point in my career, and feeling optimistic for the future and that of my family. Now, Gatsby on the other hand, and in fact all of the characters in this production, are tragically doomed…' He went on to explain the themes and how he explored them with his direction, then wrapped up the interview quickly by saying he had to go and congratulate the actors on another brilliant performance.

But he made a point of glaring at Russell as he passed him, and said coldly, 'No more interviews.'

-

Before the evening performance, Alex hurried towards the sound booth at the back of the theatre where he usually sat and took notes during the performance. At some point he would have to let go of this production. That was what most directors did, watch one or two performances, give some notes, and then move on. After all, once a production was smoothly up and running there was little else for a director to do.

Unless he became a resident director – but Richie had said Russell wasn't keen on that idea. He wanted Alex for his big name, and then gone. Why then, was Alex still here, with no plans to leave? Did he want to be sure of the play's success, or his own?

It was probably both. He had no idea what he was going to do after this. Nobody was approaching him for more projects, which was no surprise considering the amount of heat he was currently under what with Liam and Savannah's upcoming wedding.

Richie had suggested going back to LA, meeting some producers and seeing what happened. But he didn't want to leave London; it would feel like accepting he wasn't good enough – again. Theatre directing was meant to be his fresh start, a new career separate from his family's movie star lives. The production was going well and had already received critical acclaim. Not selling as much as he'd hoped, granted, but there was little he could do about that other than hope the positive reviews had worked their magic.

The ushers had opened the auditorium doors and the audience were slowly making their way in, so Alex raised his hood and quickened his pace as he made his way up the stairs two at a time. A canary-yellow dress and a shapely figure on the opposite staircase happened to catch his eye. His foot missed a step, and he had to grab the handrail to stop himself falling forward.

Ellie was here! His heart immediately raced wildly at the sight of her. She was as bright as a summer's day, her dark hair falling in soft waves down her shoulders and over a fluffy white cardigan.

The sundress fitted her like a glove and brought out the olive tone of her skin. Like a 1950s Italian bombshell, she seemed to dominate the space, all dramatic curves and sexy cleavage that flounced enticingly as she moved.

The fluffy cardigan was to soften her look and more importantly, keep her warm in London's ever-changing spring weather. Clutching a raincoat and a vintage purse to her stomach, he noticed her squinting at the row's letters and chair numbers as she tried to find her seat. She needn't have worried. It wasn't a full house and most of the audience had bought tickets near the front or middle to get the best view. If he'd known she was coming he would have comped her ticket.

Gingerly she began to sidestep down her row, her round hips swaying as she navigated the narrow space and apologised to the couple of people who had to move to let her pass. She'd not noticed Alex on the stairs opposite her. He took several deep breaths to slow down the jittery excitement pulsing through his veins, before he practically ran down the aisle to join her. Thankfully, there was no one else in the row to slow his progress.

Ellie had come to see his play! He felt like he'd won the lottery.

None of his family had come, but Ellie had. A woman he'd only met two nights ago was more of a friend to him than his own flesh and blood.

Am I crazy to feel so happy about it?

'Ellie,' he called softly, hoping not to frighten her, but she jumped anyway.

'Alex! Oh God, you must think I'm a stalker, but I could only really come today, I'm working nights next week,' she blurted out as her face flushed pink, her eyes darting around the theatre fearfully, as if she expected the cops to drag her away in handcuffs.

'No, I'm glad you're here,' he whispered, taking the empty seat next to her. The lights lowered to signal the start of the show, and an electric silence descended over the audience, who were tense with anticipation. He looked around at the many empty seats around them and winced. Sadly, there'd not been a great immediate uptake in sales despite the glowing reviews they'd received since opening night, but maybe they just needed a little more time to get the word out?

Ellie's whisper distracted him from that depressing thought. 'It sounded so good. I had to come and see it.'

'I'm glad you did.'

She leaned close and licked her lips, sending a shiver of awareness down his spine. 'I'm sorry about yesterday,' she said, her eyes pained.

'Don't be.'

'It was Mark.' She barely drew breath before continuing in a rush, 'My brother. He told the press. I'm *so* sorry. He didn't realise how bad it would be, and he's worried about money, and they paid him. Although that's no excuse, and I think he realises that now. He's promised never to do it again. Not that there will be an *again*. But you know...'

'Look, don't worry, it's fine.' He reached for her hand and squeezed her warm fingers, the touch so natural and right that he held them for a little longer than he'd intended. Her eyes dropped to their entwined hands and she released a heavy breath.

'Thank you. You're so nice.'

No man liked to hear that. Hadn't Savannah called him that when they'd broken up – *nice*? Nice was boring, lacklustre, nothing special. He was sick of being nice. As he eased back in his seat, their hands naturally broke apart. Nothing lasts, he reminded himself, and other than a couple of heated looks there was nothing in Ellie's behaviour to suggest she wanted anything more from their friendship. Was he allowing his loneliness to get the better of him? Expecting too much from Ellie in return? He could lose her friendship before it even had a chance to begin.

The curtains opened, the actors locked in position for a moment of breathless stillness and then the play began.

For the first time, he didn't take notes during the performance. Usually, he was busy jotting down areas to improve, issues that needed fixing, as well as praise. From being an actor himself, he knew a director's feedback could make or break the morale of the cast and crew. But tonight, his notebook stayed firmly in his hoodie's pocket. Instead he stole glances at Ellie to gauge the success of his show.

She laughed at all the appropriate moments and gasped with awe at the spectacular party scenes. Things would take more of a depressing turn after the interval, and as the curtain closed on the first half, he knew he'd sit through the rest of it with her.

To stroke his fragile ego further, he couldn't help but ask, 'Did you like it?' Then he held a tight breath as he waited for her verdict.

As she turned towards him, her signature megawatt smile blew away all the shadows in his mind. 'You know I did, I think you watched me more than the actors.'

That was true, and he gave a wry shrug at her observation. 'It's good to see the audience's reaction.' Except he'd only been watching Ellie. 'I've watched it so many times I could play every part. Watching you meant I could see things I might have otherwise missed. Like when you frowned at Myrtle's first scene. Didn't you like her performance?'

'What? No, she was great. The sets are amazing. That party scene? Wowza! It made me want to throw on a sequin dress and dance.'

'I'm glad. But you're avoiding my question.'

Ellie tossed her head to one side thoughtfully. It was reassuring to be with someone so inherently open. He'd lived his life beside excellent, award-winning actors, and it was hard to know what was real emotion and what was acting bullshit. He'd found it almost impossible to know when people were genuinely sorry, angry or, even, in love, but Ellie in contrast was passionately open about her emotions. 'Look,' she said firmly, 'it's brilliant, fantastic even. I totally understand why your reviews are so good, you show the disillusion of the American dream beautifully. But…'

He nudged her elbow. 'Come on, what didn't you like about that scene?'

She threw up her hands in defeat. 'Myrtle's not the villain!'

He'd not expected that. 'I know. She's more of a tragic character. A prisoner of circumstance, like you said the other night. All the characters have their own tragedy.'

'But she's like a caricature of a trashy woman, with her knock-off designer gear and bad make-up. She's lewd and tacky. It's clear you think she's as fake as the bags she swings around, and that somehow a woman's adultery is worse than a man's. I dunno, maybe it'd be interesting to see her vulnerability occasionally, especially when she's abused by both her husband and her lover… But, what would I know?' Obviously uncomfortable, she looked away as she spoke. Was it because he'd been cheated on, or because she didn't want to tell him how to do his job, or both? 'But she isn't worse than them. She's in an abusive relationship, living in a poor neighbourhood – something the other characters could never understand. It just seems sexist and unfair to judge her harshly.'

'But that's how she's written in the book.'

'And Gatsby is described as blond and blue-eyed. But you chose to update the play and cast a Black man to play his part. Isaac's excellent, by the way.'

'He is.'

'This is a modernisation, isn't it? Modernise the women too. Maybe Myrtle's not the trashy party girl we think she is. I imagine she sees Tom as her only chance of living the American dream. She doesn't love her husband or her lover, and I think Daisy is exactly the same. They can't love anyone, not really.'

Alex pondered her words, which smacked of a truth he'd been too blinded by pain to see clearly – until now. Was this what the interviewer had been trying to get at? Granted, in a far less caring way then Ellie. 'What makes you so sure?'

Sadness clouded her face and she looked towards the curtains as if she could see the characters beyond. 'Because they don't love themselves, and they can't escape.'

His chest tightened involuntarily, and it took him a second to catch his breath. Ellie had driven a truck straight through his heart. Was this how she felt? And, then the truck reversed and ran over his heart for a second time. Was this how *he* felt?

'You say that like you've experienced it…' He kept his voice soft, coaxing and gentle.

She took a deep breath and swivelled towards him, her brown eyes clear and strong. 'I've worked really hard to put aside those sorts of feelings. Hannah helped, especially when I faced some tough times… But my mum, she still struggles with them, and sometimes the feelings she has about herself ricochet onto me. She doesn't mean them to, and I've learned to arm myself against them. But, yeah, it's a hard thing to overcome.'

He'd need time to process, but she was definitely right. 'You know, I've always felt like there was something missing from the play. And I think you've hit the nail on the head.' He found himself telling her what he never would have admitted to anyone else. Maybe because she'd revealed something so personal to him, he felt compelled to repay her honesty in kind. He went on, 'When I was directing... maybe I did tweak my script too much. It was during my break-up. I guess I didn't have a very high opinion of adulterers.'

'Or women?'

He sank into his seat. 'Possibly.' His stomach twisted with disgust. Whether it was at himself or at his brother and Savannah, he couldn't say. 'I don't feel like that any more. I know all women are not the same.' But saying it out loud he realised that the experience had made him prejudiced. If he was ever going to find happiness again, he needed to move past Savannah and Liam's betrayal, but he wasn't sure how.

She reached over and patted his thigh. A shiver of electricity ran through the muscle, causing it to flex. 'Hey, stop looking as if you kicked a puppy. Don't feel bad, the play is fantastic!'

'Thank you.' Another thought occurred to him. 'I guess you're finding it tough being back home with your family?'

She nodded, sucking in a deep breath and letting it out with a wry chuckle. No emotion hidden in her lovely and expressive face. 'It's going to take some getting used to. But I think that's the disappointment over the flat more than anything else.' She waved her hand dismissively, obviously not wanting to discuss it further. 'Look, I'm going to nip to the loo. I'll be back in a minute – well, hopefully the queue won't be a mile long. Oh, unless you need to leave?'

'I'll be here.' He grinned.

'Great.'

She granted him another glorious, heart-melting smile before leaving.

—

The second half was much darker in mood than the first. The car crash was offstage, but the production team had created outstanding special effects with light and sound to horrify the audience. It caused the beautiful woman next to him to shiver. If they'd been dating, he would have put his arm around Ellie.

But they weren't dating, and a seed of unease had been planted in his mind.

He couldn't date. He wasn't over Savannah. Starting a relationship now would be dooming it to failure. It would be a rebound, nothing more, and someone like Ellie deserved better. Hadn't she said she'd been hurt in the past? Rejected because she dared to want a serious partner. He refused to hurt her like that.

Better to be friends... he *needed* a friend.

The play drew to a close, honouring the haunting and emotional ending of the book. When Ellie wiped away a tear at the final tableau of Nick Carraway looking out at the green light of Daisy's home from Gatsby's terrace, Alex was triumphant, as if he'd won a thirteen-round fight.

Most of the audience rose to give a standing ovation, but with only half the theatre filled it didn't last long. Ellie clapped the longest.

'It's brilliant, your parents must be so proud!'

Embarrassment clawed up his neck. 'Oh, they're not coming to see it.' All the proof he needed to know they didn't think him good enough.

'Really?' She looked genuinely horrified on his behalf.

He couldn't take it. 'Drink?' he asked, wondering how best to stop this night from ending. She'd still not confirmed about the awards night. After everything that had happened with the press, would she even want to go?

She bit her lip. 'I don't think I can drink again after last night, and I've got a shift tomorrow night…'

He chuckled. 'To be honest, I don't think I can either. But there's a nice Lebanese down the road that's open till late. We could get a bite to eat instead? Unless you need an early night?' To his surprise, he instinctively held his breath as he waited the two seconds it took for her to break out into a grin.

'Oh, go on then, you've twisted my arm.'

He spotted Russell coming up the auditorium stairs, heading to the sound booth, probably looking for him, potentially with another lecture about promotion. Alex ducked down close to Ellie's lap. She gasped in surprise, but didn't say anything.

'It's my boss,' he whispered.

'Oh, okay.' Her fingers clenched into fists. 'And you don't want to see him?'

'No, he'll try and convince me to do more interviews.'

Her hands relaxed. 'I see. He's gone past us.'

Alex grabbed her hand and her raincoat, then pulled her up. She chest-bumped against him, and he tried to ignore the tingle of pleasure that shot down to his groin at the feel of her pressed against him. He needed to focus, couldn't let his attraction to her spoil things between them.

'Got everything?'

She gave a bemused nod.

'Let's go.'

They hurried down the row and jogged down the steps, then swept through a closed door marked *private*.

'I feel like we're on the run!' Ellie whispered with a breathless giggle.

Alex's fingers tightened around her hand. He felt unwilling to let go of her even though they'd escaped the theatre and Russell. 'It's always like this.'

I'm always running away.

Chapter Eight

'This looks lush!' Ellie didn't even care if she couldn't eat out again for a month; this feast was worth every penny.

Moroccan lamps hung from the ceiling of the restaurant and glittered against fringed textiles. The walls were red and gold, and a mosaic water feature bubbled gently in the centre of the room, which added to its glamorous-kitsch charm.

An array of small, pretty, jewel-coloured plates arrived, piled with delicious food. Perfectly grilled chicken shish, and lamb koftas sprinkled with coriander. Herby falafels sat in a ring of steaming rice with pomegranate seeds scattered like rubies over the top. A mountain of fresh pitta spiked with nigella seeds sat to the side of their mains, with little bowls of buttery houmos, rich umami moutabal, as well as a cool yoghurt and garlic dip.

They both dug in with happy sighs.

'So, what made you choose nursing?' asked Alex.

She tried desperately to chew the chunk of bread she'd stuffed in her mouth and not choke before answering. 'To be honest, I kind of thought I'd end up in our flower shop, although Mark always seemed more interested in running the business then me. But one day, there was a bad accident a couple of streets from our house involving a cyclist and a van. It was awful.' Her blood ran cold as she remembered the shock of walking in on that scene. The twisted bike with its wheel still spinning, the man crumpled in a pool of blood, the van driver slumped across his wheel, the front of his van buried in a lamppost. 'Hannah and I were about fifteen and we tried our best to help. We called an ambulance and got blankets – the van driver was in shock. We tried to keep the cyclist comfortable and to stop the bleeding but he was very hurt, and everything we did was only a drop in the ocean. When the paramedics arrived, they were so calm and efficient. A few months later, the cyclist came back to thank us, he said we'd helped him just by being there. We'd made a difference, even without realising it – we'd comforted someone in one of the worst moments of their lives. Hannah felt the same as me and we decided to train as nurses when we left school. It gave us both a purpose. I'm kind of glad it happened, in a weird way.'

'I envy you.'

She hadn't expected that. Most people thought her career was worthwhile, but no one had ever said they *envied* her. Most of the time, they'd said the opposite: '*Tough job*,' '*Poor you*,' '*You must have a strong stomach*.' And if they'd done some of her worst shifts she might have agreed with them. But Alex *envied* her. 'Why?'

'The certainty. You know exactly what you want in life.'

Her stomach twisted. She felt like a hypocrite. 'Well, not really. I've been thinking of changing career, actually. Trying something different. The long hours of A&E are beginning to take their toll, and I want something more sociable, community nursing or teaching possibly...'

Alex dipped his bread in the houmos, scooping out a large dollop. 'Sure, that makes sense. Realising you need a change is half the battle. All you need to do now is focus on what you want.' He popped the bread in his mouth and she tried not to notice his groan of pleasure or the way the rumble of sound made her thighs clench.

'Yeah, I guess...' She took a sip of her water and avoided his eyes. He made it seem so easy. But sometimes it didn't matter how much you focused on a goal. Life could still pull the rug from under you at any time... drain your savings in the blink of an eye.

'Everything okay?' He adjusted his glasses as if trying to see her better.

A flush heated her cheeks. 'Saving for my flat deposit is looking a bit more of a long-term goal than I originally planned.'

Alex shifted awkwardly in his seat, and she immediately regretted mentioning it. *Don't talk about your money troubles to a rich man!*

She smiled, even though her heart wasn't in it. 'I'm just being impatient. I'll do some overtime, take on some more shifts...'

They ate in silence for a moment before Alex said thoughtfully, 'Tell me more about your job. It might help you decide on your next career choice, knowing what you do and don't like about the current one.'

Ellie was glad of the distraction. 'Okay. I work in the A&E at the Royal – you'd call it an emergency room – so it's always different and challenging, which I like. But the mountain of paperwork? I hate that. The physical and verbal abuse? No, thanks. I dunno... A&E can be really rewarding and exciting, but it's also pretty ridiculous at times.'

'Ridiculous?'

Mischievously she leaned a little closer and whispered, 'Oh, there's no end of things people will shove up them.'

Alex's hand stilled halfway to his mouth, the heap of dip on his bread sliding off to plop onto the plate below. 'Like what?'

With a smirk, she sank back into her seat. 'Oh, anything. Toys – both kinds, before you ask – vegetables, tools, lightbulbs.'

He put his bread back on his plate. '*Lightbulbs?* Damn!'

'But people always forget…' She sighed dramatically. 'Hungry bums.'

Alex choked. 'What?'

She gave a sage nod. 'Hungry bums. One of the first things you learn in A&E. Bums can behave like a vacuum and suck anything straight up. If that happens, it's tongs, laxatives or, worst case, surgery.'

'Fuck.' He took a sip of his mint tea with a horrified expression.

'Quite.'

Their eyes met and a moment later they were both roaring with laughter.

When she'd caught her breath, she said, 'You know what? That's reminded me, life is precious, ridiculous and strange, and I need to start enjoying myself more.'

He grinned, raising his tea. 'Good for you. Shall we say cheers to that?'

'Bottoms up!' She clinked her ornate silver tea glass.

There was a buzzing sound and Alex awkwardly shifted his hips to get his phone out. 'Sorry, I'll turn it off.'

'No, go ahead and take it. I'm popping to the loo anyway.' She slid out of the booth, accidentally noticing by the caller ID that it was Richie calling.

By the time she'd returned from the bathroom, Alex had ended his call, and the corners of his lips were pulled down in a frown.

'Everything all right?' asked Ellie quietly as she slid back into the booth.

Alex lifted his head. He looked like a man about to face a firing squad. 'I need your help.'

'*My* help? What's happened?'

'Perhaps I should order something stronger, you might need it.' The drawl of his accent coupled with the intensity of his gaze caused her mouth to dry.

'Go on,' she said slowly.

'So, erm, I've the Olivier Awards coming up—'

Called it. Ellie quickly raised her hand to interrupt before it got any more bloody awkward. 'No worries! If you don't need me any more that's perfectly fine by me.'

Alex's brow furrowed and he pushed his glasses up with his index finger in a nervous gesture. 'No! I still need you.' He cleared his throat. 'I mean, if you're still willing to come to the awards ceremony that'd be great – Savannah was meant to be my plus one, but she's too busy arranging her wedding to my brother.' Ellie's heart squeezed at the sourness of his tone. 'I need to ask you something, well, *beg* you for a favour... Oh man, it's going to sound so weird.'

This was the weird part? Every moment with Alex had been strange, but, she had to admit, it was also exciting and frightening. Didn't she want to live her life to the full? She tried to lighten the mood with a joke. 'You're not going to ask me to dress up in my uniform and nurse you back to life, are you?'

He jerked backwards. 'What? Oh man, did someone ask you to do that?'

'Yep. So, it can't be as weird as that. Can it?'

He took his glasses off briefly and scrubbed a hand down his face, looking both awkward and utterly gorgeous at the same time. 'I guess not, but it's still pretty weird.'

'Spit it out.'

'I want you to be my girlfriend.'

Ellie's universe shrank to nothing, and then expanded with a force as great as the Big Bang. She could hear every drop of water as it splashed in the nearby fountain, could feel her pulse thrumming and the blood rush with dizzying speed around her ears. A blast of heat washed over her from head to toe.

Okay, it's not real – it's a misunderstanding, surely? He means just as friends. Nothing more. Americans call their friends girl-friends, right? Although, wasn't that usually women who said that, about their platonic female friendships? 'Alex, what do you mean by "girlfriend"?'

Alex sighed, looking torn. 'According to Richie, I need to be dating someone. He says my profile has been nosediving since the scandal. People are saying I'm toxic, controlling and emotionally abusive. Normally, I wouldn't give a damn what the press says about me, but Richie says it's affecting the success of the play, and it might also be why I've not been offered any more projects. Richie agents my whole family – including Savannah now, apparently.' His lips thinned with disapproval. 'He needs to look after all of our interests, and he needs to change the current narrative of a love triangle with warring brothers and broken hearts. He's worried their wedding might seem a little *insensitive* and they could be perceived as the villains here.'

Ellie scoffed at the injustice and Alex threw her a tired but grateful smile, taking a moment to remove off his glasses again and rub his eyes before putting them back on.

'While I might agree with that sentiment, I don't want them to lose everything they've worked so hard to build, and I don't want anyone's pity. You probably think me nuts saying that. But for some reason I'm still... loyal to them.'

'I understand. Families are complicated.'

Alex's back straightened and he placed his hands on the table and leaned forward. 'Please, be my girlfriend,' he pleaded. 'Just for a short time. Richie says I need to distract the press. Show them that I'm happily in love with someone else and don't give a shit about their wedding or that they're together. It will solve all of our problems, and the awards ceremony can be our relationship debut – the big reveal. You saw how things were earlier outside your house, how they stopped asking about Liam and Savannah and started asking about you. It worked really well, didn't it?'

'Sure.' If you liked to be the centre of attention, which she didn't. But then again, it must have been a relief for Alex.

He took a deep breath. 'After the wedding, everything will die down, the press will get bored and we can decide publicly to *remain friends*.' He used air quotes and winked at the last bit. It made her stomach drop – David had said they were *just friends* when he'd not wanted to admit the truth. 'You'd be doing me a real solid, Ellie.'

'Why?' she asked, unsure of how best to word the hundreds of questions scrolling before her eyes like a knock-off *Matrix*.

Why me?
Why not some actress or supermodel?
Why a plus-size nurse from the East End?
What the hell is going on?

Alex leaned forward, his expression confident for the first time since he'd ended his call. 'I can trust you. I'm not saying it won't be tough. People will have a lot to say about me dating again. There will be plenty of scrutiny...' He paused. 'But it *will* be worth it.'

She swallowed, her mouth suddenly dry. 'It will?' So far, it sounded like her worst nightmare. Dating a hot man who would ultimately reject her in front of the whole world – been there, done that.

He nodded. 'That flat you wanted? I can buy it for you... and I can give you an allowance too, for while we're together. Or a lump sum? Just name your price.'

'Oh.' Why was she disappointed? *Erm, maybe because he's turning you into an Only Fans account?* 'That seems a bit... much.'

Alex shook his head. 'It's not. You'll need a dress for the awards night – it's black tie.'

'I was going to make something. I like dressmaking... it's a hobby of mine... I made this dress that I'm wearing.' She cringed. She was babbling like a lunatic. Plus, she didn't want to admit the real reason why she made most of her clothes from scratch – because she'd spent too many of her teen years crying in clothes store changing rooms.

His eyes lit up. 'Perfect! But,' he barrelled on quickly, as if he was ripping a plaster off, quick and efficient and mildly painful, 'you're going to need money for accessories and fabric and so on. I'll get Richie to send you a cheque. And you'll have to take time off work for Savannah and Liam's wedding too, at least ten days, buy clothes for the wedding, as it's in the Bahamas. See, there's a lot of costs involved.'

'The Bahamas?' she gasped.

'Yes, and my mum will insist we all stay together at their house. I mean, it's a very big house, but I'm still not looking forward to it.'

'They have their *own* house in the Bahamas?' Why was she even surprised? His normal was so far out of her comfort zone, it was practically on another planet.

'It's their holiday home,' he said casually. 'What do you say? Ten days in the Caribbean and an apartment for the price of one fake relationship? Sounds like the deal of the century to me.' Why was he acting like a second-hand car salesman?

'This feels wrong, and a flat? That's a huge… gift.' She winced. 'Payment' would have been a more accurate word. Was she really going to sell herself and become an employed *girlfriend*? She cleared her throat. 'And what about buying your own place?'

'I can do both.'

'Show-off,' she grumbled. 'Look, why me? You could get any one of your celebrity friends to help you.'

Alex winced. 'I don't have that many friends. Not anyone I could trust, at least.' That hit her hard; and then he leaned closer, a teasing glint in his eyes that was utterly charming. 'Not people who would protect me from the paparazzi in only a bathrobe and slippers.'

'Don't remind me,' she groaned.

'Please? You can have a great vacation, a home of your own in just a few weeks. No need for overtime, or waiting years to build up a deposit. You can choose whatever path you want in life and not have to worry about a mortgage.'

'I said I wouldn't date again,' she whispered weakly.

Alex visibly sobered, the light in his electric eyes dimming slightly. Did he realise how hard she was finding it to pretend she felt nothing for him other than friendship? How close she was to falling?

'It wouldn't be real, and afterwards you'll be in a position to settle down, just like you always wanted.'

'With my cat,' she whispered, and he grinned.

'With your cat.'

She bit her lip, and he stared at her with a knowing confidence, as if he knew how difficult it would be to refuse him – how difficult it would be for anyone to refuse him anything.

My own home. No more living at home with the family – and if she was mortgage-free? Well, that opened up a world of opportunity. Spare money to save, help out at the shop, travel and visit Hannah. It would be life-changing – but weirdly, most of all, she didn't want to disappoint him.

Could she bear another break-up like the one she'd had with David?

She had to think of her vulnerable heart. She was only just getting over Hannah leaving and was now dealing with her family's financial worries; she wasn't sure she could cope with any more disappointment or humiliation. But, her own home? How could she say no?

'So, if it's not real… Do you think people will believe it?' She squeezed her hands together beneath the table. Of course people wouldn't believe it. Someone like her with a Hollywood star? Seriously?

Alex's blue eyes glittered like sapphires in the candlelight, promising endless possibilities if only she were brave enough to agree. 'We'd have to pretend in public. I know you've never done professional acting, but I've seen you sneak past security with no problems. You just need to fake it. Look at me like you're in love. A few kisses here and there.'

Her face went numb. 'Kisses?'

'Purely Disney kisses. Nothing X-rated, don't worry,' he reassured her quickly.

She gave an emphatic nod, followed by a wheezing nervous laugh. 'Yes, of course, thank God, was a bit nervous there for a minute!'

For fuck's sake, I may as well have said, 'No sex for me, please.'

'Good.' He nodded quickly and her heart sank. 'It'll be better all round this way. Nobody will get hurt.' Ellie wasn't sure about that; she was already a little hurt and they'd not even started. 'However, I don't want my family to know that it's not real. In public and in front of them, I'd like for us to pretend we are dating. If they found out I was lying, it would be humiliating, and if it got out to the press? They'd tear us to shreds.'

'Yeah, I get it.' She didn't. It was one thing to lie to nosey strangers, but lying to his family felt wrong. However, who was she to judge? She couldn't wait to escape hers. 'But, are you sure you want to lie to your family? I'm sure they'd understand if you talked to them about how much this has affected you.'

'Look, I love them, for all their faults, and they love me. But they walk on eggshells around me and it's driving me crazy. I can't bear their pity.' He looked genuinely exhausted, and Ellie's heart softened. She knew what it felt like to be drained emotionally by those who loved you. 'If you came with me, they'd stop fussing. I know it's a hell of a lot to ask. Anyone else would sell the story of me even asking you to do this.'

'I would never do that.'

'I know, and that's why I insist you have something in return for helping me. Hell, you can come and help me pick out a home for each of us. Whatever you want. Seems wrong that you should struggle to save for a place of your own, when I can afford more than one house. Or name a figure if you don't want to decide now, and I'll have it in your account before Liam and Savannah say I do.' If it wasn't for the pulse she could see fluttering rapidly at the base of his throat, she'd have assumed he propositioned women like this all the time. 'Deal?'

Ellie was torn. Her friend needed her. Her closest friend right now, with Hannah gone. How could she not help?

'Then…' She reached forward, about to take his hand in hers.

'Dessert?' asked the waitress, who had seemed to pop up from nowhere.

'Jesus Christ!' Ellie yelled, and then tried to hide her mortification with an overly bright smile. 'Sorry.'

'Would you like to take a look at the dessert menu?' She offered them two little gold embossed cards that reminded Ellie of wedding invitations, and her stomach churned in response.

'No harm taking a look,' she squeaked in reply, snatching both cards and not even bothering to check with Alex first, desperate to get rid of the waitress.

Shit, what if she overheard Alex's proposal?

By the benign expression on the waitress's face before she turned away to leave them alone once more, she'd guess not.

'Ellie?'

She met his eyes for a split second before she stared down at the menu and tried her best to concentrate on the words swimming in front of her. 'Oh, erm, I didn't really want dessert,' she answered swiftly. After a moment, she realised he was still holding out his hand to her.

'Deal?'

She slipped her hand into his, the warmth of his skin sending a shiver up her arm. 'I'm in. Deal.'

Have I really just said yes to fake-dating Alex King?

Yes, and not because of the trip to the Bahamas, although a holiday from her life would certainly be nice, and not because in one fell swoop he'd solved her housing issue.

No. The real reason was because he needed her, and she was a sucker when it came to people needing her.

Chapter Nine

Alex had just finished his post-show talk when Isaac raised his hand and asked, 'Will you be watching tomorrow night's performance?'

He thought for a moment, and realised that it was time to let go. His tweaks had been in place for a week now and the show was running smoothly. 'You know what? I think you guys are doing brilliantly without me watching every night.' He chuckled at the relieved sighs, but understood it was more because they feared the reason he stayed was because he wasn't happy with the show.

Deciding to lavish some more praise on his hard-working actors, he added, 'Sasha and Louise have really taken on board my suggestions and run with them. There's a real depth and authenticity to your characters now that blows me away – it's fantastic. The whole production is doing an incredible job. You should all be proud, I know I am.'

Sasha, who played Myrtle, brightened at his words. 'I hope you thanked Ellie for that,' she teased.

Alex grinned. 'You got it.' He'd ordered flowers for his leading actors through Jones Floristry and told Ellie's nanna to ensure that there was an extra bunch for her granddaughter, as her insight had really lifted the production to a whole new level.

He stood up from his seat on one of the set chairs. 'Well, break a leg. I'll come to a couple more shows here and there, just to check in and keep in touch. But either way, I'll see you all at the Olivier Awards.'

The cast and crew cheered. The Oliviers were a highlight for many of them who had never been invited before as they were still so early on in their careers.

As he was walking offstage, Russell appeared from behind one of the giant party sets – a huge sparkly clamshell – not exactly the Aphrodite he'd want or hope for. 'Hello, Alex. May I bend your ear for a minute?'

Instantly suspicious, Alex nonetheless moved out of the way of the rest of the cast as they hurried to their dressing rooms so he could stay behind with Russell.

'Well, I'm pleased to tell you, we've had a little uptake in sales recently. Your *Arts Review* interview certainly piqued public interest. I have to say, it seemed a nicely balanced write-up, despite some of the leading questions.' He gave an awkward chuckle, aware of how sore that issue was for Alex – he'd kept his word about no more interviews and not done another since. 'Many of our patrons seem keen to spot you in the audience again.'

'I was with a friend that night,' Alex said coldly. He was aware from Richie that there was at least one grainy picture of Ellie and himself watching the performance. Snapped on someone's cell several rows behind them in the interval, the photo only showed his side profile and the back of Ellie's head. Richie had forwarded him the post asking if it was his date, and Alex had ignored him.

'Yes, well. If you are so inclined, feel free to do so again.'

'Like I said, I'll come and see a few more shows during the run. But I don't want my presence to distract from the performance.' It was a polite way of saying that Alex wouldn't be sitting in the auditorium again, and Russell's hopeful expression faded.

Alex's phone began to buzz in his pocket. Grateful for an excuse to leave this awkward conversation, he took it out and glanced at the caller ID. 'Sorry, my mom is calling. Is that everything?'

Russell seemed more concerned about keeping his mother waiting then annoying Alex, and waved him away. 'Of course, and, if she ever fancies treading the boards in London, let her know our doors are always open. Wide open!'

Alex strode away, not entirely sure if he'd left one awkward moment simply to jump into another far worse one. 'Hiya, Mom.'

'Hello, darling, so glad to get a hold of you.' His mother's voice skipped down the line with forced joviality, as if she hadn't heard from him in months. Granted he'd ignored a couple of calls from her, but that was normal; their family was always busy and often in different time zones.

Alex rolled his eyes. 'Everything okay?'

'Sure...' She paused. 'Your plus one for the wedding. What's her name again?'

'I never gave you her name, and you won't know her anyway.'

There was another pause, and then a deep exhale. 'Alex. I would like to know the name of the person coming to stay in my own home. Security will want to do their usual checks, and there's the jet to organise, and the seating plan for the wedding breakfast and rehearsal dinner.'

Alex stiffened, reluctant to give her Ellie's name. As soon as he did, his family would know all there was to know about her, and that felt like an invasion of her privacy. 'I am not entirely sure of her legal name, but I'll email it over as soon as I can,' he lied. He knew Ellie's full name; he'd needed it for their deal, to sort out the flat and payments.

Eliza Dorothy Jones. He thought it the cutest name on the planet, as adorable as the woman who owned it.

Appeased, his mother replied, 'If she's using a stage name that's fine, just give us both names for the checks.' Of course she would presume he was dating an actress. 'Let me know as soon as you have it, there's still so much to do...' She sighed, as if it was her swansong, and Alex chuckled. He suspected she loved the party planning. Savannah didn't have much family, so he supposed his mom was doing all of the heavy lifting when it came to planning the wedding.

'It'll be fine. I've gotta go, speak soon,' he lied again, and quickly ending the call.

He ducked into one of the rehearsal spaces and took a moment to check through his emails. The mention of a security check had got him thinking about the press. He should probably check what the latest gossip magazines and sites were saying about him.

Richie had set up an automatic alert for his name, so that whenever he was mentioned online it would send him an email with the links. Long ago he'd set up an inbox folder that immediately filed all of the alerts. There were thousands, mostly unread, but occasionally when he needed to check something, like now, he would go into that folder.

The last ones he'd opened were from a couple of months ago when the story about Savannah and Liam's engagement had first broken. At the time, he'd only managed to read a few lines before he'd felt physically sick. Thankfully, when he opened the folder today, his stomach no longer lurched at the headlines.

ALEX KING'S BRUTAL HUMILIATION!

TWO KINGS, ONLY ONE QUEEN

THE TRUTH BEHIND ALEX & SAVANNAH'S TOXIC RELATIONSHIP

LIAM KING SAVES SAVANNAH FROM HIS TOXIC BROTHER – 'She just couldn't take it any more,' says Liam's close personal friend.

Alex snorted. Most of these supposed journalists made up their own quotes. He looked at the recent alerts and clicked on one that had been published the day after the party.

HAS ALEX KING FINALLY LOST IT?

Alex King spotted leaving an East London florist after a drunken night at his play's opening night afterparty. Mr M. Jones of Jones Floristry stated, 'He's on my sofa, never seen him before – at least not in real life. But it's definitely him. Think my sister brought him home, just like her to bring in a stray…'

> A close source informed PAPPED: 'Alex forgot his hotel details, and was taken in by a kindly nurse, who happens to be a sibling of Mr M. Jones.'
>
> PAPPED can't help but wonder if Alex King is drowning his sorrows, after poor sales of his theatre-directing debut of The Great Gatsby, and his recent split—

Alex closed the alert. He didn't need to read PAPPED's opinion on his split with Savannah; it was the usual clickbait. He was just relieved that there'd been no mention of Ellie. The *kindly nurse* made her sound elderly. Alex, on the other hand, sounded like some drunken loser – which wasn't completely off the mark, but he didn't mind that if it saved Ellie's family from further scrutiny.

Even the photos were mostly of him looking stupidly confused, or the back of Ellie's bath-robed figure as they ran back inside. He suspected she'd been too close to the photographers while opening the gate to be distinguishable in the photos, which was a relief – he imagined Ellie wouldn't appreciate them publishing clear images of her in her bathrobe and bunny slippers.

He opened the next alert. It was the grainy photo from the theatre.

> ## IS ALEX KING FINALLY PULLING HIMSELF TOGETHER?
>
> Alex King was spotted with an unidentified woman at a recent performance of his theatre-directing debut, The Great Gatsby. Onlookers described Alex as unable to take

his eyes off his date throughout the performance. In a recent interview with the Arts Review, Alex described himself as 'optimistic for the future'. Perhaps Alex's new mystery lady is leading him towards a more hopeful future? Sources close to Alex have informed us that he is even considering purchasing a home in London.

Speculation and half-truths. Alex could cope with that. What he was most concerned about was how Ellie would cope with the inevitable press attention when her name broke, which it certainly would after the Olivier Awards.

His leg began to bounce with anxiety. Was he doing the right thing? He'd lived with this kind of attention his whole life, but how would Ellie cope? Alex knew it was wrong of him to put such a burden on her. After all, he had experienced how hellish it could be, how the constant scrutiny and speculation could wear down even the most resilient of people, break them.

He hadn't been joking when he'd said there was no one else he could trust to pull off this facade. The first girl he'd ever kissed had sold her story and bought herself a car with the proceeds. She hadn't been the last romantic interest or close friend to betray him like that – he'd just never expected his brother to be one of them. His celebrity friends were as fickle as the wind. They'd all quickly chosen Savannah and Liam's side. After all, he was the lesser brother, the less likely to get them any further on in their career. Not only that, but his parents had been quick to take 'no sides'– which may as well have been a public pardon.

But was he being fair to Ellie? She had no idea of the burden it would place on her and her family.

Would everything in his life turn to shit like it always did? And would he unwittingly drag Ellie down too?

He opened his messages and texted Ellie.

> You probably won't see this until after your nightshift. Did you see my earlier txt? You might see a photo of us online from our theatre night. It looks like the news of our dating will break soon... are you still okay with that? I understand if you wanna call it off.

To his surprise the message was read immediately, and she began typing a reply. The three dots flashing caused his heart to thunder in his chest.

> Oh, that? Yeah, Mum showed it me. She's practically your stalker now – soz. I'm just on my way to work. But I'm still up for it... If you are? I wasn't sure about giving you my bank details. Not because I don't trust you, LOL. But wanted to be sure you were still okay with it too?

Alex took a deep breath, relief and guilt washing through him in equal measure.

I'm 100% sure, he replied.

Ellie responded straight away: *London flats aren't cheap though. Look, I'll send you the link of the flat I like. Feel free to back out.*

She posted a link and he clicked through. The flat was just as she had described, and the price didn't faze him. With a smug smile, he typed his reply.

> I think we can do better.

Chapter Ten

'Christ, this is a house. Like a proper *house* house – actually no, it's a bloody mansion!'

Ellie rifled through the pile of housing brochures Alex had received from the estate agent. Martin's cab turned down a side street, causing her to grapple with the papers to stop them from sliding off her lap. The two had been texting over the week, and there had been something marvellously exhilarating about receiving text messages from Alex during a dull night shift. Every time she had a break, she'd sneak off into a quiet corner and check her messages. He was a bit of a night owl himself and would usually sign off from their little chats at around 1 a.m. They had chatted about everything and anything – how her shift was going, the tweaks he'd made to his characters and script and, of course, house-hunting.

'The realtor did say there was a wide variety in my budget.'

'This is huge!' she exclaimed, only half-listening, tearing through the pile like a maniac as she flicked through them. 'And this one. Bloody hell! Is that the price?'

Each property had a sales price above two million pounds, but this one was double-figure millions. She wasn't sure whether to laugh or cry.

Alex leaned towards her to take a closer look.

'Yeah, I wasn't sure about that one.' He was so close she could smell his intoxicating aftershave. Sandalwood, rich and musky, spiced with the tears of a thousand heart-broken virgins. She tried to stifle a moan of pleasure as she drank in the scent of him. *I really need to cool my libido!*

She caught Martin's raised brow in the rear-view mirror, and immediately burst into flames of embarrassment. *Busted!*

Why did Alex have to hire Hannah's dad as his driver for the day? Although, she had to admit, it was kind of sweet of him to remember Martin from the paparazzi incident. In fact, according to Martin, Alex had been hiring him regularly after that day, and, as he paid so well, Martin was more than happy to be at his beck and call.

'I'd have to sell my property in New York and my house in LA if I want this house,' Alex continued. 'I'd rather not do that, but if it's the one…' He shrugged his shoulders miserably, the epitome of indecision.

'You have a house in New York?'

'No, an apartment. I have a house in LA, but that's not really mine.'

'What do you mean?'

'Well, my parents bought me and my brother a house when we turned twenty-one. They weren't big on spoiling us with cars or credit cards, but they wanted us all to have a solid start.'

Amazing, her lifelong dream, handed to him in a twenty-first birthday card. 'I forget your parents were successful actors too.'

'Yeah, they've pretty much retired now. They only take on a project if their hearts are a hundred per cent in it. Plus, their production company takes up a lot of their time.' He avoided her gaze and shifted in his seat.

'Their production company pretty much launched all of our careers, and I'm so grateful for all they've done for me. But it's a bit weird living in a house your mum and dad picked out for you. That's why I moved to New York. I wanted – no, I needed to go it alone, you know?'

Ellie bit her tongue. *Oh, hun, you really need to readjust your idea of 'going it alone'.*

'I can imagine,' she said. But could she? Time to change the subject before she said something mean. 'So, which properties have you narrowed it down to?'

'Those are my top ten.'

She stared at him in shock. 'And how many are we viewing today?'

'Uh… Ten?' He gave her a hopeful smile.

Her mouth dropped open. 'You don't do anything by halves, do you?' She'd be exhausted by the end of the day; the viewings were dotted all over central London.

'They all looked nice… You don't mind, do you? Martin will drive us to each one. Hopefully it won't take too long.'

'Hey, he's paying me per hour, so don't short-change me, love,' joked Martin from the front of the cab, and he gave her a playful wink in the mirror.

'Have you heard from Hannah lately?' she asked, leaning towards the partition so that she could hear him better.

'Yeah, my sister's spoiling her rotten, taking her to the beach every day. She's learning how to surf. Can you believe it, our Hannah, learning to surf!'

'Ha-ha, I'd heard. Good for her, I'm so glad she's trying it. She deserves a break and a bit of fun.'

'So do you, love,' he replied softly, his kind eyes catching hers in the rear-view mirror.

'I've booked a little holiday, actually.' She glanced at Alex. He'd given her the dates for the Bahamas and taken her passport details for the flights, so she was ready to go. But it didn't feel real. None of this felt real; it was as if she were living in some parallel universe.

Martin raised an eyebrow in quiet disbelief – she'd booked time off before and always ended up working regardless. Alex gave her a thoughtful look as if he were filing away some factoid about her for later use.

'Here we are,' said Martin, as he swung into a parking space in front of an imposing white stucco villa with iron railings, situated on a quiet tree-lined avenue. The quintessential Holland Park townhouse.

They stepped out onto the pavement, Alex frowning between the building and its brochure. 'I hope it's worth it. This is the very top of my budget.'

A woman in her late fifties came skipping down the steps to meet them, which seemed a little odd. But with so much commission almost in the bank, who could blame her? She wore a twinset and had an Eighties perm, but she had a sharp and uncompromising gaze that reminded her of Martha Stewart, and Ellie suspected she wouldn't mess around when it came to business.

'Alex! So wonderful to meet you in person.' She gave Alex a double-handed shake and then turned to Ellie with an equally warm expression.

'Hi, I'm Ellie. I'm here as moral support.' She gave a limp-wristed wave.

The woman gave her a slow calculating smile. 'Then it's really *you* we should be trying to impress. I'm Barbara, lovely to meet you.' Ellie was treated to one of her brisk double handshakes.

Barbara spun on her heel and marched up to the villa, cheerfully chatting back to them without missing a step. 'Alex, I believe you're not familiar with the area? Holland Park is a much sought-after location. The beautiful Japanese Kyoto Garden, and walled spring tulip garden, are just a short stroll away in that direction. The schools – if you're interested…' she paused, her gaze flicking curiously between them, before she turned back to unlock the door, 'are *outstanding*. The best in London. And this being a popular choice for those in the public eye ensures a safe and most importantly *private* area in which to live.'

Ellie remembered the way her line manager, Hazel, had warned her yesterday about inappropriate behaviour in her personal life. She'd pushed the dressing-gown photo of Ellie in a tabloid towards her like it was a leaky specimen, and given her the following warning, '*If you want to go into mentoring or teaching, you might want to watch your professional reputation… No more messy nights out with celebrities.*' It had been a timely reminder that, even if you weren't a celebrity like Alex, you had to be careful.

Barbara swung open the door and they stepped into a blue-carpeted, narrow corridor that made nothing of the high ceilings and ornate cornicing.

'This used to be an embassy. It's empty at the moment, so you can really get a sense of the potential space, but I'm afraid the whole property will need extensive refurbishment throughout.'

'It still needs work, even with that price tag?' Ellie muttered to Alex out of the corner of her mouth, and he grimaced in response. She imagined home improvements weren't at the top of his list, no matter the amazing *potential*.

Barbara turned her steel gaze on her. 'Oh, don't worry. I'll negotiate a crackingly good deal for you if you *do* like it.'

They were shown around room after gigantic room, each with more hideous carpets and curtains than the last. The whole time Barbara was pointing out the beautiful original features and huge potential, Alex was very quiet, nodding occasionally and seeming to agree with everything she said, not once offering any ideas of his own.

'Now, the garden does need some imagination…'

For once, Ellie couldn't be snarky. An actual garden? They stepped out onto a large patio and looked down at a sea of overgrown grass at the bottom of the steps.

'I'll be at the front door. Take your time, explore or revisit any of the rooms and let me know what you think after.'

Barbara left and Ellie glanced up at Alex. She tried to read the perplexed expression on his face, but came up blank.

'It's got a lot of potential,' she said, then winced when she realised she sounded just like Barbara. Had she been brainwashed by bouncy Barb? Next, she'd be waxing lyrical over it being a bargain.

'Yes, lots of potential… and charm,' he said weakly.

Okay, time to get to the heart of the matter. 'Yes, especially if you like ye-olde-crumbling-down-embassy charm. In fact, we could negotiate keeping the bucket in bedroom seven. Now *that* has a lot of potential.'

He laughed, inhaling deeply and then letting out the air in one long sigh. 'It's horrible.'

'Yes, it is.'

'And… kind of overwhelming?'

'Those huge rooms give me the heebie-jeebies. How many ambassadors jumped from balcony three? That's what I want to know.'

'Far too many. Right, let's get out of here.'

To Barbara's expectant face a moment later, Alex said, 'It's lovely, but too much of a project. I want to move in quickly and... Look, this is going to sound crazy, but anything above six bedrooms, for just me? Well, it's just a bit *too* big.'

Barbara barely blinked, instead nodding enthusiastically at every word. 'Of course. That's really great, Alex. You've really narrowed the search down for me. I'll not bother taking you to the ones in Mayfair, and let's cancel the viewings in Camden too. They also need a lot of work, or have too many bedrooms.' She smiled as if pain-in-the-arse clients who didn't know what they wanted were a regular occurrence, which, in her line of work, they probably were.

They all bundled back into Martin's cab, Alex having insisted Barbara join them and leave her car behind, and offered Martin's services to drive her back to pick it up.

'Wonderful! Saves me finding places to park,' she declared cheerfully, as she typed lightning-speed instructions to her office – presumably to tell the billionaires no one was coming to see their house today. Ellie wondered if Barbara was the most optimistic woman she'd ever met. 'Next stop St Katharine Docks.'

Despite the usual choking London traffic, Martin made quick work of ducking and diving through the streets to the marina – black cabbies were worth their weight in gold, Ellie thought with a smile.

They stopped outside a huge redbrick Victorian warehouse, and Barbara was the first out. 'This beautiful warehouse conversion has a four-bed penthouse with beautiful views over the marina. If you have a yacht, I can negotiate the docking costs. There's a daytime porter, residential lift, and an underground car park with two allocated spaces. It's close to the tube – if you wish – as well as all the high-end bars, shops and restaurants that are so abundant here.'

'*And* there's one less number on the price tag,' whispered Ellie, tapping the brochure as they followed her into the building.

Alex's blue eyes sparkled behind his glasses. 'No need to sell my other properties after all.'

'Wouldn't want to burden yourself financially now, would we?' she teased, and he gave a good-natured laugh.

'Fair point. Thanks for reminding me of how much of a douche I sound sometimes.'

She smiled sweetly. 'Any time, except, you're such an adorable douche.' She tried to add to the friendly banter by giving him a playful punch on the bicep. Her knuckles met with the formidable muscle of his arm and her body warmed in several places as she imagined how good those arms would feel wrapped around her.

It took her several minutes to get over it.

The inside of the penthouse was a wonderful mix of modern luxury and original features. Exposed brick walls, double-height ceilings, arched windows and doors that made the building light and airy. The master suite had a walk-in wardrobe and an ensuite; the spare bedrooms were all double, if not triple, the size of her own bedroom at home.

The kitchen was stylish, with a large dining area to the side. The lounge had beautiful double doors out onto the first of two terraces, and it was the terraces that took her breath away. The one from the lounge came out into a lovely little seating area overlooking the shiny yachts in the marina, while the other faced out towards the city and river, and also had a hot tub and bar.

'Well, it's a real bachelor pad,' said Ellie, nodding towards the hot tub, her mouth drying at the thought of Alex and his muscular arms relaxing after a long day. She tried to imagine herself beside him.

No, he'd have actresses and starlets beside him, not her. She'd probably be making margaritas at the bar.

'With both terrace doors open, the breeze can run right through the apartment, creating that light and airy atmosphere you mentioned in your email,' enthused Barbara.

Alex smirked at Ellie, unrepentant. 'Sorry, I ripped off one of your wishlist points.'

It was one of the ways she'd described the flat she wanted. 'Why not? I have excellent taste. I really like this one.'

Barbara was beaming at them like a proud mum. 'I'll give you a minute. See you at the front door when you're ready.'

After she'd gone, Ellie said, 'You could have some awesome parties here.'

Alex snorted. 'I don't really entertain.'

Ellie turned to face him, trying to read his reaction. 'But do you want to?'

He looked out at the harbour and then back at her. 'Not really, that time of my life is over. But I can imagine living here. It reminds me of my New York place.'

'Well, that's good, right?'

'It's a maybe…'

'Talk to me,' said Barbara as they approached her at the apartment's entrance.

'It's a possibility,' said Alex.

'Well, there's only one left on our list, but it's a cracking property and in your first-choice area. Spitalfields.'

Ellie sniggered at the now-blushing Alex and dared to swat his arm once more. Yep, still like a muscly block of granite.

'In my defence, you made it sound so great.' He shrugged.

They arrived outside a neo-Georgian townhouse that looked stunning with its arches, orange-red brick and huge black-leaded windows. The road it was nestled in was one of those sleepy side streets that you don't realise exist in London until you happened to get lost and find one.

This was Ellie's dream home – if she ever allowed herself to dream *this* big.

'Now, this home is bursting at the seams with original features, but also has a real liveable feel. I know one of your requirements was to have a house with a sense of history, but this isn't austere like the first house I showed you,' said Barbara, who seemed to instinctively know that Ellie was already falling in love with this building. She nodded with approval at Ellie's gasp when they entered the beautiful square-tiled entrance with its sweeping staircase.

They walked through the house slowly, almost reverently. Each room was decorated in warm neutrals, but filled with unique and vibrant artwork that wouldn't have looked out of place in Tate Modern.

Ellie hadn't seen this brochure. Perhaps it had been at the bottom of the pile, waiting patiently for its time to shine.

A family home.

The ground-floor rooms had wooden floors, original cosy fireplaces, a large farmhouse kitchen and a dining area with gorgeous windows looking out onto a mature courtyard garden, which even had a rope swing attached to a crab apple tree in its centre. The bedrooms were all spacious; even the smallest bedroom was huge, and was currently set up as a nursery. After a quick, awkward glance in, they moved on; Ellie didn't dare look at Alex.

As they walked from room to room, both she and Alex were silent for the first time that day.

There were five floors in total, the top one being a huge room with bi-folding doors onto a roof terrace, which when opened – as they were now – gave stunning views of Christ Church's spire. When they reached it, they paused and stared at the sunny rooftops of London and the spires in the distance. Alex spoke first.

'It's perfect, but I don't think I'm ready for this. I mean, I was… But not now.'

She was surprised by the hot stinging in her eyes. Her heart was a dead weight in her chest. 'I understand.'

And she did.

Except, this was something she *was* ready for. She'd just not met her forever person yet, and increasingly wondered if she ever would. Her heart was so filled with longing, she could have sworn it was tearing at the seams. She wanted a family, a partner, someone to grow old with. A quick sidelong look at Alex's pained, handsome profile made those seams tear a little wider.

There was nothing worse than having a dream ripped apart.

And they both knew the bitterness of that first hand.

'So, perhaps the bachelor pad?' she asked.

'Perhaps.' Alex turned towards her with sudden enthusiasm. 'Shall I ask Barbara to make an offer on your flat in Point Clear? Unless you want me to buy you this... I mean, I can tell you like it—'

'No!' Ellie jolted as if she'd been punched awake. 'There's no way I could afford the bills for this place. Plus, it's a family home...'

'So, flat four it is?'

Ellie took a deep breath. They'd been back and forth over text about the available flats in Point Clear, the building her ideal flat was in. She'd already viewed the building a hundred times with Hannah or on her own. Every time something had come up for sale she'd viewed it, so she knew the building inside and out. Two flats were currently on the market, and Alex had wanted her to get the larger one, flat four – the one she'd originally wanted to buy with Hannah. 'The one-bed is plenty of room for me, and it will be far more manageable bills-wise.'

'Yes,' said Alex, and she could tell he was about to argue his case. 'But the two-bed will give you room to grow. You could always get a flatmate – share the cost of the bills and earn a little extra from their rent. And what if Hannah comes back? She could move in with you just as you'd originally planned.'

That was a good point. If Hannah did come back, it would suck if they couldn't return to being flatmates. 'True... Okay, let's go for number four then, the two-bed. Thank you.'

'Great, I'll get Barbara on it.'

Ellie chuckled. 'Go Barb! She'll be skipping all the way to the bank when her commission comes through. She deserves it though – that's one challenge ticked off both our lists.'

Alex's face sobered, and he ran his hand through his hair. Immediately Ellie knew she was in trouble. 'I've been thinking...' he said lightly, before fixing her with a devastatingly intense look. 'We should probably practise a kiss.'

Ellie gulped.

Alex took off his glasses, and used the corner of his t-shirt to clean them. The fabric lifted, revealing a strong stomach, the black waistband of his boxers and a line of dark hair above his belt buckle. Her mouth watered, and she couldn't help but imagine how heavenly it would feel to have his body pressed against hers. 'Just so you know what to expect and it seems natural when we do it in public. Are you okay with that?' he asked casually, putting his glasses back on.

Embarrassed that he might have caught her ogling, Ellie turned and stared out at the beautiful view from the perfect house, and nodded. This whole day had felt like fantasy land and make-believe. Like they were role-playing lives they didn't actually have. *In for a penny...* 'All right.'

Firm, strong hands turned her towards him. 'You sure?' His eyes were gentle, and her shoulders relaxed as she looked up into his kind and handsome face, the spring sun warming her flushed cheeks. A muscle in his jaw feathered as his expression became more serious, and his blue eyes slowly shifted from her eyes, down to her mouth and up again.

'Yes.' She breathed out the word, warmth spreading out from her belly in anticipation. His eyes brightened and he stepped forward, her chest brushing against his and causing her nipples to tighten.

She closed her eyes, but the sudden darkness did nothing to ease her pounding heart. The breeze ruffled her hair, and a large warm hand cupped her jaw. Soft, full lips pressed against hers in a chaste kiss, that still caused fireworks to burst behind her eyelids. She had to battle with every nerve in her body to stop herself from leaning into him, wrapping her arms around his neck and pulling him close.

He pulled away, and her eyes blinked open, dazzled by the aching lust racing through her body at such a simple touch.

'Good, just like that,' he said, his voice husky and breathless for some reason, and she wasn't sure if he was explaining the PG nature of their kiss or the fact that she was looking at him like a lovesick puppy.

Desperate to regain control over the situation and her racing heart, she said, 'Good. Great. PG kisses only, hand-holding, hugs. No tongues, or sex, right?'

Alex's eyes widened and he gave a gruff cough – no doubt shocked and horrified by the suggestion – and she wished she would just shut up, but her mouth was like a runaway train.

'Of course not. Why would we use tongues? Or have sex? We should have some boundaries, right? So we do nothing that could lead to hurt feelings or awkwardness later on.'

He nodded dumbly, and she took a deep cleansing breath before forcing a cheerful expression. 'We're friends... I'd hate to lose that.'

It would break her.

His expression turned solemn and he took her hands in his, giving them a light but heartfelt squeeze. 'I'd hate to lose you as a friend. You mean a lot to me.'

Her chest tightened painfully, but she resolutely ignored it. 'Well, we should probably get going before Barbs sends out a search party.'

Chapter Eleven

Alex's heart leapt like an excited teenager's – as it always did when he saw Ellie's name on his list of notifications. He knew it was wrong, but he couldn't stop thinking about that kiss on the roof terrace. How he'd felt for a moment as if he were living the life he was supposed to… with Ellie.

But it wasn't real, and it was blatantly obvious from what she'd said that she just wanted to remain as friends. He could understand that, suspected she'd been hurt in the past, and not just by the jerks who'd stood her up. There was something else lurking deeper behind her bravado. He wasn't sure what, or if he even had any right to pry. No, he definitely didn't have any right to pry.

It was better this way. No hurt feelings, for either of them.

Ignoring his other messages, he got off the treadmill and sat on a nearby weights bench. It was early, so no one else was using the hotel gym, and he preferred it that way. Not only for privacy, but because he'd also be awake for Ellie's first message of the day – or the end of the night, as it would be for her.

> Did you get your offer accepted on that cool bachelor pad?

It had been almost three weeks since they'd viewed the houses, and he'd still not made any firm decisions.

> Yep. Although. now I'm not so sure. Maybe I should just rent a place instead?

He waited anxiously for her reply, wondering if he should have called her instead. It was so hard to get his thoughts across, and he was still in two minds. The Spitalfields house kept popping into his head at random moments – or, more specifically, Ellie's reactions to the house: the way she'd gasped with wonder as she walked in, the stroke of her fingertips along the marble countertops, her face filled with longing when she'd stared into the nursery.

He'd meant what he'd said; he would have bought it for her, if she'd let him.

The house was beautiful, homely, and perfect for a family. If he'd seen a house like that when he'd still been with Savannah, he probably would have bought it.

Life was different now. He was alone, and he should adapt. He had the horrible feeling that it was a case of the right property at the wrong time. But he wasn't sure he wanted the bachelor lifestyle either. Could he see himself sitting alone in a hot tub overlooking the city and marina, a bunch of celebrities and wannabes fawning next to him? He hated that idea; he'd grown up amongst that set, and none of them had particularly cared for him. He remembered one famous actor had called him *the boring brother.*

He wanted a home like Ellie's, family photos lining the walls, a place with history and permanence. He'd moved so much, most of his stuff was in storage – or in the New York apartment, and he hadn't stepped foot in there for months.

Ellie took longer than normal to reply and he wondered if he'd overstepped an invisible boundary. After all, he'd dragged her around London to help him find a home, and he was still dragging his feet. He must seem so petulant and spoilt to her.

> Well, if you're not sure, maybe it's best you rent. Take the pressure off any big decisions.

He wasn't sure if he liked that idea either, even if it was by far the most sensible option.

What had he wanted her to say, that he should buy the Spitalfields house? The one she'd fallen in love with but couldn't afford, rub some more salt in her wounds?

He'd told Ellie that he wasn't ready for a family, but the truth was he was *too* ready. Even despite all the red flags in his relationship with Savannah, he'd been ready to take that leap. But they'd ended in disaster before they'd even begun.

Savannah had wanted his brother instead, the golden, perfect child of his family. She'd accused him of being cold and uncompromising, of being selfish, and he was – look at how he'd manipulated Ellie into helping him. Had he done the same with Savannah? Started dating her because it was convenient to his plans? Yes.

But then, hadn't Savannah done the same thing to him?

A chill ran down his spine when he thought of how blind he'd been.

They'd spent little time together in New York, especially after he'd agreed to the London production. He'd wanted her in London with him, but she wouldn't risk even a short break in her film career, and she hadn't wanted to leave her dogs.

He rolled his eyes. How many did she have now? Ten? Twelve? All fluffy yapping things with ugly squished faces. He was admittedly petty enough to feel no small amount of wicked satisfaction, knowing how much Liam disliked dogs. Hopefully, he was enjoying being woken up every day by ten dogs nibbling on his toes and shitting in his Japanese-inspired garden.

He refocused on his chat with Ellie.

> Everything okay with the paperwork Barb sent you?

She replied immediately:

> Yes. So relieved they accepted your offer. Only three months until we exchange. Go Barb!

He texted back:

> Go Barb! How's work going?
>
> Urgh, okay. I'm shattered. But only two more days till the Olivier Awards. And then it's straight to the Bahamas!

Her message was immediately followed by a face-slapping emoji.

> Sorry... Bet you're not excited about that at all. I'm more excited about the time off to be honest.

He smiled and replied:

> I get it. Don't worry, you deserve a holiday. It's the least I can do for all your help.

And she had helped him, in so many ways, big and small. But the Olivier Awards 'reveal' of their relationship was fast approaching, and he hadn't stopped checking the alerts on his phone.

The press was becoming more frenzied and ridiculous, each website and gossip magazine claiming to have the inside scoop on his new relationship. Every female cast member in his production had been suggested as his latest fling. There were also several British pop stars and influencers who'd been named as being seen with him. One grainy photo showed a TV presenter holding hands with someone in a baseball cap, and he'd been named as the mystery man and her boyfriend. He'd never even met her.

A woman's shrill voice brought him back to the present. 'Oh. MY. GOD!'

He glanced up to see a young woman rushing towards him wearing head-to-toe designer workout wear and wild eyes. He immediately stood up and grabbed his t-shirt from the treadmill. Damn, this was awkward, meeting a fan topless.

'I knew I'd seen you in the lobby. You're Alex King!' she shouted, and her voice echoed around the silent gym. 'Can I get a selfie?'

She'd already grabbed his arm and taken the picture before he'd had a chance to answer.

'Sorry, I've gotta go,' he said, untangling himself from her vice-like grip quickly and striding out of the gym as fast as his legs could carry him.

After he got back to his suite, he called Richie. 'I need to change hotels – better yet, rent me an apartment. A similar set-up to my New York place, plenty of security.'

Richie was used to panicked calls. 'No longer buying?' he asked smugly, and Alex's jaw tightened.

'I'm not sure yet.'

'Hmm, well, no problem, I can sort that out for you in no time. By the way, does your date for the awards need a stylist?'

Alex smiled for the first time since the incident with the woman in the gym. 'No, she's got enough style for the both of us.'

'Hmm,' repeated Richie, unimpressed. 'Well, *you* will definitely need a stylist. For your hair, if nothing else.'

Alex glanced at himself in the mirror. 'What's wrong with my hair?'

'You look like a hobo, like you can't cope. Is that the impression you want to give your family when they next see you?'

'Fine, book the stylist,' snapped Alex.

'I really wish you'd give me the name of your new girl. I need to shape the narrative, remember? I hope it's someone who will show off your softer side. Prove to people that you've changed, that what happened with Savannah and your brother actually helped you grow as a person.'

Alex had had enough. 'I thought you were meant to be on my side too? You know what, fuck the narrative. The world will just have to accept us as we are.'

He ended the call and threw his phone on the bed before storming into the bathroom. He needed a cold shower to cool off.

Chapter Twelve

On the day of the Olivier Awards, Ellie sat in her room quietly losing her mind.

There was no backing out now. Today was the day their fake relationship would be revealed.

The cramped space of her box room was dominated by moving boxes, as well as the bric-a-brac furnishings from the flat she'd shared with Hannah. She looked like one of those secret hoarders, surrounded by all of her shit.

Her suitcase for the Bahamas was by the door, already packed, as was her hand luggage. The essential toiletries bag sat on top of them, so she could still dip in and out of them when needed. In two days, she'd be last minute squishing it into her suitcase and jetting off to a tropical paradise.

Her hands began to tremble and she flicked her wrists to try to dispel some of her nervous energy, before placing her elbow firmly on the dressing table. 'Right, come on! Draw a fecking straight line.' Five minutes later she was admiring her reasonably straight eyeliner.

The mannequin in the corner kept drawing her gaze, and she took a minute to admire the dress waiting for her.

The dress mannequin was still the best investment Ellie had ever made. The sections could be adjusted individually for any measurement rather than dress size, which meant she could tailor it exactly to her body – important when you were making a silk scarlet dress that clung to every curve. She was going for a Grecian style, something Venus might have rocked after stepping out of her clamshell if she'd had a lot of red silk going spare.

'Soon, my love,' she cooed, more to entertain herself than anything else. She winced when she remembered her mother's reaction a few days ago to the half-finished dress, as if it were a patch of black mould on the wall.

'Is that your dress?'

'Yep,' Ellie had mumbled, concentrating on hand-stitching the beads she'd bought to glam up one of her clutches.

'It doesn't look very forgiving on the hips.' Her mum had frowned at the dress in the same way she'd always done when Ellie had eaten a dessert.

'It'll fit just as well as everything else I've ever made for myself.'

'Yes, and you're very good at making things to flatter a fuller figure, but for such a *big* event wouldn't you rather something a bit less… clingy? And the straps! You won't be able to wear a normal bra, and strapless bras are always so uncomfortable. You've got a few more days, why don't you join me on that soldier's diet? You're meant to be able to lose half a stone in just five days.'

Ellie had counted to ten in her head, but it still hadn't been long enough. Why did her mum always have to bring up her weight like this? As if it were a hurdle to overcome, a shame to hide.

'No, thanks. I'd rather eat more than a boiled egg for every meal.'

When her mum had continued to grimace at her dress, Ellie had had to put her needle down to stop herself from stabbing her. 'I'm never going to be skinny, Mum.' She'd almost added, 'and neither are you,' but that would have been unkind.

'Only because you refuse to do anything about it!'

Which was rich considering Ellie had spent years undoing the damage caused by her mother's constant yo-yo dieting and negative comments. It was a vicious cycle of reward and punishment that never ended. Her mother would fall into depression about her weight, then start one of her hideous diets that were so unhealthy she would immediately jump back on the wagon for sheer survival.

Ellie's own self-esteem and eating habits had only become more balanced once she'd moved in with Hannah and had taken positive steps to focus on being healthy rather than thin.

What people never seemed to understand was that being thin didn't necessarily mean you were healthy. Ellie at her slimmest had been exercising until she'd felt faint, saving her diet points for alcohol and chocolate, nutritionally starving herself because she couldn't cope with such a strict calorie deficit, and always needing some kind of small treat to get her through the week.

Her body had been broken, and Hannah had helped heal her relationship with food, because she'd had issues of her own. They'd worked together to overcome their problems.

Ellie had lost weight, though not as much as her mother insisted she should. But she'd finally arrived at a place that she was happy with, through a healthy balance of nutritious food, enjoyable light exercise, and just allowing herself to *bloody live*. She never regulated treats any more, or wallowed in guilt after an indulgence, and weirdly she ate less because of it.

But her mum had never understood that. 'There's going to be models there. You'll look like a whale against some of those twiglets.'

Ellie's needle slipped and she pricked her finger. Unfortunately, this wasn't a fairytale and she didn't slip into a coma, unable to hear her mother's words.

'I'm fine as I am, Mum. I exercise, I eat and drink whatever I like because it makes me happy. I may never complete a marathon, but I can always run for a bus, or dance the night away, or whatever. I'm happy with my body as it is. Yes, I'd love to get into some skinny jeans and not look like a link of sausages, but that's not my figure. I've got massive boobs, a nice waist and strong legs. Everyone has to work with what they've got. And, honestly, I'm going to look so hot in this dress, so please don't worry about me.'

Ellie knew that, just as some people were naturally slim like Hannah, she would always be a plus size by today's standards.

Frankly, she was done with hating herself. Unfortunately, her mum hadn't got the memo. She was still searching for the impossible, soul-destroying, *ideal* BMI. A calculation invented nearly two hundred years ago by a man – of course – who wasn't a doctor, but a mathematician.

'But the straps...' her mum had grumbled, pointing an accusing finger at the offending material.

Ellie had turned her back in silent dismissal. 'I'll be wearing enough tit tape to raise Tower Bridge. So stop worrying.'

Today the dress was complete and waiting patiently for her. Ellie peeked beneath her fluffy dressing gown and chuckled. She really was wearing enough tit tape to raise Tower Bridge. She rose and put on the dress, and was delighted when it slipped into place and hid the tape perfectly.

She gave a little squeal of delight as she spun around in front of her tiny bedroom mirror, giggling to herself as she almost got her heel stuck in the rug. She then contorted her spine to check out her bum, and grinned. She looked *hot*.

She'd had her hair and nails done that morning, then spent hours doing her make-up and securing her boobs – she'd had to rope poor old Nanna into helping her with that. But it was so worth it.

'Oh, you look gorgeous, love!' said Nanna, grinning when Ellie entered the kitchen.

'Thank you.' She tottered over to where Nanna was sitting and bent down to give her a squeeze.

'Your mum will be so impressed.'

'Hmm...' murmured Ellie, unconvinced, as she put her lipstick and phone into her hand-decorated purse.

'Of course she will.' Nanna stood and smoothed a stray hair from Ellie's carefully blow-dried hair. 'You look like a Hollywood star.'

Nanna was always the peacemaker between Ellie and her mum. A thankless task.

Her phone buzzed, and she scrambled to check it. 'He's five minutes away. I best head down.'

Nanna's voice stopped her at the door, brooking no argument. 'Go show your mum first.'

She gave a huff of acknowledgement, and stomped into the lounge on her way down, her sky-high heels punching into the carpet. 'Mum, I'm leaving,' she said from the doorway. They'd barely spoken since last week.

Her mum and Mark were watching the telly. He glanced up at her, and grunted, 'You look nice.' Then he turned back to the screen. *Typical brother.*

Her mum stood and stared at her open-mouthed. 'Oh, love, you look lovely... All secure?' She eyed Ellie's substantial cleavage as if it were a bomb.

Ellie jumped up and down, causing her bosom to bounce, but, importantly, not to fall out. 'Locked and loaded.'

Her mum's eyes became a little misty. 'You really do look gorgeous, darling.' She came over and gave her a light peck on the cheek and a squeeze to her arm.

Unused to compliments from her mother, Ellie backed out of the room. 'Well, best head out. It'll take me for ever in these heels.'

Her mum blinked. 'You won't be taller than Alex, will you?'

And normal Mum was back. 'Nope. Alex is huge, remember? Even with these on, I'll come up no higher than his nose.' Her phone beeped. 'Ah, that's him, best get a wiggle on. Bye, Nanna,' she shouted up the stairs, and then gave a little wave to her mum and brother before heading down to the ground floor.

Alex was waiting inside the yard; she'd left the gate open earlier in case he was followed by paparazzi, though judging by his laid-back stance he'd not had any trouble.

He stared at her and gave a low whistle that may as well have been a full-on kiss for all the goosebumps it gave her. 'You look so beautiful! Did you really make that?'

A blush rushed up her face and she did a joyful spin on her heels. 'Yes, and thank you, I'm glad you like it.'

'Like it?' He chuckled. 'I love it!'

She took the arm he offered her, and then she realised he also looked different – still hot, but more sleek-hot than casual-hot. 'Are you wearing contacts? And, have you had your hair cut.'

He nodded. 'Richie insisted, said I was starting to look like a hobo.'

'I'll cut out his tongue,' she said with mock horror, and Alex chuckled.

'So, you don't mind me as a hobo?'

She grinned. 'You're perfect in every version.' As they stepped out into the back street, she waved at the cab driver. 'Hey, Martin!' He waved back. In a lower voice she asked Alex, 'Do you have Martin on speed dial, or what?'

'Pretty much. He gives me great restaurant recommendations too.' Alex opened the cab door for her and she felt like a princess.

Richie was waiting for them to arrive and had given them strict instructions for when and where to pull up outside the Royal Albert Hall. To her surprise they were quite far away from the entrance, but, when she looked at the set-up as they circled around, she realised why.

The crowds!

The entrance, the terracotta and cream dome of the Hall perched at the top of a huge stone staircase, looked miles away. The 'red carpet' was actually green, an environmentally friendly grass carpet that rippled down the steps with photographers and reporters rammed either side held back by cattle railings. At the bottom, the carpet pooled to the side, with a spot for yet more photographs, this time in front of a walled backdrop plastered with the Olivier Awards logo and branded sponsors.

It was a terrifying gauntlet she wasn't sure she could run, especially in heels.

An usher opened Alex's door, and a dazzling cacophony of cameras flashed. The light burned her retinas and she shrank back from the glare, suddenly feeling very exposed in her bright and slinky dress. No woman looked her best bent over and shuffling out of a black cab. The door beside her opened as well, and Richie's face dipped down to stare at her.

'What the fuck! It's you,' he hissed, looking appalled to see her, and Alex turned in his seat with a lethal expression.

'Richie.' Alex barked his name like a warning. 'She's *my* choice.'

Richie blinked. 'Fine.' He gave her another one of his hideous up-and-down looks, before offering her his hand. 'I'll make it work,' he added with a huff, which meant she'd somehow passed muster on this occasion.

It may have been childish, but Ellie gave him an up-and-down appraisal of her own. 'Looking not so bad yourself, Richie. Scrubbed up nicely.'

Richie scowled, but didn't respond to her comment on his appearance. 'It's always best for ladies to get out of cars turned away from the cameras. Be grateful I'm here to guide you.'

Alex got out at the same time as she did, on the opposite side. There was a riot of sound, as if everyone were shouting at once.

Richie spoke into her ear, his words filled with warning. 'Take my advice. Always remember, he's the star, not you. Ordinary people don't last long in this business – they don't fit the part.'

He moved away before she could answer, and a prickle of fear ran down her spine. Fans and photographers were buzzing around and she'd never felt so exposed in her life. Cold to the bone, she shivered.

Vaguely aware of Martin shouting her a cheery goodbye as he pulled away, she walked towards Alex. Richie hurried ahead, disappearing into a throng of crews and planners that were beavering away in the background while the glamorous celebrities shone in the limelight.

Alex stood poised and confident, his legs wide and his spine straight as he patiently waited for her. His whole body was facing towards her, oblivious to the chaos behind, and an enigmatic smile graced his perfect sculpted lips.

He'd kissed her not that long ago, and her mouth tingled with the memory. She focused on his smile, hoping it would give her the strength to keep walking forward with her head held high.

Time slowed, and she reached out for Alex. His handsome face brightened and his hand met hers, pulling her close as the cameras popped and flashed around them. He looped her arm gracefully around the soft fold of his tuxedoed elbow as if she were a queen, his warmth seeping through the fabric to her chilled skin and reassuring her this was really happening.

Nurse Ellie is on a date with a Hollywood star!

She gathered up the silk of her dress with one hand, and they climbed up the kerb to the first waiting area – the logo-crowded backdrop.

'Sorry about this,' Alex murmured in her ear. 'It's really weird, but you have to stop and give them a good picture. Sometimes it stops them hassling you later.'

She nodded, her throat too dry to speak.

A queue of stars were waiting to be photographed, all of them making their slow progression towards the entrance. An acclaimed Shakespearean veteran stood between where they, and a musical star further up the steps, stood. At intervals, the stars would stop for interviews, photos or autograph signing.

It was the weirdest queue she'd ever been in, and she'd gone to the *Sound of Music* Sing-a-long last year where one group of people had dressed up as the lonely goatherd and his goats. They'd even had wire frames above their heads to look like puppet strings. This felt much the same, people nonchalantly waiting in line while wearing a variety of outfits from black tie to Met Gala outrageous.

Alex guided them to a position that was marked with a tiny black-taped cross on the carpet. Unsure of what she should do, she stood awkwardly at his side, shifting on the spikes of her heels.

Cameras flashed and clicked once more in a frenzy of light that made her turn her face instinctively away, leaving her temporarily blind as a roar of shouts rang in her ears. The shouts were all confusing instructions that contradicted one another.

'ALEX, OVER TO THE LEFT.'

'WHO IS SHE?'

'RIGHT!'

'WHO'S YOUR DATE?'

'SMILE, LOVE, FOR GOD'S SAKE!'

'LOOK LEFT.'

'WHO IS SHE?'

'LOOK AHEAD.'
'RIGHT!'

Her panic and uncertainty were so unlike her, she had a weird sense of losing herself, like she was experiencing the moment outside of her body.

Alex's knuckle stroked beneath her chin, gently guiding her face to tilt upwards and look into his ocean eyes. Suddenly the noise of the press disappeared, and all she could see was Alex, the sharp cut of his jaw in stark contrast to the softness of his expression.

'Just remember the posing advice you gave Hannah.' The low rumble of his voice rippled over her like a comforting blanket.

'Yes,' she answered weakly, followed by a much stronger, 'yes.'

She could do this. A few photographers were nothing. She'd dealt with worse. She'd not even blinked when a builder had walked up to her in A&E carrying his hand in a Tupperware box. If she could handle that, she could handle anything. She straightened her spine, shifted her feet and moved her free hand to her hip, slipping into a more confident and hopefully glamorous pose.

The shouts grew more incessant.

'YES! LEFT, LEFT!'
'RIGHT, RIGHT!'
'STRAIGHT AHEAD, LOVE!'

Alex dipped his dark head to her ear and a shuddering heat ran through her. 'You're a natural, so beautiful.'

It was like a shot of pure adrenaline, flooding her body with confidence and joy. She gave the crowd a beaming smile, but it was Alex and not the photographers who'd made it happen.

The brush of Alex's hand skimming up her back to her nape made her look at him again. Piercing blue eyes flicked between hers, and then his head dipped slowly forward. He wasn't going to kiss her here, was he? Hypnotised, she wasn't sure if she was up or down. Her only anchor was Alex and she wanted to cling on to him for dear life, but she was afraid he would disappear in a puff of smoke.

This wasn't like the sweet kiss on the roof terrace.

There was heat and passion as his arm swooped around her waist and drew her against him, his lips pressed firm against her mouth. She gasped and his tongue teased at the open invitation, almost breaking their rule.

This was going to end badly, and not for the Hollywood star. No, it would end badly for her, the *ordinary* Ellie Jones. He was going to break her heart if he kept kissing her like that.

Remember, it's not real. At least this time she knew it was fake, and she'd be getting her lovely two-bed flat at the end of it.

Nobody would laugh this time. No, Ellie Jones had nothing to be ashamed of.

She pulled away, blinking rapidly against the flashing cameras, still shocked by his kiss. He led her away gently, as if she were the most precious woman in the world.

Was he acting? He had to be.

The crowd of photographers were going wild. But Ellie couldn't hear a word they said; in her mind they were cheering, and she was finally being accepted for who she was. Alex had kissed her publicly – declaring them as a couple, claiming her as his own – and, even if it wasn't real, she didn't care.

Plus-size, ordinary Ellie had finally triumphed. Alex's kiss had stuck up a middle finger to every person who'd ever made her think she wasn't good enough. David, Richie, even her mum.

Richie beckoned them impatiently from the side and they moved on.

A scream of noise and light came from behind them and Ellie had the sudden horrifying thought that one of her duct-taped boobs might have fallen out of her dress. But no, it was for the glamorous and tiny woman who had just stepped out of a limousine and was currently walking up to the position they'd just left.

'Is that— Oh my God!'

Alex grinned. 'Get used to it. I'm not the biggest name here, not by a long shot.'

Wild-eyed, Ellie whispered, 'Don't leave me alone. I'll end up doing something ridiculous, like beg her to kiss my hand or sing my name.'

They walked up the steps towards the scarlet and gilded archway and the memorial statue guarding its royal entrance.

'I'm having such a great time,' gasped Ellie, holding on to Alex's arm tightly.

His eyebrow quirked up playfully. 'It's only just begun.'

'I know, but if I forget later, I just want you to know that I had the best time!' She beamed up at him, her heart thundering in her chest. If this were a dream, she never wanted to wake up.

Chapter Thirteen

Alex was grateful that Richie always knew what to do. Smoothing the way ahead of them, speaking to the reporters – telling them what they could and couldn't ask. Shaping the damn narrative, and threatening to blacklist the journalists who didn't play ball. Which was why an official event like this was the ideal place to publicise their fake relationship, and also why Richie was paid so well, despite the fact that he could be a complete asshole at times.

Alex had been furious with Richie's rudeness to Ellie in the car. It was Alex's fault for not telling Richie her name. In fact, he'd only confirmed her full name with his mother that morning, after she'd threatened to contact a private detective. He'd delayed telling them because he knew that, once he revealed who she was, the entire family would be looking into her, and their safe little bubble of privacy would be gone for good. He also didn't want to give Richie an opportunity to talk Ellie out of helping him, and he couldn't trust his mother not to tell Richie.

A journalist was asking him about his latest production, and he reeled off all of his planned talking points, in well-rehearsed answers, steering the conversation to the talent of his actors and crew. As always, the interviewer then turned to Ellie and asked a question to draw her into the conversation. This time it was the very benign, 'Who are you wearing?' question.

Ellie gave a sexy pivot on her elegant heels, her hips seductively tilting with the movement and causing his mouth to dry. 'Me, of course.' She giggled.

'You're a designer?' gasped the interviewer with admiration.

Ellie shook her head with a sweet blush.

Alex was quick to interrupt before she dismissed her abilities. 'It's one of her passions – her designs are fantastic, don't you think?'

The interviewer gushed enthusiastically in agreement, and Ellie was obviously flattered by the praise. Richie came over and quickly ended the interview, then ushered them on to the next. The earlier green-carpet viewing area had only been the beginning. Camera crews, interviewers and photographers filled the entrance area, assistants and agents flying around like tennis balls arranging interviews.

'Bloody hell, are we *ever* going to get inside the theatre?' quipped Ellie, as they walked away from yet another reporter.

'You're doing brilliantly, and don't worry, we'll be going in soon,' he said, and he meant it – she was a natural in interviews. Bubbly and friendly, but not overbearing. She took a back seat and let him do most of the talking, only answering questions when they were directed specifically at her, or if he asked for her opinion, which he often did.

'One more,' said Richie firmly, and directed them towards a familiar face – at least to Alex – the *Arts Review* journalist, Mei. Today she wore a black cocktail dress with dramatic puffy sleeves. The design was probably a deliberate choice, as it seemed to keep the other reporters at bay, despite their jostling forward with their own microphones and lenses.

Alex stiffened and tucked Ellie's arm under his more firmly, as if he could somehow guard her from the indomitable Mei. He was prepared to drag Ellie away if she played one of her tricks again.

'Hello again, Alex.' Mei beamed, not an ounce of guilt on her perfectly made-up face. She had a TV cameraman beside her today.

'Hello...' He glanced at Richie, who gave a *see how it goes* head-nod.

'And who's your gorgeously vivacious lady in red?' asked Mei with a flash of canines.

He slipped his arm around Ellie's waist and pulled her closer as she answered cheerfully, 'I'm Ellie.'

'Ellie?'

'Ellie Jones.'

'Ellie Jones.' Mei breathed out the name with a puff of satisfaction. 'What's that short for? Elizabeth?'

'Eliza.'

Damn, thought Alex; Mei had gotten her full name faster than his mom. Still, it was bound to happen eventually.

A slow, Cheshire Cat smile spread across Mei's face. 'How delightful. I hear you're a nurse? This must be a change from bedpans and patients, yes?'

Alex was about to interrupt when Ellie laughed. 'It's certainly more glamorous. But tonight is about Alex's line of work, not mine.'

'Oh, I don't know about that,' said Mei slyly. 'Everyone is so thrilled to hear that Alex is dating again. Alex, you previously mentioned you were looking forward to the future – is Ellie the reason for that?'

Alex nodded, his fingertips stroking the silky warmth of Ellie's curvy waist. 'Like I said, I'm optimistic about the future, both professionally and personally.'

'Great, and how long have you two been together?'

His eyes locked with Ellie's. In the past he'd always found it better to stick as close to the truth as possible. But Richie had said it would work better if they already seemed committed, so it was probably best to be vague. 'Oh, a little while, but it's like we've known each other for ever,' he answered, and Ellie's lips twitched.

'Well, aren't you two just the cutest,' declared Mei, and then, with a wink at Ellie, she added with a merry laugh, 'you've given all of us ordinary ladies hope. Who'd have thought Alex King would be into curvy girls now – you must feel very lucky.'

Outrage seared through him and he was about to pull Ellie away, but her grip on his arm tightened and she kept him firmly at his side as she replied, 'I think we're lucky to have found each other, don't you?' She tilted her head up at him, and he was tempted to kiss her again, and not only to shut Mei up.

'Yes, I'm the luckiest guy alive.' He turned back to Mei, and said with a charming but firm look, 'I think Ellie's the hottest, kindest, funniest, and best damn woman I've ever met.'

As Mei opened her mouth to ask another question, he gave a brisk and cheerful goodbye, before leading Ellie away. 'I'm so sorry,' he said, leaning towards her in case any cameras picked up his words later with a lip-reader.

Ellie stopped walking and turned to face him. To his relief she wasn't visibly upset by Mei's rudeness; in fact, her jaw tilted up with confident defiance. 'Don't be. That's not the worst thing anyone's ever said to me.'

Anger fizzed in his veins. What was the worst thing? Who had dared to hurt her? 'I'm sorry, people are assholes, especially in this industry.'

Ellie squeezed his arm and rested her head on his shoulder lightly. An oddly comforting gesture considering that she should be the one needing support, not him.

'Thank you, but don't worry about defending me. I'm tougher than I look. When it's strangers making those kinds of comments, it's not too bad and I can deal with it. It's kind of you, but you don't need to defend me, honestly.'

An ache settled low in Alex's stomach, and his throat tightened as he thought about what Ellie might have suffered in the past, and not only by strangers, but by people she'd trusted and loved. He knew she had a difficult relationship with her mother, but he had a feeling that she wasn't the only person who'd let her down.

Was it his place to ask? He suspected now wasn't the right time to ask, regardless. They strolled away from the interviewers. The sun was beginning to set and turning the sky above the Royal Albert Hall slate grey. The warm lights from within the historic building seemed to be calling to him, offering them shelter and warmth.

The pop princess was close on their heels, so the press quickly lost interest in them, and they were finally able to go inside to take their seats.

He'd almost forgotten the point of the evening, after spending so long working through the press.

'Alex!' cried Isaac, slapping him on the shoulder excitedly.

'Shouldn't you be backstage?' asked Alex.

'Just about to go. Getting in took longer than I'd expected,' said Isaac with a slightly bewildered expression, as if he still had camera flashes going off behind his eyes.

'You're performing tonight?' asked Ellie.

Isaac nodded. 'Yeah, the big party number, can't believe you managed to get us in, Alex. Thanks so much, the cast are thrilled. Scared witless too,' he joked, 'but thrilled.'

Alex gave his leading man a supportive clap on the shoulder. 'You'll be great. Now, get backstage quick, before people start to panic.'

Isaac hurried off, going the wrong way at first, and then quickly correcting his direction with a panicked expression.

Alex smothered a laugh. He knew those jittery nerves well.

'You really care about them, don't you?' Ellie was beaming up at him with obvious admiration.

'I know what it's like early on in your career. It's a whirlwind, and you have no idea what you're doing half the time. I had my parents' support, but many young actors don't have that. I'd like to think I can help them.'

Ellie nodded with approval. 'I'm sure you are. Getting them here must be a huge help.'

'Hopefully. It's only a small slot, but Russell and I pulled every string we could think of to get them this gig. Not only will it boost sales, but it'll get them well known in the industry for their next job. I'm trying to get Isaac a meeting with another producer I know.'

Ellie pressed a hand to her chest. 'That's really good of you. You should be proud.'

His chest expanded with a glowing warmth. He was proud of both himself and Russell – who he was getting along much better with these days. Probably because Alex had heard about the last-minute cancellation at the awards programme and had been the first on the phone to the organisers begging for the free slot.

'Come on,' said Alex, and he led Ellie into the huge glittering awards space. Rows of ruby seats were gathered around the shiny black presentation and performance stage. Their seats were positioned at the end of a row, a helpful tag on them proclaiming, *Alex King* and *Alex King's Guest*.

'Sorry,' he said. Ellie must think him so disorganised.

'I'm happy to be here. Don't apologise.'

They sat down amongst the stars and waited for the rest of the audience to arrive, which didn't take long as a flurry of people began to pour in all at the same time. Ellie moved out of the way so that a famous actress, Dame Mary Woodhouse, could take her seat. She barely glanced at Alex, but to his delight she stopped to compliment Ellie on her dress. 'Stunning, darling,' she declared, with an upper-crust pout, and Ellie thanked her with a blush.

'Wish I hadn't picked something so bloody wide!' huffed the actress, flapping frustratedly at her sweeping purple skirt. 'I'm going to be up and down to the loo like a yo-yo – nervous bladder and all. So, apologies in advance.'

Alex tried to stifle a chuckle. He found the Brits so adorable with their variety of accents and phrases.

'That's no trouble,' said Ellie hurriedly, more than a little star-struck, but then she appeared to gather her composure, and added cheerfully, 'I'll keep my fingers crossed for you.'

'Thank you, darling.'

The pair of them chatted for a little longer, Ellie explaining who they were and why they were here. She constantly referred to Alex's 'amazing production *The Great Gatsby*', but the dame seemed more intrigued about where Ellie was from.

'My family was born on that street!' she declared with wide eyes.

'Really? Oh, my nanna would be thrilled to hear that. She's lived there since she was a little girl.'

They chatted a little more, and then, when the dame started speaking with another actor to the other side of her, Ellie turned to Alex and whispered, 'Who'd have thought Dame Mary would be nervous. She's an absolute icon. Goes to show, we're all just human.'

Alex nodded and then took her hand in his and squeezed it, proud of her ability to triumph on any occasion. 'It gets very intense. I get nervous and I'm not even up for anything.'

'Not this year… But maybe next,' she said with a playful grin before returning the squeeze.

He tried to imagine his life a year from now, potentially nominated for an award and waiting nervously to hear the announcement. Would he be alone?

The evening began. The awards were being presented by a well-known British comedian who gave a light-hearted spin to the proceedings. The awards were interspersed with outstanding performances by West End shows and musicals.

Ellie kept turning to him and saying, 'I've got to see that one,' after each performance.

'Me too,' he replied, and he hoped they would see them together, that they would remain friends even after their deal had ended. That she wouldn't walk away and never want to see him again.

When his cast performed their number, he was so nervous he almost couldn't bear to watch. However, he needn't have worried; they were awesome, and when they took their bow he and Ellie leapt up to give a standing ovation, and even Dame Mary rose from her seat in support.

'Bravo,' she declared, and turned her manicured clap towards him. Which was more than a little flattering.

'They were brilliant,' squealed Ellie. She gave him a quick hug, pressing her soft body against his, and tilting her bright and beautiful face to look up at him, eclipsing the crowd's applause with her radiant cherry-red smile. 'Well done!'

More than anything he wanted to kiss her again, but the ceremony was already moving on, and they had to retake their seats. Dame Mary caught his eye as he sat down, and flicked her wrist in a whimsical gesture. 'Ahh, to be young and in love.'

He only wished they were.

Chapter Fourteen

Ellie glanced at the clock on her phone for the hundredth time.

Any minute now, she reassured herself.

Soon, Alex and Martin would arrive and whisk her away to the airport. She couldn't wait. Her suitcase was already waiting in the yard downstairs. Her hand luggage, a large straw tote that would double as a beach bag, sat on the empty chair beside her, filled to the brim with travel essentials including her passport.

She wished she'd stayed in her room until Alex arrived, but Nanna had wanted her to eat well before the journey. Needless to say, her pile of toast was barely touched; she was too excited to eat.

'This is ridiculous!' snapped her mum, thumping down the gossip magazine in her hand. It had only been two days since the awards, but the press had been quick to run with the announcement of Alex's relationship with her. 'I can't believe you're putting yourself through this. Again!'

'I'm not.' There was no point explaining how this situation would be different from the mistakes of her past.

'Have you seen what they're saying?'

Ellie glanced across at what her mum had spread out on the kitchen table, rolled her eyes, and went back to playing Scrabble on her phone – she was losing badly, too distracted to concentrate.

'Then don't read it. I'm not.'

Her mum karate-chopped the morning paper like it was a stack of wood. '*Alex King's mystery woman* flaunted *her curves in a scarlet dress of her own design at the Olivier Awards.*' More dramatic gestures followed, Ellie leaning back to avoid a finger in the eye. '*Alex couldn't keep his hands off the* vivacious *brunette, with* some *sources describing them* kissing passionately *throughout the night.*' Her mum collapsed back in her chair, as if she were a lawyer putting in her final closing argument. 'Ellie, I mean, *seriously*?' She shook her head in disbelief, and followed it with a deeply disappointed sigh – the ultimate closing argument of any mother.

Unwilling to be beaten, Ellie held her mother's stare. 'I did nothing to be ashamed of.'

'Good girl,' said Nanna with a chuckle followed by a wink, which received a scathing look from her mother.

'I'm off,' said Mark, tightening the lid on his Thermos of tea ready to make a quick getaway. 'Have a nice time, Sis.'

'Thanks.'

Her mum was not to be put off by the lack of support from the rest of her family. She was a dog with a tabloid bone. 'Flaunting!' she shrieked. 'What does that even mean?'

'I've no idea,' Ellie answered dryly. But she could guess.

'It's provocative. Gets the people going,' said Nanna sagely, and Ellie snorted at her obscure Will Ferrell reference.

'It's just the usual nonsense.' Honestly, she *was* used to it – albeit on a much smaller scale, and not in the public eye. If you had a large bust and large hips you were immediately sexualised in a provocative way.

You were never *pretty* – you were a *femme fatale*.

You were never *healthy and strong*. You were *curvy and vivacious* at best, and simply *fat and lazy* at worst. Despite the fact that she could work twelve hours straight on her feet and lift patients twice her size.

'I don't understand why you're doing this.' Her mum's brow was furrowed, a mix of frustration, confusion and worry, as if Ellie wasn't a thirty-year-old woman entitled to do whatever the hell she pleased, and quite frankly it wasn't anyone else's business, including her mother's.

Still, she didn't see why she should lie to her family. 'It's for the press mainly, and,' – she'd have to explain it at some point – 'he's bought me a flat.'

Her mother's eyes bulged out of her head. 'WHAT? You're prostituting yourself?'

'No.' However, Ellie's next words only made her look worse. 'It's a business deal between friends. This just helps take the heat off him. His brother's marrying his ex-girlfriend, and, well, he wants to show them that he's happy with someone else.'

There, done.

Nanna and her mum exchanged a concerned look, but of course it was her mum who spoke first. 'The article says you were kissing each other. Couldn't take your hands off each other.' She tapped the paper for dramatic effect. 'That's what it says. Right here, in black and white.'

'It was just a peck, nothing serious. Just for show.'

Nanna raised a snowy eyebrow and Ellie took a sip of her water. A telltale flush crept up her neck. Nothing about that kiss had been casual – she still didn't understand it.

Nanna placed a hand on her arm. 'We're only worried, darlin'. This sounds like you're playing with fire, and David—'

'This is not the same!' she yelled, and her nanna's hand retreated. Immediately, she apologised. 'I'm sorry, I know you both mean well. But it's not the same.'

She'd had a wonderful night at the Olivier Awards. Sure, the press were making comments about her body, but that was to be expected. She would ignore them, and have a magical holiday with Alex.

She was happy. Why did her mother have to spoil everything?

'And all this time you've taken off work, to run away on holiday with him. You're putting your life on hold, for a man you barely know, and what's to guarantee he's going to keep his promise about the flat?' asked her mum, trying to play good cop for a change.

Ellie pursed her lips at that, and her nanna gave her a look of warning. How many times had her mother bent over backwards for the men in her life? And those men hadn't even offered to buy milk. Her mum's relationships had been a hellish merry-go-round of hope and despair, with her kids picking up the pieces of her broken heart every time.

'Even if he doesn't buy me a flat, I'm still going to the Bahamas, aren't I? That alone would be worth it. It's not like we're rolling in money, is it?' She suspected her mum already knew about the money troubles with the shop. She'd also bet that her mum knew she was helping Mark financially. She'd seen them talking over his business plans the other day, and she'd stepped out of the room again as if it were completely normal, even though Ellie had never been involved in the big decisions before. It was infuriating that her mother was happy to throw around opinions on stuff that didn't matter, but was tight-lipped when it came to the fate of their family business.

Her mum paused, her face flaming. 'But you have to ask yourself. Why did he pick *you*?'

'Angela, that's enough!' exclaimed Nanna, but it was already far too late.

Regardless of the cold looks from both sides of the table, her mum continued, 'I'm just making sure she understands the risk. She could be made into a laughing-stock again, and for what? Some man she barely knows.'

Ellie dropped her phone in her bag, stood, and slung it over her shoulder. She didn't care if she had to stand outside waiting to be picked up for an hour. She wouldn't take another minute of this. 'David was a coward and an arse. You act like I was to blame for what he did, that I somehow deserved it. Why?'

Her mum became flustered. 'I just don't want you to be taken advantage of again—'

'No. You think that someone like Alex couldn't possibly want to be with someone like me. I must be a joke, right?' The white heat of anger and resentment boiled through her veins.

'She's not saying that, love,' said Nanna, reaching for her arm.

Ellie walked towards the door, knocking down her sunglasses from the top of her head to hide the tears that were already threatening to fall. 'I am not unhealthy. I am not ugly. I am not hideous.' She swallowed the burning lump in her throat as she opened the door and turned to face them. 'I am a *good* person, and I deserve to be happy.'

'I know that,' said her mum with a defensive huff.

'Really?' she asked, her voice strained. 'Because you never say it. There always seems to be room for improvement. You'd be pretty, Ellie, if only you lost another twenty pounds. Try this, try that. Starve yourself and then someone might be able to love you, right?'

Her mum looked down miserably at the single boiled egg on her plate. No toast, no butter. A lonely egg in a *Morning Sunshine* cup. 'I'm just looking out for you,' she muttered.

'Thanks, but I'm a grown woman and I can look after myself. I'm off to eat, drink and wear that skimpy bikini we saw in the shops last week.' She wanted to live her life, not hate it.

'Oh God, not the polka dot one!' gasped her mum, her eyes wide as if an axe-wielding clown had entered the kitchen.

Ellie had admired one in a shop window – and her mother had lamented for ten minutes about how they *both* could never wear such a thing. Ellie had ordered it online that same night.

'Shut up, Angela,' Nanna practically growled across the table at her.

Ellie pushed the door fully open. 'Right, I'm off to the Bahamas. Did I tell you? We're flying Business.'

She flicked her hair as she walked away, but her nerves were brittle and her chest tight.

—

Mark must have heard her yelling because he popped his head through the shop doorway as she stomped down the stairs. 'All right?'

'Yeah,' she said with little enthusiasm.

'Ignore her.'

She nodded.

'Have a good time.'

'Thanks.'

He closed the door and went back into the shop.

Typical brother, she thought with a roll of her eyes, and went out into the yard. Her phone buzzed. It was Alex:

> Just coming down your road.

Ellie squealed, grabbed her giant suitcase and wheeled it towards the yard gate. She was swinging the gate open as Martin's cab pulled up outside.

Alex jumped out, grabbed her case and hauled it into the cab, not moaning once about the weight of it – unlike Mark, who'd cursed her packing down each flight of stairs. Then, like a gentleman, Alex waved her inside first.

'Oh, you're spoiling me!' she exclaimed, as she spotted a little Harrods bag on the floor filled with chocolates, two flutes and a bottle of Moët with a branded freezer jacket to keep it cool.

Alex crawled back into the cab and his big body filled the limited space as he settled beside her on the back seat. 'Martin helped.'

'Of course he did. What would you do without him? All right, Martin?' she called out in greeting, buckling her seat belt.

Martin chuckled and waved from the front. 'Yes, love. You got your passport? Hannah was convinced she'd forgotten hers halfway to the airport. Almost had to turn around until she realised it was in her coat pocket, silly pickle.'

'I've got it.' She waved her passport at him for confirmation and he pulled away.

'He checked me for mine too,' said Alex and chuckled. He reached for the champagne and popped the cork. 'I didn't have it. Left it in the hotel safe. We had to go back – sorry, that's why I'm a bit late.'

Ellie held out the glasses for him to pour, and said loudly, 'Thank you, Martin. You're a life saver.'

They toasted each other and took a sip.

'So, when do you go back to work?' Alex asked conversationally.

Relief and the fizz of champagne flooded her veins. They were back to their easy friendship, despite the drama of the awards and their heated kiss. At least, Alex was; she found herself unable to stop staring at his sultry mouth as he took another sip of his drink, and watching the bob of his throat as he swallowed the liquid.

Staring at him was a habit she really needed to break.

Like now... *What did he say? Oh, work, yes!*

'Well, I've plenty of unused holiday, so I've booked a bit of time off after too. Just to have a think about my next steps and get over any jet lag.' Ellie sipped her bubbly and sank into the leather seat with a happy wiggle, her fight with her mum already fading into a distant memory.

'That sounds like a good idea. It's a long trip, what with the connecting flight and the boat.'

Ellie almost choked on her perfectly chilled champagne. 'I'm sorry, what?'

She really should have paid more attention to the details. But she'd spent all of her spare time on sewing her award show and summer outfits. She'd made nearly everything from scratch, with only a few exceptions

– like the scandalous teeny-weeny-not-yellow-but-blue-polka-dot-bikini. She suspected she would never be brave enough to wear it, but she'd packed it anyway. There were always her usual one-pieces if she felt shy, and she had plenty of beach kaftans and throws to cover up with.

Alex's voice brought her head back from the inside of her suitcase to the hunk beside her. 'Yeah, sorry. The house is in Exuma, it's an archipelago of cays and islands about thirty-five miles from Nassau. We've a connecting flight, but it's less than an hour.' He gave her a sheepish look, as if he was sorry his luxury holiday home was such a ball-ache to get to. 'Then we'll take the boat to my parents' house, which is only another forty minutes, and it's a scenic journey – you get to see the smaller islands, stingrays, turtles, that sort of thing.'

'Seriously, that sounds amazing. And that's just the journey there? Brilliant!'

Alex winced. 'You might feel differently when you meet my family.'

It was Ellie's turn to cringe – she shouldn't be so excited for something that Alex was going to find so hard.

'It will be fine, I promise.' She offered her glass, and he tapped it gently with his own.

She only prayed that they wouldn't let each other down, because right now she was *really* out of her depth.

Chapter Fifteen

Flying with Ellie had been the most fun Alex had *ever* had travelling. She made everyone laugh around her, filling the plane with cheerful holiday vibes that would make even the most hardened traveller crack a smile.

Every aspect of his luxury lifestyle had filled her with wonder, from the VIP lounge and quick security passes – to the fact that they turned left when they got on the plane and she discovered a whole new world of private cubicles and spacious seats.

'We've got a cubicle each. Oh my God! Look, that guy's flattening it out, it turns into a bed!' She was practically vibrating out of her skin as they were shown to their seats.

Alex grinned at her over his partition. 'I'm glad you like it.' Now he felt bad that he'd not accepted his mother's offer of the private jet for the entire journey. Ellie would have probably fainted.

'Like it? I love it,' she said with a teasing wink, followed by a gasp. 'They've given us a blanket and a load of knick-knacks too.' She began to tear through the amenity kit, pulling out each item with increasing excitement. 'Oh man, I know I should sleep. But look at all this stuff!' She gestured to the bag and the entertainment screen like it was the eighth wonder of the world.

Shaking his head, he said decisively, 'I'm choosing sleep.'

'I'll do a bit of both,' she said after a moment of thought. 'Quick, show me how to recline this thing, I want to veg out.'

Alex moved to help her, but the flight attendant arrived first, and efficiently flattened down her seat. After she'd gone, he leaned into her booth and asked in an admittedly terrible French accent, 'Champagne, mademoiselle?'

'Yes, please.' Ellie's brown eyes sparkled. 'I am *officially* living my best life!'

—

They arrived in sunny Nassau at two in the afternoon local time. As Alex had promised, the connecting flight to Exuma was short, and made more palatable by the fact that it was in his mother's private jet. Ready and waiting to go within minutes of their arrival, that, combined with the private cars to and from the airports, had been almost too much for Ellie to bear.

When they arrived at Exuma's harbour and boarded his parents' boat, she side-eyed him. 'Seriously? I thought you meant we were catching a ferry, not a freaking private yacht.'

'It's only fifty feet, so not a big one.'

'Ah yeah, it's pretty much a dinghy.' Ellie stifled a yawn, and he imagined all the champagne and lack of sleep was beginning to catch up with her.

'Come on, let's get you a drink and set you up with a nice view.'

Moments later they were settled on one of the padded benches, each with a bottle of chilled water in hand, as they whipped through the glorious ocean spray. Ellie immediately perked up, especially when the captain stopped the boat so they could watch a school of stingrays sail majestically by. She said she would have gladly spent all day watching them, but then Alex had pointed out a shark and she'd been quick to suggest they 'crack on'.

'Everything's so much brighter here,' she said with a sigh of pleasure, lifting her face to the sun and allowing the breeze to run through her hair. 'I'm sure thirty years of London pollution has just been swept out of my lungs. I always thought I was a city girl at heart, but this really is paradise.'

He couldn't agree more; the colours were sharp and vivid in the Caribbean, the sand whiter, the aqua blue of the ocean somehow more radiant than any other place on earth and the salty breeze a gentle kiss in the shimmering heat of the day. Awe-inspiring wildlife and natural beauty combined in perfect harmony.

Experiencing the Bahamas through Ellie's eyes was inspiring, giving him a new and greater appreciation of its exceptional beauty.

Luminous green palm trees swayed on beaches of islands dotted with luxurious homes. Beaches with shallow crystal-clear waters stretched into the never-ending horizon.

She was right, they really were in paradise, but he wouldn't have been grateful for any of it without Ellie by his side.

'I think this must be the most beautiful place on earth,' she said reverently, turning to face him.

'It's pretty spectacular, isn't it,' he said softly, thinking how beautiful her olive skin looked in the afternoon sun. She had changed in the small bedroom of the jet from her sweatpants and t-shirt to a white linen dress she'd kept rolled up in her hand luggage. The wind pressed the material against her body and his appreciation of the scenery moved from the landscape to the sweeping curves of Ellie's body. He would never tire of looking at her.

They anchored at the quay of his parents' sprawling holiday home. The yellow mansion was just visible through the tropical gardens, white imposing pillars stood on either side of the large front doors and a white wooden veranda flowed around every side of the house. The beach, landscaped gardens and shiny moorings only added to the opulent luxury.

'Christ! From a distance I thought it was another one of those hotels we've passed.' She paused, as if realising something for the first time. 'Is this… their private island?'

Uncomfortable, he nodded, unsure of what to say.

'Damn, your family are riiiiiiiccchhhh,' she drawled, and he couldn't help the blush that crept up his neck.

'My parents both had a successful thirty-year career in films. They're…' He paused, searching for the right phrase, and then shrugged with defeat. '*Very* rich. But I'm not. I just enjoy the perks occasionally.'

Ellie reached over and touched his arm. 'Hun, I hate to break it to you. But you're all very rich. And that's okay, I'm honestly not judging you.'

'None of these places ever feel like home,' he confessed. 'Not like yours. There's no love or history. They're empty shells that my parents hop between like hermit crabs. I don't remember half of them, and when my parents are bored they'll just discard it and move on. This is their third house here.'

A flash of understanding crossed her face. 'Is that why you were looking for a house with a bit of history behind it?'

Alex swallowed. 'We lived in so many different places while I was growing up. I just want to feel settled for once.'

Ellie searched his eyes. 'I get it.'

Despite their obvious differences, Alex knew that she did understand. They had similar values, if not upbringings. They both cared about their families – even though they drove them mad – and they both wanted a place where they could be themselves.

He was dreading introducing Ellie to his family. It would be like introducing her to a school of sharks. To them, success was measured in awards and accolades; to be ordinary was to be less, and he couldn't stand their silent judgement.

They'd proven how shallow and uncaring they could be, choosing his lying, cheating brother instead of him. Alex clenched and unclenched his fists, trying to relieve some of the tension building up inside him.

He'd managed to lock away the bitterness and hurt until this moment. Meeting Ellie had definitely helped, but now that he was about to face them again all his old insecurities and demons came flooding to the surface.

This may be paradise, but seeing his family again would be hell.

Chapter Sixteen

Two men in crisp white shorts and matching polos pulled up in golf buggies and started piling their luggage into a little trailer attached. Well, her luggage; Alex only had one battered suitcase, while she had her giant case, her hand luggage and a bag of shopping. She'd treated herself and her family to make-up and perfume from the onboard duty free. Her stuffed plastic carrier bag looked like an afront to nature in this setting, and she shoved it deep into the belly of her straw tote.

'Want to walk to the house or take the buggy?' asked Alex, in between greeting the men.

'Oh, let's walk. I don't think I can bear sitting down a minute longer.'

'I'll give you a little tour on the way,' he said, helping her off the boat.

They strolled up the polished wooden pier and through the gardens, using a sandy path that looked like a trail of brown sugar. As they reached a fork in the path, Alex gestured to the right. 'That goes direct to the house, and this one goes everywhere else.'

They took the fork to everywhere else, and she breathed in the scent of tropical flowers and salty ocean.

She flicked Alex a playful look. 'Couldn't they have bought something a bit nicer?'

'I know what you mean. It's so small.'

'Yeah, absolutely tiny, and so… basic.' She frowned at the beautiful palm trees and gardens as if they were offensive.

Alex gave a solemn nod. 'It sure is.' Their eyes caught one another's and Alex roared with laughter, and Ellie collapsed into a fit of giggles.

'This is a nice place to hang out,' he said, pointing to a pristine beach to the side of them, the sun sparkling across the white sand. A couple of hammocks swayed in the trees, and the turquoise water gently lapped against the land. It was all so peaceful and tranquil. The gardens on this side of the island grew a little wilder. There were fruit and palm trees, with colourful birds flitting between them. A little lime-green lizard sped across their path and Ellie grinned.

Next, they passed a tennis court and the staff lodges, before heading towards the back of the house, with its kidney-shaped pool, sandstone steps and a fountain with stone dolphins leaping through the air, spurting water out of their blowholes. When they reached the house, they walked along its veranda, complete with rattan furniture and porch swings, and arrived back at the front of the house.

He opened the tall double doors and stepped aside to wave her into the marble hotel-sized lobby.

'Your parents don't lock their front door?'

'Oh, don't worry, my parents have plenty of security. You just don't see them.'

Ellie looked around and spotted a camera up in the corner of the ceiling. She gave a little wave, and then immediately felt like an idiot.

'Alex!' cried a jubilant voice from the massive, curved staircase above. Ellie gulped as Hollywood star and legend

Jessica King skipped down the stairs like a gazelle in a relaxed kaftan. She could have passed for Ellie's more glamorous – and only slightly older – sister, with nary a wrinkle or dark circle on her perfectly smooth face. In contrast to Alex's dark hair, his mum's was caramel blonde and shoulder length, and her soft blue eyes were a little lighter than her son's.

'Darling...' Jessica King cooed, reaching for Alex, and embracing him with a grasping hug, Parisian kisses and jangle of boho-chic jewellery.

'Mom, meet my girlfriend, Ellie Jones.'

'Hello, thank you for having me,' said Ellie, as if she were a schoolgirl on a playdate.

'Oh, sweetheart, aren't you just gorgeous!'

Ellie was grabbed by the shoulders and pulled forward into a warm embrace followed by another sweet bookend of Parisian air kisses.

'Don't crush her, Mom. She's been travelling for over twelve hours.'

'Oh, my darlings, you must be exhausted. Come, I'll sort out some refreshments for you. We're all in the sun room. Maggie!' A brunette in her early forties, wearing an apron and smart uniform dress, appeared from one of the doorways. 'Could we have some drinks brought to the sun room? Then a light dinner? Thank you.' She turned back to them, her colourfully embroidered kaftan swirling around her gold-sandalled feet. 'Eddie has taken your luggage to your usual room. If you two prefer, you can freshen up first before meeting everyone?'

'What would you prefer, Ellie?' asked Alex. His expression was tight and pale, and she could tell he was hoping she'd say unpack, because he kept looking towards the stairs.

She didn't want to be unkind, but she knew sometimes it was better to be quick and efficient when it came to painful situations. Delaying only built up anxiety. 'Maybe we should say a quick hello? I probably won't be able to stay awake for very long. I'm shattered.'

His shoulders slumped, but he gave her a quick nod.

'Great idea.' Jessica King – she literally couldn't think of her as anything other than the full billboard name at this moment – swept them down a corridor before Alex had a chance to respond.

They passed elegant, airy rooms until they finally reached the back of the house and the beautiful sun room, filled with lush plants, comfy seating and low, glass-topped tables. Huge bi-folding shuttered doors opened out to a gorgeous vista of the gardens. The room was a mixture of white panelling and yellow walls.

Draped on the cushions was the elegant star Ellie recognised as Savannah Lochlan. She was as luminescent and breathtaking in real life as she was in her films. Light-blonde hair fell about her narrow shoulders in choppy waves and her thighs were so slender they would most definitely not touch in those denim cut-offs she wore. She had a large, pouty mouth that dominated her face and gave her an extraordinarily beautiful smile, which dropped the second she spotted them.

Beside her sat the caramel-blond-haired version of Alex who was obviously the action-hero star Liam King. Off screen, Liam was noticeably slimmer than Alex and shorter by a couple of inches. Absently, Ellie thought he looked like the stereotypical version of Gatsby, all suave glamour and golden looks.

As Alex and Ellie entered, Liam and Savannah both sat up a little straighter. Savannah's fingers dug into the cushions, and Liam looked at her with concern deeply etched onto his handsome features.

Ellie felt as if she were intruding on a private moment by even looking at them. Alex stared at Savannah with a blank expression, giving away nothing of his emotions – she was strangely proud of him for that, but also worried at what might be lurking beneath the surface.

A rustle of a magazine drew their attention to the other side of the room.

Alex's father, Robert King, who was a silver-fox version of Alex, sat in an armchair in stylish white linen, a film magazine in his hands. No doubt checking up on what the bright young things were producing these days. He had a sprawling, muscular physique most men in their thirties would have been jealous of.

There were a few other people she didn't recognise, but she presumed they were part of the wedding party. All of them looked like they'd just stepped out of a Californian surfing commercial. Her initial thought was that they were all so slim and perfect, and, while she hated herself for doing that, comparing herself to them, some habits were hard to beat. A few sly smirks passed between Savannah's friends, and Ellie could tell they thought her pairing with Alex was odd. Which, to be fair, it was, even to Ellie.

'You have a beautiful home, Mrs…' *Don't say her full name like some weirdo.* '…Mrs King.' She felt like a dirty chimney sweep in comparison to the beautiful surroundings and people around her.

'Call me Jessica, sweetheart.'

Ellie swallowed, and turned to face the happy couple. Her nanna's drilled-in manners demanded that she be a polite guest – even though it warred against her heart to do. 'Thank you for inviting me to your wedding, Liam…

and Savannah. I know I'm a bit last-minute, so I hope I've not caused any problems for you.'

They blinked at her like baby owls, before Savannah answered cautiously, 'No... No problem at all.' Her voice was low and husky, like a New York version of an M&S advert; this wasn't just *any* sexy voice, this was an *M&S* sexy voice.

'Oh my God, I love your accent,' drawled a dark-haired woman in head-to-toe pink over in the corner. Her voice and features were very similar to Savannah's – a sister or cousin possibly? 'You sound like Dick Van Dyke!'

Well, that served her right for mentally taking the piss out of Savannah's voice. 'Err, thanks?'

'Dick Van Dyke wasn't even British,' grumbled Alex beside her, only adding to the awkwardness.

Jessica King – *Jessica*, for fuck's sake – saved the day by quickly making introductions.

'Ellie, that's Savannah's sister, Holly, she's the maid of honour. These are Savannah's other bridesmaids, Caitlyn and Keira. That's Liam's best man, Tony. And here's my husband, Robert.'

'Nice to meet you,' he said, his voice rich and warm. Hadn't he played God in his last film?

'Likewise,' replied Ellie, realising she was putting on airs and graces because she was so nervous.

'She's so polite.' Holly cackled, as if manners were a quaint tradition – she'd been the Dick Van Dyke commentator earlier.

'She's British, remember?' said Caitlyn, a redhead who looked like a bouncy cheerleader. Keira nodded as if that explained everything. She looked like a supermodel with her long, slender limbs, dark-brown glossy skin and gorgeously full features.

'Ignore these fools. You're wonderful, darling!' Jessica King declared warmly, giving her arm a quick squeeze.

The 'fools' all laughed good-naturedly and Ellie relaxed. She could handle a bit of light ribbing; she was from the East End, after all.

She glanced at Alex, who was scowling, and looped her arm through his, hoping to distract him from wanting to kill his ex and/or his brother. He glanced down at her and gave her a lopsided smile that she could have bathed in all day.

Refreshments arrived and they sat sipping Bahama Mamas, a local favourite according to Jessica King – *damn it, Jessica!* – a hearty punch of dark rum, coconut liqueur and grenadine, topped with fresh pineapple, orange and lime juice.

The conversation flowed over and around them like the breeze from the veranda, but Alex remained largely silent. His mother made up for his lack of conversation by going through the wedding plans in great detail: who was flying in and when, what still needed to be arranged for the wedding. It sounded a lot. There was an array of stylists, designers, and not one, but two wedding planners were mentioned several times. It sounded like a secret army were actually the ones beavering away in the background. Ellie felt as if she were in a bubble of luxury, so far from the comfort of the East End it may as well have been a different planet.

Several gold food carts were wheeled in, filled with an assortment of sandwiches, salads, pastries and cakes.

'Just a light meal tonight, as we've the big rehearsal dinner tomorrow,' explained Jessica, as if the idea of two big meals in as many days was unheard of – it probably was to this family.

Ellie kept her head down as she waited for everyone else to move first. Thankfully, Alex was the first to grab himself a plate.

'How about a tennis tournament tomorrow? Bride's team against groom's – although, let's split Jessica and Robert so it's fair,' chirped Holly. She began to count on her fingers. 'So that'll be Savannah, me, Keira, Caitlyn and say Jessica on team bride, and Robert, Liam, Tony, Alex and Ellie on team groom. You must play tennis, Ellie, what with Wimbledon being on your doorstep.'

Ellie swallowed her bite of smoked salmon bagel carefully, hoping she wouldn't choke. 'Well, I don't know if you'd want me to play, I—'

'Count me out,' interrupted Alex, and the group flinched from the frostbite in his tone.

'Oh, but that's such a pain!' cried Holly petulantly. 'The numbers are so nice and even. Look, even if Ellie's not very good, it doesn't matter – it's just for fun. Come on, Ellie, say you'll play!' Holly stared at Ellie bad-temperedly, as if she had single-handedly ruined her plans, even though it had been Alex who had said he didn't want to play.

She shrugged, uncertain. 'I don't mind either way.'

'Good,' said Holly. 'Now you have to play, Alex, otherwise our numbers will be out.'

Savannah rolled her eyes. 'Leave them be, Holly, they've only just arrived. And, honestly, I don't know if smashing tennis balls around only days before my wedding is a good idea.'

Holly pouted. 'Then, if anyone should sit it out, it's you and Liam.'

There was an awkward silence before Jessica brightly asked Tony about his latest project. He was a film director

– Ellie had seen some of his films, all action-packed disaster movies. Holly in particular seemed keen to know about the different parts and storyline. Ellie couldn't help but notice that no one had asked Alex once about his play.

The food, cocktails and gentle hum of conversation as the sun began to set made Ellie sleepy. The hours of travel and the jet lag were finally catching up with her, and she had to cover a yawn more than once.

Alex jumped at the chance when he saw her try to hide it for the third time. 'Ellie's exhausted. Good night.' He grabbed her arm to half-help, half-drag her out of her seat and then frog-marched them out into the corridor before Ellie had time to mutter anything more than a vague, 'Bye,' and they made their escape upstairs.

—

They entered Alex's usual room, which was more of a suite in Ellie's mind. There was a living area with a desk, chair, sofa and coffee table. Two full-length shutter windows were open and letting in the sun and cool ocean breeze, making the room pleasantly balmy. There was nothing personal in it except for Alex's laptop placed neatly on the desk… and was that her e-reader on top?

Through an archway was the bedroom, with a four-poster bed wreathed in an artfully draped mosquito net that honestly looked more like it was for style than functionality.

As if it called to her, she walked into the bedroom, while Alex downed some of the bottled water left on the coffee table. She should probably have done the same, but she was too tired, and the bed looked too inviting. The en suite beyond was all coastal elegance, with white wooden furnishings and gleaming double sinks. Her toiletries were on one side, and – presumably – Alex's on the other, as well as a glorious free-standing bath and separate shower.

She noticed that her make-up bags were set out carefully on the dressing table, and her manky old bunny-eared slippers had been placed carefully beneath her fluffy dressing gown hung on the back of the ensuite door. She opened the wardrobe and sure enough her clothes were all hung up or folded neatly on shelves, some of them looking in better condition than when she'd packed them.

'Erm… Someone unpacked our stuff… and ironed it.'

Alex kicked off his shoes and flopped on the bed. 'That sounds like Eddie. He takes his job very seriously. I think he'd be offended if we didn't let him do it.'

'Not sure how I feel about it to be honest.' She looked pointedly at the three shelves of her neatly folded underwear, her bras and swimwear hung on scented silk hangers.

Thank God it was all brand-new stuff.

'You'll get used to it.'

'Hmm.' She wasn't entirely convinced on that front. She was sure Eddie was a lovely man and all, but it was a bit weird to think of a stranger folding her knickers. There was living in luxury, and there was also something called personal boundaries.

'Your suitcase is in the top of the wardrobe. Anything you don't want him to clean, put straight in there. Otherwise, he'll be searching the room when we're out for stuff to launder.'

Yep, that was where she'd be stashing her smalls from now on. Sorry, Eddie.

She removed her earrings and, out of habit, opened the drawer on the bedside table, thinking to place them somewhere safe. Staring back at her was an extra-large pack of condoms. She picked it up dumbly and stared at Alex. Suddenly, she realised something that should have been obvious from the start; she'd been too distracted by Eddie the secret knicker elf to notice.

The bed.

The bed, with a very large, very male Alex sprawled across it. He'd taken off his glasses and left them on the bedside table. He looked like a gorgeous backpacking model with his floppy black hair, rumpled shorts and t-shirt that had risen just enough to show his tanned, strong stomach. Her mouth became dry as she stood and stared at him.

Aqua eyes the same colour as the ocean outside their window opened and stared back at her, as if he'd sensed a shift in the pleasant atmosphere – a tropical storm building despite this clear and beautiful day.

'Do we have Eddie to thank for these too?' She shook the box.

Alex's eyes widened and his face flushed. 'Yeah, he always puts them there... That's weird, right?'

'Totally.' She tossed them back in the drawer. 'But I guess it's nice he cares. Better safe than sorry... Not that we need them, of course.'

He raised himself up onto his elbows, looking more adorable and hotter than ever – if that were possible – his biceps flexing as he adjusted his position. A slow mortification dawned across his face. 'Of course! I'll sleep on the sofa. I just lay here out of habit.'

'No!' Wow, did she have to sound so desperate? 'I mean... We don't want Eddie to know the truth, do we? He might tell your family. And this bed is huge. I don't mind sharing if you don't.' Unsure of what else to say without sounding as if she were begging him to stay, she grabbed her pjs and stumbled into the bathroom to get ready for the night.

She was so tired, she rushed through a quick five-minute shower, removed her make-up, brushed her hair and teeth, and then put on her pjs. A shorts and t-shirt set that had a print of tropical fruit doing the tango across her breasts – she was beginning to regret her stupid sense of humour. She was also beginning to have doubts about how relaxing this holiday would be.

Well, too late now.

When she came back in, Alex was still lying on top of the bed, fully dressed and pensive, brooding like Heathcliff, despite the glorious pink and lavender sunset framed in the window. At the sound of the door opening, his gaze shifted over to her, and he smiled.

That small gesture was breathtaking, mainly because she realised that in some small way she'd made him feel better. She hurried over to the bed, quickly slipped beneath the crisp sheets, then turned towards him, a good arm's length between them. 'See, it's huge. No different to the flight really, just no partition.'

Except, of course, it definitely was different.

Chapter Seventeen

Every nerve in Alex's body was aware of Ellie lying next to him, in a cute and revealing pyjama set.

Man, he was an idiot sometimes. So much for respecting her boundaries – the first thing he'd done was jump straight in her bed. In his defence, he'd got so used to her company that it was beginning to feel like they were dating for real. They'd slept next to each other on the plane, followed by hours chatting happily together, and it wasn't just the journey here. Recently, they'd got into the habit of calling or texting each other daily.

The only thing they hadn't done since the awards ceremony was kiss. He'd almost broken their Disney rule that night. How on earth was he going to make their relationship look real in front of his family, while also not breaking Ellie's boundaries?

That kiss had ruined him. The way she'd melted in his arms and opened up for him with careless abandon, proving without a shadow of doubt that their attraction was mutual. The realisation was both devastating and euphoric. Ellie wanted him, possibly not emotionally, but physically she couldn't deny it, and he longed to break their stupid rules – but he couldn't. He wouldn't.

'I'm sorry, that punch cocktail has wiped me out,' she said through a yawn. 'Wow, these sheets are heavenly. Eddie did well!'

He couldn't help but laugh, relieved to be distracted from his spiralling by her delight at the simplest things.

Maybe he should appreciate his life and privileges a little more. The fact that he could come to places like this, and had a butler who unpacked and folded his underwear... She must think him a pampered idiot. He'd never thought it strange until she'd pointed it out.

'Are you okay after seeing them?' Ellie's gentle voice cut through his distracted thoughts, and it took him a second to realise what she meant.

He fiddled with his glasses, pushing them higher on his nose. 'It wasn't so bad, I guess – I'm glad it's done.'

She turned on her side to face him and he did the same, as if they were teenagers at a sleepover. 'That's why I suggested doing it straight away – like with injections, sometimes it's best to do it quickly. No time to overthink.'

He nodded. They were only inches away from one another, and the intimacy of their position was not lost on him. She was so cute, he wanted to wrap his arms around her and hold her tight. Take comfort in her presence.

If he was being honest with himself, he wanted to do more than hug her. Even after travelling for hours, he couldn't get enough of her. He could have lain on the couch or gone for a walk, given her some privacy, but instead he'd refused to part from her for even a moment.

Why could he never keep his distance? He was like a moth to a flame, hypnotised by her even when she looked tired and jet-lagged. She stifled a yawn, and he could tell it wouldn't be long before she was fast asleep.

'You're right, and I thought it would be a lot worse. I mean, Holly's as annoying as ever, but don't let her get to you.' He was relieved when Ellie gave an unbothered shrug. He'd been worried that Holly's nasty teasing had hurt her.

'What about Liam and Savannah?'

He took a deep breath. Strangely, with Ellie by his side he'd not minded the confrontation as much as he'd thought. 'Seeing them together doesn't hurt like it used to. I mean, I didn't punch him again – so that's an improvement.'

Ellie winced. 'I can't imagine you punching anyone.'

'I'm not proud of it. I let my anger get the better of me.' His stomach rolled just remembering the way his fist had crunched into Liam's jaw. 'Tonight when I saw them, I was still angry and bitter, but the initial heartache and pain? That's no longer there.'

'That's good, right?' A small wrinkle appeared between her brows and he longed to kiss it smooth.

'Today was the first time I've seen them since New York. They ambushed me in my apartment. Sat me down and explained that the rumours in the tabloids, for once, were true. They were sorry. Their on-screen love affair had developed into something real.' The betrayal had been a white-hot poker straight through his heart. 'Savannah got upset and Liam told her to leave. That's when he asked me if I wanted to hit him – as if that would make everything right between us. But I did hit him. Hard.'

Ellie's hand reached out to rub his shoulder, fingers pressing into muscle he hadn't noticed growing tight.

That day had been the first and only time he'd punched someone, and it had hurt like hell, both physically and emotionally. Because seeing his brother's split lip and feeling the ache of his knuckles hadn't helped. Nothing would ever make things right between them. His brother had lied to him, and broken the one thing he'd thought he could always rely on: his family.

'I told Liam I never wanted to see him again. My family have always had one rule. To put the family first. Above jobs, money, friends, girlfriends… Liam broke that rule, and I stupidly thought my parents would take my side. But they wanted me to forgive Liam and move on, and now they think I should pretend I'm delighted my brother is marrying my ex. I'm beginning to realise that, when they said family should come first, they only meant their golden boy Liam.' Rolling onto his back, he stared up at the ceiling. 'Maybe they're right. Maybe I am overreacting, and I should let go of all this anger and bitterness. After all, it's making me unhappy. I just don't know how.'

Ellie raised herself onto her elbow. 'Just because they want you to move on doesn't mean you can or should. You need time.'

'But I want to. I don't want to feel this way any more, every time I look at them…' His words died. He was unsure of how to voice his anger, jealousy and bitterness — and it wasn't all directed at Liam and Savannah either. Seeing his parents today had also been difficult. He couldn't understand why they never supported him, never took his side in anything.

Ellie's face was filled with sympathetic understanding. 'They broke your trust, and I know exactly how that feels. I faced something similar once, and I found it— No, I *still* find it difficult to talk about.' She couldn't meet his eyes. 'I should have told you about it sooner. But honestly, I'm still ashamed, even though I know now it wasn't my fault.'

He shifted a little, so that he could catch her eye. She looked so vulnerable. As if she were afraid he wouldn't be able to handle her secret. 'Go on.'

She blew out a breath. 'I haven't had many serious relationships, except one. David. I met him at the gym – that's relevant, by the way. He was a proper gym rat, obsessed with body-building and his image. *That* should have been the first red flag. Anyway, we got talking one night – I was there late because of my shifts, and he said he preferred the quieter times. We exchanged numbers, texted every day and started dating pretty quickly. David was pretty intense, but incredibly romantic – he told me he loved me within a couple of weeks. Honestly, I was flattered by all his attention and fell for him quickly. I was stupidly desperate to fall in love and start my happily-ever-after. I was an idiot.'

'Why? You sound brave!' Alex had always been cautious and slow to trust in relationships. But he'd still ended up hurt, hadn't he?

'I ignored all of my doubts – all the red flags. The fact that he didn't want me to meet his family and friends, or talk to me in the gym during the day. I gave excuses to Hannah every time she pointed out how weird his behaviour was, that he was busy with work or wanted to concentrate on his training.'

Ellie laughed, and the sound was so bitter that Alex's hands twitched with the urge to gather her close.

'Turns out,' she continued, 'he had a fiancée. She came storming into the gym when she found our texts. She was the complete physical opposite of me and I think David cheating on her with someone who looked like me—'

'There is nothing wrong with you,' snapped Alex, his rage threatening to boil over.

'Well, rightly or wrongly, seeing me humiliated her. She didn't take it very well. Started screaming at me and chasing me around the gym. David had to drag her out eventually, all while trying to explain that I didn't mean anything to him. All of his friends were laughing and filming the whole thing. They couldn't believe he was a secret chubby-chaser.'

Alex's stomach flipped at the casual way she'd said such a cruel and derogatory phrase. But he'd worked long enough in Hollywood to understand about unrealistic beauty standards and the horrors they inflicted on people.

'I think I went viral on TikTok for a couple of weeks. Thankfully you couldn't see my face too clearly, and the video was mocking David more than me—'

'Fucking assholes,' Alex growled.

Ellie took a deep breath. 'Anyway, that was over a year ago, and I'm only just getting over it. So, don't be tough on yourself, it's still early. Give yourself time.'

Alex knew he was opening himself up for another brutal rejection, but he couldn't allow Ellie not to know the truth. 'You're gorgeous, Ellie. Anyone who can't see that must be blind.'

She reached out and placed her hand over his heart. The touch was affectionate, but also subtly reminding him of their invisible boundary. He could understand why. Their relationship wasn't real, and she'd been hurt once before by a liar – he knew how brutal that could be. 'Thank you. But I'm not stupid, I know I don't fit the ideal body type. That's why people think they can say abusive shit and get away with it. I'm not under any illusions with you, so don't worry.'

'I think you are beautiful and incredibly sexy,' he said, unable to let her think otherwise. 'You didn't think I'd choose just anyone to be my fake girlfriend, did you?'

Her chocolate eyes widened, and she was too sweet, too delicious for him to resist. He sat up and twisted his body over hers until she flopped onto her back with surprise. Leaning forward, desperate for her to see the truth in his feelings for her, he pressed his mouth firmly against hers, and she softened beneath him.

Boundaries, he reminded himself harshly and raised his head. 'I want you to know that, even if our relationship isn't real, my attraction to you is, and I don't give a fuck about beauty standards, I know what I like, and it's you.'

Shock, confusion and arousal filled her face as she stared up at him.

He brushed aside some of her hair, allowing himself to feel the silky softness between his fingers. 'Go to sleep, you'll need your rest to face Holly's tournament tomorrow.'

She closed her eyes, her full black lashes fanning across her olive cheeks. She'd once told him that her family was a melting pot of different cultures, just like the East End. English, Welsh, Spanish, Polish and Greek were all part of her tapestry of heritage. So many countries, in fact, that she didn't know them all. *That's London for you*, she'd told him cheerfully. Everything about her was uniquely wonderful.

Alex got up from the bed, but didn't move to the bathroom immediately, instead allowing himself the indulgence of admiring her now that her eyes were closed. She was beautiful and warm, and the kindest woman he'd ever met. Even exhausted, she'd been attentive and gracious with his family, including Savannah's overbearing younger sister Holly, who he suspected wanted to build a film career to rival her sister's and wasn't afraid to walk over people in the process.

He needed to keep an eye on Holly's nasty teasing, and make sure she didn't bully Ellie. He went into the lounge area of their suite and noticed that they'd already drunk a lot of the bottled water. Ellie would probably be thirsty when she woke up after all those punch cocktails, so he decided to go and replenish their supplies.

Downstairs was quiet, and he presumed everyone had decided to spend the rest of the evening in their own suites. He grabbed a large bottle of mineral water from the kitchen, and was about to head upstairs when he noticed the veranda doors were still open in the sun room.

He'd always liked sitting out on the veranda in the evening, so he went outside to the swing and, after placing the water on a nearby table, checked his phone.

There were hundreds of alerts about his relationship with Ellie. Most were positive, some were a little strange, and a few were downright cruel – the sort of horrible bullshit Ellie had described earlier when she'd told him about David. Criticism over her curves and suggestions that Alex was some kind of pervert for finding a woman with a shapely figure attractive, or, worse, that he was encouraging her into an unhealthy lifestyle.

Alex immediately dismissed it as the usual Hollywood nonsense. Growing up, he'd regularly seen the scrutiny and pressure his mother had faced about her appearance. Too fat, too thin, too old… the criticism never ended. He also knew that Ellie's health and attitude towards food and exercise was far better than his mother's; she'd been hospitalised several times for anaemia and had developed osteoporosis due to her poor diet. Ironic, that thinness was always deemed healthier when a lot of the actresses he knew barely had enough body fat to function normally.

One particularly odd article stood out.

ALEX KING PUTS HIS TOXIC PAST BEHIND HIM AND FINDS NEW LOVE

He frowned as he scrolled through the article. Still spouting the same old lies – Alex as controlling towards Savannah but, having realised the errors of his ways, now dating with a more relaxed and open mind. Dating an ordinary, plus-size woman was apparently proof that he'd changed.

What the hell was that supposed to mean? That he'd only dated a woman like Ellie to improve his reputation? He flinched, because there was some truth to it; he was dating Ellie to make himself look better – but he'd picked her because he liked and trusted her.

No, more than that. The truth was he found Ellie very attractive, had done from the first moment he'd set eyes on her. If anything, Savannah had never been his type – they'd just fallen into a relationship with one another.

Why had they even started dating in the first place? Hadn't Richie organised their first date – something to do with promoting their latest films?

A shadow moved across the swing and instinctively Alex swiped away the articles before looking up at the person who'd come outside. Liam stood beside him with two crystal tumblers in his hands.

'Do you still struggle to wind down after a flight?' he asked, sitting down beside Alex on the swing and offering him one of the glasses of Scotch.

Alex grunted in acknowledgement, unsure why his brother would approach him like this. 'Just long haul.' He took the offered glass and swirled the liquor around. Smooth and smoky, it would have been the perfect drink to help him wind down – if his pain in the ass brother hadn't been the one to ruin it by joining him.

'Ellie seems lovely.'

Did he want to get punched again? 'She is, so don't get any ideas.'

Liam's lips thinned, and he took a sip before answering. 'I just meant that she suits you.'

Alex couldn't argue with that; he'd been thinking the same not long ago. But he'd be damned if he'd ever admit his brother was right. 'Well, leave her alone. Don't let Holly drag her into anything she doesn't want to do.'

'Savannah will have a word with Holly.'

Alex scoffed and took a large sip of the Scotch. 'Cus that's worked so well in the past, right?' Holly had never paid any attention to Savannah's advice in the past. She thought she knew better than her older sister in every way.

Liam didn't reply.

'Why did you even want me here?' Alex asked tiredly, removing his glasses and pinching the top of his nose, fighting the sudden exhaustion that threatened to overwhelm him.

Liam's face became pained. 'You're my brother... It wouldn't have felt right without you.'

Alex turned away, his jaw aching with tension. He didn't bother to hide the brittle anger in his voice. 'I'm only here because Mom insisted.'

Why was he the one that always had to make amends and do the right thing, while Liam got to do whatever he wanted, no matter who got hurt along the way.

'I messed things up between us, didn't I?'

Alex put his glasses back on and scrutinised his brother's face – how could he ever trust a word he said? His cheekbones were more prominent than normal, and there were dark lines under his eyes, or was that just the moonlight playing tricks on him? His brother always looked so confident, so calm, but tonight he seemed nervous.

'Yeah, you did.' Why should he pretend like all was well between them? He'd done nothing wrong, and he'd still come to this dumb wedding of theirs. What more did they want?

They both stared straight ahead into the darkness as the cicadas hummed loudly in the tropical night.

'I'm sorry.'

Alex glared at him. 'Why couldn't you just wait? Let her break up with me first. Just a couple of months – that's all it would have taken. Why go behind my back? Why lie?'

Liam took a deep breath. 'I couldn't think clearly... I kept telling myself it was already over between the two of you. And it was, wasn't it? You hadn't even spoken to each other in weeks.'

Alex shook his head in disbelief. 'You think that makes it all right? I *trusted* you. You're my brother, the one person who should have had my back. You think I care about losing Savannah? I don't. I care that I lost the one person I believed in and looked up to. You made me look like a fool in front of the entire world, and you're still doing it now with this wedding. But I guess, as always with this family, you were too self-centred to give a shit about anyone but yourself!'

'I'm sorry,' Liam said quietly, unable to give any more excuses.

Alex took a sip and let the heat burn down his throat, a comforting pain that always reminded him of when he was younger and he and Liam used to steal sips from their dad's liquor cabinet. One time, he'd drunk too much and been as sick as dog. Liam had told their mom he'd swallowed too much seawater while swimming. Alex didn't drink alcohol again for years after that, and Liam had never revealed his secret.

There'd been a time when nothing could have come between them. When Liam had been the only one in his family to have his back.

'I'll get over it, eventually,' he said, and for once he actually believed it, although he didn't want to let Liam off the hook just yet. The asshole needed to feel guilty for a few more days at least. He deserved it. 'Just don't expect me to be cheering you down the fucking aisle.'

He knocked back the rest of his Scotch, put the glass on the table with a thud and picked up the bottle of mineral water before leaving.

To his surprise his dad stood in the doorway, a sad and disappointed look on his face. 'Son—'

'Save it, Dad.' Alex waved the bottle of water at him dismissively as he walked past. 'Ellie needs this water, and I'm not up for a heart-to-heart right now. Besides, we all know whose side you're on, anyway.'

His dad's expression turned into a scowl. 'There's no sides—'

Alex laughed bitterly, throwing back his last words casually, his arms spread wide. 'Oh, come on! We all know Liam can do no wrong in this family and that he always comes first in the pecking order. Look, I'm playing ball, just be grateful I'm here. God forbid the perfect Kings look bad to the rest of the world.'

His dad frowned but couldn't argue with him. When Liam's first feature film was filmed in Brazil, the entire family had moved there to support him through it, because Liam had always struggled with anxiety. But when Alex had got accepted into Juilliard, they'd clapped him on the back and sent him on his way, letting him move to New York alone while they focused their energy on Liam's latest project in LA. It was one of the many times his parents had subtly chosen Liam over him.

Before, he'd always considered it a petty jealousy he needed to control, but now he wondered if his feelings had been justified.

When had they ever put him first?

Alex's shoulders were a little looser as he climbed the stairs. His words probably wouldn't make any difference. His dad was probably commiserating with Liam even now, but it felt good to get some of it off his chest.

Back at his rooms, he placed the bottle of water and a clean glass by Ellie's side of the bed. She'd left the bedside light on for him, and his heart ached with longing when she gave a happy sigh of contentment in her sleep.

He quietly opened the bedside table's drawer and took out one of the supplies Eddie had left for them, then popped it into his wallet for safe keeping before gently closing the drawer.

Not that he'd ever get to use it – he should be so lucky. But the possibility that he might gave him hope that he might be able to move on after all.

Chapter Eighteen

Ellie woke up refreshed after her extra-long sleep. Who knew that travelling could wipe you out so much? Or perhaps it was the constant shift work and overtime catching up with her?

Either way, she woke up in the most comfortable bed she'd ever slept in, with tropical sunlight streaming in through chalk-white shutters. When she turned, Alex was sleeping peacefully beside her.

Was she in heaven?

But then she realised her mouth was drier than the Sahara. Thankfully, there was a bottle of water on the table beside her. She couldn't remember seeing that last night, she'd been so dead on her feet. She cracked open the bottle and poured herself a large glass, being careful not to make too much noise and wake Alex.

Alex had kissed her last night. Not because they were in public or putting a show on in front of his family, but because he'd wanted to... Had apparently *always* wanted to.

She gulped back the water and then crept from the bed. Not only did she need the loo, she also needed to put some distance between herself and the man beside her. She grabbed some clothes from the wardrobe and hurried to the bathroom, locking the door firmly behind her.

Yesterday had been a revelation in so many ways, from Alex's luxurious lifestyle to his family and the obvious fractures within it. His poor mum was battling to patch up and gloss over the cracks, everyone else pretending like nothing had happened, while Alex's bitterness and anger radiated through every interaction he'd had with his brother.

There was a lot going on and she wasn't even sure how she could help. Then, after confessing the worst time in her own life, Alex had kissed her. *Alex King*, star of film and theatre, fancied her.

Surely he was just being kind? After listening to her horrendous confession about David, he was probably trying to boost her confidence, make her feel better about that humiliating disaster.

But that kiss… Still completely PG – but also more. As if he were asking her a question, but she was too dumb to know the answer. Did he want more from their relationship? Could she give more? Her attraction to Alex was unquestionable, but she'd locked it away in a box marked *SECRET! Open at your own peril.*

She stared in the bathroom mirror at the fruit dancing on her pyjama top, and decided that Alex couldn't have been serious.

Pretend like it never happened. There was no point in embarrassing herself over a silly compliment. They'd sworn to stay friends for a reason. No hurt feelings – most importantly, *her* hurt feelings.

After getting ready she left the bathroom, to find Alex awake. He was sat up in bed frowning at his phone, but quickly put it aside with a thump when she walked in. He'd slept in just his boxers, or at least she hoped he was wearing boxers beneath the covers. The bare chest on display was enough to short-circuit her brain for several seconds.

'Hey,' he said brightly, almost guiltily.

'Everything okay?'

He glanced back at his phone on the bedside table, and groaned. 'I'm falling into the alert trap.'

'Eh?'

'I get alerts sent to my email whenever my name is used online. You know, gossip columns, tabloids, that sort of thing. I usually put them in a separate folder and forget about them. But now I've read a few, I can't stop.'

Ellie nodded understandingly. 'How about we leave your phone here for the day? Go cold turkey.'

'Good idea.' He pulled back the covers and she was only a little relieved to see he was indeed wearing boxers. Averting her gaze, she hurried into the lounge of their suite, feeling a lot like a Victorian Miss who'd just been scandalised. 'I'll just be waiting in here for you!' she squeaked.

—

Breakfast was a delicious buffet served in the 'casual' dining room, which looked a hell of a lot like a formal dining room in Ellie's humble opinion. Everyone was already eating when they arrived, which was surprising as it was so early, and the room was buzzing with excitement for the rehearsal dinner that evening.

'I thought you had the rehearsal dinner the night before the wedding?' Ellie whispered to Alex, wondering if she'd misunderstood.

'Not always. Besides, this is more of a welcome barbecue.'

Ellie relaxed. Alex had said the island they were staying on didn't have any fancy restaurants, and she'd presumed that meant no fancy clothes, so she'd only brought one formal outfit for the wedding. Now she was here, surrounded by luxury on a private island, she was beginning to think she might have made a mistake with her packing. Today she'd put on a pair of long linen cream shorts and a khaki vest, with a shirt, also in cream linen, open over the top. She didn't want her shoulders to burn and was conscious that Holly had threatened a tennis tournament, and this was the sportiest outfit she'd packed.

Holly was literally dressed for Wimbledon, in one of those tennis dresses she'd seen famous players wear, a little visor cap on her head with her ponytail sticking out of the back. The rest of the group seemed far more casual, and Alex's mum was wearing another spectacularly bright and stylish kaftan.

'Ready for tennis?' asked Holly expectantly as people began to push aside their plates or prepared to leave the table.

Savannah leaned towards her sister. 'Perhaps not everyone—'

'Oh, come on. It's going to be so boring if we don't do anything to break up the day. Just a few quick games and then we can start getting ready for later.'

Savannah looked helplessly at Liam, who opened his mouth to speak, but Ellie interrupted him. She had a feeling they were conscious of what Alex had said last night. 'I'll play. But not too many games – the hammock on the beach is calling me!'

Holly smirked like the cat that had got the cream. 'Still don't want to play, Alex? Your *girlfriend* apparently does.' Why did she say the word girlfriend like an insult?

Alex shrugged and grumbled. 'Fine.'

—

A short time later they were gathered at the tennis court, preparing for the tournament. Savannah and Liam had also decided to join, despite Savannah's fear of flying balls, and Ellie suspected it was to try to keep Holly in check.

Caitlyn frowned as they all lined up. 'It's not very fair, there's all men on team groom, except for Ellie.'

Holly shrugged. 'Not everyone will be good at tennis. It's a skills game really, so I'm sure it'll even out.'

Ellie let the comment wash over her. She could tell Holly had been thinking of her as the weakest link in team groom.

Alex was the first to pick up a racket. 'So, who am I up against? You, Holly?' he asked with a lift of his brow.

'Keen to go against me, Alex?' She giggled, and then shook her head. 'Age before beauty. Robert and Jessica first.'

Alex's parents dutifully did as they were told. Jessica didn't know how to serve, so by default Robert had to. The match was quick, with a lot of good-natured ribbing and laughing at the expense of their parents' equally bad skills.

'My parents only built the tennis court for their friends and us. They're useless,' explained Alex, but Ellie was pleased to see that he was enjoying the tournament despite his earlier reservations.

Robert was declared the winner, and Jessica gratefully bowed out of the tournament. Tony and Caitlyn played next – Caitlyn was delighted when she won. Tony was apparently more of a running man, the type to enjoy silence and solitude rather than team sports.

Liam played against Savannah and won – a light-hearted and easy-going game, as it was clear neither wanted to incur an injury before their big day. Holly then declared that she would play against Ellie next. They tossed a coin to see who would serve, and Ellie was secretly pleased when she won the toss.

Holly looked incredibly smug as she took a position near the middle of the court. She began to slide her hips from side to side like a pro.

Ellie took a deep breath, tossed the ball in the air and smashed it as hard as she could. Caitlyn had to leap out of the way as it smacked into the fence on the other side of the court, having bounced just once within the lines. Holly, on the other hand, was still clutching her racket and clearly wondering what the hell had happened. Alex cheered.

'Wow,' shouted Keira, 'that's one hell of a serve!'

Ellie shrugged lightly at the scowl on Holly's face. 'I did warn you that you might not want me to play.'

The rest of the match followed a similar pattern, with Ellie hitting the ball so hard and fast that Holly could never react quickly enough. She only managed to return the ball once, and Ellie took great pleasure in tapping it over the net lightly before Holly could sprint back for it.

'Team groom wins again!' Liam said, calling an end to the match.

Alex roared with approval and ran on to the court to lift her in a bear hug as if she were a champion player, and she dropped her racket in shock. Ellie gulped with fear as he swung her in a circle before setting her down. At least he'd managed it without any grunting or straining, which was delightful in itself.

'Serves her right.' He snorted as Holly stomped away with a furious scowl on her face. 'You were fantastic.'

Ellie fought to get her breathing back under control, though she wasn't sure if her elevated heart rate was due to running around on the court or being wrapped in Alex's embrace. 'Mark played for the school. We used to practise at a court in Hackney. I'm actually not that good, but Mark liked me to serve to him so he could practise his volleys.'

'I thought you didn't want to play. You should have said you were the third Williams sister.'

She blushed and swatted his arm lightly, but he refused to let go of her. The silliness of the moment evaporated. Everything fell away but the summery breeze and his ocean eyes. His head was turned away from his family, so they couldn't see him when he said quietly, 'Now feels like a perfect time to kiss you.'

Excitement raced through her veins and she nodded. 'It is.'

His head bent and his mouth pressed against hers in their practised Disney kiss. Her heart leapt in her chest, and courage and need rushed through her in equal measure, buoyed by Alex's confession last night.

The last two days had changed something between them. The chemistry that had always been fizzing between them seemed to have reached a tipping point. They were simply dancing along the edge of the precipice, afraid to leap, and yet too far gone to step back.

Wickedly, she pressed closer, her fingers daring to snake to his hips and ever so slightly pull him closer. He tensed, and she was afraid she'd pushed him too far, but then a low moan rumbled in his chest and his mouth opened and his tongue slowly stroked hers, causing a moan of her own to escape.

It was the best kiss she'd ever had. Fantasy and anticipation melting into perfect harmony. She was lost in his arms, and happy to stay that way for as long as he kissed her back.

But reality intervened and he pulled away. 'My parents are watching,' he said, chuckling, but looking as shaken as she felt.

Oh God! What was she thinking? She glanced over to his family and saw the surprise on all of their faces, as well as the absolute disgust on Holly's. The hatred in her eyes burned through Ellie, and a hot wave of shame flooded her cheeks. She'd seen that look before, on David's fiancée's face.

'Sorry,' she mumbled, shuffling awkwardly out of his hug. But Alex didn't fully let her go, just moved one arm to drape across her shoulders as they walked back to team bride and groom.

She lowered her head, feeling guilty, and mumbled, 'Sorry, I got carried away... Let's remember our boundaries in future, yeah?'

Alex's arm dropped from her shoulder. 'Sure, if that's what you want?'

She smiled, even though it hurt to do so. 'Might be for the best. Don't you think?'

Alex had to play against Keira next, and he won. Holly's persistent thunderous face brought down everyone's mood and, in the end, everyone was grateful to part ways and enjoy the rest of their day alone before the rehearsal barbecue.

Ellie and Alex did the same, Ellie muttering about wanting to read through the career information she'd printed out and brought with her. Alex nodded, an unspoken agreement that they would take some time apart.

Chapter Nineteen

'Could this get any more awkward?' whispered Ellie. She was staring at the giant seating plan placed on an ornate gold stand in front of them.

Honestly, Alex had been worried sick about overstepping the mark with her at the tennis match. But seeing her cracking jokes again eased some of his worries.

Some, at least; he couldn't shake the feeling he'd messed up somehow, and, to make matters worse, the rehearsal dinner had arrived with terrifying speed. He'd dreaded it almost as much as the wedding itself.

He glanced at the plan over her shoulder. 'What's wrong?' he asked, although he could already guess the answer.

She stabbed at their names with a scarlet fingernail. 'For a start, there's a top table, and we're on it.'

Her eyes darted around the guests milling about in the sun room and drinking champagne. The doors had been folded back to create a smooth transition between the sun room and the garden, but most people were outside. Over two hundred guests were invited to the rehearsal dinner and wedding, so by the current number there were still more to arrive. Alex shook his head, in awe at the speed with which the staff had turned their island home into a glamorous event space, with tropical flower arrangements placed on every cloth-draped table and barbecue stations manned by chefs in tall white hats, ready to go.

'This is super formal. I mean, I knew Americans have rehearsal dinners and we don't in the UK, but...' Ellie nervously adjusted the strap on her halter-neck dress. The colourful fabric pressed her breasts together in an enticing way and he found himself in a constant battle to keep his eyes above her neckline. 'Are you sure I look all right? I thought this was just a relaxed barbecue-thingy?'

'It is.'

Ellie flapped her hand aggressively at the garden. 'There are three chef stations, and is that a whole pig roasting on a spit? I thought the American rehearsal dinner was for close friends and family only? Seriously, what happened to just having a curry the night before? Why do you always have to be so *extra*!' Her voice was getting higher-pitched with every word, and he was worried that she might pass out. He probably should have warned her about this. But the truth was, he'd been afraid she'd say no.

He took hold of her arms and turned her to face him. 'Look at me.' Brown eyes full of worry and doubt stared back. 'It's going to be fine.'

She did a strange half-snort half-cry and he gave her a brilliant smile, hoping to calm her nerves. Begrudgingly, she took a few deep breaths. 'I'm sorry. I'm meant to be supporting you tonight. It's just far more glamorous than I thought it would be. There are *actual* Hollywood stars here... I mean, as well as you and your family. It's all so much.'

She gestured around at the garden. There were about fifteen large tables dotted around the manicured lawn, lit with flaming torches, and formally attired waiting staff flowed between groups with silver trays of champagne flutes and canapés. The indigo sky sparkled with stars, while the ocean waves crashed softly in the background.

It was beautifully and thoughtfully designed, as all of his mother's parties were. Nothing unusual to his mind, but then again Ellie wasn't used to this.

She bit her bottom lip and looked down at herself. 'I'm just worried I look out of place.'

'Not at all. Firstly, you look gorgeous.' He didn't need to fudge any truths there, at least. Her bright yellow-and-orange African-print maxi-dress set off her hair and skin beautifully. He had to keep forcing his eyes not to linger too long on her impressive cleavage, because he was definitely getting a more than friendly reaction to her luscious body, and she'd already reminded him about their boundaries more than once.

'Secondly—' He blinked, pushing up his glasses while he tried to remember the point he was trying to make. 'Secondly, it's a small wedding, so most of the people arriving today will be at the wedding too. My mom loves a party.'

Ellie gave him a shaky smile, but her spine straightened and she was looking more like her usual confident self by the second. 'This isn't what I'd call small... Are they all staying here?'

'Only Richie, the bridesmaids and the best man, who you met earlier. The rest have their own holiday home nearby or have rented a place at one of the resorts. Those without transport are being ferried back and forth by the staff.' He pointed towards the marina, where a yacht and some speedboats were anchored. Ellie swallowed deeply at the sight of them.

'I wish you'd told me it was going to be this swanky. I only brought one formal dress and that's for the wedding.' She huffed, and he realised it was the first time she'd ever been truly annoyed at him, and he knew that he shouldn't find it so adorable, but he did.

'There's no actual dress code. Some people just decided to dress up.' A group of his parents' friends sailed past in tuxedos and silk evening gowns.

Ellie turned and glared at him pointedly.

'Look, I haven't dressed up either!' He gestured at his pale linen shirt and trousers, even lifted a trouser leg to show off his leather sandals.

Unconvinced, she snapped, 'Men get away with it. Women don't.'

'I promise,' he attempted to placate her, 'this is the only big event before the wedding. The next five days will be sun, sea and sand. Now, regarding your last worry. The seating plan.' He leaned forward and made a big gesture of squinting at it. 'Yep. Next to my parents. How else did you think it was going to be?'

She looked like she was going to slug him and he couldn't help but chuckle.

'I *thought*,' she hissed through gritted teeth, 'that the *bride* would have some common *sense* and put us on a separate table. Like, the kids' table probably. I would have preferred that.'

He shook his head, took her arm and led them through the sun room towards the garden party, collecting a flute of champagne for each of them on the way. 'No way. My mom cares only about appearances. Proving the Kings are still a united family will be her number one goal.'

'But your mum's lovely,' Ellie said, with a pained expression. 'Surely she must realise how horrible this is for you.'

He knocked back a deep gulp of the champagne. 'She does. But she wants everyone to be happy too, and in her mind, that means I have to suck it up.'

She stopped walking and stroked his arm. 'I'm sorry.'

He couldn't resist. Bending down, he gave her lips a chaste kiss. They were warm and velvety soft, and left him with the faint taste of her strawberry lip balm. When he raised his head, her face was flushed and her eyes were wide with shock. They'd not spoken about the last couple of kisses – especially the one that had almost floored him on the tennis court.

He murmured softly, 'For our audience.' But his parents' arrival in the garden had only been an excuse. He wanted to kiss her, well and often.

The only problem was she didn't feel the same, because she stiffened. 'Of course, I wondered what you were doing for a second.' The smile didn't quite meet her eyes, and it wasn't the bright sunshine that he'd become accustomed to over the last few weeks. Immediately he regretted kissing her; the last thing he wanted to do was make her uncomfortable.

'The final boat has arrived!' called his mother, gesturing for them to take their seats at the top table.

Holly sauntered past them in a full-length gold sequinned dress and sky-high heels. 'Cute dress,' she said, but her tone was snide. 'Did you make it yourself? I hear you like dressmaking. I've never been good at arts and crafts. I prefer to leave it to the professionals – Versace never lets me down.' She smoothed a hand down her body for emphasis. 'But then again, designer clothes aren't an option for every*body*, are they?'

Alex couldn't stand her sneering. 'No, and if it wasn't for your sister, I doubt they would have been an option for you either!'

Holly glared at him and strutted away with a toss of her hair to join his mother at the top table.

'Ignore her. She's been sponging off her sister's fame and wealth for years – she's got no reason to be so proud.' But to his horror, Ellie's eyes were shining with unshed tears and she quickly ducked behind the seating plan. He quickly turned to shield her as much as possible. 'Are you okay?'

Ellie nodded, blinking rapidly with an awkward laugh. 'Sorry, I know I shouldn't let people like her get to me. She just touched a nerve is all.'

'Damn, it's all my fault. I should have been clearer about tonight.' He felt like his heart was breaking, seeing strong, confident Ellie brought to tears, and he wasn't sure how to fix it. 'I'm so sorry. If you want to change into your other dress, you can, I'll make them delay. And I can take you to the mainland and buy you another for the wedding. There's a few designer boutiques there – my treat!'

Ellie stopped him with a hand to his chest and a shake of her head. 'I don't think you realise what she meant by "an option" – she wasn't talking about wealth. She means skinny privilege, that's why she emphasised the *body*.'

'Oh…' What a jerk, he'd not noticed until Ellie had pointed it out.

'I'm just a little overwhelmed and I let her get the better of me. The fashion industry is designed for people like her and she knows it.' She looked embarrassed and leaned closer to him to explain. 'My nanna taught me how to make clothes – because she was sick of me crying in dressing rooms whenever we went shopping. Plus-size fashion is a bit better now, but when I was younger nothing fitted properly, or it just looked plain ridiculous on a tall and curvier girl. A sixteen-year-old with E-cups does not need to wear a t-shirt that says *Babe* in silver sequins.' She rolled her eyes at her own joke, but he could tell the memories were still painful. 'Nanna made a point of telling me that it was the clothes that were the problem and not my body. I'll always love her for doing that. She took something that hurt me and turned it into a hobby I love. Honestly, I don't know what's wrong with me. A bitchy comment like that normally wouldn't have bothered me.'

'I'm so sorry... for what she said and for the shitty world we live in, and for not understanding sooner.'

Her eyes warmed. 'You don't have to understand. You've been kind and that's enough.'

But it wasn't, was it? 'Everything is going to be fine,' he promised.

'Alex!' called his mother, sounding a little more panicky this time.

'Okay, let's do this,' said Ellie, raising her chin and stepping out from the shadow of the seating plan.

His mother and Ellie exchanged polite greetings as they settled in their chairs, although he could tell Ellie was uncomfortable.

'Where's the happy couple? Shouldn't they be here by now?' he asked, unable to keep the snide tone out of his voice.

His mother frowned and his father took a deep sip of his single-malt Scotch.

'They'll be down in a minute. So tell me, how did you two meet?' She posed the question not to him, but to Ellie.

Ellie's face fell and she lowered her glass slowly. 'Erm… I gate-crashed his opening-night party.'

Alex's mother, ever the professional, smiled without missing a beat, the quick glance towards him the only indicator of her surprise.

'So, you haven't been together long?'

'No.' Ellie paled and looked up at him for reassurance. 'No, I guess it's been a bit of a whirlwind.'

His mother's pleasant expression remained fixed, but her eyes sharpened. 'I forgot to ask. Do you plan to enter the business at some point?'

Ellie blinked, and Alex added for clarity, 'Show business.'

He could tell by his mother's sudden change in demeanour that she was worried. Even though she would have learned from the security checks that Ellie was a nurse, she still might suspect her of being hungry for fame and using him as a stepping stone to becoming famous – it wouldn't be the first time. Several of his previous girlfriends had done that, and in the end he'd switched to only dating women who were already successful within the industry. But that hadn't worked out either; Savannah was proof of that.

Ellie looked at him and then his mother and laughed, the joyous smile he'd come to love finally gracing her lips. 'Me? Oh God, no! As if.' She swallowed nervously and took a shaky breath. 'Nothing wrong with it of course… I mean, well… just not my bag. Nursing is enough drama for me.'

His mother paused a moment, obviously surprised. He could literally see her mind churning: doesn't everybody want this? *No*, he wanted to shout. Not everybody wanted their lives to be lived in public. He didn't. Had hated it as a kid, and had fallen into acting anyway – even though he'd always preferred writing and directing.

His mother recovered quickly. 'Oh, I played a nurse once – Nurse Wahler, or Walker, something like that. It was hard work.'

He rolled his eyes. Sometimes he wondered if she remembered what the real world was actually like. 'That's not the same, Mom.'

'Close enough,' Ellie said with an unbothered shrug. 'Was it a film?'

'No, one of my first TV series actually. A long time ago, when I first started out. We had a lovely doctor and nurse consultant who gave us all the juicy stories.'

'I bet,' Ellie said warmly.

But their conversation immediately died when his mother noticed the arrival of Savannah and Liam, sparking a flame of irritation in his chest that their arrival would automatically halt her conversation with Ellie. Although she didn't seem to mind, and instead looked concerned about him.

Savannah and Liam made their way over to the top table and were greeted by a round of applause from their guests. Savannah was wearing some baby-pink frothy designer number, and his brother was wearing a linen suit, not dissimilar to his own except it was in the same colour as Savannah's dress, with a frilly white shirt beneath, and a baby-pink bow tie at the neck.

At that moment, Alex knew with complete certainty that he'd dodged a bullet.

His parents stood and welcomed them both with hugs and air kisses. Savannah's mother had died a few years ago, and her relationship with her father was strained, so he wasn't surprised that he hadn't come.

Alex took a deep breath and, after glancing at Ellie for silent reassurance, they stood. He gave Savannah's cheek a quick awkward air kiss and then gave his brother a firm handshake before sitting back down as quickly as possible. Ellie – incapable of behaving unkindly to anyone – complimented Savannah's dress and beamed cheerfully at his brother.

As they returned to their seats, his mom and dad remained standing and turned to their audience, commanding the room easily without saying a word.

His father was the first to speak. 'We are so delighted to welcome you all here for Savannah and Liam's wedding. We know some of you have travelled a great distance: Monte Carlo, South Africa and even from Australia – thank you, Margot and Rocco. I can speak for all of us when I say we are so pleased to have you with us on such a wonderful occasion.'

His mother spoke next. Neither of his parents had speech cards; the smoothness of their delivery was down to their talent as actors, combined with their close relationship as a couple – a winning team who loved each other deeply.

How had he thought Savannah was the one? Was he truly so blind? Was he falling blindly again with Ellie, with another woman who didn't really want him?

'Savannah and Liam are perfect for each other,' continued his mom.

His dad followed, 'Anyone can see that, and we are all delighted to welcome Savannah into our family.'

Neither looked at him as they spoke and he got the distinct impression that this was how all of the wedding events would pan out, everyone pretending nothing had happened. His fingers clenched into fists beneath the table and his jaw tightened painfully.

His thoughts, his feelings, ignored as always.

A warm hand was laid on top of his own.

He looked up into the chocolate pools of Ellie's eyes, and slowly the tension faded away, falling off his shoulders like a heavy coat dropping to the floor.

She understood and she saw him. But she didn't want him, not really. Lust was a powerful thing, but love? He'd never managed to get that, not with Savannah or any of his previous flings. No one stayed; they all got bored, or sought out better opportunities and left him behind, and he'd never missed them. But Ellie? He knew he would miss her when all of this was over.

'…which brings me on to our wedding gift.' His mother beamed indulgently as she passed the couple an envelope.

Liam and Savannah opened it with curious smiles. After a second of confusion, Savannah burst into sobbing tears and jumped up to hug his mom. His dad was given a bear hug by Liam, and Alex tried very hard not to roll his eyes.

'They've gifted us a honeymoon island!' cried Savannah, wiping gently at her tears with a napkin.

Holly jumped up and down as if she'd won a carnival prize. 'What, your own island? You have to let me stay!'

His mom chuckled. 'We told you that we would sort out the honeymoon, and we have. The Bahamas will always have a special place in your hearts and ours, so we thought it only right that you should have your own place here. We hope it's a special start to a beautiful life together.'

There was more emotional gushing from Savannah, followed by hugs, while the guests watched with captivated gasps of wonder and sentimental sighs.

Ellie squeezed his fingers lightly and he returned the touch, hoping to reassure her. He wasn't surprised by his parents' actions. When you've bought houses for your kid's twenty-first birthdays, what else can you buy them as a wedding gift?

An island, of course.

Raw jealousy clawed at his throat and he struggled to swallow it down. He knew it was a wedding gift and the occasion demanded extravagance. But, for all their display of familial affection, not one of them had come to see his play. How could they buy an island for one brother, and not even a plane ticket for the other? Like salt poured onto an open wound, it hurt like hell, but was also strangely cleansing.

If they didn't care, why should he?

The bitter rage that had been simmering since his arrival boiled over. He let go of Ellie's hand and drained his glass in one swig. He then picked up the bottle from the centre of the table and repoured his glass, not caring when some of it sloshed onto the tablecloth.

'Oh, my babies are going to love it!' cried Savannah, hugging Alex's mother once more.

'Babies?' asked Ellie quietly.

'Her dogs,' Alex replied gruffly, not caring to lower his voice. They could pretend he didn't exist, but he wasn't going to make it easy for them.

Savannah glanced their way and giggled nervously. 'I've quite a few… I have a bit of an obsession.'

Alex snorted. 'That's putting it mildly.'

Savannah blinked and turned away. Liam glared at him but Alex simply shrugged.

His dad, sensing the dangerous turn in the mood, quickly ended the speech. 'Right. It looks like the food is ready. Help yourselves to the meat, fish and vegan barbecue stations over there. There's a buffet of sides to your left. Enjoy!' He nodded at the calypso band stationed at the edge of the lawn and they began to play a cheerful song, the trumpets and jaunty rhythm trying their best to drown out the obvious tension.

'Savannah, tell me about your next film?' gushed Caitlyn.

Savannah's eyes brightened. 'I play a genetically enhanced doctor who creates a cyborg soldier – played by Liam. We have to save the planet from self-destruction. The film tackles the issues of climate change in a fun yet thought-provoking way.'

Alex hadn't realised he'd scoffed out loud until all of their heads swivelled towards him. Why were they looking at him like he was the bad guy? They'd all flown in on private jets for this wedding. He'd never heard anything so hypocritical.

'There are rumours it's Oscar-worthy. Another trophy to add to Liam and Savannah's collection!' Holly said smugly. 'I'm hoping to get a part in it.' She glanced over at Richie who was sat at one of the tables closest to them, he gave a non-committal shrug.

Alex rolled his eyes. 'Oscar-worthy already? Before it's even been fully cast? Impressive.'

'Shall we go get something to eat?' Ellie asked briskly, rising from her seat.

'Not right now. I've lost my appetite.' He eased back in his chair, and Ellie sank back in hers with a hopeless expression. He knew he was making everyone uncomfortable, but why the hell should he leave? They were the ones who wanted him here.

'Come on, baby,' prodded Savannah, and dragged a furious-looking Liam away from the table. A short time later everyone had dispersed, leaving Ellie and Alex alone.

'Are you okay?' she asked.

'I'm fine.'

'You don't look fine.'

He sighed. 'I'm just a little… pissed off.'

'That's understandable. It must be hard seeing them together.' She looked over at Liam and Savannah at one of the barbecue tables with a pained expression. 'I mean, you loved her, didn't you?'

Did I?

He didn't answer. It would sound so stupid and petulant to tell her the truth. That he was jealous of his brother. That his pride and his feelings had been hurt because everyone in his family had chosen him last, again. After everything they'd done, Savannah and Liam still had his parents' love and affection, and he had to just accept the humiliation in silence. 'Go, get something to eat. I just need a minute alone.'

'Okay, if you're sure?'

He nodded and drank some more champagne. It tasted sour and acidic on his tongue, as Ellie, the only person to actually care about his feelings, walked away.

—

'Maybe you should slow down, darling.'

His mother was standing beside him, a plate of food in her hands. She lowered herself serenely into her chair, as if she hadn't just scolded her adult son on his excessive drinking.

Everyone was queueing at the various stations to collect their meals. Ellie was at the buffet table piling up two plates. No doubt she'd ignored him when he'd said he wasn't hungry and had gone ahead and made him up a plate anyway.

'Why? Are you worried I'll embarrass you?' he spat, and took another long sip of his drink out of spite. 'That's what you want, right? For everything to be nice and easy. No bad press.'

His mother sighed. 'What I want is for things to be better between you and Liam. Which it can't be if you continue to behave like this.'

'How do you want me to behave? Happy? After what they did? How can you ask me to just forget it, like it never happened?' *Like I don't even matter.*

'I know it's hard. But you can't keep punishing them for it. I was hoping that by now you'd have both moved on.'

'You think that because now I've got Ellie I can forget what they did?' The laughter that sprang from him had an almost cruel edge to it. 'They lied to me. They *betrayed* me. I'm here, aren't I? You can't expect more than that.'

'They love each other. Surely you see that?' she beseeched him. 'Savannah and you were never happy together. Not like they are.' She looked over at Liam and Savannah. They were feeding each other shrimp – the same colour as their matching outfits. His stomach churned with nausea.

'And now they've found each other, I should be happy for them?'

His mother looked him dead in the eye and answered with a hard tone, 'Yes.'

'How can you say that?'

Her eyes narrowed and she stared at him as if he were a child again and she was reprimanding him. 'Because it's the only way you can be happy too. You need to let go of all this anger and jealousy. We love you both *equally*, and all I want is for you to be happy.'

Her words reverberated through him, shaking his foundations and shifting his perspective with dizzying speed. He still didn't believe they loved him equally to Liam, but he was beginning to wonder if he should just let go of all this pointless bitterness. It wasn't helping him, and his bad behaviour wasn't fair on Ellie either.

As if reading his mind, his mother added, 'She's worried about you,' gesturing with her chin at Ellie, who was halfway up the veranda stairs with two plates in her hands and eyes overflowing with concern.

Holly was walking up the steps beside her, and he noticed her give Ellie a sneering side-eye before asking, 'Hungry?'

Ellie blushed, but nodded towards him. 'One's for Alex.'

A pang of guilt hit the pit of his stomach, and he pushed away his glass. No matter what, she was still his friend, and that counted for something. He needed to protect her from this den of vipers.

Chapter Twenty

Ellie was beginning to think that this whole holiday-fake-relationship thing was a bad idea. Alex's usually charming smile had twisted into a brooding scowl that had everyone's nerves on edge.

Yes, Savannah and Liam had done a terrible thing, and yes, he had a right to be angry. But did he have to be such a... dick?

His behaviour during and after the speech had made her skin crawl with embarrassment. Free holiday be damned – she would start swimming back to the East End now if this was how the rest of the week was going to pan out, and she didn't even care about the shark-infested waters.

Thankfully, he'd not said anything else after they'd all gone to get their food. She'd noticed his mum had had a word with him. Hopefully, she'd reminded him about his manners.

What had happened to him? He'd been so happy after the tennis game. Granted, she'd had to repeat their agreed boundaries, and thank God she had – by his current behaviour, it was perfectly clear that he wasn't over Savannah.

She could understand his pain. Of course he wasn't going to be all sunshine and rainbows about the wedding. He'd obviously loved Savannah deeply; his silence when she'd asked him about it had been answer enough.

Which meant that her suspicions had been right all along. Their attraction to each other was a passing crush, nothing more. When Alex finally moved on from his disappointment with Savannah, he would realise Ellie had simply been a nice comforting distraction. While she would be left hurt and as broken as she'd been after David... Except much, much worse.

She pushed around the delicious food on her plate. She'd lost her appetite. Holly's fatphobic comments had been the icing on the cake of this crappy evening.

'Would you like to dance?'

Ellie's head shot up so fast she wondered if she'd given herself whiplash. 'What?'

Alex smiled, and her heart fluttered back to life when she recognised it as his first genuinely happy emotion since the start of the meal. 'Come on.' He held out his hand.

She shook her head, glancing towards the couples dancing expertly on the wooden decking in the centre of the garden. Pretty lights were strung up around the square, and the music rolled through the crowd as their hips swayed in time to the calypso beat. She had no hope of emulating those moves – she was more used to stomping around her handbag to Little Mix or grinding to some Rihanna.

'I don't know how to dance, not to this, sorry.'

'Let me show you,' he said, taking her hand in his and tugging her towards the deck. She stumbled after him, terrified at the prospect of making a fool of herself in front of this crowd. But also elated at the welcome change in Alex's attitude.

Did his mum slip him a Prozac earlier?

He started to show her the basic steps, and after a few false starts she managed to almost get a dance routine going.

He twirled her around with one arm in the air and she spun awkwardly around him, bumping her hips against his, until they both laughed. Then his face sobered and he pulled her close, his hips still swaying in time with the music. 'I'm sorry. I don't know what came over me earlier.'

'I understand,' she said immediately, although, if she were honest, she was more than a little relieved that he regretted his earlier behaviour. It had been so unlike him.

He pulled her close, the spicy scent of his sandalwood aftershave mixing with the smoke of the barbecues to create an intoxicating blend. 'I've been a bit self-indulgent,' he said sheepishly.

She was glad to have him back – her friend. 'I'd have said you were behaving like a dick – but self-indulgent works too.'

'You're right. But I'm going to try and get over it.' He chuckled, and she could feel it vibrate through his chest and into hers as they swayed along the deck.

Cicadas, twinkling fairy lights and music combined in the mild heat of the evening to create the perfect romantic atmosphere. It was a shame they were just friends, because at this moment the only thing that would have made her any happier would have been if he'd kissed her – for real. Not to play to an audience or because he needed a distraction, but because he wanted a relationship with her... loved her.

She patted his bicep and tried not to shiver at the strength of muscle beneath her fingers. 'That's all anyone can ask of you.' She tried to remind herself they were just friends. 'Everything is going to be fine.' She repeated the words he'd said to her earlier, longing to kiss him but knowing she couldn't; she wasn't an actor, and, no matter how much she pretended to be happy about this facade, she knew it would hurt her in the end.

'Thank you,' he sighed. He rested his chin on the top of her head, drawing her even closer. Their hips slowed with the beat, and she closed her eyes.

All was forgiven.

The music shifted to a party number and so did Alex, whisking her around until her head was spinning and she was giggling uncontrollably. His hips moved languidly and he had a natural rhythm, which she tried her best to match.

Eventually she had to beg for a break. Panting, they made their way back to the top table. Alex offered to get her a drink and she accepted with a gasping nod. Man, he had a lot of energy – *I bet he's amazing in bed*, she thought wistfully, as he bounded off to get them some fruit punch.

His mum glided down into the seat beside her with swan-like elegance. 'I'm so glad he met you, Ellie. Frankly we were more than a little worried about how he was going to react this week. We wanted him here, of course, but we were worried he might... *misbehave*. He had a bit of a shaky start tonight, but you've managed to pull him around.'

Ellie bristled at the implication that Alex was to blame for all of it. He'd been cheated on – with his brother, of all people. 'Oh, I don't think that's fair. Maybe he shouldn't have said what he said, but he has a right to be upset.'

'Has he?' Jessica replied shrewdly, her eyes piercing Ellie's soul, just like her son's always did. 'I would have thought he'd have gotten over it by now. He's with you, after all.' She raised a single blonde eyebrow. Obviously that wasn't what she'd expected to hear from his current girlfriend.

Ellie squirmed with discomfort at the possibility that she'd outed herself, and their lies. After all, who was she kidding? Anyone with half a brain cell would realise Nurse Ellie couldn't possibly be the love of Alex King's life. 'He still needs time to forgive them, especially Liam.'

It was his mother's turn to bristle. 'Liam never meant to hurt him.'

'Of course not,' Ellie agreed. Then couldn't help adding more firmly, 'But he did.'

Jessica King sighed miserably, leaning back into her seat and crossing her impossibly long, sleek legs. 'I know.'

'The sibling rivalry thing probably doesn't help either. Alex must feel as if Liam's the golden child who can do no wrong.'

Jessica's spine stiffened and she shifted towards her, perfectly manicured hands crossing in her lap. 'What do you mean?'

Fuck.

When would she learn to keep her big mouth shut? She looked around for Alex, praying he was on his way back to help drag her out of this hole. Unfortunately, he looked as if he'd been collared by an older lady in a glittering turquoise sari and equally glittering jewels.

'Oh, you know how those two are…' She gave a vague wave of her hand. But Jessica was not so easily fobbed off.

'No. Enlighten me.'

Ellie braced herself. In for a penny, as the saying went. 'I guess Alex feels as if he's never good enough. I mean, Liam has done so well with his career, and he can't help but compare himself.'

'Alex has always wished to forge his own path. We've always encouraged that.'

Ellie remembered his face in the Lebanese restaurant just a couple of weeks ago. The disappointment, the bitterness. 'None of you came to see his play.'

'He wanted to be independent.' Jessica all but choked on her indignation, but her hands uncrossed and she leaned forward with concern. 'He made it *very* clear that he wanted to do it all alone. Richie said he'd be offended if we'd stuck our noses in. The press would have gone mad and we would have distracted from his art.'

Ellie knew she was walking a very fine line between defending Alex and pissing off her host, but she couldn't help raise an only-slightly-sarcastic eyebrow at Jessica's comments. 'And there was no other way to support your son's new, independent venture?'

Jessica sank back in her chair, looking as if she'd just discovered her diamond necklace was fake.

Alex arrived back at the table, two glasses in hand. Before his mum could say anything that put Ellie any more in the shit, she grabbed his arm and steered him away. 'Can we take a walk on the beach with these?'

'Sure, no problem,' he mumbled with a glance over his shoulder at his unusually subdued mother.

'What were you two talking about?'

'I was talking to her about your play. Any more news on ticket sales?'

'The weekends are beginning to sell out, and Russell is hopeful for the rest of the run. But I really should have tackled the publicity issue earlier.'

'You'll know for next time.'

He remained silent and she felt bad for bringing it up. He was always so hard on himself. They walked onto the sand, her sandals sinking into the soft powder. A few torches had been lit to illuminate the beach, but no one was there except them. She supposed this crowd saw breathtaking natural beauty like this all the time. 'Can we sit here a moment?'

'Sure, there's some loungers around here somewhere...'

'I'm happy to sit on the sand.'

'No worries.' They sat down, their shoulders brushing against each other. Ellie crossed her legs beneath her maxi and sipped her rum punch, staring blankly out into darkness and enjoying the sounds of the surf. The stars and torches cast glittering shadows on the cresting waves, and a few faint lights shone in the distance from the surrounding islands.

'I've never been anywhere as beautiful as this.'

'It's nicer in the daylight.'

'Maybe, but you see the true heart of a place at night, and this really is paradise.'

They sat in companionable silence for a while until the quiet darkness gave her the confidence to speak.

'How do you want to play it, this week? If you want to avoid them like the plague, I don't mind, but we'd probably need a plan of action. It's a small island.'

'I'm ashamed of how I acted earlier. I shouldn't have made you worry like that. I think I just needed to get some of that bitterness off my chest, you know? It drives me crazy that they keep pretending like nothing happened, but I guess they just want to move on, and I should do the same.'

'Hmmm.' She wasn't convinced. If anything it made her worry that there was a lot more emotion hidden beneath the surface. Not just for Alex, but for the entire family.

'Honestly, I'm feeling a whole lot better about it. We don't have to avoid them.'

'You're honestly okay about your ex marrying your brother?'

He paused, considering, then the air rushed out of his lungs in a sigh of relief. 'Yeah, I think I am. I have to be – not just for them, but for me too.'

'Did the matching pink outfits help?'

They both started laughing and Alex bumped her shoulder with his.

'Definitely.'

—

The following morning, after awkwardly shuffling around each other getting ready, they met everyone for breakfast downstairs. This time in the *formal* dining room, as the staff were busy cleaning up the sun room, informal dining room and garden from the night before.

The formal dining room was bigger than her family's shop, but so were most of the rooms in this mansion.

A continental buffet was laid out for them. Everyone was there, including Richie, in what she supposed was his attempt at leisure wear – tailored shorts, a muted Hawaiian shirt, a Bloody Mary in one hand and his phone in the other. Apparently he'd arrived during the party, although she didn't really remember seeing him.

Alex's family, as well as the rest of their entourage, were decked out in a variety of safari and hiking outfits.

If she was to take a quick guess, she'd say they'd had some serious plans for the day.

'We're going to see Savannah and Liam's island after breakfast. Would you two like to join us?' asked Jessica, sipping her coffee delicately.

She glanced at Alex, but by the look on his face the answer was a definite *hell no*.

Alex's father looked up from some business documents, saw the lay of the land, and quickly returned to burying his head in the sand. So, there was no help there either. Everyone else had dived into their pastry selections as if they were backpacking around Europe and this was their only meal for the day.

The tension in her shoulders eased when Alex finally piped up.

'No, I think we'll just have a quiet day today.' He then surprised her by adding, 'But what are your plans for the rest of the week? It's Ellie's first time in the Bahamas, and I'd love to take her to see Big Major Cay. Maybe go snorkelling too. Just let us know when you're not using the boat.'

His mum bit her lip with a pained expression. 'Maybe I should buy another boat... There are a lot of us, and it might make things easier.'

Jesus, one look at me and they need a bigger boat.

'Oh, don't do that,' cried Ellie. 'Honestly, I'm fine. This island is beautiful. Why go anywhere else, right?'

'You can't come all the way to the Bahamas and not see Pig Island,' said Holly enthusiastically. Was Ellie imagining it or had she emphasised the word pig?

Savannah looked tentatively at Alex, her husky voice hopeful and earnest. 'We were thinking of going tomorrow. It would be great if you guys came along. We could get to know each other better...'

'Pig Island?' Ellie asked tentatively, half-afraid she was back in school and any minute now Savannah or Holly would shout, '*Pig Island, that's where you're from! Oink, oink!*' But thankfully Savannah wasn't a stupid teenage bully who abused others to make themselves feel better. Holly on the other hand...

Caitlyn and Keira were nice, but she had the impression they weren't very interested in getting to know her, and Tony was the quietest man she'd ever met. He'd said fewer than two words to her – or anyone for that matter – and yet people still fawned over him like a prince. She supposed he'd directed enough blockbusters to justify his silence.

'It's a must,' Savannah said eagerly.

'You have to go,' agreed Alex's mum, giving Alex an *agree to take her or else* glare.

Alex shifted in his seat. 'It's an uninhabited island with native pigs. They're quite tame and paddle about in the sea. People feed them and pet them.'

Ellie gasped. 'Oh my God. We're close to it? I think I read about it in the plane's brochures.' Her excitement was closely followed by guilt. Alex would probably find a day trip with his family awkward. 'Although, honestly, I don't mind either way.'

To her surprise, Alex grinned. 'I think that's a yes.'

Savannah sank back into her chair with visible relief, exchanging a pleased smile with Liam. The whole table seemed a little lighter in spirit, and Ellie was proud to sit by Alex's side.

After the rest of the household left on the boat, Alex and Ellie spent their morning properly exploring his parents' island. Well, Ellie explored, Alex was just joining her for the ride. After lunch the heat of the day crept up to unbearable levels, and they lounged in hammocks on the beach and chatted about Ellie's career. She'd read through the information she'd printed off and had narrowed down her options. But talking them through with Alex was the boost she needed. She didn't think there was anything nicer than top-and-tailing in a hammock with Alex, chatting about possible futures with a tropical fruit juice in hand, provided by staff who seemed to pop out from nowhere and then disappear with equal speed.

The rest of the party returned bright-eyed with excitement in the late afternoon. After everyone had showered, they returned to the dining room to eat a delicious meal of rock lobster with a creole sauce and plenty of fresh crisp salad. This was followed by juicy fruit platters and yet more rum punch on the porch.

Caitlyn and Keira were as excitable as teenagers and constantly talked at Tony about how much they loved his films. Ellie was beginning to suspect that they were after roles on his next project. Holly, in contrast, seemed a little quieter than normal, as if she'd not been quite as pleased with visiting her sister's new island as the rest of them. Savannah was treating her like a grumpy child, with forced joviality and constant praise.

Ellie found them more than a little strange, but also fascinating. She'd always thought beautiful, successful people wouldn't have a care in the world, and in some ways they didn't. They talked about luxury travel, flashy cars and designer handbags with carefree abandon. Work was a passion and a lifestyle that they had to maintain daily. None of them had any idea about struggle, but they were also like little birds with broken wings. Fragile and desperate to avoid falling from the nest.

The afternoon stretched slowly into evening, the sun dipping to a burnt orange as it sank below the horizon and the insects began to sing their lullaby. The mood of the group was content and relaxed. As lamps automatically switched on, Ellie went to the loo. On her way back to the porch she noticed several people making their way up to bed, and found herself returning at the same time as Liam, who was carrying two herbal teas from the drinks cart back out onto the porch.

'How's your new island?' she asked even though all she'd heard about for most of the evening was him gushing enthusiastically about his little slice of heaven and making plans to renovate the house. Apparently, it was dated, and she'd grinned at Alex and whispered, *like the embassy*? Alex had laughed. *I doubt it.*

'All right as islands go.' Liam smiled, his perfect teeth flashing in the dim light. It made him look a lot like Alex and it disarmed her for a moment.

'No native pigs?'

'No, afraid not.'

'Ahh well, there's always a compromise.'

Her teasing wasn't lost on him, and he gave her a wink as they walked out onto the porch together. She would say this for the Kings, they didn't take themselves as seriously as she might have expected from billionaire celebrities.

Alex was sitting on the porch swing, and he looked up with narrowed eyes as they approached.

Oh dear, fraternising with the enemy.

'I might head up,' she told him. They'd agreed that morning to stagger their bedtime routine so they each had time alone to change, and, in Ellie's case, hide her underwear from eager Eddie. He'd already washed her slippers and pyjamas twice, and she'd still not spoken to the man.

Alex gave her puppy-dog eyes. 'I'll be up in a minute, darling.' He looked at Liam pointedly as he said the endearment, and Ellie tried not to roll her eyes.

'Okay, hun,' she said with a yawn as she sloped away, then realised belatedly that her endearment hadn't been a ruse. She had to be more careful. She was leaning further and further over the precipice, and if she fell, their friendship and her last shred of hope would be lost for ever.

Chapter Twenty-One

The next day, very bright and very early – so they'd miss the tourists – they all boarded the boat or yacht, whatever it was called, and headed over to piggy island – as Ellie was calling it in her head. Everyone except Richie; he had some work calls that day and had settled on a sun lounger with a Bloody Mary in hand. Ellie had been relieved, as she still hadn't forgiven him for the money-waving.

Yes, she held grudges.

The boat had a little kitchen below and Ellie watched in surprise as Eddie and his team steadily filled it with plenty of ice, food, wine and general supplies. You'd think they were going for a fortnight and not a day trip.

Ellie had her straw beach bag with a change of clothes, a sun hat, dark glasses and sunscreen. She wore her swimming costume beneath another one of her maxi-dresses. The one-piece, of course – she wasn't sure if she was ready to reveal her teeny-weeny bikini just yet. Looking at the real-life Barbies skipping onto the boat, she wasn't sure if she'd ever be ready. Next to them she was like the BFG – Big Friendly Girlfriend. All those years of training herself to be body positive were threatening to get washed away by a single flood of well-waxed Californian women in designer bikinis. But wasn't that always the way?

And it wasn't just their bodies, although that played a huge part. They genuinely *belonged* here, to this life of yachts, champagne, celebrities and luxurious islands.

She, frankly, didn't. This was a holiday, not a lifestyle. She couldn't allow herself to believe otherwise; it would only make the return home to her real life even harder.

They all piled onto the boat, comfortably stretching out across its full length with plenty of room between the different groups. Alex's parents, Liam and Tony stood at the wheel – she wasn't sure what you called it, but it was definitely the part that ran things and so she knew to steer clear of it. Savannah and her gaggle of girls sat at the very front of the boat, while she and Alex perched midway between the two. Oddly, she found herself relaxing significantly when she realised Alex must feel just as out of place as she did.

The day was glorious, but when wasn't it in the Bahamas? Ellie could have happily spent the whole day sailing around to nowhere in particular, but the boat skipped through the ocean and they arrived at Pig Island in no time.

As they came close, she was surprised to see how sparse the island was. Shaped like a straggly horseshoe, it had very little in the way of shelter, just a few bushes and some low wispy trees. They anchored at the entrance to the beach, where the water was so clear you could see the white sand beneath, tinged by only a hint of the turquoise water.

In the distance, little four-legged bodies began to emerge from the shrubs and trees of the island. Smudges of pink, black, brown and orange happily trotted out into the water. Soon she could see the wild troop of pigs more clearly. Some were huge, others clearly no older than a few months. All were adorable.

The boat became a frenzy of activity as people chucked off their clothes and handed around vegetables to feed their hungry porcine guests, who were now halfway between the beach and the boat. Ellie dumped out the contents of her beach bag and filled it with carrots, lettuce and apples. Everyone was making their way down the steel ladder and into the water. Alex, bless him, was waiting patiently for her, eyeing up the loaded bag with amusement.

'I don't want them to go hungry.'

'Oh, believe me, they won't.' He stripped off his t-shirt and shoes and headed to the ladder.

Ellie stared at the half-naked Alex. Her heart skipped, then stalled like a broken-down car, then jump-started back to life again, all in a matter of seconds. He was truly breathtaking, just like a Hollywood star – *he is a Hollywood star, you doughnut!*

The grunts and snorts were getting closer. Ellie went to the side of the boat. Everyone was now swimming towards the pigs. Liam had managed to swim far enough in to be able to stand and was wading through the shallows, greeting some of the faster pigs with a head of lettuce.

'You best get down there.' Alex grinned. 'It'll only be a matter of time before they realise they should have carried more food with them. And, as much as I'd like them to eat Liam, I think my mom would be pretty heartbroken.'

After a deep breath, she threw off her own dress with a muttered, 'Fuck it.'

She clambered down the ladder gingerly, her straw beach bag slung over one shoulder. Alex followed after, and she was treated to the sight of strong thick legs and a pert bum as he descended.

The sea was a pleasantly balmy temperature and Ellie blissfully treaded water and waited for Alex. The swim didn't take long, just a few minutes doggy-paddling and then they were wading over to the others. A few piggy stragglers came paddling over towards them.

She couldn't get over the variety of their rough coats. A mottled black, tan and ginger pig with tusks came towards her, snorting. She reached in her bag and drew out a long carrot.

'Do I just throw it at them?' she asked nervously, eyeing up the tusks of the *little piggy*, who suddenly looked more like a very big, very feral piggy. She was going to call him Motley.

'They'll take it from your hands. Just hold it out, like this.' He took the hand that held the carrot and offered it to Motley.

Motley took a huge bite, barely pausing in his paddling as he gulped it down with an appreciative snort and slobber.

'Bahamians take the wellbeing of these pigs very seriously. You should only feed them healthy food, and only in the water.'

'Why only in the water?'

'Some pigs were found dead from ingesting too much sand because of eating on the beach.'

'Oh, how sad,' Ellie gasped, then quickly delved into her bag for more treats as they were rapidly surrounded by more happy pigs nuzzling at them with varying degrees of force.

'Some tourists are complete trash, trying to feed them alcohol and picking them up for photos. But the tour operators have clamped down on that sort of thing.'

'Good.'

'Ellie, do you have any more vegetables? This one has cleaned us out,' Savannah said cheerfully as she waded over, her narrow hips swinging below her washboard stomach.

Ellie rummaged around in her bag and handed her two lettuces and a carrot. Savannah shared them around to the rest of the group. 'Thanks, you're an angel.'

She didn't feel like an angel. She felt as if she were an alien on a planet populated by only supermodels. They were gorgeous people who jumped in oceans and knew that someone else would always be lugging a bag of vegetables behind them.

Holly's voice interrupted her thoughts and she turned to face her. 'Someone take a photo of me with my little buddy!' The baby pig did not look amused with his new *friend*.

'You're not meant to pick them up,' Alex said sternly.

But Holly ignored him. 'Keira! Take a picture! Isn't he adorable?'

'Put it *down*,' Savannah shouted, looking uncharacteristically annoyed at her sister's antics as she stood obliviously holding up a small pink pig, its trotters kicking the air furiously as it squealed and jerked with distress.

Alex started to wade towards her.

'Oh my God, chill, Savannah. You're not *Mom*.' Holly pouted indignantly at her sister, completely unaware of a much larger pig swimming up behind her. At a guess this larger pink pig was in fact Mummy Pig, and Mummy Pig was not happy about seeing her wee little piggy being manhandled.

So much so, in fact…

'OWWWW!' screeched Holly, and Alex swooped in to catch the falling piglet and then smoothly released it back into the water. It swam merrily to its defensive mother. Holly was now hiding behind Alex's broad shoulders clutching her bum. '*It bit me!*'

Ellie decided to quickly feed Mummy Pig a very large apple before she turned on her as well. In a sea of skinny women, she was beginning to feel a little nervous. She must look a lot like a prime rib-eye right now, and didn't pigs eat everything? She began to feed them more liberally, occasionally scratching one behind the ear in an attempt to befriend them.

Savannah sloshed over to her sister, inspected her rump and declared, 'You're *fine*.'

'Everything okay?' asked Jessica, looking freaking hot in her white bikini and wide-brimmed hat, with an equally dashing Robert beside her.

Ellie vowed to always wear sunscreen and give Pilates another go.

Who was she kidding? She *hated* Pilates.

After another quick rummage in her bag, she admitted defeat. 'I'm all out.'

Holly eyed Mummy Pig while rubbing her own bottom. 'I want to go back to the boat.'

Savannah glared at her sister, but nodded in agreement. Turning back to them with an apologetic look, she said, 'We'll head back and prepare brunch.'

There was a bit of chatting amongst the group until it was decided that Savannah, Liam, Tony and Holly would go back to the boat while the rest of them would head to the beach for a while, until the tourist boats began to arrive. When that happened, they all agreed, they would go back too, to avoid becoming the tourist attraction themselves.

Ellie and Alex headed to a shady area on the beach and settled down to watch the pigs. Now that their food was gone, most of the animals had lost interest in them, although some continued to play in the surf, while others also sought out the shady areas of the beach to sleep away the morning until their next meal.

Keira and Caitlyn splashed in the shallows like they were on a fashion shoot, and Ellie strategically placed her bag across her thighs, feeling more than a little self-conscious.

'Everything okay?' asked Alex. He was leaning against a gnarled old tree trunk, drawing shapes in the sand with a stick.

'Yeah, of course,' she yelped, embarrassed that he'd noticed her dip in mood. She reminded herself that she was in one of the most beautiful places on the planet, experiencing stuff that many people couldn't even dare to imagine.

'Is it the pigs? Honestly, they're fine as long as you don't maul them like Holly did.'

She chuckled at the absurdity of it all. 'I love the pigs. I probably have more in common with them than anyone else here.'

Alex frowned out at the sea. She had the uneasy feeling she'd insulted him in some way, which was ridiculous.

'I mean, I'm not one of you beautiful Hollywood people, am I?' The fake laugh stuck in her throat, and came out as an awkward cough.

'What do you see when you look at them?' He pointed his ridiculously chiselled chin over at Caitlyn and Keira.

'Supermodels,' she replied, without missing a beat.

He nodded sombrely, and then tilted his head thoughtfully. 'True. But I also see hours of strict diet and rigid exercise regimes. I see a team of nutritionists, chefs and personal trainers. I see a lot of hard work and restriction, combined with genetics that naturally lean towards a slimmer build. And there's nothing wrong with that. But I worked with Keira once – she hasn't eaten bread since she was seven.'

'Bread is life!' gasped Ellie, unable to restrain her horror.

'Yes, it is,' Alex agreed with a whimsical smile. 'I like bread too much to have Liam's physique.'

Ellie blinked. Liam was slimmer, but he didn't have Alex's broad shoulders or powerful thighs. She tried not to sigh with pleasure as she admired his physique. She'd never found anyone more gorgeous than Alex, with his Clark Kent glasses and beefcake arms.

'I prefer your body. Six-packs are overrated,' she said, before she could manage to stop herself. A blush crept up her neck, and she suddenly wished the pigs would eat her alive after all. Anything to escape Alex's piercing blue eyes.

A slow, sexy smile spread across his face. 'Glad to hear it.'

She gazed out at the pure white sand and turquoise sea. So beautiful it was almost painful to look at. She thought of the boats and planes she'd had to get on to even get here. Paradise and perfection weren't easy to come by, and even these lucky pigs who'd found themselves on this island by mistake or chance had their own hardships to face.

After a pause, she asked, 'What do you see when you look at me?'

As soon as she asked, she regretted it. *What was I thinking?*

He gave her a heated look, and she bit her lip, her nerves fizzing with excitement and arousal. 'A natural, unique beauty who's confident in who she is.'

'Hmmm, that sounds like, *she doesn't make any effort*,' grumbled Ellie. 'But that's sadly not the case. It takes a lot of work to make me look this *natural and confident*.' She leaned back against the tree, so their shoulders rested against each other. She wasn't even joking, although she'd said it with her usual flippancy. After David, her confidence had nosedived until she'd finally accepted her curves and become healthier. But all of that hard work, inside and out, hadn't mattered; she still wasn't good enough for some people, and never would be.

'And yet you make it look easy. I've never managed that,' he said, softly with a tinge of sadness, and she wondered if he always compared himself to his older brother.

She hoped not.

Chapter Twenty-Two

When the tourist boats started to arrive, they headed back to the yacht, his mom explaining to Ellie that once the public realised who they were, the paparazzi would descend on them quickly, ruining the rest of their plans for the day. Their security, who Ellie would probably never see, kept them largely away from the public eye but they couldn't guarantee anonymity when they left the safety of their island.

One of the main reasons why Alex had moved away from acting was because he couldn't stand the suffocating lens of the press. Whatever you said or did was picked apart online. He'd once lost a contact lens at a premiere and had been accused of snubbing a co-star when in fact he hadn't noticed them.

In some ways, his family were trapped by their fame. They bought islands and yachts not to show off, but to retain some level of privacy. Liam had had some frightening stalkers over the years, which had played a large part in his own battles with anxiety. Alex hoped Ellie understood that sometimes extravagance was necessary for their safety.

They sailed out to one of the smaller reefs, which was part of Exuma's nature reserve, and stopped for lunch. Eddie's team had done an impressive buffet of cold meats, shrimp, salad and rice dishes, as well as wines, fruit punch, beers and juices.

He and Ellie returned to their previous spot on the deck and spent a pleasant afternoon eating, chatting and spotting colourful fish in the sea.

'Anyone for snorkelling? We've only four snorkels, but you guys are welcome to go first,' asked Liam, waving the gear at them cheerfully.

'Oh, not for me, thanks,' Ellie replied, shaking her head.

'Are you sure? If you're nervous…' Alex asked quietly, surprised that she would refuse after she'd seemed to enjoy spotting fish from the side of the boat.

She shook her head fervently, and then leaned towards him with a mischievous glint in her eye. 'It's not that. It just feels… rude to the fish.'

'Rude? Well, that was the last thing I expected you to say.'

'Yeah. I mean the pigs, it was their island, but they got some food out of us going to visit them. But the fish? They're just living their life, in their beautiful home. The last thing they need is some massive goggled face getting up close in their business.'

'You've got a point.'

'I don't mind a swim though, if you're up for that? That's not intrusive to the reef, right?'

'No. We're too close to the surface to bother them, and I'd love a swim.' They made their way to the side of the boat. Liam and Savannah had given them firm reminders about the nature reserve's strict 'no touching, no taking' policy, as well as advice on snorkelling techniques.

So while the others struggled with the snorkelling gear, he and Ellie sank into the warm waters of the reef with happy sighs of pleasure.

As if in thanks, they were gifted with the arrival of a sea turtle, its shell scarred and chipped, its eyes bright and curious. The turtle paddled around them, its copper and brown markings catching the light like polished metal. Ellie watched in awe, her dark eyes sparkling with wonder in the sunshine.

Alex shook his head in astonishment and they exchanged excited looks as they watched the turtle majestically swim around them without a care in the world. They didn't speak, just watched, afraid to frighten the animal away.

After a few minutes of circling, it dipped its head and launched itself with surprising speed into the depths of the water. In only a few strokes they'd lost sight of it.

'Oh, damn, we missed a turtle!' cried Savannah as she made her way to the side of the boat, her flippers slapping as she walked. She jumped down into the water feet first, causing a huge splash.

Alex wiped the moisture from his face, glad that he'd taken the worst of it. He gave Ellie a conspiratorial nod of agreement. She was right – sometimes it was better to leave things be and mind your own business.

'Shall we go back up?' he asked.

Three more flipper-dives rocked the water around them.

'Good plan,' she replied, with a barely suppressed giggle.

Rain was falling heavily by the time they returned to his parents' house, signalling the start of a tropical storm.

They all piled off the yacht as soon as it docked, and ran indoors laughing. They were drenched, but it didn't matter; they'd been in and out of the water all day anyway, and it had been a refreshing change to the tropical heat.

The day had been surprisingly enjoyable, mostly due to Ellie's presence, but he was grateful for the excuse to go straight to their room.

He grabbed two towels from the bathroom and began to rough-dry his hair with one, having passed Ellie the other. Her hair swung around her in dripping tendrils, laughter kissing her lips as she stared back at him with bright eyes and flushed cheeks from the sprint indoors.

He had a horrible feeling that he'd been staring at her for far longer than necessary. And had he taken a step closer?

'Shall we have a movie night?' he asked.

Ellie blinked in surprise. 'Errr...'

'It looks like it's going to rain for a while.' He pointed towards the window, as if the rain running down the glass would convince her to stay with him. 'I could get us some snacks. Or we could just stay in here and chill. Have a break from my family.' Avoiding his family was an excuse, a valid one, but still an excuse. He wanted to be alone with her. To shut out the world and curl up with Ellie.

'Oh, sure,' Ellie replied, a little breathlessly, and then with a blush headed towards the bathroom. 'I'll just have a shower and put my pjs on.'

'Great.' He was rooted to the spot until the bathroom door closed. Then he punched the air with a silent cheer. After a moment, with a shake of his still-wet hair, he gathered his wits and headed down to the kitchen.

He almost turned tail when he saw his brother rummaging around in the cupboards, a tray of fruit and Savannah's vegan crackers beside him. Liam stilled, as if he'd been caught red-handed.

'Hey…'

'Hey…'

Liam set a chilled bottle of champagne and two glasses on the tray. 'I think the others are going to do some games in the sun room. If you're interested?'

'No, we thought we'd have a quiet night. Watch films and… chill.' Jeez, he may as well have said, I'm off to have sex. Which wasn't actually true… *Unfortunately.*

'Cool. Same,' said Liam, staring at the champagne and looking more than a little awkward. He *was* off to have sex, by the looks of it… with Alex's ex.

Strangely, it didn't bother Alex any more. He'd actually rather spend an evening not having sex with Ellie than be in Liam's shoes. Savannah and he had always been… tepid.

'Are you using the boat tomorrow? I thought I might take Ellie to one of the islands.' He wasn't sure why he'd asked, maybe to break the weird atmosphere growing between them. Plus, it sounded like something a loving boyfriend would do with his girlfriend.

'Oh. Sorry. We need the boat tomorrow. Eddie's got to pick up the flowers Savannah's having flown in from New England.'

Alex's eyes ached from trying not to roll them. 'Ah, yes. The pink English tea roses and peonies? She always insisted on them for her trailer. No matter the season.' He tried to hide the scathing criticism in his voice, but obviously failed, because Liam glared at him with barely concealed rage.

'You know why she likes them, don't you? Or was that another thing you never bothered to ask?'

Alex stared at Liam in shock. Partly because his perfect brother was finally snapping at him for a change, and partly because he was right. He had never bothered to ask Savannah why she insisted on having pink tea roses. Why hadn't he? He remained silent, unable to say anything unless it incriminated him further, and he had the uneasy feeling that it *would* reflect badly on him.

Liam tutted. The bastard actually tutted. 'No, of course you didn't. You act like I stole her from you, but you never even knew her. Not really.' He picked up the tray, before looking at Alex with narrowed eyes. 'They're her favourite because they were her mother's favourite flowers.'

Guilt swept over Alex with enough force to knock him back a step. Savannah had only mentioned her mother once; she'd died of breast cancer before Savannah's first feature film. He'd never met her, and Savannah had said she didn't like to talk about it. So he'd never asked, never bothered to find out more.

If that had been Ellie, he would have.

Liam was right. He was a jerk.

Unfortunately for him, Liam wasn't done.

'She called Savannah her flower because she was pregnant with her on her wedding day – she carried a bunch of roses and peonies in her bridal bouquet. When she died, she asked to be buried with roses and peonies. That's why she loves them. That's why she always has them with her. But I'm sure you knew that already…'

As the silence stretched, the air thickened around them, the tropical storm lashing against the kitchen windows wildly.

'I'm sorry. I was being a jerk.'

Liam sighed and balanced the tray with one hand as he ran his fingers through his hair in such a familiar way that it was almost like looking in a mirror. 'I love her. I love her flowers, and her silly dancing, and her hundred dogs. I love everything about her. And I'm sorry that it's hurt you, but you never loved her like I do.'

Liam began to walk away, but Alex grabbed him by the elbow, the champagne flutes jiggling precariously as he stared into his brother's eyes.

'You're right. And... I'm sorry.'

Liam took a deep and shaken breath. 'Thank you, and I'm sorry too. Not for being with Savannah, but for how I treated you. You're my brother, and you deserved better.' He left the room.

Alex remained rooted to the floor, staring at the door, long after his brother was gone, struck by the realisation that he'd never loved Savannah.

—

Back in the room, Ellie sat curled up on the couch, her magnificent hair dried and piled on top of her head in a messy bun. She wore long silky pyjama trousers and a white vest top that had black cat whiskers and a pink nose across her breasts.

It was very cute and very distracting.

Just like Ellie.

He put the tray of snacks down on the coffee table.

'Wow. You really went to town.'

He'd grabbed everything he could think of: popcorn, nachos and dip, sweets, chocolate, two cans of soda, as well as a pot of tea for Ellie and a latte for himself.

'Yeah, I needed time to compute my brother pointing out that I'm an asshole.'

Ellie sat up with an outraged gasp. 'What? How dare he have a go at you!'

Flattered by her immediate and unconditional defence, he admitted the truth quickly, before she marched out of the room to knock his brother out. 'He was right, in this case.'

She relaxed a little and eased back on the couch with a teasing raise of her brow. 'Did you steal all of his movie snacks?'

'Funny, but no. He pointed out the truth that I didn't really know Savannah that well. I guess I wasn't a great boyfriend to her. I was obsessed with rehearsing the play and my own plans for striking out solo. I never really thought about her. I never asked about her life, supported her goals, understood her past... nothing.'

Ellie pondered his words, plucking a few pieces of popcorn from the bowl and popping them in her mouth. 'I see.' As always there was no judgement, only acceptance. He was confessing he'd messed up, and she was listening. When had anyone else ever done that in his family? To fail was to be ordinary, and the Kings were never ordinary.

Solemnly, he said, 'I don't think I've ever been a good boyfriend, to anyone.'

'Except me,' she replied with a loyalty he didn't deserve, and placed her hand on his arm, causing goose-bumps to shiver across his skin.

He shook his head to clear the racing hormones. 'I'd had girlfriends before Savannah. Some of them were obviously just using me for industry contacts. And I let them. I didn't like being on my own, so in a way I used them too. But I never bothered to get to know them, and eventually they got tired of me.'

'How could anyone ever tire of you?'

He wanted to kiss her so badly. But the last time he'd kissed her spontaneously it hadn't gone down well.

Instead, he gave her a sad smile. 'This isn't real, remember?'

She shrugged. 'You've still been the best boyfriend I've ever had.'

'Then I feel sorry for you.' He laughed, but the sound died in his throat when she stiffened. 'I only meant because I'm useless.'

'Most blokes find me... hard work. I want too much, too soon, and I guess I frighten them away. When I met David, I thought I'd met someone just like me. But that was a lie too. I was just too blinded by hope to realise it.'

'Men don't know what they want half the time. We pretend like we do, but we don't have a fucking clue. I was the same with Savannah. Falling into a relationship with her before I even really knew her. I was the one pushing for the next stage, without ever learning who she was.'

What had he ever seen in Savannah? They'd had nothing in common except the business. He could now understand her reluctance about joining him in London; he'd been deciding their next steps as a couple, but he didn't even know why she loved her favourite flower.

'At least now I know where I went wrong. I'll do better next time.' He subtly tried to catch her eye, but she was avoiding his gaze.

Should he ask her out for real?

Would she even say yes? And if she said yes, would he ruin it all over again?

He didn't trust himself, and he knew it was cowardly, but he couldn't bring himself to take the final step. Not until he was certain she wanted the same.

The moment passed with painful awareness on both sides.

Ellie dragged a cushion across her middle like a shield and reached for the remote. 'What shall we watch? I fancy a comedy.'

'Sounds good.' He eased back into the couch, worried that, just like with Savannah, he didn't understand Ellie at all.

Chapter Twenty-Three

They had a nice routine now. Taking it in turns to use the bathroom in the morning, before going downstairs together for breakfast. At night they did the same, both piling their clothes for the next day in the bathroom so there'd be no awkward shifting about in the bedroom.

'My turn,' Ellie said brightly, setting down her cup of coffee, as Alex left the bathroom in nothing more than a pair of colourful swim shorts. Thick chest and strong limbs on full display. She doubted she'd ever get bored of seeing him.

Christ, the man had no idea what his body did to her libido!

Ellie suspected Alex was just going along with her privacy routine to make her feel less awkward about her insecurities. He never seemed bothered about his nakedness, and slept in nothing more than boxers each night, while Ellie had a variety of pyjamas. She supposed that was why he had a small suitcase and she had a giant one.

The rest of the day was spent together, which was never a hardship. They never seemed to tire of each other's company, and even when they ran out of things to say the silence never felt awkward. Alex seemed content to do whatever she suggested, whether it was lie in hammocks or, like today, spend it at the pool with the others.

Did he always agree to her suggestions because he didn't mind, or was it because he wanted to maintain the facade of their relationship? She wasn't sure, because even when they were alone their fake dating felt real. A fact that frightened and excited her wishful heart. Was she going mad? Was it just the fact that they'd been stuck in the suite together, or were they becoming close, like a weird consensual version of Stockholm syndrome? Or was there something genuine beneath their fake happiness?

After all, it was true – she'd never had a better boyfriend than Alex. Never been happier to live a lie. Alex was kind, considerate, fun and the sexiest man she'd ever met. When she was with him, she felt cherished and respected. But of course he had to behave like that in front of his parents. The soft looks he gave her, the time they spent together, it was all for someone else's benefit, and he *was* an actor. This was nothing more than a performance.

Except, sometimes he stared at her with such... yearning. Had she imagined those hot looks he'd given her last night during their movie night? More than once, she'd wondered if he was going to kiss her, and this time they'd been alone in their room, with no audience to speak of. But he'd not kissed her, and surely that was answer enough?

She had to remember his words: *I'll do better next time.* Alex planned to date again, and it wasn't going to be with her. Perhaps their time together had simply awakened his libido – as it had hers. It wasn't that serious, just a powerful calculation of hormones + proximity = desire.

But Ellie wasn't the type to have a casual romance; she could never leave her heart out of the bedroom. If she allowed things to happen between them, it would only end in disaster.

No, she couldn't bear it.

Alex had already admitted he'd never been able to make a proper connection with his previous girlfriends. What on earth made her any different? She'd promised to be his friend, nothing more. The worst thing she could do right now would be to ruin this blissful time by exploding a reality bomb in both their faces.

There was no point hoping for more or acting on their fleeting desires; it would only ruin a beautiful holiday. Better to keep her mouth shut. Then, when the holiday ended and they inevitably drifted apart, she could look back on this friendship with kinder eyes, and, most of all, be grateful that she hadn't humiliated herself.

She'd done that too many times in the past – jumped in with both feet, only to find herself looking like a prize idiot.

Ellie stared down at her polka dot bikini with a frown.
It's now or never.

If she didn't wear it today, she might as well throw it in the bin. Alex was right, the lifestyle of Hollywood starlets wasn't possible for most women.

Ellie and every other plus-size person on the planet knew the truth. Genetics, appetite, medical conditions and mental health were all factors in body shape. No points plan, burpees or calorie deficit could eradicate obesity, because obesity was the symptom of far more complex issues.

The last time she'd worn a bikini was when she went on a girls' holiday with Hannah to Tenerife to celebrate passing their nursing degree, and a lot of years had passed between then and now. A twinge of sadness hit her at that realisation. No wonder Hannah had run off to Australia; they'd not been on a decent holiday in years – all because she'd insisted on saving for the flat. Maybe she should have lived her life, instead of planning for a future that had never been guaranteed.

Still, did living your best life really have to involve wearing a bikini? Many people wore those hideous plastic Crocs; just because you could didn't mean you should.

She thought of Jessica, who'd gone swimming with pigs in a gold lamé bikini and an open see-through kaftan. She'd not given two hoots about the bright young things around her – she'd rocked her older body without a care in the world.

Why shouldn't Ellie? How many years had she spent improving her relationship with her body, only to fall apart at the first sight of a couple of supermodels?

She needed to practise what she preached.

Forget self-doubt.

Embrace her body and love the skin she was in.

She picked the scraps of material up off the bathroom dresser – because of course there was room for a dresser in this huge bathroom. She held the top against her and looked in the mirror. There would be nipple coverage, but not much else.

A quick glance at the bottoms confirmed there wasn't much difference in the quantity of fabric. The ties on both bottoms and top were silly thin strings with silver beads at the ends. She'd picked the style because she could then adjust the tightness of the ties, and hopefully ensure it stayed in place.

'Fuck it!' she whispered, and ripped off the hygiene crotch sticker with one quick whip of her wrist. She stared in horror at the plastic strip, as if she'd just scalped a navy-blue puppy.

Too late now.

Horrified and elated, she quickly put the bikini on, then stepped back as far as she could to view as much of herself in the bathroom mirror as was possible.

What should have been such a small thing – wearing a bikini – felt like a pole vault to Ellie. She may as well have been competing in the Olympics, because putting aside all her fears and doubts was a huge leap of faith. A jump she could only make successfully if she trusted in herself and left the past behind.

She knotted and re-knotted the ties a hundred times, adjusting and then readjusting the straps until she was happy. There was a fine line between securely covering her privates and cutting off her circulation, but she'd managed it.

After a deep breath, she left the safety of the bathroom to face the consequences of her spiteful rebellion.

'Ready to go...' Alex's question died with a strangled cough as she walked into the bedroom. She fought the urge to cover herself.

The look on his face sealed the bikini's fate.

Alex's mouth was slack and his gaze burned with lust. Ellie grinned, a blush of pleasure flaming her cheeks.

'I'm ready.'

Alex quickly turned away from her, gathering up her beach bag and towels as if his life depended on it.

'Great,' he said, clutching the beach bag in front of his lower body in a suspicious way.

—

'Damn, girl...' Caitlyn said with an easy grin as they arrived at the pool. Ellie gave her a cheeky wink. The bikini was now the best purchase of her entire life.

'I brought everyone an inflatable. I thought we could have races,' said Savannah merrily, as she pointed out several massive inflatable lilos in a range of different shapes.

'I want the unicorn!' shouted Holly.

Everyone gathered around to pick out their inflatable, and Liam blew each one up with a whiny electric pump.

Ellie wasn't sure how much her bikini would hold up in a race. 'I think I'm going to read that book you recommended, Savannah. I downloaded it to my Kindle last night.' She made her way over to the loungers and settled down. Alex came to join her.

'You don't want to race on the hot dog?' she asked with mock surprise.

Alex sank leisurely onto the lounger beside hers, his body fully turned towards her. 'I'd rather stay here with you. The view's better.' He lowered his glasses in a coy way, a seductive smile on his lips.

Heat engulfed her from the tips of her toes to the top of her head, igniting a responding lust within her as she stared at the beautiful man in front of her in disbelief. Then again, they weren't alone – perhaps it was all an act?

Unconvinced that he meant it, she said confidently, 'All right, Mr Lothario. Enjoy the view while I enjoy my book.'

She smoothed some deep conditioning treatment through her hair and tied it up in a headscarf. She wanted her hair in tip-top condition for the wedding; there were only a couple of days to go until the big day, and all the sea and sun had frazzled her ends.

After the races ended, everyone flopped back onto the sun loungers for a rest.

Richie came out to the pool and started talking to Alex about a new script he'd just received from a top

Hollywood producer. Alex kept giving her side looks, as if seeking her approval, which she deliberately ignored.

'Listen, this would be a guaranteed blockbuster,' snapped Richie, obviously irritated by Alex's lack of attention.

'But a move back to LA?' Alex glanced at Ellie. 'I'm not sure if that's what I want.'

Why was he looking at her? She had no right to an opinion when it came to his next career move. Of course she wanted him to stay in London, but friendship wasn't enough of a reason for him to stay.

'Things change,' Richie said thoughtfully. 'This would only be for a few months, if that…'

She didn't want to listen to Richie any more. The inflatable unicorn called to her and, after pondering how she'd actually get in it, she realised that she could sit on it from beside the pool and then launch herself like a Viking ship, using only her feet. There was a helpful cup holder and headrest built in, so she could relax for a while before she had to paddle back to the side.

She launched, and was so pleased with herself that she took a sip of her drink and leaned her head back against the headrest with a heavy exhale of satisfaction.

This was the life.

Until, of course, it suddenly wasn't.

Her bikini strap with its dangling beads was digging into her hip, so she wiggled her bum to free it. Unfortunately, that caused a chain reaction of epic proportions.

She tipped to the side uncontrollably with a plastic farty squelch, and held up her drink trying to save it – why that suddenly seemed so important to her, she wasn't entirely sure. But the lilo made a terrible screech and swayed too far. She threw her body back, desperate to stop herself sliding into the water. Icy, sticky cocktail sloshed across her sun-soaked chest, causing her to gasp and rock once again on the infernal lido, this time backwards, her legs flipping up and over her head. And then, with a final 'OH GOD!' she was gone.

Ankles over headscarf. Arse over tit. A full backwards roly-poly, straight into the shockingly cold water, the cocktail still clutched in her hand.

Adding further insult to injury, when she surfaced she was smothered by the lilo now floating above her, white unicorn plastic surrounding her. The artfully placed headscarf was now a wet sloppy mass. She struck out at the unicorn, wishing the glass in her hand was a knife.

The unicorn had the audacity to bounce off the side of the pool and smack her right back in the face, dunking her once again under a wave of plastic and water. There was a chorus of gasps and sniggers from the side of the pool as she resurfaced, but she couldn't quite see clearly through the headscarf's soggy fabric. A messy cloud of orange cocktail and creamy hair conditioner floated in the water around her.

'Are you okay, Ellie?' called Alex, as a mostly horrified cast of Hollywood stars looked on from their sun loungers. Of course, hateful Holly was cackling loudly, but honestly, that wasn't unexpected – she was surprised they weren't all in hysterics.

'I'm fine.' She whipped the unravelling scarf off her head, and half swam, half doggy-paddled to the steps, unable to do either very well with her hands full.

As she strode up the steps, there a sudden and dangerous loosening of her bikini bottoms fabric. She stopped dead and clamped her thighs together as if she were about to wet herself. 'No!'

Jessica and Robert King – Hollywood legends – were directly in front of her on their sun loungers. They leaned forward with obvious concern. 'What's wrong, darling?' drawled Jessica.

The other side of her bikini gave up its hold on her hip and dropped as well, the beads slapping wetly against her thigh.

'NO!' She hunched forward to protect her privates, clutching the glass and scarf to her front. But her bottom? There was nothing she could do – all hope was lost.

The tropical breeze fanned over her wet and naked bum cheeks. Mortified, Ellie wondered what the hell she was going to do. If she bent to put down the glass and scarf, she risked exposing herself in an even more terrible way to the Hollywood stars behind her. If she dropped the glass, it would shatter all over the pool steps and cut her feet to shreds. She wasn't even convinced that, if she dropped the scarf, the glass wouldn't fall too – it was all so tangled together.

She heard Alex shout from behind, 'I'm coming!', followed by a splash. A quick glance behind her shoulder showed that he was cutting through the water like an arrow.

'I hope not,' muttered a deep voice, and there were a couple more stifled sniggers, then a slap followed by an 'Ouch!' and then a 'Behave!'

Was that his parents?

Like an Adonis from the sea Alex emerged dripping wet, golden and beautiful. He strode towards her huddled form and with calm efficiency re-tied the straps on her bikini bottoms.

'Am I dead?' she whispered.

'No.'

'That's a pity.'

He laughed.

'Wow, I thought that flip was funny. But damn, I didn't expect her to put on a show!' cackled Holly from the side, and Ellie's stomach churned.

'Shut it,' hissed Savannah, and then louder she asked, 'Are you okay, Ellie?'

Ellie swallowed the bile rising in her throat and shook her head. 'Not really...' She turned her head to whisper to Alex. 'You know what? I think I'd like to go inside for lunch.'

'No problem.'

'Maybe I should go eat in our room. For the rest of the day or, like, for ever.'

Chapter Twenty-Four

Alex had taken Ellie back to their room, where she could lick her wounds. After changing out of her bikini she'd thrown it in the bathroom bin, but he'd insisted on fishing it out and hanging it up to dry. There was no way he'd let her get rid of something she'd looked so stunning in. He'd managed to convince her by pointing out that she only had to double-knot the ties in future.

'More like triple,' she'd grumbled, flopping on the bed and staring up at the ceiling with a miserable expression.

'I'll go fix you some lunch,' he said, and left quietly, so she could have some time to think. She was obviously embarrassed and shaken up by the lilo accident. Alex made his way downstairs feeling a little guilty that he'd been so turned on by her accidental flashing. But... *Man, she has a great ass.*

All plump and round, something he could really grab hold of in bed. He flushed at his wayward thoughts. Seeing Ellie in her bikini today had really pushed all of his buttons. She was gorgeous already, but put her curvaceous hourglass in a tiny bikini and she became a goddess. He'd spent most of the day staring intently into her face to avoid another erection.

He swallowed the knot in his throat. His attraction to her was getting out of control.

Dare he take it any further? More than once he'd caught her looking at him with similar desire, and they were already good friends. Could the natural progression to a romantic relationship be the perfect solution for both of them?

But she'd told him at the start she wasn't ready to date again, and they'd made a deal. There was only the wedding and then a couple of days left in the Bahamas before they went home. It would be wiser to wait, to see how it changed when they were away from the romance and drama of the islands.

He began to rummage through the fridge helpfully labelled *lunch*. A variety of sandwiches, salads and fruit platters were waiting inside for anyone who wanted them.

'How's Ellie?' asked Savannah, and the slice of watermelon Alex was about to take a bite of stopped inches from his mouth. He turned towards her, uncertain.

To be fair, he reminded himself, Savannah had been nothing but kind to Ellie since she'd arrived. Unfortunately, he couldn't say the same thing about his own manners towards his ex.

'She's fine. A little embarrassed about mooning you all, but she'll get over it. I think she'd like to pretend it never happened – could you tell the others?'

'No problem,' she said firmly. 'Consider it done.'

'Thanks.'

He thought she'd leave then, but she hovered around, watching him as he plated up lunch for him and Ellie. For once, he didn't mind her presence; it didn't prick at his skin as it might have done before. But it was still a little odd. He waited, giving her the space to speak if she wanted to.

'Alex, I'm sorry,' she finally said, her voice hushed and fragile.

'It's fine.'

'But you've never let me explain.' She rushed the words as if a dam had been broken between them and she was scared to miss her opportunity to speak.

'I said, it's fine,' he said with a sigh, grabbing the tray of snacks and heading towards the door. Savannah's fingers grabbed his arm and stalled him.

'It's not fine, and I'm sorry for that. Please don't blame Liam. It was my fault. I told him that things were over between us… and they were, weren't they? We'd not seen each other in over two months, barely talked, and when we did, we didn't have much to say to each other. We were never suited and, well, I presumed you'd moved on and not told me.'

'We never broke up!' snapped Alex, frustrated that they were only now having this conversation. He took a deep breath, before adding more calmly, 'We never even talked about breaking up. You cheated on me, Savannah. And with my *brother* of all people. I know I wasn't the best boyfriend, but I didn't deserve the lies. I didn't deserve all of this only a few months later!' He threw his hands wide as if he could describe the effect all their plans had had on him.

Savannah winced. 'We had to improve the narrative. A wedding was the perfect distraction.'

Narrative… distraction… he'd heard those words before. Were all of their lives smoke and mirrors?

'Do you even want to get married?'

'Of course,' Savannah gasped. 'But what we did—'

'Cheating on me with my brother?'

She nodded, her face pale. She was so delicate and nervous, and he realised he'd never been attracted to her – he'd thought she was the perfect woman, but she wasn't, not for him. For Liam, probably, but not him. 'We didn't want it to be for nothing. We wanted to show you and the rest of the world that we did it for a reason. That we love each other – otherwise, we never would have done what we did.'

'You should have talked to me. Told me you were unhappy. I would have understood. But instead, you started dating Liam behind my back! Whether you thought it was over or not, neither of you spoke to me about it. You just did what *you* wanted, like you always do. Neither of you cared how I felt. Hell, none of this family gives a shit how I feel!'

This was what he'd always burned to say. The betrayal and pain he felt was because of how his family had behaved towards him, not because of any love he'd had for Savannah.

'We never talked much about anything! You were so focused on setting up your play in London, while I was building my career in LA. We never once discussed anything, not properly. We just told each other our separate plans and got on with it,' Savannah said defensively, but then she sighed miserably. 'We were never going to work together. But, you're right. I should have ended it sooner. What I did was unforgivable. But I still want you to know that I'm sorry. Not for falling in love with Liam, but for how I treated you both. Liam is devastated about it. Please, I understand if you can't forgive me, but please talk to him.'

Turning to face her, he said gently, 'I do forgive you, Savannah. We were never right for one another, I see that.

But Liam is my brother. I trusted him to have my back. And now everyone expects me to just get over his betrayal of my trust like it was nothing. I'm going to need time to forgive him. I know I will in the end. Just, don't ever cheat on Liam – that's one thing I could never forgive.'

Her chin wobbled.

'Don't cry!' he pleaded, removing her hand from his arm and giving it a gentle squeeze before releasing it.

She gave him a watery smile. 'I love him so much.'

'Then I'm glad, because he really loves you, too.'

To his surprise, he meant every word.

—

After they'd eaten lunch, Ellie seemed a little brighter about the bikini incident.

'I can't hide away for ever,' she said resolutely, before wincing. 'But maybe not the pool again just yet. Actually, you know what? I'd like to learn to cook something. The meals here are so lush, do you think your chef will give me some recipes?'

'Erm... probably.' He couldn't even remember the name of his parents' current chef.

'That curried lobster dish we had was fantastic. I wonder if I could recreate it with king prawns for Mark's birthday. He'd love it.'

'Doesn't he like lobster?'

Ellie rolled her eyes. 'Our wallets don't like lobster.'

'Ahh, sorry.'

Ellie merely chuckled, unbothered by his stupid statement.

They walked into the kitchen and found the chef humming to herself. She looked to be in her mid-thirties.

Her dark skin contrasted against the crisp chef's whites and her hair was wrapped in a colourful headscarf.

When she noticed them, her brow wrinkled in confusion. 'Is there a problem, Mr King? Lunch today is a buffet in fridge one. I was told no formal dining.'

Alex immediately raised his hand in reassurance. 'No, no problem. Lunch was as delicious as always... Alyssa.'

The tension in her face evaporated and she rewarded him with a grin. He relaxed as well. He hadn't been a hundred per cent sure of her name, but surely she would have corrected him if he'd been wrong?

'Hi, I'm Ellie,' said Ellie, going over to shake Alyssa's hand with the bright and easy manner that he always found so refreshing. 'Your food is *amazing*. I know you're very busy, but I was really hoping you could give me the recipe for that lobster dish we had the other night? My brother would absolutely love it, and I really love trying to cook new dishes. Only if you don't mind?'

'Of course I don't mind.' Alyssa dismissed her worry with a wave of her wrist. 'I'll write it down for you right now. Unless you would rather try making it? I'm preparing the dishes for tonight and Mrs King requested that dish again. She said one of her guests loved it.'

'Guilty as charged.' Ellie held up her hand. 'And I would absolutely love to make it.' She turned to Alex, her eyes shining with enthusiasm. 'You can go do your own thing if you'd prefer?'

Honestly, if she'd asked him to go dumpster-diving naked, he would have said yes. Her smile was like an aphrodisiac, and he could never deny her anything.

'Sounds great.'

'I might even make a fruit punch or cake for your family, just as a little thank-you for having me.'

'You don't need to. But if you'd like to, I'd be happy to help.'

'I'd like to,' she said lightly as she tied back her hair.

He was both bewildered and pleased by the current turn of events. To think he was worried about them being bored on his parents' island. He was never bored with Ellie around.

Chapter Twenty-Five

As Ellie and Alex washed their hands and put on white aprons, Alyssa wrote out the instructions for the curry, explaining a few of the techniques and trickier elements to Ellie as she went and patiently answering her questions. Then she said, 'I'll be grilling on the barbecue outside if you need me. Everything I need for the meal tonight is fridge one. But feel free to take anything you want from the pantry. I'm afraid fridge two and three are for the wedding. Have fun!' Alyssa walked out of the kitchen back door with a cheery wave.

'Ready?' asked Ellie, re-tying her apron.

He looked around the huge kitchen, uncertain of what to do. He'd never been much of a cook. Had never needed to be. There were always personal chefs, nutritionists, restaurants and room service that could do a better job than him, and he'd never felt the inclination to even try.

Before he had a chance to regret his life choices, Ellie had gotten him straight to work preparing the vegetables. As he was trying to peel a slippery onion, he felt her eyes on him.

'What?' he asked.

Her lips were twitching as if she were trying to stop herself from laughing. 'Is that how you peel an onion?'

He rotated the brown vegetable thoughtfully. He'd never peeled an onion before and he hadn't realised there could be a wrong way.

'You're peeling it like a banana.' Ellie stared at him as if he had two heads.

'How do you do it then?'

She nudged him with her hip and he took a step backwards, unsure if he could trust himself around her. She grabbed the sad half-peeled onion from his hands, her fingers gentle yet confident. She'd plaited her hair down her back and he fought a ridiculous urge to stroke the braid as it swung between her shoulder blades. She was so full of vitality and feminine power that she almost dropped him to his knees.

'Like this, you great big idiot.' She giggled, and he watched over her shoulder as she chopped off the tail and top. As the layers were released, they fell like petals across the wooden chopping board. Turning a little, her dark eyes sparkling with humour, she said, 'See.'

'Oh,' he whispered. More in reaction to her close proximity than his ignorance.

Her gaze softened, flicking down to his mouth momentarily. It was an open invitation and he leaned closer, but she took a step away from him, visibly shaking off the tension with a shiver of her shoulders. 'God, you make me... laugh,' she said with a weak chuckle, her cheeks warming to a rosy pink.

A sense of pride radiated from his chest straight down his spine. He shouldn't be so pleased that Ellie found him attractive, but he was. Relieved and glad that he wasn't the only one unsettled by the chemistry between them.

Except, he was beginning to crave more. Every day, little by little, the fire between them burned hotter and brighter, and he wanted more. Despite his fears and the potentially terrible consequences that might follow.

'I'm useless in the kitchen. You need to give me exact instructions.'

'Don't you cook for yourself?'

'Nope, except breakfast. I'll always make you a nice breakfast.' He couldn't resist giving her a cheeky wink. If only to see her flush once more.

When she did his body reacted instinctively and he became light-headed as all the blood rushed to his groin. A physical reaction that he most definitely shouldn't be having while chopping root vegetables.

He tried to refocus on the task at hand, and it didn't take long to prepare the ingredients. Admittedly, Ellie had been the one to do the majority of the work. He'd been too busy staring at the curve of her neck and the strand of hair she'd missed when tying it up, longing to feel the silky softness run through his fingers. Thankfully, she was unaware of how awkwardly he was chopping things into the wrong size or shape. She didn't seem to mind his poor offerings, just helped him with the patience of a saint until all of the ingredients were ready and sat in orderly piles awaiting fire and spice to become something new and wonderful. They just had to throw it together and hope for the best.

'Penny for your thoughts?' asked Ellie softly.

'Nothing really. It reminds me of directing.' He gestured to the piles. 'Everything prepared and ready to go. Endless possibilities. That's what I've always liked about being behind the scenes. My family always wants to be the centre of attention, but there's something magical and beautiful about being the one in charge of bringing it all together.'

If he hadn't been watching her so intently, he would have missed the way her pupils expanded, and her tongue poked out to wet her lips. 'You're such a romantic,' she said huskily.

His heart stuttered in his chest. Everything was better with her. Whether it was house-hunting, swimming with pigs, watching a film or even cooking.

She always made it *better*.

He was already lost to her. There was no denying it, he wanted desperately to kiss her. The only thing holding him back was his fear of losing her friendship.

His hesitation cost him another opportunity, because she shifted a step away and turned on the gas to heat the oil, leaving him bereft and kicking himself.

They cooked up the flour and spices first, Ellie following the instructions while he was in charge of stirring. Although he suspected that was more of a token job, like asking a kid to hold the bowl.

She added the coconut milk, her shoulder brushing against his lightly. 'Just the lobster meat and lemon juice to add now.'

He went to the fridge to grab the ingredients, and handed the fruit to her helplessly, as he wasn't entirely sure how you juiced a lemon and worried it would go the same way as the onion. He was glad of his decision when Ellie grabbed a knife and something that looked like a mini medieval torture device from the kitchen drawer. She was already at home in the kitchen, he noticed; she instinctively knew where everything was, and her confidence astounded him.

She added the last of the ingredients, then balanced a wooden spoon on the lip of the pan. 'To stop it boiling over.'

Alex nodded, although he had no idea how a spoon would manage that. The curry bubbled gently, perfuming the air with delicious spice, and his mouth watered.

'So, that's done. Want to make a rum cake with me?' Ellie asked.

'Sure, sounds fun.' He would have said or done anything to stay by her side.

'We're such geeks!' Ellie grinned.

'Shall we make a punch cocktail for everyone too?' He was better with drinks.

'Why not, sounds fun.'

They set to work on the cake and when they put it in the oven the curry was done, so she turned off the heat.

Unable to resist, Alex took a clean spoon from the drawer and dipped it into the luscious sauce.

Ellie stared at him expectantly as he tasted it.

'I hope Alyssa approves of it for dinner tonight. I'd hate for her to have to make it again.'

Alyssa had an open budget when it came to meal planning, and could probably fly in chocolate from Switzerland if she needed to. But he didn't want to sound any more like a spoilt brat; besides, he was too busy sipping the sauce, and groaning with pleasure. Warm spice, creamy coconut and salty-sweet lobster made the perfect combination.

'Good?'

He rolled his eyes heavenward, steam on his glasses. 'Mmmm-hmmm. Try it,' he said, holding out the rest for her. Easing forward, she placed her lips against the spoon. A dainty sip, followed by a soft sigh of pleasure that made his body stiffen.

'Gorgeous,' she whispered, and he wetted his lips, his mouth suddenly dry.

She'd looked like this after they'd kissed. The urge to press her body against his was almost overwhelming. But this wasn't the time or the place.

Clearing his throat loudly, he busied himself with putting the spoon in the nearby sink, embarrassed by his inability to control himself, as if he were a nervous teenager and not a fully grown man.

Ellie seemed to be fascinated by the label on the rum bottle, and was smoothing her thumb over where the label was peeling. 'Everyone will need a drink after me exposing myself earlier,' she joked sourly.

'Don't say that,' he said firmly. 'I enjoyed you exposing yourself. In fact, I think you should make a habit of it.'

She smacked him on the arm, but at least her smile was genuine and no longer embarrassed. He moved closer, his hip brushing against the curve of her waist.

'Do you think you should talk to your family, about how you feel? It sounds like talking to Savannah earlier helped. Maybe you can explain the real reason I'm here. It might even help them understand what you've been going through.'

He frowned at the sudden change of subject. Why would she bring them up now? Granted he'd told her about his conversation with Savannah, and how it had helped close the door on some of his conflicted feelings, but the last thing he wanted to think about now was his fractured relationship with his family.

It was almost like she wanted to put him off. Remind him of the real reason they were here.

'Perhaps...' he said, unsure if she were testing him or not. 'But after the wedding. I don't want to spoil their wedding day with my issues.'

'Hmm, well, whenever you're ready.' She headed to the pantry, her voice overly bubbly. 'Let's get everything out and start making up our marvellous medicine.'

The strange moment had passed by the time they returned from the pantry, their arms brimming with ingredients. He supposed, if she didn't want a relationship with him, he couldn't blame her. The paparazzi alone would be enough to put any sane woman off him for life.

One of her rules had been that no one would get hurt. Could he guarantee that when his family were constantly in the tabloids and on social media?

She took out a large jug from a cupboard and began chopping fruit.

'How can I help?'

'Chop these.' She handed him an orange. He could definitely chop an orange.

'Into slices…' she added, and made a sawing motion with her hand. He turned the knife above the orange and she gave an approving nod, followed by an indulgent chuckle.

Maybe he'd always act this dumb in the kitchen. He liked making her laugh. Plus, who was he kidding? He *was* dumb in the kitchen.

The juice, rum and bitters were added one splosh at a time. Every now and then she would sample the punch and bite her lip and ask him what he thought it needed. He made suggestions and they tweaked the ingredients. Eventually she was happy with the mix, and he thought it the best cocktail he'd ever tasted in his life.

'You sure it doesn't need more syrup?'

'It's perfect. Just like you,' he said.

She grinned back at him and he felt fifty feet tall.

Alex's family were impressed when they walked into the sun room with their big batch of afternoon punch and rum cake.

'Darling, you made this?' gasped Jessica, her gold bangles clinking delightfully as she gestured at their bounty. He didn't think his mother could have been any more impressed if he'd walked in with a freshly caught shark.

'The cake sank a bit in the middle,' he grumbled. It had been his fault. He'd opened the oven door to check on it, and all of the heat had escaped, causing the cake to flop.

'Only a tiny bit, it's barely noticeable,' said Ellie, as she placed the jug of punch down beside the tray of glasses and cake he'd brought in.

Richie looked up from his phone as they entered, but quickly returned to it with an unimpressed frown. He was always on his phone. Alex was glad he and Ellie had put theirs away. He found life easier without any social media or emails distracting him. The pressures of the real world disappeared when he wasn't being confronted by them constantly.

Ellie had timed the late-afternoon break well. Savannah and Liam were slumped on the sofa looking defeated. Savannah's eyes were red and hollow, as if she were on the verge of tears, but they brightened a little when she saw the afternoon treats. 'Oh, that's so kind of you guys. I could do with a drink after the news we've had.'

'What happened?' asked Ellie, pouring drinks.

Savannah gave a shake of her head and tucked her head closer to Liam's chest, leaving him to answer. 'It looks like the flowers have gotten lost in transit. I've chartered a boat to bring them here as soon as they find them, and our wedding planners are on the case. Don't worry, honey, it's going to be fine.'

Ellie cut a generous slice of cake and handed it to Savannah. 'I'm sure they'll arrive in time. Flowers are not easy to lose. They'll soon turn up.'

Savannah's bottom lip trembled, but she took a deep breath as if to steady herself. 'Yeah, you're probably right.'

Dinner was a little sombre after that, and he couldn't help but wonder what other disasters might befall the Kings between now and the wedding.

Chapter Twenty-Six

The night before the wedding, dinner was served in the formal dining room. A few magnums of Dom Pérignon chilled in a giant gold champagne bath in the corner of the room. The chandeliers sparkled overhead, but in contrast everyone was dressed casually. Alex wore a battered pair of denim shorts and a Hawaiian shirt; Ellie wore white linen trousers and a floral halter-neck. Everyone else was dressed in similar laid-back tropical style, just as Alex had reassured her they would be, putting her nerves to rest.

Well, at least until his dad took one look at her and said, 'Ellie, you're looking a little overdressed this evening.'

Raucous hoots of laughter erupted in the room, and, even though her face was in flames, she forced herself to face it – albeit with a grimace. 'Yes, and hopefully I'll stay that way.'

'Spoilsport,' replied Robert with a grin, causing more chuckles around the room.

'To be fair, your backflip was pretty impressive. I don't know if you could recreate that even if you tried,' said Savannah cheerfully as they all took their seats. Robert and Liam began pouring the champagne and handing it around.

'We thought we'd have a simple supper tonight before the festivities tomorrow. Something light and delicious to prepare our stomachs for tomorrow,' Jessica said as they took their seats.

Ellie had to hide her smile behind her crystal flute. Alex's family were so extra, she doubted they could ever manage a *simple* supper. Alex gave her a subtle wink while he sipped from his own glass, and a moment of understanding passed between them. It was nice that he finally seemed to understand his privilege, and, rather than be embarrassed or ashamed, he now accepted it for what it was. She wondered if it was her influence, but she suspected he would have realised it on his own eventually. He was a good man.

'I just want you all to know how happy we are that you're all here,' continued Jessica, her bottom lip trembling, as she raised her glass. She made a point of looking at Ellie and Alex. 'This wouldn't have been the same without you.'

After a deep steadying breath, she turned to Liam and Savannah. 'We love you both so much and, while things weren't easy at the start of your relationship, I want you to know… We… I…' Her words died and Alex tensed beside her. Ellie's heart lurched for both mother and son.

Alex stood and raised his glass, his voice as clear as a bell. 'Welcome to the family, Savannah. To Liam and Savannah!' A chorus of cheers filled the room, causing the atmosphere of the whole group to sing with joy. Even Richie looked positively thrilled, and she'd never seen him even quirk a lip since she'd met him.

Savannah grabbed Liam's arm and kissed his dazed face while his mother beamed at all of her children proudly, and wiped away her tears with the Versace handkerchief passed to her by her husband. Robert gave Alex an appreciative and approving nod.

Ellie was so proud of him she whispered, 'You did good!' as he sat back down.

Alex shrugged. 'I'm happy for them.'

Leaning closer, she whispered, 'Really?'

She followed his gaze to Liam and Savannah, their faces shining with love and excitement, their hands clasped together.

'Yeah...' He turned towards her, covering her hand with his. 'I am.'

—

The meal passed pleasantly, which was shocking in itself. Alex was laughing and joking with his family, telling them stories about his stay in London, in which she made a surprising number of appearances. There were no awkward silences, no terrible moments. In fact, if Ellie hadn't known about their history, she would have imagined this was like any other family dinner – chandeliers, champagne and Hollywood stars excepted.

Alex was charming, relaxed and... *loved up*.

That was the most disconcerting thing of all: how he behaved. He would hold her hand, or press his cheek gently against her shoulder, and once he even brushed a stray hair away from her face in a loving caress.

It was nice. She couldn't deny that. But a small part of her was still uneasy, as if she were waiting for it all to go wrong. Hadn't she said they should confess the truth? Why would he behave like this, if in a few days' time they'd reveal it as a lie?

Was he trying to make Savannah jealous? But no, he seemed relaxed, easy-going. There was nothing contrived in his behaviour; it seemed *real*.

But it couldn't be. Unless… was she the rebound girl?

She'd played that role in the past too. The comic light-relief girlfriend – *fun-time Ellie*. Until things – she – turned more serious, and they'd run for the hills, turned off by her eager plans. She'd thought laying her heart bare as Alex's friend would protect her against that pain. That he knew how much she wanted to settle down, and would know how cruel it was to raise her hopes.

Because they were friends first, BFFs.

To give herself a moment to think, she excused herself and went to the loo. When she came out a few moments later she was surprised to see Holly waiting outside. There were hundreds of bathrooms in this place. So why was Holly waiting for her?

'You all right?' she asked cheerfully, praying she wasn't about to be ambushed.

Holly's smile turned predatory, and Ellie felt as if she were a mouse that had been caught by a bored cat. 'I knew Alex was a good actor, but you really should go into the business, Ellie.'

Her heart plummeted to her toes. 'What?'

Holly sniggered. 'I thought your relationship was a little too convenient. Alex King falling in love with a fat girl? After all those rumours about him being toxic over Savannah's weight? I mean, I didn't get it at first, but now it's obvious why he picked you. It would have worked too, if Alex could keep it in his pants for five minutes.' She flashed her phone at her, and there was a grainy picture of a bare-chested and sweaty Alex, taking a selfie with a smiling young woman. *MY UNEXPECTED ENCOUNTER WITH ALEX KING*, the picture proclaimed.

Ellie felt sick. His hair was long, like it had been before the Olivier Awards.

'Oh no!' cried Holly with a mocking laugh. 'I thought you were in on it. Don't tell me you thought this was all real?' Her eyes narrowed and Ellie recoiled from the vicious hatred swirling within. 'I happened to catch a look at Richie's emails today, all about how he was going to work the fat angle.'

You're a fool, Ellie. You've proven it, time and time again. He doesn't want you, nobody wants you, screamed the cruel voices inside her head – the ones she'd thought she'd silenced long ago.

Holly wasn't finished with her vitriol. 'All this body-positivity shit makes me sick. People like you are just lazy and gross, always acting like the victim, when you've never had to put in any real work. I've worked for this body! Alex would never have looked twice at someone like you if it wasn't a PR ploy.' She screeched the last few words in a frenzy, and Ellie instantly recognised Holly for who she was.

A woman who believed that beauty was earned through starvation and constant exercise, who sought validation through the eyes of others. That was why she hated Ellie so much; Ellie hadn't earned the right to have a man like Alex on her arm, to have friends and people who liked her.

She's right, sneered the voice in her head.

Ellie struggled to contain her whirling thoughts. Even if her heart and pride were wounded, she wouldn't give Holly the satisfaction of seeing her break. 'I wouldn't believe everything you read, Holly. Isn't that the first rule in the business? I'm sure your sister knows that better than anyone.'

As she walked away a brittle coldness swept through her, and her spine stiffened. She lost track of the conversations at dinner, allowing them to flow around her while she drowned in a sea of her own intrusive thoughts.

By the end of the dinner her emotions were so frayed and ragged she feared she would shatter like glass as she rose from the table. Alex took her elbow as they made their good nights. Ellie did her best to pretend she was happy, that this was *normal*.

They'd been pretending this whole time. She could make it a couple more days.

As soon as the door to their room clicked closed, she shrugged out of his hold and strode towards the bathroom, eager to put some space between them.

'What's wrong?' he asked, his voice sounding genuinely confused.

'I'm fine.'

Alex groaned as if he'd been shot in the gut. 'Now I know I'm in trouble. What did I do?'

She spun on her heel, and was momentarily shocked by how close he was. He loomed over her, not in a threatening way but still dangerous all the same. 'You can stop now. We're alone.'

'Stop what?' he asked with an adorable floppy-haired frown, as he pushed his glasses up with one finger.

'Pretending you like me.'

'I do like you.'

'Fancy me then – or whatever. Just stop it.' She turned to walk away, but the soft touch of his hand on her bicep made her pause.

'But I do.' He pulled her close to him, the power of his intense gaze stealing her breath and causing her heart to pound fiercely.

With a strangled snort, she stared down at their feet. Afraid that if she didn't, she would spill her hopes and silent dreams all over the floor, only to be trampled over and spat on.

'There's a photo of you half naked with a woman on the internet. Your hair was longer, so it must have been before the awards, and I'm pretty sure if a woman was going to brag about a one-night stand she'd do it straight after.'

'What are you talking about?' He walked over to the desk and took out his phone, tapped it quickly, and then shook his head with disbelief.

'Have you read it?' he asked quietly. 'Properly?'

Ellie crossed her arms. 'I didn't have time. Holly was too busy rubbing my face in it!'

Alex sighed, and then read from his phone. '*I was delighted when Alex King took a selfie with me at the gym.*' He raised his phone so that she could see it. 'You can even see the gym equipment in the background. Hardly a one-night stand, and I was texting you at the time – otherwise I would have gotten away from her sooner.'

Ellie swallowed. She'd not paid attention to the rest of the photo, and now she'd made a fool of herself by complaining about it. Defensively, she added, 'Well, no, I didn't see that. But apparently Richie is spinning the "fat angle" of our relationship to fight the rumours of you being toxic about Savannah's weight.'

Alex tossed his phone back on the desk with a heavy thud. 'Fucking Richie and his goddamn narrative!'

'So it's true.'

Alex met her eyes. 'I don't know. But probably, because that's what Richie does. He makes choices that *work* for the press. It's not what I asked him to do, and, if you must know, I've never said anything about Savannah's weight, toxic or otherwise. The press have constantly, because that's what they do.'

She believed him and yet more shame and embarrassment crawled up her neck. 'I'm sorry. I let my insecurities get the better of me.'

He moved closer and stroked his hands down her arms lightly in a soothing gesture. 'Ellie, I haven't lied to you. In fact, I want…' He hesitated, took a deep breath, and then said, 'More.'

Her stomach flipped as if she'd taken a nosedive on a rollercoaster. She dared to peek up at him. His eyes were pinched closed as if he were afraid to look at her, but after a quick inhale he opened them again.

'What do you want?' he asked.

You. There was a horrible moment when she wondered if she'd spoken her confession out loud, but Alex continued to wait for her answer, and her mother's voice filled the silence in her head with a sharp dose of reality. *You have to ask yourself… Why did he pick* you?

'Why?' Why would Alex King want her? Yes, she was a good person. But what did someone like him really see in her?

And there it was, in his easy sweet answer, 'Because you're loyal, kind—'

'Like a friend.' *Or a dog*, she thought bitterly.

'No. I want more than that.' He cleared his throat and rubbed the back of his neck. 'I was hoping you felt the same.'

'I'm not breaking our rules, Alex,' she said firmly, trying to ignore the heartbreaking way his shoulders sagged. 'I'd rather we remained friends. This was all just for show. No one was meant to get hurt.' *Me. I don't want* me *to get hurt*. 'None of this is real. I think you've forgotten that.'

He sucked in a breath as if she'd really punched him in the gut this time. As he tilted his head up at the ceiling his lips thinned, and he spoke without emotion: 'You're right. I'm sorry.'

Ellie couldn't bear it any longer. 'I'm going to get ready for bed.' When she left the bathroom a short time later, the bedroom was empty.

For the first time since their arrival, Alex slept on the sofa.

Chapter Twenty-Seven

Alex didn't sleep well that night, and it wasn't just because he'd crammed his long limbs onto the too-short couch. He'd been thinking over and over about Ellie's jealous reaction to the gym picture. If she really didn't feel anything for him, then why had she been so upset?

Unable to stand staring at the ceiling a moment longer, he dressed in the same clothes as the night before, shoved on his glasses and went downstairs, stopping at one of the many bathrooms along the way to freshen up, as he didn't want to disturb Ellie, who was still asleep.

The staff were hurrying around already, preparing for the big day, and after grabbing a coffee he went out onto the porch to sit on his favourite swing.

His father was there, sitting on one of the deckchairs with his paper and a coffee.

'Hey, Dad,' he said, sitting on the swing and lightly rocking it with his foot. Eddie and his team were grappling with a gazebo frame on the lawn. 'Eddie needs a pay rise.'

'Probably,' said his father, lowering the corner of his paper thoughtfully. 'The florist and wedding planner got in a car accident chasing down the missing flowers. So it's all hands on deck.'

Alex's coffee cup stopped halfway to his mouth. 'What?'

His father barrelled on as if he were actually a sea captain: 'Good news is, they found the flowers.'

'And they're okay?'

'Not sure yet, they weren't stored properly.'

'I meant the florist and the wedding planner.'

'Oh, yeah, they're both fine. Well, reasonably fine. Joseph, the wedding planner, is on his way here with a fractured wrist. But the florist hit her head and has to stay in hospital under supervision until she gets the all-clear – so won't be able to make it at all.'

'Jeez!' Alex finally sipped his coffee. He needed it.

There was a moment of silence as they imagined the chaos and panic that was probably already happening upstairs.

'Ellie's a lovely young woman,' said his dad conversationally, before going back to reading his paper.

Alex stayed silent for a moment, unsure if his father expected a reply. He'd never once complimented any of his girlfriends in the past. Not even Savannah, who he obviously liked a lot. 'Yeah, she's great.' *Shame she wants nothing to do with me after this.*

His father lowered his paper ever so slightly. 'Your mom and I were thinking. Maybe we should come to London. If you do another play there, or if there's still time before the end of your current run. We'd like to see it.'

He almost choked on his second sip of coffee. It was the first time his parents had offered to support him in one of his own endeavours. A welcome surprise, but it still shocked the hell out of him. 'Are you sure? Sales have been slow. It wasn't as much of a success at the start as it should have been.'

'They picked up though, didn't they? Last time I checked, you were sold out every weekend until the end of the run.'

Alex's heart doubled in size as he realised his father had been keeping an eye on his production sales – it meant he cared. 'I was hoping the theatre might offer me a resident director position, but they haven't yet.'

His father lowered his paper further. 'Then approach another theatre, or a film company based in the UK. Sometimes you have to make your own opportunities. Especially when you've got a good reason to stay.'

Alex nodded, unable to speak, choked up by his father's insight and support. He *did* have a good reason to stay in London. But did Ellie have a good reason to be with him?

His father wasn't done. 'And do us a favour... Help Tony with his speech? It sounds like a trailer for one of his action films. Give him some proper stories to add to it.'

Alex chuckled. 'Sure.'

'And go see Liam at some point. I think if anything else goes wrong, he's going to pass out from stress. Poor boy's a bundle of nerves.'

Alex sipped his coffee thoughtfully. 'Does he still get bad stage fright? I would have thought he'd gotten over that by now.'

'You never get over it. Your mum still gets jittery before starting a film even now. You're like me, always calm under pressure. We never worried about your nerves when you were performing.' His dad gave him a pointed look. 'We never thought to worry about you.'

Alex shrugged. 'That's because my heart wasn't in it – acting. But my directing, that's always meant a lot to me – the nerves are different, but they're still there.'

His dad looked sad for a moment, and he put down his paper. 'I'm sorry we weren't there for you. We didn't understand why you wanted to do something so... different.'

Alex smothered a smile. His acting dynasty family would never understand why he preferred a backstage role in a London theatre, compared to the buzz and glare of LA fame. 'It's okay, and I'd love for you to come and see it.'

They were both momentarily distracted by the fiasco of the gazebo on the lawn. Eddie was running across the grass trying to catch the silk cover that had been blown out of someone's hands, and the gazebo was wobbling precariously, as if it were missing some much-needed screws.

His father's voice brought him back to the present. 'You should have been his best man, not Tony. He needs you.'

'I'll do what I can.'

His father reached across and patted his shoulder, a surprisingly gentle look in his eyes. 'Thanks, son.' He slapped his thighs and stood up. 'Right, I think it's about time we helped. Don't you?'

Alex rose from the swing. 'I think so. We don't want Eddie quitting on us now, do we?'

His father's eyes widened with genuine horror. 'God, no!'

—

Alex spent the rest of the morning helping with the decorations, Tony's speech, and calming his brother's nerves.

He'd got dressed for the wedding in his suite, as he needed to put in his contacts, and on the way back he'd caught a glimpse of Ellie running down the corridor to the bridal suite. She didn't see him, as he was at the other end of the corridor and she was distracted. But he was glad to finally see her – after spending so much time together this past week, he was lost without her presence, and he was still worried about how upset she'd been last night.

After this wedding was over, Alex vowed, he would break away from Richie for good. He didn't appreciate how he'd treated Ellie or how he'd managed this entire situation between him, Liam and Savannah. But Richie was also a close friend of his parents, so he'd have to be careful how he ended it. Hopefully, the new London theatre career would mean a natural break from his Hollywood ties.

He'd already taken his father's advice and spent an hour today putting out some feelers to see what other options he might have. Now, as he drank in the sight of Ellie like a man dying of thirst, he knew he'd made the right call. She hurried down the corridor in her heels, her luscious curves bouncing with each step. She wore a Fifties swing dress in emerald green, which brought out the sparkle in her chocolate eyes and the warmth of her olive skin.

She turned and entered the bridal suite, and he saw that half of her hair had been pinned up and the rest was cascading down her backless dress like a waterfall of mahogany.

He'd never wanted a woman more. Her rejection stung, but he would have accepted it if it hadn't been for her jealous reaction to the photo in the gym.

He needed to talk to her properly, clear the air. If she did just want to be friends, then that was fine – even if it hurt like hell. But something about her jealous behaviour and her previous kisses made him wonder.

Perhaps Ellie did want more, but was too afraid to confess it?

After all, she'd been let down so many times in the past that she must be as cautious as he was to put her heart on the line again. In which case, it was up to him to reassure her that he was a safe bet.

Chapter Twenty-Eight

'Oh God, they look awful!' wailed Savannah, a bouquet of wilted flowers drooping sadly from her hands. 'The heat's killed them. I should have listened to you, Joseph. Who plans a tropical wedding with roses and peonies?'

Joseph waved away her concerns with his one good arm – the other was in a sling – while he desperately searched for a local florist on his tablet.

Ellie wasn't sure if it would even be possible this close to the wedding. They were surrounded by private islands, for goodness' sake. The nearest florist would be back on the mainland, surely?

Savannah began to pace, her embroidered dressing gown flapping around her ankles in the breeze from the bedroom balcony. 'You said they wouldn't last the journey from the mainland and you were right. Why don't I ever listen? I ruin everything.' She slumped on the bed and burst into tears. 'I just wanted the same flowers as Mom had on her wedding day,' she sobbed, looking at her sister – who for once seemed to have a heart, and now dropped to her knees beside her to rub her back with a soothing, 'We'll sort it out, don't worry!'

The bouquet slipped from Savannah's hands and dropped on the plush carpet, scattering petals in its final defeat.

'Surely they're not all dead,' said Jessica, sweeping them up with a desperate expression and prodding the stems gently.

'It's too late,' Joseph said, as if he were a doctor delivering bad news. Sweat was dripping down his face, and he swallowed deeply, looking like he might throw up. 'They're all gone. We tried to save them, but it was too late.'

Ellie edged a little closer, and had to admit the same. Although they'd once been beautiful, the car accident and the bad storage in the tropical heat had made them wilt and brown, shedding some of their petals and shrivelling the foliage.

Ellie hadn't meant to intrude, but she'd heard Caitlyn and Keira legging it down the corridor to the bride's room, gasping something about flowers, and that had been enough to get her to follow them. So far, she'd spent most of her morning with the other female members of the wedding party in one room or another. Savannah had insisted she join them for the manicures, pedicures, make-up and general preening. At first, she'd felt awkward, especially after her reality check with Alex last night.

But now, she was glad. The chaos had kept her mind off Alex and the way he'd looked last night – as if she'd broken his heart.

'They'll be fine,' she said, with an authority she didn't feel, bustling in with her Nurse Ellie confidence. She took the bouquet gently from Jessica and examined it more closely. 'I can save them. Bit of sugar water in a cool room for a couple of hours and they'll be perfect.'

'Really?' Savannah looked up with a flicker of hope in her mascara-smudged eyes. Poor thing would need her make-up doing all over again. At least that gave her time to fix the flowers, though, and no bride was ever on time to her own wedding.

'Of course. I grew up in a flower shop. Flowers are hardier than they look.'

That wasn't strictly true. But she wasn't going to worry the bride any more than she needed to. 'And I'm sure I can tidy them up with some flowers from the garden to make them look even more beautiful. After all, it's the blending of two families, right? What better way to express that than with flowers?'

Savannah leapt up from the bed and gripped her in a fierce hug. 'Thank you!'

'No problem.'

Joseph stood, swaying on his Cuban heels and making the sign of the cross. He was probably high on pain medication, because he was looking at her as if she were a saint. 'Are you sure it can be done?'

She gave a quick nod, then turned to the rest of the women and gave them a hard Nurse Ellie stare. 'You sort her out, ladies. And I'll sort these little fellas out.' The bridal party flew into action, relieved to have a mission, and shouting things like, 'Get the snail mask!' and 'Cucumber, we *need* cucumber!'

Alex's mum followed her out, being careful to close the door behind them and talk quietly. 'Are you sure they can be saved? I could still get an order from the mainland arranged. It might mean delaying the wedding by a couple more hours...' She winced, and Ellie knew that couple more hours was going to be more like five.

'Nah, besides, she wants her mother's flowers, and that's understandable. I'll sort them out, if you're sure it's okay to use some of your flowers from the garden to beef it up a bit. I might need the bridesmaid posies too...'

'Of course, take anything you need. I'll get Alex to help you. He needs a distraction today.'

She tried not to bristle at that comment – she knew Jessica meant well, but why did they all think they had to walk on eggshells around Alex? He'd shown them he was over it last night.

Or did they realise something she didn't?

Alex joined her in the kitchen a few minutes later, suave and sophisticated in his cream linen suit. The cut of the jacket made it hang off his broad shoulders perfectly, and the colour brought out his holiday tan. He wasn't wearing his glasses today, and the brightness of his blue eyes was startling, especially when they were focused on her so intently.

The staff were furiously busy preparing for the wedding breakfast, but Alyssa had given her the quiet corner sink to use. She'd taken one look at the flowers and wished her luck.

'Thanks for doing this.' Alex came to stand beside her. 'You must think it strange trying to save a bouquet when there are so many beautiful flowers already here, but Savannah's mother—'

'I get it,' she interrupted him, her attention focused on filling the sink with cool water and sugar syrup. 'She wants to keep her mother's memory alive. Flowers are such a great way of doing that, although I'm probably biased.'

'You knew?' he asked softly, coming to stand beside her. 'You've only known her a week. I didn't know even after months of dating her. I guess that only proves what a shitty boyfriend I can be.'

He sounded so depressed that she dared to meet his eyes. 'We all make mistakes.'

Oh God, what was she saying? That she'd made a mistake by saying they should remain friends? *Had* she made a mistake?

She shook her head. 'Sorry, but I need to concentrate, one minute.' Clearing her throat, she tried to focus on what kind of arrangement she could salvage, before placing all of the flowers – including the bridesmaid posies – gently in the filled sink. 'Right, I'm going to leave these to rest. Let's go pick some flowers. Your mum said to take whatever I needed.'

They stepped out of the kitchen's back doors and began to walk the gardens, dodging the guests and picking a myriad of flowers and foliage. Ellie kept cutting the flowers until Alex's arms were full and he twitched his nose with a smile, the variety of scents wrapping them in a bubble of heady perfume.

When they returned to the kitchen the bouquet looked a little better, but still beaten up and sad. *How on earth am I going to assemble them into any kind of order?* She took a deep breath and tried to channel her nanna and mum's green fingers and remember all of their advice and wisdom over the years.

'How can I help?' Alex asked.

'Cut these to there, and for these strip the leaves from here.'

He nodded and followed her instructions to the letter. Thankfully, he seemed to understand the value of not ballsing up a bride's bouquet as much as she did.

She began to work, pulling apart the old bouquet and rearranging the stems. A waterfall of flowers with the roses and peonies in the centre might work.

'I bet Savannah is thanking her lucky stars that I brought you here,' said Alex, gesturing towards the growing bouquet in her hand. 'It already looks a hundred times better.'

Ellie laughed as she plucked out some of the dead leaves. 'We'll see, she might kill me when she sees it. It's been a while since I did an arrangement as big as this.'

At the end she smiled triumphantly, and, honestly, she had the right to. She'd done a spectacular job – even if she did think so herself.

The majority of the peonies and roses were gathered in the heart-shaped centre, fanned by large tropical leaves that only highlighted the contrasting delicate pinks in the centre. To add more colour, and balance out the green, she'd added a waterfall of lush, vibrant pink-toned flowers, and dotted a few around the outer leaves of the heart to draw it all together.

'A bit of sugar water. Some bougainvillea, some hibiscus, a few leaves… and voila, a bridal bouquet fit for a Hollywood star. Plus, I've enough to bulk up the bridesmaids' posies – I had to steal some of the roses from theirs for the bride.' She turned to Alex, the bouquet clutched to her chest as she fluttered her lashes dramatically. 'How does it look?'

He didn't react as she'd thought he would, just looked at her with a yearning she'd have thought impossible a few weeks ago. 'Beautiful,' he said. 'Just like you.'

Heat flooded her face, and she turned away and inspected the bouquet with a more critical eye. 'Well, it's nothing compared to what my mum or nanna could have made. I haven't been able to save all of the flowers, but I've made sure the best roses and peonies take centre stage in the bridal bouquet. I'm not sure how long they'll last though.' She picked up a can of hairspray from the counter and began liberally spraying the flowers. 'This will help. But they'll need to get as many photos done as quickly as possible while they still look good. Can you tell the photographer, and ask for a bride ETA?'

'You're amazing, you know that, right?'

She swallowed, unsure of what to say or if she could cope with any more emotional drama right now. She gave a dismissive shrug. 'Fake it until you make it, right? My motto in life.'

A muscle in his jaw flexed and his brows knitted together with displeasure. 'You're wrong.'

'What?' The vehemence in his voice startled her.

'You're wrong. You're not fake. You're beautiful, resourceful, funny and most of all kind. You don't need to pretend you're fine when you're not – you can just be yourself. I know who you are, and you're perfect.'

Wobbling on her heel, she took a step back, and he wrapped an arm around her waist to steady her. She opened her mouth to speak, but a male shriek from the doorway startled them.

Joseph and Richie stood in the doorway. Well, Joseph mainly, as Richie appeared to be passing through on his way to the garden, phone in hand as always.

'LADY! You are an *artist*. Thank you, you beautiful angel! Thank you!' Joseph exclaimed in a rapid fire of gasps and screams. 'Come, you gorgeous, beautiful, talented lady! Come, come!'

'Oh... okay,' said Ellie, shaking her head as if awakening from a dream. The wedding planner rushed her out of the room as if she were the president, but she glanced back at Alex before she left. 'We'll talk later, okay? Like, hold that thought.'

Alex grinned, obvious relief relaxing the tension in his shoulders, and he gave her a salute. 'I sure will!'

The wedding planner pulled her out of the kitchen, his heels clattering on the marble like castanets as he continued shouting, 'Come, you beautiful lady! Come! Show them how magnificent you are!'

The wedding ceremony decorations were beautiful, and pink... very pink. But Ellie admired Savannah's commitment to the theme.

Liam waited beneath a baby-pink gazebo on the pristine beach. As well as the pink silk draped over it to create shade, the wedding arch was also decorated with more hastily draped garden foliage and tropical flowers. Ellie was relieved and proud that they looked so good. After sorting out the bouquets, Joseph had quickly set her to work on the rest of the flower arrangements. Again, most of the delicate peonies and roses hadn't survived transport, but there were just enough to keep the bride's original theme alive.

She had to admire Joseph's ingenuity; he'd called the new theme *fusion* and it actually worked. When the guests arrived on the beach, they all commented on the unique aesthetic and stunning arch and Joseph answered with the wisdom of a prophet, '*Fusion*, darling.'

The wedding planner, who'd she'd become quite friendly with over the course of the morning – probably because he still called her *beautiful lady* every five minutes in his gorgeous Bahamian accent – had whispered to her, 'Use enough swagger and people will believe anything!'

Didn't she know it. Her whole relationship with Alex was based on her ability to swagger, and to lie. And not just to Alex's family; she was beginning to lie to herself, beginning to think there might be a future for herself and Alex if only she had the courage to grab it.

She was on dangerous ground, but she wasn't sure whether it was better to run and hide, or give in and allow herself to fall.

She peeked at Alex, sitting beside her on the front row of the white-draped chairs with pink bows. The tropical breeze lightly fluttered through his dark hair, and as if sensing her looking, he turned towards her and smiled softly.

They stared at each other quietly, the sound of the ocean the only whisper in the space between them.

She couldn't bear it. Had he really meant what he'd said earlier? That she was perfect?

'Liam looks nervous,' she said, for want of anything better to say.

Alex glanced at Liam, who thankfully did look nervous – he kept adjusting and readjusting the peony on his white linen suit.

'He's going to destroy it if he carries on fiddling with it,' she whispered.

To her surprise, Alex stood up, walked over to his brother and rested both palms on his shoulders. He then murmured something quietly to him. She couldn't hear what he was saying, but by Liam's immediately relaxed shoulders and deep inhale of calming breath she knew he'd said the right thing, whatever it was.

It was so damn sweet.

A band of twelve musicians began to play a romantic song that she instantly recognised as a slowed-down version of Liam's first Oscar-winning action film's theme song. And… was that Hans Zimmer conducting them?

Considering it had been an action film, the instrumental version was surprisingly poignant. The tender notes swept around them, building up the anticipation of the bride's arrival, until the wedding guests were swaying to the melody.

At the celebrant's gesture, the guests rose in their seats. With a brotherly slap to Liam's bicep, Alex returned to Ellie's side.

They all turned to watch the bridal party emerge from the garden path. Caitlyn and Keira catwalked down the aisle with the sure-footed gait of women who weren't strangers to modelling.

Then came Holly in a frothy dress that was meant to resemble the head of a peony flower, which on anyone other than Holly would have looked like they'd fallen into a candyfloss machine. She was carrying the surprise gift from Liam to his bride, which had arrived with another guest that morning: a fluffy Pomeranian puppy, its fur dyed baby pink. Ellie couldn't help but 'awww' with the rest of the guests as it wagged its tail cheerfully in Holly's arms. Holly didn't seem entirely pleased about carrying the excited bundle of fur, especially when its collar kept blinding her with the sun's reflection. Unlike the dog, the collar had arrived with its own security guard – according to Joseph – as it was made with real diamonds.

Jesus, they're so extra. She couldn't help but smile about it. Savannah and Liam were as mad as a box of frogs, but they were also loving and sweet. She could only admire and respect their honest and open devotion to one another.

Ellie had to subtly brush away a tear as Savannah walked down the aisle. A modern-day princess, the ivory column dress fitted tightly over her slim frame. It wasn't as fussy as the bridesmaid dresses, or even the dress she'd worn at the rehearsal dinner. This gown oozed class and sophistication. A fine layer of lace and crystals embellished the simple low v-neck cut of the gown. Ellie gave her an excited wave as she passed, and Savannah responded with an elegant wave of her own.

Then the sadness hit her hard, as she realised Savannah had walked down the aisle alone. Ellie was glad more than ever that she'd helped with her bouquet, so Savannah wouldn't feel so alone as she walked to meet her husband-to-be, carrying the memory of her mother with her. The waterproof mascara was working overtime as she dabbed at her eyes for the second time.

The ceremony, like most non-religious weddings, was surprisingly short. The couple had written their own vows, which were more than a little bit soppy. But somehow, on a beautiful beach in the Bahamas, the words fitted perfectly. By the time they walked back towards the house hand in hand, their puppy yapping on its lead in front of them, everyone was wiping away tears, and Ellie was grateful for the pocket handkerchief Alex had pressed into her palm.

'Are you okay?' Alex chuckled as he stood and offered her his arm.

She nodded, not trusting herself to speak. Weddings usually set her off; the combination of love, families and her own hopes always made her emotional. She didn't have a chance in hell at a super-romantic wedding like this.

They walked back to the garden, where the tables and chef stations were set up a lot like the rehearsal dinner barbecue, Savannah and Liam having chosen a more casual set-up over a formal sit-down dinner. Instead of a hog roast, though, it was steak, lobster and delicious vegan kebabs on the menu tonight. The decorations and entertainment were also more formal and elegant, fairy lights glittered in the trees, and the silver service gleamed in the light of the large candelabras placed on each table.

Music from the band played from the beach – although this time they weren't being led by a famous composer.

'You okay now?' asked Alex, as they took their seats at the top table.

'I'm not sure, am I? Has my mascara run? I should probably go up to the room to fix it.' She offered up her face for his inspection.

To her surprise, he ran a finger lightly over her cheek. 'Perfect.'

Her heart stuttered and then ran full pelt. Confused and disorientated, she tried to focus on reality and pull her head out of the clouds. The day had been a rollercoaster of emotions and drama, but back at home in London this fairytale would inevitably end, and Alex would realise that Ellie didn't suit this life, or him. 'Don't say that. I'm far from perfect.'

His father began tapping a knife against a champagne flute to announce the upcoming speeches, but Alex didn't look away.

'You are to me,' he said, and then turned to watch his father give his speech.

'We always wanted a big *Waltons*-style family, but it wasn't meant to be.' Robert paused to look lovingly at his wife, who gave a sad smile in return. 'However, we have always considered ourselves very lucky and grateful to have Liam and Alex. They have both exceeded our hopes for them, and have turned into fine young men who we are extremely proud of. Both in their careers and in their private lives. And now, we are so pleased to welcome Savannah officially into our family, who we already know and love as a daughter. But I'm sure she won't be our only daughter for long...' Everyone's eyes flickered to Ellie, and she wondered if she'd spontaneously combust with embarrassment.

'Is no one going to mention me? I'm actually family, after all,' grumbled Holly, and Savannah shot her a glare.

Robert continued smoothly, as if he hadn't heard her. 'And, of course, we'd also happily adopt Holly and Tony, who've both done amazing jobs as maid of honour and best man. So now, we are delighted to say we have the big family we always wanted. Dreams can come true and we wish you all the happiness and joy for the future. May your dreams, like ours, come true, even if it's not in the way you first imagined. We love you. Everyone, please raise a glass... to Liam and Savannah King!'

'Liam and Savannah!' repeated everyone with a cheer.

Liam gave his dad a hug, and then took the mic for his own speech. 'Thanks, Dad. We love you too. *So*, you may have noticed a running theme with our wedding, the peonies and roses hidden amongst all the beautiful decorations. Earlier today we thought all was lost, but luckily we were saved in the end, by one person's ingenuity – thank you, Ellie.' She gave him a dismissive wave, hoping he'd quickly move on. 'Well, *my wife and I*...' – Liam paused at the rapturous applause – 'thank you from the bottom of our hearts. These flowers mean the world to us. They were Savannah's mom's favourites. Savannah once told me that it would always feel a little wrong to get married without her here.' Liam turned to his bride, who looked to be on the verge of tears. 'I hope you'll agree with me when I say that I believe she *is* with us today. And I'm certain that she loves you, is proud of you, and thinks you are the most beautiful bride she's ever seen, because that's how I feel. Savannah, I love you with all my heart. The only thing that could ever be wrong for me would be to be without you.'

Savannah, unable to control her emotions a moment longer, sobbed prettily, clutching her little puppy to her chest and staring up at Liam with wide adoring eyes.

'Oh man, right in the feels,' whispered Ellie, wiping away her own fresh tears.

Next was a joint speech from Holly and Tony, which was jam-packed with light but embarrassing stories about Liam and Savannah, right from childhood up until last week – she suspected Alex might have helped Tony with some of them. At the end, everyone was smiling, and stood up to cheer the happy couple with raised champagne flutes.

Alex's mum turned to Ellie and gave her a warm smile of approval that she would take to her grave. 'I've been meaning to say all day, I love your dress, Ellie. Who's the designer?'

'Ellie. She made it herself – as you saw with the flowers, she's a natural artist,' said Alex, draping his arm around her in a way that was both possessive and proud. A thrill of excitement ran up and down her spine on a wave of heated longing.

'Only because I struggle to find clothes that suit my figure,' she explained, already hating herself for saying it, because it suggested she was some kind of monster. But she was damned if Holly would be the one to point it out first, which she was about to do going by the way she opened her sour-puss mouth.

'Well, you're fantastic! You should go into fashion. There's a lot of curvy actresses coming into the industry – a change I wholeheartedly agree with. But they really struggle to find red carpet dresses for the Oscars and Golden Globes. You'd make a killing with your designs.'

Ellie laughed. 'I'm a nurse, not a designer.'

Jessica gave her a firm look that suggested she never gave empty flattery. 'Believe me, you can be whatever you want to be. I'm not saying it isn't hard work, but no dream is impossible. And who says you can't be both?'

NHS staff shortages, lack of money, lack of sleep? But Ellie didn't bother Jessica with those mundane hurdles. Instead, she gave her an appreciative nod. 'Thank you.' She meant it, because it was nice to have Alex's mum believe in her. When had her own mum believed in or encouraged her?

A quick glance at Alex showed he agreed with his mother. Ellie had always faked her own confidence, choosing positivity over negativity, but there had been limits. Not only with work but in her personal life too. A glass ceiling that she was too scared to smash through, in case she plummeted to the bottom and was forced to start again.

Dare she aim higher, hope for the impossible?

Chapter Twenty-Nine

Twilight began to descend around them like an indigo curtain, while in contrast the party atmosphere rose considerably with the arrival of a swing band. The bride and groom had their first dance, and cut their pink tiered cake, which was taller than Hannah – Ellie snapped some photos and sent them to her.

Everyone ate and drank, the tables mixing and mingling with an easy and exuberant mood that made Ellie drunk with possibility. Here, everyone was equal; there were no self-centred divas – she imagined the Kings would refuse to be close friends with anyone like that anyway. Instead, a world-renowned singer was prodded to sing a ballad, while an Oscar-winning actor played the guitar. The crowd and singer laughed good-naturedly when he missed a chord.

'Shall we go for a walk?' Alex asked huskily and a tingle of awareness ran down her spine as he offered her his hand. He was incredibly dashing when he wanted to be.

Ellie could do with a change of scene. The party was lovely, but also a little overwhelming with so many famous faces. She was sure she'd bumped into a rock star coming out of the loo just now.

They walked down to the beach, the water glistening in the moonlight. The lapping of the waves grew louder as the sounds of the party faded. Alex's warm hand wrapped around hers, his thumb idly stroking her skin in a loving caress.

Ellie sighed, wondering how she'd feel when she returned to the city noise of car horns, millions of people and trains.

The island was beautiful, but also unreal. Like she was living in a dream that would inevitably end. She didn't want it to – not because she didn't want to leave this island; she was resigned to that fate. Besides, her colleagues and patients needed her, her family needed her.

Most of all, she didn't want to lose Alex. Her chest became tight when she thought of life without him, even as she worried if she could keep up with this facade. Reality and dreams were blurring into one, and she was afraid she would lose herself.

Alex's behaviour over the last couple of days – especially in front of his family – had made it seem like his feelings were, at least partially, real. Ellie was worried that he was beginning to believe his own lies – after all, he'd said that was how he'd fallen into the relationship with Savannah.

She sank down to sit on the sand. 'This has been the best holiday of my life. I'm going to be so sad when it's over.'

Alex plopped down next to her. 'It doesn't have to end.'

'All holidays end. You can't hide from the real world for ever.'

'This *is* my real world. It could be yours too, if you wanted it to be.' His hand reached for hers, the brush of his thumb a seductive promise.

The moon was so bright and so low she wondered if she could reach out and take it from the sky as a memento of this whole experience. She allowed herself the pleasure of staring at Alex. Admiring his black hair shifting in the gentle breeze like a raven's feathers, she reached out and stroked it away from his eyes. She couldn't decide if she preferred him wearing contacts like today, or with glasses. His face turned to hers and she smiled. She didn't want the moon, she wanted Alex, and both seemed within her grasp in this magical moment.

She leaned forward and pressed her cool lips to his heated mouth. A reckless question as well as a kiss.

'You're breaking your own rules, Ellie.'

'Should I stop?'

'God, no, I couldn't bear it.' His hands swept into her hair as he pushed against her, rocking her onto her back into the warm sand beneath. His mouth, hips and chest pressed against hers in a strength of desire that she found thrilling and she returned his passion wholeheartedly.

Drunk on Alex's kiss, she didn't hear the commotion to the side until he pulled away from her. Bleary-eyed, she followed his gaze to the rest of the guests making their way to the specially chartered speedboat that would be taking Savannah and Liam to their honeymoon island.

'Should we go and say goodbye?' asked Ellie, her breath ragged.

His lips glistened in the moonlight, wet from their kiss. 'They won't miss us.' With a quick glance to the intruding guests, Alex took her hand, pulled her to her feet and led her deeper into the shadows of the gardens towards the house. A bird flew between the foliage, causing Ellie to jump with fright, scared it might be one of the guests stumbling upon them.

Which was ridiculous – they'd been (fake*)* dating this whole time. Who would care if they found them walking alone in the gardens? Still, Ellie couldn't shake the fear that he was secretly embarrassed by her, wanted to hide her away, like some guilty pleasure.

A cool breeze made her shiver and she stopped, letting go of his hand. 'Maybe this is a mistake… The wedding, the romantic setting, maybe we're getting a bit too carried away.' She wrapped her arms around herself. The ferns that looked so beautiful in the light of day were suddenly black serrated blades in the dark, poised to strike at any moment.

He shifted towards her, and she swallowed the sudden dryness in her throat. She stepped backwards, but he kept coming. His arms came up, caging her against a palm tree as he pressed his body into hers, surrounding her with his heat, his broad shoulders blocking out the lights of the stars and the party. Cautious thoughts scattered like half-remembered dreams into the tropical night.

'There's nothing wrong with romance,' he whispered against her lips, his voice rough and deep. 'I've been going crazy for days wanting you, needing you. Thinking about every way I want to make love to you.'

He kissed her deeply and she clung to him as if he were her anchor to this world. His hands gripped her hips as he pressed himself against her. The hard length of his erection rubbed against her inner thighs and she moaned into his mouth, desperate for more. More of his passion, his weight, his words. More of everything. What did it matter if it didn't last? At least she would have these memories to treasure.

'Well, I am on holiday,' she managed to gasp out between kisses. It was a happy surrender though; she had never craved anything more in her life than Alex's sexy voice and drugging kisses. With dizzying speed, he threw off his linen jacket, as if he couldn't bear the fabric separating them.

She took a step back, breathless, her naked back pressing against the rough trunk of the palm swooping above their heads.

'I've wanted to do this for so long,' he groaned, his breath coming out in hot pants against her neck as she tugged at his trousers and his hands traced up her thighs.

Their fingers fumbled in the darkness, pulling at buttons and ties, impatient for heated flesh to meet with heated flesh. A small, vulnerable part of Ellie was grateful for the darkness; she could allow herself to drown in the sensation of Alex's body claiming hers without fear.

The clouds rolled away from the moon and a pool of silvery light opened around them. She had one curvaceous thigh wrapped around his waist, her skirt indecently hitched around her hips and her halter-neck undone, exposing the globes of her breasts.

Had the moon shone a light on her faults to punish her for daring to reach for the stars? Flinching, she pushed away from him, covering her breasts with both arms, and turned away from him. The same burning humiliation she'd felt after the lido incident the other day rushed through her. Fear churned with self-doubt, becoming something darker and crueller. He'd said security was always watching, were they watching her now, laughing at her?

'Don't.' Alex's voice was gruff, raw. Carefully, he pulled her arms away. 'Don't hide yourself from me. You look gorgeous in your dress. You're beautiful.'

'Are there security cameras here?'

'No, not here,' he reassured her.

Unwrapping her slowly, he eased the dress down her body and over her hips to puddle on the ground.

She fought the urge to suck in her belly or make a joke. A part of her needed to know if he really meant what he said. He took a step closer and stared at her hard. Black dilated pupils shone in the moonlight, and his breathing was ragged.

A male huff of pleasure was enough to get her pulse back into racing gear. 'Gorgeous... you look even better out of your dress. Christ, that was worth the wait.'

One hand went to the curve of her waist, the other tentatively reached and then cupped one large breast. His thumb smoothed over the tight bud of her nipple and she bit her bottom lip to stop herself crying out from the shuddering pleasure of it.

She'd never wanted a man so badly in her life.

Heat radiated from the palm of his hand as it lowered from the dip of her waist to the flare of her hip. His thumb snagged under the band of her lace knickers and he tested the elastic with a light tug.

'You're so fucking sexy,' he growled against her lips, gloriously carnal and filling her with powerful feminine confidence.

He pulled her close, reaching around to her bottom and squeezing it gently. The hard jut of his erection pressed against her groin and she moaned. She adjusted her legs slightly to press him closer to her core, but wobbled precariously. Belatedly, she realised she was still wearing her heels, her knickers and nothing else.

Despite the unsteadiness of her heels, she knew she was safe in Alex's arms. Cupping the sides of his face, she pulled him down towards her for a brief, passionate kiss that made her toes curl. Panting, she pushed him gently away. 'Your turn. I want to see your body now,' she said, her voice a husky promise.

She took her time unbuttoning his shirt, delighting in how his tense muscles twitched with every brush of her fingers, how his heart thundered beneath her touch and a moan slipped between his lips when she grazed his nipple. Once she was done, she trailed her palms up his torso, from the dusting of rough hair in the centre of his stomach up to the broad plates of his chest.

Her core clenched with arousal. He wanted her as much as she wanted him, and that was the greatest aphrodisiac of all time. She pushed the shirt over the peaks of his wide shoulders and the fabric slumped down in heavy folds to gather at his wrists. 'You're so lush,' she sighed, her fingers scoring lightly down his chest.

Alex chuckled, the sounds strained, and there was a rustling sound as he shook off the sleeves of his shirt. 'Lie down. I can't wait any longer.'

An irrational blush burned her cheeks. This wasn't the first time she'd been with a man. This wasn't even her first attempt at casual sex; not that she would describe this as casual – spontaneous, yes, but not casual. Sex had never been casual for her, and that was part of the problem. But she'd never felt so vulnerable or so excited in her life, and she knew that, if she lay down and surrendered to the moment, there would be no going back.

As she lay down on his clothes, she kicked off her heels. Alex lowered himself over her, taking the brunt of his weight on his thick arms. Her hands glided up them, revelling in the knots and cords of his muscles.

Alex wasn't just muscular, he was solid, stocky, huge. The fine dusting of his dark body hair tickled her skin and, unable to resist, she buried her nose in the gorgeous sandalwood smell of him, licked and mouthed at his skin, desperate to feel him on her tongue.

One of his hands smoothed down her leg, and began to stroke behind her knee, and she gasped in surprise as goosebumps sizzled up her thigh.

Who would have thought that was an erogenous zone?

Or maybe it was simply because she was with Alex, and her entire body was naturally sensitive to his touch. She squirmed beneath him and with a harsh groan he pressed his hips against hers and silenced her movements with the weight of his desire. She moaned in pleasure, her body having just enough common sense left to spread her legs wider in welcome.

Alex cursed under his breath and began kissing her with furious need, his lips sweeping down her neck and latching onto her nipple. After he'd sucked it into a stiff peak, he moved his dark head to bathe the other nipple in similar affection. Ellie was lost in sensation as she ran her hands through his hair and rubbed her aching body against the ridge of him with longing.

'More,' she whispered in a daze.

His head dipped lower and she bit her lip in anticipation. Strong rough fingers wrapped around the black lace of her underwear and pulled. She raised her hips to help him, not caring any more about her stupid hangups and insecurities. Only that she needed whatever intense pleasure he could give her.

The lace scratched lightly down her thighs and calves until he was able to slip off the scrap of fabric and toss it aside. His blue eyes caught in the moonlight, a smug smile on his handsome face.

He lowered his head to her leg, kissing his way to that special spot he'd found behind her knee, and she jerked a little at the overwhelming sensitivity of his tongue as it swirled over her skin. When she was panting with needy moans, he moved higher, licking and teasing the inside of her thigh until she thought she couldn't take it any more.

'Please,' she uttered on a guttural moan.

He took pity on her, moving his head and shoulders between her thighs. Easing her legs wider with a nudge of his arms, she complied eagerly and draped her thick thighs over his equally thick shoulders. He laved his tongue against her clitoris with eager abandon, her hips pressing against him with each swirl of his mouth.

She was so ready for him she cried out in pleasure the first time his tongue dipped inside her. He gave a satisfied chuckle and kept moving with an enthusiasm she found liberating.

In only a handful of moments, she was riding wave after shattering wave of climax. Shocked by the force of her release, she cried out again, her hand gripping his hair and tugging him closer as the tension within her burst into a thousand falling stars behind her eyes.

Afterwards, she was nothing more than a boneless pool of satisfaction, her skin still tingling and her heart still racing.

Never had it been like this.

Never.

Chapter Thirty

Alex grinned at Ellie, so sexy in the moonlight, her lush figure all relaxed and thoroughly satisfied, like a cat stretching in front of the fire.

As if she'd gifted him an Academy Award in lovemaking, her responses had been so passionate and raw that they'd driven him to the edge of madness. But he was determined to do right by her, to give her as much pleasure as he could before he took his own. He wondered if he could make her come again. He hoped so.

He slipped off his trousers and boxer shorts, then took out the packet he'd conveniently stashed in his wallet and opened it carefully.

'An Eddie special?' Ellie commented, her voice husky and breathless.

He paused. 'Yes. Are you okay for... more?'

'*God yes.*'

He grinned at her reply and quickly rolled the condom down his cock. When he looked up, Ellie was staring at him with slack-jawed admiration, and a wave of dizzying excitement rushed down his body until he was aching beneath her hot gaze.

She was going to be the death of him... but what a way to go.

Ellie raised herself up onto her elbows, her large breasts distracting him from her pretty face as they bobbed with her movement. Her velvet lips pressed against his own and he gladly fell back into the spiralling passion that so readily built between them. With a groan he moved forward, needing her softness against his hardness. The need to possess her and thrust himself inside her was almost overwhelming.

He wanted her wrapped around him, whimpering his name and clawing his back as they made love. He wanted her waking up next to him every day, and reaching for him at night.

He wanted all of this and more.

Pinning her down, he rained kisses on her face, breasts and hips. His fingers brushed against her clitoris and came away slick with wetness. He positioned her legs and hips just how he wanted them, then grasped himself and eased into her soft body, gritting his teeth to stop from coming too soon. She welcomed him with a moan, and it was all the permission he needed to press into her hard and take what she offered. Her hips rocked against his, seeking release, and he tempered his thrusts in the hope of wringing out more pleasure from her body. When she began to tighten around him, their bodies were so slick with sweat and desire that they slid against one another easily. A familiar heat began to build within him and he plunged harder, using her moans and cries as a road map to their climax.

She stiffened, arching against him like a bow, her inner muscles spasming around his cock. Relieved and elated, he gathered her in his arms and joined her, grinding wildly until with a shuddering groan he allowed his own orgasm to rip through him.

He collapsed into her embrace and nuzzled into her soft hair, breathing in the musky, salty scent of her skin and perfume. His fingers unconsciously tightened on her, unwilling to let go of her for the moment.

'This is the *best* holiday,' she teased softly, but her words caused the sweat on his skin to chill, and he shivered as he lifted his weight onto his arms and off her.

He didn't want it to be just a holiday.

Was that what she wanted – for it to be a casual fling, forgotten about in a few short days, once their tans had worn off? He sat up, feeling like a prize idiot. He'd been so certain this time that Ellie was the right woman for him, that she had also decided she wanted more. But was that a mistake, wishful thinking? Had he opened his heart to yet more betrayal and disappointment?

'It'll be a shame to get back to normality,' he said, testing her response. Hoping that she'd… what? Say that she wanted him for ever?

Pathetic.

'Your life isn't normal, Alex. I don't think it could ever be normal.' Her voice was quiet, sad almost, but he couldn't see her expression fully in the darkness.

Was it his lifestyle she didn't want? The constant running from paparazzi, the shallow luxury, and lack of privacy. Where Eddies were all over your personal belongings and sexual health. Where blatant lies were snowballed into gossip and intrigue.

Who would want his life? He didn't.

For once, he'd allowed a woman to see the real him, pulled out his trust issues and opened his heart fully, shown her the man beneath all the gloss and the bullshit. But he still wasn't enough.

He dressed and helped Ellie back into her clothes, ignoring the sensation that his heart was splintering inside his chest. They stumbled back to the house and he went into their bathroom to dispose of the condom.

After washing his hands, he headed back into the bedroom, and snuggled into Ellie's warmth, throwing a blanket over the pair of them.

'I want more than just a holiday,' he whispered, but he could tell by her soft, shallow breaths that she was already asleep. He resolved to talk fully with her tomorrow. He didn't want a fling; he wanted Ellie.

All of her, for ever.

He knew she was afraid of being hurt again, and that he couldn't defend her from the press, no matter how much he wanted to. But surely, as long as they were together, everything would be fine.

Unable to quiet his thoughts, he crept from the bed and went into the lounge area to check his phone. There were no new notifications in his alert folder. But there was one particular email that surprised him, and he immediately clicked on it. Legendary actress Francesca Tatiana was interested in working with him – and it was an offer he couldn't refuse.

Chapter Thirty-One

Ellie woke up with Alex's beautiful face inches away from hers.

Had she really had sex with him last night? By the look of the naked Adonis next to her, she'd have to say that, *yes*, she had. Without a shadow of a doubt, Ellie Jones had had sex with Alex King last night, and it had been fantastic!

Straight off the back of that realisation, regret began to climb like rising damp up through her bones. Not because it hadn't been one of the best and most liberating sexual experiences of her life. No, what she regretted was the inevitable change in their relationship. Last night had ruined any hope of her getting out of this situation unburned.

She slipped out of the bed and went to shower. It was one thing to have passionate, wild sex with your best friend, quite another to wake up to the same best friend the morning after.

As she washed away the scent of their lovemaking, Ellie tried to process what had happened.

Alex was only just getting over his break-up with Savannah.

Yes, he seemed a lot better about the whole thing, but yesterday must have still been emotional for him. No wonder he'd sought comfort and *romance* – as he called it – with her, and, well, she was only human.

A gorgeous, kind and generally awesome man sweeps you off your feet, telling you that you're *sexy and perfect*... Well, it's a tale as old as time. Of course she'd had sex with him.

Ellie rolled her eyes as she finished drying herself off. Now she had to think about damage control. *Her* damage, because how many times had she read into something like this only to be disappointed by the eventual outcome? Too many to count. And even worse, this time she'd known from the start it was going to lead to nothing, and she'd still let it happen regardless, like a bloody moron.

How should she play it? Cool and relaxed? *We had fun. I'm a cool, independent woman. Of course I can enjoy holiday sex without expecting more.*

Ellie frowned. She was none of those things. She was the type of woman who slept with a guy and then practised writing out her future married name to get the signature just right.

Fuck. No wonder she was single.

She put on a swimsuit and kaftan that had been drying on the towel rail, hoping that some exercise would help clear her head, and left the bathroom.

Alex was awake but still in bed. He turned his head towards her as she entered. His dark hair flopped adorably as he rubbed his eyes and sat up. 'Hey, beautiful,' he said with a gentle, hesitant smile.

Ellie's stomach did a somersault. 'Hey...' she replied weakly.

He scraped his hand through his hair, and leaned back. 'So, about last night...'

NO! She couldn't deal with this right now! She forced herself to smile, but it felt more like a grimace. 'Oh, man, you were amazing. Thank you.' Bloody hell, did she really just thank him? 'Erm, so great night had by all.' *Stop, Ellie, please.* 'Let's not ruin it by talking about it, yeah? I'm going for a swim now. See you at breakfast?'

He nodded slowly, his brow creased with concern. 'Okay, if you're sure…'

'Great!' She grabbed her beach bag from the lounge area as she made a hasty exit, and got all the way to the empty loungers before she realised she'd forgotten her sunglasses, which wasn't a big deal, but she liked to read her Kindle after a swim and the glare from the sun could be annoying. Maybe Alex would be in the shower by now?

With a resigned huff, she trudged back to their room. As she quietly entered their suite, she could hear Alex talking on the phone. He was stood by the window, his back towards her and his laptop open on the coffee table. He'd thrown on his linen trousers from last night, but was otherwise bare. He had a lovely back, she thought wistfully. Wide at the top and then tapering down to narrow hips in a dramatic V-shape. She had to shake her head to focus on the task at hand, her sunglasses, which she quickly spotted beside his laptop.

Not wanting to disturb him on a call – an obviously important work call, going by the serious and professional tone of his voice – she tiptoed towards the coffee table.

'Yes. I'd be delighted.' He laughed, and her ears pricked. 'Thank you, I was worried you were never going to ask…' She grinned, hoping it was the theatre asking him to do another production.

She was ready to give Alex a thumbs-up if he happened to turn around. But his next words caused the delight to curdle in her stomach. 'I'll book a flight to LA immediately. Oh, that. Yes, I saw the photos… it's all nonsense, a distraction… Likewise, can't wait to meet her – yes,

Francesca would be a perfect match... I agree... it's for the best. I've really figured out my priorities.'

He's going back to LA? She remembered the film script that Richie had been pushing at him the other day. Had he accepted it? Bile rose in her throat.

Of course he'd accepted. Why on earth would he stay in London? Why on earth would he stay with her?

She snatched up her sunglasses and silently slunk away. She wasn't ready to face him yet. She needed time alone before she faced this latest humiliation.

Was she the distraction he'd mentioned? Was she the... nonsense?

Their relationship *was* based on a lie. He'd picked up a nobody in a bar and passed her off to the world as his girlfriend, all so that he wouldn't look a loser in front of his family.

Well, who was the loser now?

What a joke.

A distraction, one which had allowed him to get his fucking priorities straight.

Good-time, funny, curvy Ellie. Always the girl you went on a few dates with, but was never good enough to keep for ever.

Memories flashed through her mind. The sniggers of the gym bros, the disgust on David's fiancée's face, Holly's hate-filled eyes. She couldn't go through another public humiliation. Not again. Alex had said they would have a mutual, friendly split. But wouldn't it be better to just fade away, without any drama and without the shame?

She needed to plan her escape with as much dignity as possible. She barely even noticed Richie as she passed him in the corridor, her eyes too blinded by tears. No doubt he was on his way to finalise the details of Alex's return to the States.

—

She walked along the beach until she was certain enough time had passed for Alex to have left their room. Then she headed back, going through the kitchen to avoid as many people as possible.

It was only a couple of days until their scheduled return flight. That was enough time for her to mentally prepare herself for being dumped by Alex.

How would he do it? She tortured herself with all the possible scenarios. He wouldn't want to make a scene in front of his family or on the flight home. So, in the cab on the way to her house? *'I've had such a great time, but I think we want different things in life.'*

Or maybe a text? *'Let's remain friends.'*

Or maybe... Nothing.

She'd had that before.

Ghosted. Which sounded like an action-movie stunt, as if the person put on a jumpsuit, fired-up their proton pack and blasted the bad relationship back to hell, rather than the act of cowardice it truly was.

She couldn't go through this again. She dug out her phone; there were several texts as well as a few missed calls. She'd look at those later, but first she needed to protect her future self – she found Alex's number and deleted it, then blocked it for good measure. No way would she embarrass herself further by sending him 2 a.m. texts asking why he'd stopped caring, what she'd done wrong.

Even the flat he promised her... she didn't want it, although she now suspected that had been her hush money all along. Perhaps the keys would come with an NDA? He would walk away without a single stain on his character, while Ellie would always be the reject, the joke.

A wave of nausea washed over her, and she leaned against the closed door of their bedroom, glad that Alex had indeed gone down to breakfast already.

No, she couldn't stomach his excuses, the awkward *chat*. A wave goodbye at the airport and then to never see him again – that would be the kindest goodbye. Maybe she could even pretend she was asleep the entire journey back.

How the hell was she going to get through the next couple of days?

Her phone began to vibrate in her hand, and she jumped with surprise, almost dropping it. There was no way her mum would call her while she was abroad – it cost too much – not unless it was urgent. Dread twisted inside her gut as she raised the phone to her ear. 'Is everyone okay?'

'We're all fine. But... how are you, darling?' Her mum was being gentle – she was never gentle.

'What do you mean?'

The silence was deafening.

'Mum, this call must be costing you a bomb. What's going on?'

Her mum took a deep breath and then opened the floodgates. 'I can't believe he's not even had the decency to tell you! It's all come out, Ellie. The fake relationship to make his ex jealous, and, well, there's some awful pictures of you... mooning his ex. What on earth possessed you to wear that bikini? You can't trust a bikini! I've always said it's safer and more flattering to wear a one-piece. Oh God, the photos... and they're saying terrible things – that you stalked him and gate-crashed a party to meet him. Possibly even *roofied* him to sleep with him – because as a nurse you'd have access to the drugs to do it – and then you blackmailed him into taking you to this wedding and buying you a flat. But worse than that...'

Ellie wasn't sure what could be worse than drugging, sexually assaulting and blackmailing someone, but she waited to hear it all the same.

'They say you tore up her *bridal bouquet*. We own a florist. I know you would never, *never* do something so awful. But they say you've been making a mess of Savannah's wedding – ruining it out of jealousy. That you've done it before, ruined a man's relationship by spreading lies and stalking him. Do they mean David? But... that's not what happened. He cheated on you. You didn't know about his fiancée, did you? They say you even refused to say goodbye to Savannah when they left on honeymoon. That's not you. That's not my Ellie! I know you wouldn't do that, and I've told them, but they just won't listen, and we've had to close the shop because reporters are constantly here... and... Oh, Ellie it's awful!' She broke down into sobs while Ellie slumped against the back of the door and dropped to a heap on the lush carpet, her hands shaking uncontrollably.

'W-what? How...'

An exasperated hiss rattled down the line, and Ellie could tell her mum had switched from despair to anger in the huff of a breath.

'I *warned* you, Ellie! I warned you that this would all end in tears. He's made a fool out of you, and for what? He's going to be fine, according to the papers. He's just landed a major Hollywood film franchise with Francesca Tatiana. The bastard starts filming in the next few weeks.

But what about us? We've been left to deal with this… embarrassment alone! We could lose the shop. We could lose everything!'

Ellie's mind raced, trying and failing to keep up with her shattered heart as it exploded inside her chest.

How had they got pictures? Had she been wrong about the Kings? Did they all think of her as a joke?

She tried to sound in control, but her voice trembled. 'Mum, this is the first I've heard about this. What happened in the pool was an accident. And I was helping with the flowers – they'd arrived damaged, and I reworked the bouquet. I'm sure Savannah and Liam will explain everything.' Unless they'd sent the photos? Had this all been a ruse to fix the Kings' reputation? A way to change the narrative? She certainly sounded like the only person to come off badly in all of this.

'Come home!' begged her mum. 'The sooner you're away from them the better. Mark says you should tell your side, clear your name. Tell them that it was all him, that he put you up to it. You've got to look after yourself for a change, Ellie.'

Her spine stiffened. Even now she couldn't hurt him. 'I'm not going to do that.'

'Well, either way it's best you come back. Once you're home they'll realise it's all over anyway, and they'll lose interest. I'm going to send you the online articles, so you're prepared. I don't want him fobbing you off. Nanna is beside herself with worry. You need to come home.'

She promised her mum she'd return soon and ended the call.

The first article she opened showed pictures of her mooning the horrified happy couple. She quickly closed the web page, and then viewed several social media videos that were trending. All were speculating on her crimes and the motives behind them; none of them painted her in a pleasant light. One had even stuck up a picture of her at the Olivier Awards in her scarlet dress, and drawn devil eyes and horns on her, and was calling her Nurse Stalker.

In a fit of weakness, she decided to go and find Alex.

Even if he didn't want her, surely he cared enough about her to at least try to help her with this mess of a situation. She gripped her phone tightly in her hand, and rushed down the stairs to find him.

Richie was walking down the corridor again. But this time he stepped in front of her, his sallow face pulled into a sympathetic mask, one she didn't quite believe. 'I take it you've seen the pictures?'

She stopped dead, her heart hammering in her chest. 'My mum called. Does Alex know?'

He scoffed. 'Of course he knows. He thought it best not to worry you about it. It'll all blow over, especially when he returns to LA.'

How could he keep this from her?

'So, it's true? He's going back to LA.'

'Of course. London was only ever a trial, and why would he turn down a Hollywood franchise?' His eyes gleamed. 'If you'd prefer to go home now, I could easily arrange that for you. But like I said, it'll blow over in a few months anyway.'

'Months?' Ellie gasped. *No.* 'There's no way I'm putting my family through this for months.'

'I know it sounds strange, but it's probably the easiest path all round. Otherwise, it can get very ugly... very litigious...'

She pushed past Richie and headed towards the sun room. He followed, his footsteps thudding on the marble behind her.

Alex and his father sat in chairs facing the open doors to the garden. The script she'd seen earlier was on the table between them. They raised glasses of orange juice and toasted each other. Ellie paused in the doorway, the shadow of Richie stopping beside her.

Could she face Alex?

Could she face the humiliation?

She turned and walked back out without saying a word.

'Ellie, darling,' Richie said, and the endearment made her skin crawl, but she looked at him through her tears, hoping for any good news he might offer her.

He took her by the elbow and guided her into the library. 'Things change. Especially in show business, and it's always us mere mortals that have to pick up the pieces.' He gently pushed her towards the desk.

On top of a freshly printed document was a pen and a signed cheque for £10,000 made out to her, and signed by Alex weeks ago according to the date on it. Absently she wondered if he'd always planned it to end this way.

Thanks for playing your part, but it's over now.

Richie offered her the pen. 'It's an NDA, stating you won't comment on the Kings or the time you spent with them. There's also a little something for your trouble. I mean, that plus your apartment is a good offer, don't you think? The Kings want you to know they're really grateful for everything you've done. You've brought this family back together in a way I would never have imagined possible. It's unfortunate the media decided to follow a different narrative. Sadly, that's usually the way of it – I tried to warn you. You need to look the part to be believable. You and Alex? Are just *not believable.*'

For the first time since meeting him, she agreed with Richie.

Ellie stared down at the offer on the table. She thought about the shop being closed because of the press. How long would they last? She picked up the pen and signed the document with a trembling hand. She didn't bother reading it; she'd never talk – who would believe her?

'I need to leave,' she whispered.

False sympathy radiated from him in waves. She couldn't bear pity from someone like Richie, especially when it was obvious he didn't give one flying shit about her.

She wanted her family. 'I need to go home.'

'That's probably for the best. I can arrange everything. No need to say goodbye to the family. I'll let them know, far better to leave quietly... Less awkward.'

She nodded numbly and headed to the stairs.

They wanted her gone, because she'd served her purpose. Before she left, she picked up the memo pad from the coffee table and scrawled a note.

Chapter Thirty-Two

Alex couldn't find Ellie anywhere. She'd said she was going swimming, but she wasn't by the pool or on the hammock beach.

The talk with Russell had taken far longer than he'd expected. The theatre wanted him back as resident director and were keen to talk about upcoming projects, which was fantastic. Unbelievably, movie legend Francesca Tatiana was also keen to be involved in his next production – whatever it may be. Interestingly, she'd seen *The Great Gatsby* during a visit to London, and had liked it so much she'd asked to work with him in the future.

However, he'd had to spend half an hour this morning reassuring her agent that he wasn't going back to film acting. Apparently, there was a rumour spreading like wildfire in LA that Alex and several big names – Francesca being one of them – would be starring in a new multimillion-dollar franchise.

Of course, it wasn't true. The franchise script that Richie had been trying to ram down his throat since he'd arrived was of no interest to him, and he'd told him that more than once, but the rumours were still circulating anyway. He suspected it was another one of Richie's *distractions* combined with wishful thinking on his part.

Thankfully, Francesca was still interested in a theatre role, but wanted to speak with him personally about the projects before signing. Projects he'd not even finalised himself – but that was show business. He and Russell had agreed that as soon as he was back in London they would work like demons to pull together proposals, and then Alex would fly out to LA to ensure Francesca was on board.

Obviously, he'd miss Ellie like mad, but one week away would be worth it in the long run. Francesca's name attached to his next project was a dream come true, especially as the production wouldn't rely on his name for publicity. When he'd eventually sorted out all of the details, including booking flights – he needed to stop relying on Richie for everything – he'd looked for Ellie first, and then found himself blurting out his good news to his dad when he couldn't find her straight away.

They'd toasted to his new career and talked it over until Richie joined them. Richie had then spent an hour trying to convince him to accept the franchise instead.

The whole conversation had been difficult, with Richie constantly pushing for him to change his mind. In the end, Alex had still refused, and Richie had agreed to delay the franchise producers just in case Alex changed his mind. Which was infuriating, as he wasn't going to.

After Richie had left, his dad had said, 'Don't worry about him. He gets things into his head sometimes, and struggles to let go. He's just signed Holly too – I think she's the romantic interest in this, and that's probably why he wants you on board – a safe pair of hands so to speak. But he'll come around eventually.'

'I can't think of anything worse than filming for months, possibly even years, with Holly.' Alex grimaced at the thought. 'Honestly, Dad, I don't think I need Richie any more. He keeps pushing me towards jobs I don't want.

My heart's in the theatre; it always has been. I only did film acting because he pushed me into it.'

His dad pursed his lips thoughtfully, before breaking into a sly smile. 'So, you've decided then? London will be your new home after all. You're not tempted by the big franchise?' He gestured to the script on the table between them. There was probably a copy in every room of this house, Richie was so determined that he should fall in love with it.

'It's good money. There's no denying that.' The contract was worth millions.

His father raised an eyebrow in question. 'But?'

Alex shook his head, and sucked in a deep breath. 'I don't need it – thanks to you, I can do whatever I want, and that's not what I want. I want London and Ellie. You probably think it's too soon—'

His father interrupted him with a raised hand. 'No, you boys are like me. When you fall, you fall hard. I was the same with your mother. She wanted to work in LA, so I worked in LA. Best decision I ever made.'

Alex nodded. His parents had always balanced their careers according to their relationship. It was one of the reasons they'd moved so much when he was younger. He'd never appreciated it, but they'd moved so that they could stay together.

Now he understood what he never had before. Home meant nothing without the right person.

'Have you seen Ellie?'

His dad shook his head. 'No, but your mother and I were playing tennis first thing – she's determined to get better. So, we haven't been in the house much.'

'Okay, thanks.' Alex was about to leave when his father reached over and rested a hand on his forearm, stilling him.

'You know we are proud of you. Sometimes, in this business, we forget that not everyone wants to be a star. When you went into directing, we worried it was because you felt...'

'Inadequate?' Alex suggested, and his father winced. Alex shrugged and returned to his seat. 'I mean, you're not wrong. That's why I wanted to try something else other than acting. Theatre directing suits me.' He took a deep breath, and confessed the truth. 'I never liked acting. I did it because it was the obvious choice, and I wanted to prove to you that I could be as good as you and Liam. But the truth is, I've always hated being in the public eye. I'm much happier behind the scenes.'

His dad sighed, heavy with regret. 'I'm so sorry. Looking back, I realise how much we pressured you into acting. Liam was doing so well, we forgot that not everyone wants the same life we have. And we weren't sure how to support you without seeming like we were interfering – you were always so sure of yourself compared to Liam. We thought that by taking a step back we were allowing you room to grow. But now I see that only made you think we didn't care... and we do. We've booked tickets for your show, if you'll have us?'

'Of course I'll have you.' Alex leaned back, shocked by the contrition in his father's tone. 'I'm the one to blame. I should have talked to you about how I felt, rather than getting all bitter and twisted over it. I would love for you to come and see my work. Always. It'd be an honour.'

His dad gave his arm a squeeze and patted it, his eyes shining with raw emotion. 'Go find that gorgeous girl of yours.' He picked up the franchise movie script. 'Maybe I'd be interested in being... *Tanko, alien-lion-man from the Planet Kelton*... What do you think?'

Alex laughed. 'You'd be great, Dad. He's an awesome character.'

—

Alex followed the path that ran a circuit around the island.

Maybe she'd gone for a walk? She'd done that a couple of times when she'd grown bored of reading and sunbathing. Ellie was never still for long and he loved that about her. She was a woman of action, always optimistically moving forward no matter the struggles she faced.

He didn't see her, so he headed back towards the house via the pool area. Worry began to itch and crawl up the back of his neck when he still couldn't find her.

Had they missed each other and she was already back at the house? The pool, sun room and kitchen were all empty of her.

There was no sign of her in their bedroom suite, but something about the rooms seemed strange, although it took him several moments of standing and staring at the bathroom to realise what was so disturbing about it.

Where was Ellie's stuff?

Ellie was messy, tended to leave her hair and make-up products all over the counters. Eddie's team always tidied up – much to her chagrin, they arranged all of her clutter in neat piles. But today every surface was clean and empty.

He walked into the bedroom and checked the wardrobes. Her suitcase and clothing were all gone. He stood in the lounge area, unable to comprehend what he was seeing.

Where the fuck was she?

Had she gone on an overnight trip with one of the bridesmaids? But why wouldn't she mention it, and why take everything with her?

Had something terrible happened, news from back home? A surge of adrenaline rushed through his bloodstream, and he lurched forward, only to come to an immediate stop.

She'd have told him if something had happened to any of her family.

Wouldn't she?

He noticed a hastily written note on the coffee table, held down by a glass.

> *The holiday is over. No need to call me.*
> *Ellie*

—

'Have you tried calling her?' asked his mother over lunch.

Alex had to stop himself from snapping back at her. 'Yes, of course I have.'

In fact, he'd called her continuously most of the morning. Each time the call had failed to connect. He suspected she'd blocked him.

His eyes swivelled to Richie, who he'd almost throttled earlier when he'd discovered his part in helping Ellie escape.

Escape!

Like he was some monster that she'd had to run away from. He just couldn't understand what he'd done wrong, and he couldn't even go after her – the boat wouldn't return for a while, and anyway she was already in the air. Richie was damn efficient, he'd give the bastard that at least.

Last night had been wonderful, he hadn't imagined that. But then she'd been cold and distant in the morning.

So, was that it? They'd had sex and she'd been afraid he wanted more than the holiday fling she was willing to give? That didn't make sense. Ellie wasn't a *fling* type of girl.

Did Richie know more than he was letting on?

'Don't glare at me like that, Alex. She told me she'd had enough and wanted to go home. What was I supposed to do, force her to stay? Hold her against her will?' Richie sneered before going back to his phone and Caesar salad.

'Of course not,' said his mother with a frown. 'But maybe you could have told me at least. This is my house. I have a right to know who comes and goes.'

Richie inclined his head. 'I'm sorry, Jessica. I thought you deserved some rest after the wedding, and I was just trying to sort things out for the girl. She seemed desperate to leave.' He looked to Alex. 'Did you argue?'

'No,' Alex said miserably. 'But she left a note.'

His mom and dad exchanged a wide-eyed look. 'What did it say?'

Alex closed his eyes, but the words were burned on his retinas.

The holiday is over.

Nothing ever lasted with Alex, and Ellie had had enough of his weird lifestyle. He'd crossed the line of their friendship and tried to make it more than it was. After she'd repeatedly told him she didn't want a relationship with him. He'd taken advantage of her, bought her affection and begged her to lie for him. No wonder she'd had enough. Beneath all the luxury and lies, there was just Alex, and he wasn't enough for her.

He was never enough.

'She said not to call her.'

His mom and dad winced simultaneously and went back to pretending to eat. What was more worrying was that no one seemed surprised. They all exchanged knowing looks and kept quiet, as if they weren't surprised Ellie was gone.

Well, he'd never been very good at keeping a girlfriend, had he?

Chapter Thirty-Three

The journey home was long and tedious, far worse than her journey there. Especially when a curt text from Richie arrived while she was still bumping up and down on the speedboat, explaining that he'd had to put her in economy on the flight back to London to ensure she was on the next available flight.

But at least she'd got a window seat. She leaned against the window and turned away from the two other passengers in her row, hoping to avoid speaking to anyone for as long as possible – for ever, ideally.

She couldn't sleep, but, when she'd looked at the films available, there'd been one starring Liam and Savannah. No doubt the notorious affair film. She'd switched it off and pretended to sleep for the remainder of the flight, occasionally rising for a long overdue loo break or a bag of crisps.

Back in London, she wearily collected her baggage and got into the first available taxi. As soon as she was inside, she kicked herself for not calling Martin. He would have charged her far less and driven far more safely. Turning on her phone, which she'd had off the entire journey, she was depressed to see an influx of notifications.

Big mistake. She should have waited until she was in the safety of her own home.

There were several missed calls from her mother, which was to be expected. Her mum always seemed to forget about flights and phones. But there were also a lot of emails from her, which was unusual from her non-tech-savvy mum. She opened up the email app on her phone.

As well as the ones from her mum, there were some other names she didn't recognise, all reporters from various magazines, papers and media outlets by the look of their email addresses. The subject lines were all variations of *Tell your story*. She groaned and moved on through the list.

There was one email address she *did* recognise: Hazel, her line manager. The air in her lungs froze and her heart jerked in her chest.

Ellie immediately clicked on the email. It was very professional – which was worrying in itself. She scanned through it and then read it again in disbelief. She'd been asked to take a voluntary leave of absence until the board could determine if recent events in her *private life* qualified as gross misconduct.

Hazel had been kind enough to comment that, as she had no previous cautions and a spotless record, she was 'hopeful' this would not lead to a suspension of her nursing licence. But it would probably be 'best' for the hospital, and Ellie, if she took some time out while they investigated the complaints raised by members of the public.

They'd be in touch soon to determine a decision about her alleged alcohol and drug abuse. There was also mention of a possible police investigation, if her drug record-keeping showed any inconsistencies.

Ellie closed the email with trembling fingers. They were taking it seriously and, although she had nothing to hide, she felt as cornered as a rat in an ally.

Things were worse than she could ever have imagined.

She opened the emails from her mum, hoping for some sort of comfort or guidance, but was horrified to see several links that took her to pictures of her 'mooning' at the pool.

From this angle, and the way she was leaning forward to hold up her bikini at the front, it looked as if she was deliberately mooning a shocked and horrified Liam and Savannah. Worse still, she was clutching a cocktail glass, which didn't seem to help matters as the headline read, *DRINK-FUELLED NURSE TURNS SAVANNAH AND LIAM'S ROMANTIC WEDDING INTO A NIGHTMARE!*

There were several more images of her. *Always* with a drink in hand, occasionally with two. There was even a photo of her gleefully pulling apart a wilted bouquet, her head thrown back with almost manic laughter. Alex must have been cropped out of that photo – lucky for him.

Christ on a bike! It was horrendous; she looked crazy. She didn't even remember half of these pictures. Who had taken them?

Amongst all of the pictures there were a few captioned quotes from a 'reliable' source. The quotes swirled in front of her eyes and she dipped lower into her seat, afraid of unseen enemies and cameras. The entire world hated her, and she could see why.

> Alex met Ellie at his lowest point after his break-up with Savannah. He'd produced and directed The Great Gatsby on the London

> stage, which at first had a lukewarm reception. Life began to imitate art when he found himself falling into the arms of serial dater and party girl Eliza Dorothy Jones. Witnesses say they left together after his opening-night party, with Alex heavily under the influence of either drugs or alcohol. Close friends believe Miss Jones, a registered nurse, took advantage of Alex, possibly spiking his drink with strong medications.

There was a picture of her Tinder profile, as well as a quote from a previous 'liaison' who'd had to end his date with her early because she'd been '*too intense – wanting to make plans for marriage and children within minutes of meeting with him*'.

Presumably it was the same guy who'd bailed on her on their first date. Another reason to wish epic karma on that prick.

There was also a photo of David's fiancée, including an interview, and of course a link to the damn TikTok of her being chased around the gym. '*Eliza Jones tried to break up my relationship. She stalked my husband-to-be and trapped him with her lies. We almost split up because of it. She's an obviously deeply troubled fantasist, who is desperate for an alpha-male boyfriend, despite the fact she's probably a three at best.*'

She glanced at the comments box at the bottom of the article. A never-ending litany of hate. So many angry and sick emojis that Ellie felt personally attacked by each hateful comment.

'Ugly. Fat. Bitch! I thought it was sus that they were dating. She obviously blackmailed the poor guy.'

'What a psycho!'

'Nurse Ratched more like…'

'She's gross.'

'What a crazy fat pig!'

'Hope there's a hog roast in hell for her!'

'You couldn't pay me to f*ck that.'

'I knew it was all lies. What on earth would Alex see in THAT!'

She had hundreds of messages on her Facebook and Instagram profile, and, after a quick look at some of the hateful comments and threats, she clicked on each icon and deleted the apps completely.

Her eyes burned, awash with tears, and she was struggling to breathe. She tried to manage the panic attack with the breathing techniques she'd been taught to use with patients. But she couldn't stop herself from catastrophising.

Life was hopeless. If she could get on a flight to Australia right now, she would do it gladly, but she suspected this vitriol would follow her there too.

This was confirmed when she spotted some panicked text messages from Hannah asking if she was okay. Ellie couldn't face calling her, not yet; she didn't want to ruin Hannah's happiness with a misery of her own making.

What had Alex even seen in her? They looked ridiculous together.

All the carefully built confidence, all the body-positivity she'd spent years nurturing, evaporated, and her mother's words of caution came flooding back.

Why you?

He'd wanted a *distraction*. A holiday from his crazy, glamorous life, and he'd found it with her. He would go back to LA and his bachelor life, and she'd be left to deal with the fallout.

This was all so unfair.

She'd be alone for the rest of her life, with no job, and her family's business was probably ruined too. She'd foolishly put her life and her family business in someone else's hands, and for what, a free holiday and a flat?

Unable to stop herself, she clicked back to the article and the 'read more' button with morbid curiosity. A car crash that she couldn't seem to look away from.

She clutched her straw bag closer to her chest. The cheque within seemed to burn like a hot coal inside – her hush money. The money wouldn't last five minutes if she needed to rebuild all of their lives from scratch.

The rest of the article loaded.

> Alex, enthralled by the curvaceous seductress, made the mistake of taking her with him to his brother's wedding. Ellie then took it upon herself to spoil Savannah and Liam's wedding in a twisted act of revenge. According to our source, "Ellie left the wedding celebration early in disgrace. However, this incredibly difficult time has enabled the two brothers to overcome their previous difficulties and there are rumours

they are due to start filming a multimillion-dollar franchise together soon with movie legend Francesca Tatiana."

'Fucking marvellous!' spat Ellie, getting a curious look from her driver in the rear-view mirror. She ducked down in her seat and tucked her face into the pashmina wrapped around her neck.

All she needed was a taxi driver dishing the dirt on her next.

Chapter Thirty-Four

A day passed, maybe two, Alex wasn't sure of time any more. He spent hour after hour staring at his silent phone and replaying their last conversation over and over in his mind. Savannah and Liam returned from their island early, and his brother tried to talk to him about it. But he couldn't understand it himself.

She'd said they would remain friends... *what had changed?*

The morning after they'd slept together, she'd been obviously worried, had said they were going too fast, and he'd ignored her. As he'd done with Savannah, as he always did when people didn't fit in with his plans.

Except this time, he actually cared. Not because of hurt pride or disappointment.

He'd thought losing Savannah had broken him.

No. Losing Ellie was *real* pain.

Soul-crushing, desolate pain.

Staring up at the ceiling of the glamorous impersonal bedroom that was apparently *his*, he wondered what the hell he was supposed to do. Move on?

No, he couldn't bear life without her. Even if all they could ever be was just friends, he wanted that. She was the only real thing in his dumb life. He'd gladly change all of his plans if it meant Ellie called him back.

He should go back to London. Force her to speak with him. But what would that accomplish? Her note had been pretty clear.

His worst fear had come true – she didn't want him. She'd just been swept away by the romance and glamour of this dumb life.

Richie had suggested he return to LA for good, do the franchise and forget about London... forget about Ellie. He was almost tempted to agree. But he needed time to think before he did anything else rash.

The *holiday* might be over for her, but he'd never seen it that way. She wanted to get back to her normal life and that didn't involve Alex.

Nothing was normal with Alex, and maybe, just like his own privilege, he needed to learn how to accept that.

–

It wasn't until the next morning, after a restless night, that Alex saw the press coverage, and only then by accident. Some of the *Gatsby* cast had sent him messages asking if he was okay; Isaac had even asked if he should do a wellness check on Ellie and her family... which had immediately raised alarm bells in Alex's mind.

There'd been no alerts in his emails. In fact, there was nothing about the wedding either, which didn't seem right. He quickly realised that the alerts had been switched off somehow.

After a quick Google search, his stomach began to ache with growing nausea. This was why he avoided the vitriol of the papers and social media. It was pure evil.

Had Ellie read some of this shit? Was that why she'd left?

NURSE STALKER: BLACKMAILER AND WEDDING SABOTEUR. The headlines were shocking, and in each one Ellie's character had been dragged through the mud. The press were hounding her family, and the world was reacting like he'd been the victim of an unstable and abusive woman.

After everything she'd done to help him reconcile with his family, this was her reward?

My damn family.

A blazing-hot rage seared through him.

He knew who was to blame.

—

Alex stormed into the sun room, where his family and Richie were relaxing over the remains of a leisurely breakfast, his laptop gripped tightly in his hand and wielded like a weapon.

'What the hell did you do?' he shouted.

Liam and Savannah jumped.

'Hey, what the hell is wrong with you!' snapped Liam, jumping to his feet despite Savannah's pleading hands.

'Not you,' growled Alex, his eyes fixed on the parasite that had been leeching off his family for years. 'No one has access to my emails but you, Richie. My alerts were switched off. So I had no idea about your latest *narrative* until it was too late!'

Confused looks passed between his family, but Richie remained stony-faced and silent.

Alex passed the laptop to his father. 'I guess he's turned yours off too. Hoping you'd get the deal signed before the truth came out, right?' He pointed to yet another script on the coffee table – this time with a stapled contract beside it. 'Take a look. There's half-naked photos of Ellie by the pool. No one else could have taken them but you. Always walking around with your phone. Fucking bloodsucking leech!' He turned to Liam and Savannah, teeth gritted against his barely contained fury. 'There are stories about Ellie ruining your wedding, deliberately ripping up Savannah's bouquet. Ellie's family own a florist – this will ruin them! And that's nothing compared to all the other bullshit. Claiming she's drugged and stalked me!' He spun back to Richie. 'What the fuck were you thinking?'

Richie rolled his eyes. 'She served her purpose, and the press will soon move on, they always do. And don't feel too bad for her. You paid her, remember? Nice little flat for pretending to date you, and she was more than happy to take the cheque I gave her. She even signed an NDA,' he said, adjusting his cuffs calmly and rising to his feet. Shocked gasps rang around the room, but he shrugged. 'What does it matter, your *relationship* was all a ruse anyway. We agreed a fake girlfriend would be a good distraction for you, and would help ease some of the awkwardness of this wedding.'

'You weren't really dating?' asked his mother, pressing her hand to her chest.

Richie nodded. 'Alex, it's time you come back to LA and stop playing at this London theatre nonsense – it'll never make any money for you, not like the franchise. Be grateful that I've gotten rid of that fat little hanger-on sooner rather than later. She was a joke from the start, wasn't she? A weird choice to upset Liam and Savannah with, but a choice all the same.'

'I knew it! As if someone like her would ever end up with Alex,' cackled Holly, and Savannah smacked her in the arm.

Alex's face was numb with shock, and then his heart began to pound with such overwhelming rage his clenched fists shook. He didn't realise he was walking towards Richie until his brother's arms held him back. 'It was real to me!' he yelled. 'Have you any idea what you've done to her? People are calling her a stalker, accusing her of drugging and blackmailing me. She could lose her job and her family could lose their business – all because of your lies! I don't care what you paid her, it's not enough, she deserves better than this!'

'It's not just about you, Alex,' snarled Richie, finally losing his temper and revealing the snake beneath the carefully tailored suit. 'I have to look after *all* of your careers. Liam's popularity has taken a nosedive since the affair. And then they decided to marry, despite my advice to wait.' He took a moment to glare at Savannah, whose eyes were wide with horror. 'I *had* to ensure there was damage control. You were meant to find a pretty little thing to take the heat off your brother. Not a charity case!'

Before he knew it, Alex had barged through his brother and his fist had flown. Richie's face connected with his knuckles with a hard crack, and he was thrown back onto his chair, which tumbled backwards, sprawling Richie on the floor. It was the second time he'd hit someone, and this time it had been worth it.

His mom leapt up and his father rushed over to help hold him back. But it wasn't needed; seeing the bloody nose and the snivelling wreck of a man he thought he'd trusted was enough.

'How could you? Get out!' shouted his mom.

Richie straightened his shirt with a jerk and sat up, patting his nose with one of his silk handkerchiefs. 'That might be wise, Alex. Otherwise, you'll be hearing from my lawyer. This family has put up with your nonsense long enough. Consider your contract with me terminated, and good luck with your little theatre career. You're a joke in this industry.'

'I meant *you*, Richie!' his mom snapped coldly – to both Richie and Alex's surprise.

'What?' Richie struggled to his feet. Only Holly reached out to help him.

'You have hurt both of my children and their partners with your lying and scheming. I want you out of my house. Consider your contract with Robert and me terminated, right, Robert?'

His dad nodded firmly, his arm wrapped around his mom. 'Absolutely.'

'And mine,' snapped Liam, his jaw tight as he placed a hand on Alex's shoulder.

'And mine,' added Savannah, she stood up and hugged Liam, leaning into his embrace. Alex wasn't surprised to realise it didn't hurt to see them together any more. He smiled at them, and they gave him an emotional nod of solidarity.

They were family after all.

'Thirty years I've managed you, and this is how you repay me? You'll never work in this industry ever again. *Any of you*,' screamed a hysterical Richie as he stalked towards the door.

Holly was the only one not agreeing with them. 'Richie, you'll still put me forward for the franchise, won't you?'

Savannah grabbed Holly's arm as she tried to follow him, and forced her to stay put. 'Don't you dare! You think our mom would have approved of this?'

Holly lowered her eyes with shame. 'I just want to be like you...' she whimpered.

Savannah's eyes filled with tears and she pulled her sister close. 'We'll talk later.'

Alex's father called out to Richie just before he left the room. 'You seem to have forgotten something, Richie.'

Richie spun on his heels, looking at Robert expectantly.

Alex's father looked him dead in the eye and said calmly, 'You didn't make us. *We made you.*'

Richie left this time, with a lot less bluster.

—

After he had gone, all the eyes in the room turned expectantly to Alex. But it was his mom who spoke first. 'So... You're not together, you and Ellie – it was all a ruse?'

His shoulders slumped and he flopped down into a nearby couch. 'Yes, at first. But now I wish we were together. More than anything. I love her, Mom... and I've ruined her life.'

Alex's dad sat down beside him. 'Then go get her, make it right. I'm not allowing you back into this house until you make Ellie one of us. Understood?'

Alex could barely turn his head to look at him. His chest ached with every breath. 'After everything that's happened? I'll be surprised if she ever speaks to me again.'

Liam leaned down in front of him, and placed both hands on his shoulders, until Alex raised his eyes to meet his. Liam repeated the same words that Alex had said to him on his wedding day: 'You can do this. Everything is going to be okay. Okay?'

Alex stood, wrapped his arms around his brother, and squeezed him tightly. His family were finally supporting him in the way he'd always wanted, with love and acceptance.

Now, all he needed was Ellie, and for once he wasn't going to give up.

'I'll bring her back to us,' he said firmly. 'I promise.'

Chapter Thirty-Five

Someone was banging loudly on the shop door.

'For fuck's sake, when will they get the hint?' snapped Mark, taking an angry swig of his coffee, while his leg twitched uncontrollably beneath the kitchen table.

'I wouldn't have any more coffee if I were you,' Ellie said quietly, fully aware she wasn't in any position to give medical advice, considering she was suspended and awaiting full investigation.

'Love...' said her mum carefully, glancing at Mark before she continued, 'Mark and I have been talking and we think you should speak with one of them. One of the nice ones, at least.'

Ellie snorted. 'Nice ones? Are you mad? They're all a bunch of sharks.' She hadn't mentioned the NDA. She was ashamed of signing it, of accepting the hush money. She hadn't even deposited the cheque yet – how could she when they were trapped inside?

The banging came again, louder this time, and they all looked at each other huddled in their snug like it was the Blitz, the curtains drawn and a blanket of fear wrapped around them.

'I don't get why they're still here,' said Nanna helplessly.

'They want a story. They'll get bored soon.' Ellie huddled further into her dressing gown. She'd not dressed in days, and had only showered when Nanna insisted.

'They want an explanation,' growled her mother 'We all want an explanation.'

'I told you. We made a pact to fake-date. That's all it was, just an act to make Alex look better in front of his ex. This was never meant to happen. The press has twisted everything, but eventually they'll move on.'

Her mother bristled and threw down a tabloid article with Ellie's bum plastered across the cover. A new wave of nausea washed over her. 'He can move on. We've got to hide from the light of day like a bunch of cockroaches. What possessed you to ruin that poor girl's wedding—'

'Angela!' snapped Nanna, with an angry shake of her head.

Ellie's bottom lip trembled. 'Why do you believe the papers over me?'

'No... I...' Her mum lowered her head for a moment and then added defensively, 'You should have realised how dodgy this set-up was from the start.'

'Why?' asked Ellie bitterly, already knowing the answer.

'Men like that are not interested—'

'That's it!' yelled Nanna, and everyone stared at her in surprise. 'Angela, we've all had enough of you. I've tried to be understanding about your issues. But this has got to stop! None of this was Ellie's fault. You keep acting like Ellie deserved this, and she didn't! The first person to throw her to those wolves was her own family' – Mark's shoulders slumped in shame – 'and you think I don't know about the bills you let her pay with her savings? Ellie's been more sensible then the two of you put together!' She glared at Mark and her mum, who both squirmed under her reprimand.

'It's okay, Nanna,' Ellie said weakly, not wanting her nanna to get upset.

'No, it's not okay!' Nanna said firmly, her grey head switching between mother and son with equal ferocity in her eyes. 'We're a family, and we stick together through good times and bad. We support one another, not pull each other down. Angela, you need to stop with all the negative comments and look in a mirror. You are putting all of your fears and self-hatred on your own daughter. No wonder she's been so desperate to leave home. And, Mark, I know you're trying, darling, but at some point you need to take accountability. Stop looking for easy fixes and money from your sister to bail you out.'

Mark and her mum looked as if they'd been hit by a truck and not by a pensioner laying out some hard home truths.

'Mum's right though…' said Ellie, feeling as if all the strength had left her body. 'I was an idiot to think this wouldn't all go wrong. Nobody knows how cruel society can be like a fat girl, and well… I should have learned my lesson after David.'

Everyone looked at her with a mixture of surprise and worry, including her mother. She knew they were shocked to see her like this. Ellie was usually the optimist, but even she couldn't see the bright side of this mess.

'David was lying scum,' said Mark firmly, followed by a gentle, 'and I'm sorry, Ellie. I'll pay you back every penny, I mean it.'

'I don't want it.' Ellie shook her head miserably. She didn't want her deposit, or the flat, or her hush money, or even her job. Her stomach rolled with the sickening realisation that all she really wanted was Alex. 'I've behaved like a prize idiot, and the worst thing is… I still love him.'

Her mum moved closer and took Ellie's hand with tears in her eyes. 'You're not an idiot. We've all been there – me, more times than most...' She gave a sad chuckle as she wrapped Ellie in a hug. 'I've always been so scared for you. You're so beautiful and so full of life, I didn't want you to get hurt. I thought I was protecting you, but Nanna's right, I've just been making things worse. I'm going to work on it, I promise.' Ellie sank against her and sobbed. In a rare display of affection, her mother kissed her head.

'Thanks, Mum.' Ellie sniffed away her snotty tears.

Some gravel from their yard hit their window with a rattle that made them all leap in their seats and shriek.

'BASTARDS! They've got in the yard again.' Mark stormed over to the window and yanked aside the curtain. 'THIS IS PRIVATE PROPERTY—' His angry words died in his throat as he looked down at the person below.

'Hannah?'

Ellie lurched from her seat to join him.

Sure enough, Hannah stood with Martin in the yard below. 'Sorry. You weren't answering your phones. Let us in.' Hannah looked fearfully behind her as paparazzi began shouting and climbing the walls of the yard to get a picture.

Ellie ran down the stairs so fast she almost missed the last step. When she flung the door open, Hannah and her father barrelled in, and Martin quickly shut the door after them.

'What are you doing here?' Ellie gasped, staring at her friend in amazement, before quickly bursting into yet more tears.

'Oh hun.' Hannah wrapped her arms around her waist and snuggled close. Hannah was too little to really give hugs; she usually allowed Ellie to envelop her, as if she were a much-loved doll. Today was no different, except the hair beneath her chin was no longer mousy but a sun-bleached blonde. Ellie pulled away and mopped at her tear-swollen face so she could look at her friend more closely.

'You look amazing,' she said, and Hannah laughed.

'Trust you to compliment me at a time like this.'

'Come on, girls. Let's go put the kettle on,' said Martin, ushering them up the stairs with a nervous look over his shoulder.

A short time later, with a cup of tea in both their hands, they settled on Ellie's single bed for a more private reunion.

'Look at you, beach babe,' Ellie said, her vision blurry. It had only been a couple of months but the change was extraordinary. Hannah's body, which had always been petite, was now strong and toned, her skin a shade of honey that suited her.

Hannah smiled at the compliment, but she wasn't easily distracted. 'What the hell happened?'

Ellie couldn't keep anything from Hannah, who was more like a sister than a friend, but her body was wrung out and exhausted, and she could only mutter, 'What always happens. I made a fool of myself.'

'No, I don't believe that.' Hannah shook her head vehemently. Always so loyal.

Ellie sighed. 'I fell in love with him. I fell in love with the movie star, and almost believed he felt the same. Turns out I'm just a joke, as always.'

Sympathy rolled off Hannah in waves, and Ellie bent her head against her friend and sobbed until her throat was raw.

Eventually, she ran out of tears. They sat side by side, propped up against the wall with their feet hanging over the bed like they were kids again. 'You shouldn't have come back, you know,' said Ellie.

'Yes, I bloody should have,' replied Hannah with zero hesitation.

'It's a waste of your return ticket. How will you pay to come back at Christmas? Oh God, your mum is going to be so pissed at me.'

'It's fine.' Hannah gave an easy shrug.

'I'll buy your flight back.' Ellie's mind was whirling. She'd have to pay for it from the hush money, but, fuck it, she was still eternally grateful that Hannah was here.

'There's no need.'

'I insist.'

Hannah gave her a hard look. 'For once, just believe me when I say this – you're worth it, and if Alex doesn't realise that then he's a complete fool.'

Ellie sank against her, sagging with the weight of the world's cruel words on her shoulders. Hannah had picked her up after David, and said something similar. 'I don't think I can go through this again.'

Hannah rubbed her shoulder in a soothing gesture. 'We'll get through it together.'

'You've got your new life in Australia.'

'It can wait. You're more important.'

'I knew it!' Nanna crowed, waving a glossy magazine, as she strode into the kitchen the following day. 'I *bloody, fucking* knew it!'

'Language, Nanna!' gasped Mark.

'Sometimes you need a little sauce with your chips.'

Her mum frowned. 'Is that even a saying?'

'*Shush*,' hissed Nanna, as she triumphantly threw down the magazine like a gauntlet. 'Look, Ellie, finally, *the truth*!'

'What?' Ellie asked in a daze, a cold mug of chamomile tea in her hands that she'd been nursing for nearly an hour.

Nanna thrust the glossy spread towards her like a winning hand at a poker table. '*The truth*,' she repeated.

Ellie leaned forward and blinked at the magazine spread in front of her. Liam and Savannah's wedding photos were plastered all over the pages. Savannah had said they wouldn't publish their wedding photos to the press… *More lies?*

She almost pushed it away, but then she saw a picture of herself handing the remade bouquet to Savannah, and then another of Savannah hugging her. The caption said, *Ellie didn't ruin my wedding. She saved it.*

She peered closer, relieved that there were at least some people willing to speak up for her despite this mess. There were quotes from Joseph, the wedding planner– '*such a beautiful lady*,' as well as Caitlyn, Keira, Tony and Liam. Even Jessica and Robert King had praised her for being a wonderful guest and a close friend to the family. Alex was 'unavailable for comment' due to the fact that he was currently travelling.

LA, no doubt.

Disappointing, but what else did she expect? He was probably eager to return to his 'normal' life.

'You've been exonerated, love,' Nanna said softly, but her elation quickly turned to concern at Ellie's lack of a happy reaction.

Ellie's relief was short-lived. Her body ached, and she still felt as if she'd aged a hundred years in the last couple of days. 'Looks like it.'

'Your work will have to see sense after this. Look, they all repeatedly say that you didn't drink to excess, and that the bikini bottom thing was an accident. They're going to sue the papers and some horrible ex-agent of theirs who's been selling stories to the press about them for years. Looks like he'll never work again in Tinsel-town – his reputation and business is in tatters!' Nanna cackled with delightful abandon as she continued to point out pieces from the article. 'And here, they say that you worked hard to ensure the wedding went without a hitch. *Our flowers were ruined in transit, thank heavens Ellie was here to save them.* They've even mentioned the name of our flower shop.'

'Let's have a look.' Mark grabbed the magazine and cheered. 'Yes, Jones Floristry and Gifts.'

'That's nice,' Ellie said, and her family all looked at her with concern.

'Ellie…'

She blinked again as Nanna's hand rested over hers, bringing her back to reality. She stared at it, the tissue-paper-thin skin covered in wrinkles and age spots and the joints slightly gnarled by arthritis and hard work. Nanna's warmth and kindness seeped into her empty, numb bones.

'Everything's going to be all right, sweetheart.'

She nodded, only realising she was crying when she saw tears splashing on the back of Nanna's hand.

'Where's Hannah?' Nanna asked her mum softly.

'She's in my room. Her dad called earlier, but she missed him. She's calling him back now.'

Hannah came bursting in at that moment, her face flushed. 'Please don't kill me!'

Ellie wiped away her tears with the back of her hand. 'Why would I kill you?'

'Well, you wouldn't kill *me*. But you might kill my dad.' Hannah bit her bottom lip with nervous excitement.

Ellie sat up a little straighter. 'What? Why?'

Hannah glanced at her phone. 'Because… he's about to pull up with Alex King in the back of his cab.'

'What!' Ellie jumped up from the table, her knees banging against the top and knocking over her cold tea. Everyone stared at each other in shocked silence.

Hannah took a deep breath, and added, 'Dad says he needs to talk to you.'

There were several honks from outside, and they all ran to Ellie's bedroom and looked out of the window. Martin's cab was trying to inch through the flower market, but traffic was always slow going on market day, as the road was filled with beautiful flower stalls – and, currently, a lot of photographers.

Like a pack of hyenas, they sensed fresh news and were ready to pounce. They filled the pavement and made it impossible for Alex to make it to the house. He leaned out of the cab window as if trying to judge the situation. But then he glanced up at the house and at the window where she stood. Their eyes locked and she couldn't move, couldn't speak. A whirlwind of painful longing rushed through her like a tornado.

His blue eyes widened, and he said something to Martin, who stopped the cab with a jerk. The air rushed out of her lungs in a wheeze. Alex stepped out of the cab, but the photographers rushed forward, blocking his path.

With nowhere to go, he hauled himself up onto the cab's roof.

Martin wouldn't be pleased about that, she thought. But then she realised Martin was the person shoving him up there by pushing both hands against his bottom.

'Ellie!' Alex shouted, above the raging crowd of questions and camera flashes, and suddenly a hush descended over the street. 'Ellie, listen!' he continued. 'Richie lied. He was playing you, just like he's played all of us from the start. I don't know what he told you, but I want you. I want us to be together, for real!'

She stared at him, her heart fluttering back to life, only to be crushed by reality. She leaned out of the window, her tea-stained dressing gown squishing against the glass. 'It's not going to work,' she shouted back. 'I won't leave London. I won't leave my family. I don't want to go to LA.'

'We won't!'

'But the franchise… and I don't suit your life.'

The crowd's heads flipped back and forth between them as if they were watching Wimbledon.

'I know I haven't got everything figured out. But I know I could never leave my family or the East End. I don't want to live in LA, I wouldn't fit in there and I don't want to fit in there.' Her voice trembled at the last bit and the crowd issued a collective 'aaw' before turning back to Alex. Ellie was sure she could see them all scowling at him in disapproval.

'But I want you!' Alex yelled back. 'Wherever you are, that's where I want to be. I'm not moving to LA anyway.

I planned to go to LA in a couple of weeks, but it's just to meet with Francesca Tatiana for my next theatre project.'

The crowd gasped in excitement.

'Oh, she's good,' said Nanna with an appreciative nod.

Alex wasn't done. 'I've just accepted an in-house job at the theatre. I've decided to be like you, and follow my heart and be true to myself – wherever that may take me. But more than that, I finally worked out what I want in life… and it's you.'

One of the sellers passed him a gorgeous bunch of flowers. 'Say it properly, lad.'

Alex took the bouquet and held it up to her, even though they were still too far away to touch. 'I love you. Please say you love me too!'

Choking back a sob, she ran from the window and down the stairs. Nanna shouted down to Alex as she ran down the stairs, 'Don't panic, handsome, she's on her way!'

Ellie threw open the front door, but the photographers blocked her path. 'Get outta 'er way, ya bunch of idiots!' shouted some of the burly market sellers, most of whom she'd known her whole life. They pulled the photographers out of her path, and she walked forward as if she were Moses parting the Red Sea.

'I love you,' she shouted, her floppy-eared slippers slapping on the pavement.

Alex dropped down and ran towards her.

In a couple of seconds, the agony of longing was over. They were in each other's arms, and it was perfect. They kissed each other with all their hearts and souls, as flowers rained down on them from the cheering crowd with rapturous applause.

Chapter Thirty-Six

Eight months later

Ellie's steps echoed on the tiled entrance of her new home, her comically large suitcase wobbling precariously beside her. The rooms were unfurnished, the autumn air sweeping through the open front door and into the house breathing new life into every room.

Ellie sucked in a deep breath.

'Hello,' she whispered to the house.

Alex followed with his own suitcase from Martin's cab a few seconds later. That was all they had. A king-sized bed was arriving in a few hours, followed by a sofa the following day. But somehow their lack of furniture only added to the charm of moving in together.

They couldn't wait – as soon as they'd received the keys in their hot, greedy hands they'd grabbed their suitcases and run.

They'd only brought their clothes. Everything else would be fresh and new. Except for her dress mannequin, which would be brought over by Mark during the week – when he had a minute. The shop was flourishing now that it had been associated with the famous King wedding, and 'fusion' had been all the rage this wedding season.

Nanna and Mark had created a signature 'King bouquet' that had been doing exceedingly well the past couple of months. You could even add a full-size personalised balloon to it – if you fancied that horror show. Despite Mark's misguided love of awful balloons, Jones Floristry and Gifts remained safe and profitable for at least another generation.

Ironically, Mark hadn't even needed her flat deposit in the end, and her mum didn't need it either. She had started counselling to work on her emotional issues, and moved into the flat Alex had originally bought for Ellie, and her newfound independence was giving her the confidence that Ellie had found so freeing herself.

Maybe I should use the deposit money to build my Curvy-Couture brand?

Jessica had been right about plus-size actresses being desperate for award ceremony clothes. She'd already had two requests for dresses since Alex's mum had championed her designs to most of Hollywood and photos of Ellie at the wedding – *nice* ones – had circulated, prompting readers to ask where she'd found such a flattering design. She'd even requested that Ellie make her next dress for the Oscars, which was incredibly flattering, if daunting. She wasn't sure how she was going to fit it in with her nurse mentor training, but it was a happy predicament to be in.

She thrived on change and being busy, and so did Alex, who was flourishing in his resident director role. He had also become a mentor, and his productions specifically showcased new and developing talent, combining the inexperienced cast with one big name that would drive ticket sales. Isaac – now on Broadway – was the first in a long line of actors who would benefit from Alex's industry knowledge and contacts.

The latest production, *Boudica* with Francesca Tatiana, was greatly anticipated to be a roaring success; there were even rumours of an Olivier Award, and it hadn't even finished rehearsals yet. Now, other big-name actors were queuing up for the prestige of being the big lead in one of Alex's shows.

However, tonight she'd planned a lovely quiet night in with Alex. Just the two of them getting to know their new house. Sitting on the floor, eating fish and chips out of the paper... She couldn't have imagined a more perfect start to their new life together, and Alex agreed wholeheartedly.

The holiday hadn't ended after all.

Ellie had moved in with Alex into his rented apartment within a few weeks of their official *real* dating – which might have raised eyebrows at the time, but it had made perfect sense to them, and they'd been proven right. There were still privacy issues, though the press cared less about them with each month that passed.

Now, they had moved together into the Spitalfields house, where they'd had their first kiss... Not many couples could claim that.

Barbs had worked her magic, quickly securing them the house that they'd both fallen in love with but had dismissed as an impossible dream. The only downside had been that they'd had to wait for the family currently living there to find a place of their own, which had delayed them several months – but Alex and Ellie were willing to wait.

They were together, and this was their perfect home. Their perfect life.

Alex's suitcase thudded next to hers and then he shut the door with a soft click. His arm wrapped around her shoulders and he gave her a light squeeze. She tipped her head up and their lips met in a sweet pressing of each other's mouths and hearts.

'I still can't believe we've got it,' she said. They'd both had restless nights praying that the sale would still go through. It truly was their dream house; Ellie would be close to her family – but not too close – Alex loved the private and tucked-away location, and it offered them the family home they both craved.

Her heart was so filled with joy she feared it might burst. 'Let's have a walk around. Reacquaint ourselves with the old girl.'

Hand in hand, they walked through the house, inspecting the strange dust patches and discoloured paint that held shadows of the house's former occupants, like ghosts in a photograph. But somehow it wasn't unpleasant; it showed them the endless possibilities that awaited them. They would build their own life here, create their own history and make their mark on its walls.

They chatted as they walked.

'Let's paint this room blue.'

'What about one of those big Welsh dressers here?'

'How about a desk by the window?'

Claiming each room as their own, laughing with bewilderment at the odd pieces of furniture or pictures left by the previous owners, who according to the note '*hoped they had a use for them*'. More likely, a ploy to get rid of their last-minute junk. Alex and Ellie didn't mind; they even decided to keep one crazy picture of a parrot with a cigar in the downstairs loo as a memento of the day.

Ellie's chest tightened as they approached the nursery. She remembered Alex's statement that he wasn't ready when they'd last been here.

'We could paint it grey or white. Make it into my sewing room,' she suggested as they stood in the doorway.

Alex entered the room with one confident step and an easy smile. 'No, it's better as a nursery, don't you think? When you're ready, of course.'

Ellie cleared her throat, feeling as if the floor were tilting. She tightened her hold on his hand and followed him inside. 'I don't want you to rush into anything, especially anything you're unsure about. I love you. I can wait until you're ready, and if that's never then I'd still rather have you.'

He chuckled, wrapping his arms around her waist. 'I think you misunderstood me before. I wasn't ready to face living in a family home alone. After Savannah, the idea depressed me.'

Her insecurity reared its ugly head and whispered dark thoughts in her ear. But with Alex, she wasn't afraid to take those dark thoughts and push them into the light. 'I'm not a consolation prize?' she asked.

His hands smoothed down her spine to cup her bottom and pull her close against him. 'This is what I want. With you, and only you. I love you, Eliza Dorothy Jones, you are everything to me. Everything I will ever need and more.'

She giggled at the use of her full name. She used to hate the cliché of living in a flower shop with Eliza as a first name. But Alex thought it the most perfect name in the world, and who was she to argue with perfection? 'I love you. So much.'

He bent his head and kissed her thoroughly until her heart was racing. So different from their chaste kiss months ago on the roof. Ellie vowed to kiss Alex deeply in every room of their new home.

'Shouldn't we wait for the bed to arrive?' she giggled when he started to peel off her clothes – although her own eager fingers had already made up her mind.

'No,' replied Alex, chucking his t-shirt on the floor with a slap. 'When have we ever needed a bed?'

Ellie laughed. 'What about our dating rules? PG kisses only… no tongues… no sex.' She ran her fingers slowly up the wall of his chest.

'Fuck that,' he growled, cupping her face and tasting her mouth with a kiss that was anything but chaste.

The truth was, they didn't need a bed or rules or even the world's approval. They had each other, and *that* would always be more than enough.

Acknowledgements

A huge thank you to my writerly friends and fellow directors of the Romantic Novelists' Association; Ali Henderson, Katie Ginger, Saoirse Morrigan and Seána Catherine Tinley. Your daily support keeps me going, and without you, I'd be a hot mess!

Thanks also to Virginia Heath, Alison French, Liam Livings and Jean Fullerton for your wonderful friendship and brilliant advice.

Of course, I also need to thank my husband, Daniel, and our two gorgeous children, Rory and Alma, for always believing in me and being proud of my writing achicvements – both big and small.

A huge thank you to my editor, Emily Bedford, for picking up *The Dating Pact* at an RNA 121, and for generally being such a supportive and savvy editor. You have helped me turn this book into something really special. Can't wait to keep working with you on this Behind the Scenes series, shedding glittering light and love on the unsung heroes and heroines.

Finally, I'd like to send love to all my fellow plus-size ladies and lovers of romance. I see you, I am you, and there is nothing wrong with enjoying a happily ever after!

The world always needs more love.